THERE'S A BUG GOING AROUND

Robert Silman
&
Steven Froelich

SAMPLE NEWS ARTICLES ON AIDS VIRUS AGAINST LEUKEMIA

(10th to 13th December 2012)

GlobeNewswire
A NASDAQ OMX COMPANY

December 13th 2012

Inspiring New Documentary Short "Fire With Fire" Helps Spread Awareness About Groundbreaking Advance in Cancer Treatment

Who would dare to pit one fatal disease against another… inside the body of a seven-year-old patient? Immunologist Dr. Carl June is achieving amazing results with a medical breakthrough almost too good to believe: he and his team are reengineering the HIV virus to fight cancer cells. This groundbreaking cancer research is at the heart of a new Focus Forward short, "Fire With Fire".

The New York Times

December 9th 2012

In Girl's Last Hope, Altered Immune Cells Beat Leukemia

The experiment… used a disabled form of the virus that causes AIDS… The treatment very nearly killed her. But she emerged from it cancer-free, and… is still in complete remission.

The Telegraph

December 11th 2012

Emily Whitehead: girl whose cancer was 'cured' by HIV

A seven-year-old girl has become the first child leukaemia patient to be successfully treated by doctors using a disabled form of the virus that causes Aids to reprogramme the immune system.

Le nouvel Observateur

December 11th 2012

Cancer : une fillette en rémission grâce au sida

Une thérapie génique encore expérimentale a permis à Emma Whitehead, qui souffrait d'une leucémie avancée, de connaître un spectaculaire rétablissement.

msn now

December 10th 2012

Dying girl now cancer-free after 'breakthrough' AIDS virus experiment

The last thing you'd expect to be a cure for cancer is AIDS. And though researchers are still far from reaching that milestone, an experiment with a disabled form of the virus that causes the disease has given them great hope.

The Guardian Express

December 11th 2012

The HIV Virus as a Curative: Disabled HIV Virus Cured Emily Whitehead of Leukemia

The therapy, termed CT019, attempts to reprogram a person's T cells, in an effort to search out and kill cancerous cells.

NEWS CHANNEL 5 wptv.com

December 13th 2012

Emma Whitehead, T-cell immunotherapy treatment: Acute lymphoblastic leukemia cured with AIDs virus

An experimental treatment in which researchers reengineer a patient's own immune system to attack cancer cells seems to have worked in a 7-year old girl named Emma Whitehead.

THE INQUISITR

December 10th 2012

Doctors Use HIV To Cure 7-Year-Old's Cancer

Emma Whitehead is a 7-year-old cancer patient. After two years of battling with acute lymphoblastic leukemia, she was selected to participate in an experimental trial that uses a disabled version of HIV to "cure" cancer.

There's A Bug Going Around is a medical thriller/black comedy where the principal character is HIV, the AIDS virus.

Felix, the research scientist, needs it as a means of fulfilling his professional ambitions and for settling scores with his father. Bismarck, the homophobic President of a drug company, fears it and wants it hunted down and destroyed. Mrs Plank, the mother of a self-obsessed rock star, accepts it as a weapon in the war of belittlement against her son. Henry, the ineffectual shop assistant, is martyred because of it. Tiger, the gay militant, enlists it for political mobilisation and revenge. Finally Eldridge Kwanza, the African medic, conquers it.

WHY NOW?

Earlier this month I was phoned by a friend who said: "You remember your medical thriller about using the Leukemic virus to cure AIDS, well I've just read that someone has used the AIDS virus to cure Leukemia". As you can see from the facing page, which shows some of these news articles, my friend was right.

The core of our book was the novel idea of using one virus to fight another, fire with fire. It was written in the 1990s at the height of the AIDS epidemic when the gay community particularly was threatened with a life threatening incurable and untreatable disease. The book characterised the social *dance macabre* that surrounded this modern day plague. It also addressed the dangers of untrammelled ambition. In moderation, ambition is a virtue. It is the necessary spur to excel in sport or politics or business or art or science. But there is a difference between "excel" and "win". For example the overarching need to "win" led to the corruption and downfall of Lance Armstrong, who was otherwise an excellent sportsman. In our novel we wrote how the honourable ambition of discovering the cure for AIDS can be the cover story for an obsessive need to win the Nobel Prize at any cost, with lethal consequences.

At the time, our book was offered to all the major literary agents and publishers and was rejected by one and all. They thought the central idea of using one virus to battle another was too fanciful and eccentric to be credible. The book has lain dormant ever since.

The scientific breakthrough described on the facing page has led me to think that maybe the book is worth resurrecting. As with science, much has changed in the publishing world since the 1990s. The major agents and publishers can be bypassed; and a book can be printed and distributed within a few months.

So here it is. The text has not been changed. It is set firmly in 1990s when the paranoia around AIDS was at its height, and for you to decide whether it was worth resuscitating. And, if you arrive at the end, at the last three lines of the book, remember they were written nearly 20 years ago!

Robert Silman
30th December 2012

Tambar

Publication date: 15 May 2013
Tambar Arts Ltd
Hamilton House, Mabledon Place, Bloomsbury, London WC1H 9BB
Tel: +44 (0) 207 554 8584; Fax: +44 (0) 207 554 8501
e-mail: contact@tambar.co.uk
Reg. No. 03937329
www.tambar.co.uk

ISBN 978-0-9572966-2-6

Cover Illustration: Miles Hyman (www.mileshyman.com)
Graphic Design: Dylan Martin (www.friedbanana.co.uk)

A CIP catalogue record for this book is available from the British Library

For Annick who phoned

Contents

PART ONE: A TALE OF THREE LIVES

I:	FELIX, GENESIS OF A GENIUS	Page 9
II:	DARIUS, LIFE WITH MOM	Page 71
III:	HENRY, CALVARY IN CALIFORNIA	Page 75

PART TWO: CRIME AND PUNISHMENT

IV:	CAUSE OF DEATH	Page 89
V:	TIGER'S DREAM	Page 139
VI:	RETRIBUTION	Page 147

PART THREE: DEATH IN VENICE

VII:	LAZARUS	Page 171
VIII:	LOST TO FOLLOW UP	Page 201
IX:	GUINEVERE	Page 241

EPILOGUE: FULL CIRCLE Page 255

PART ONE

A TALE OF THREE LIVES

CHAPTER ONE

FELIX
GENESIS OF A GENIUS

Felix mounted the podium. He turned and faced his audience. He was about to address a congregation of the greatest scientists in the world.

He stood at the lectern and looked directly at his father who was sitting in the front row. Father stared at him, anxious and bewildered. Felix gave him a reassuring smile. He'd done it all for father.

Felix began to speak. There was total silence in the conference hall.

Felix told them about his discovery.

At first there were a few stifled cries and gasps. Then, one by one, the members of the audience rose to their feet. Uproar broke out. They were giving him a standing ovation. Some were clapping, others were yelling their approval.

Felix had discovered the cure for AIDS.

Even father was standing, even father was proud of him.

Felix could hardly make himself heard above the hubbub.

It was the consummation of his life's work.

****

It all started when Felix was five.

It was a bright summer's day. Felix wasn't sure of the place; it was probably out on the terrace at the rear of the castle. He had a vague memory of a blue and white China tea service laid out on the marble table with a Georgian silver tea pot reflecting the sun into his eyes and making him screw up his face. It was a glorious day; he was in his sailor's suit. His mother was sitting to one side, away from the rest of the party, in a primrose yellow silk floral dress, her auburn hair flowing down to her waist. She was like the picture of Guinevere pinned to the wall of the nursery. There were lots of other people, the servants in formal dress, and guests, friends of his father, mostly men. He couldn't remember any women except for his mother.

PART ONE: A TALE OF THREE LIVES

Felix was sitting on his father's knee. The memory was vivid, composed of intense sensations. Felix remembered running his hand down the side of his father's face, and the shock of discovering his father's skin like sandpaper. Skin should be soft and smooth like his or mother's, or furry like the dogs. His father's shaven face with its sharp bristles and solitary hairs sprouting in odd places was alien. But it didn't repel him. On the contrary, its strangeness attracted him. It was like fingering the future, touching himself as he would be in twenty years time.

But most of all he remembered the smell. His father wasn't smoking, but the powerful odour of pipe tobacco lingered in his clothes. Felix buried his face in his father's tweed jacket to savour it, a heady mixture of new mown hay and coumarin. It was like snuggling up against a hay stack.

And then suddenly he was snatched out of his father's arms. One of his father's friends, he didn't know who, had picked him up. He was held high in the air, on display to the assembled company. Felix didn't like it. He didn't like being forcibly removed from the safety of his father's hold, and he didn't like being dangled in the air.

"What do you want to be when you grow up young man?" His father's friend was bellowing the question so that everyone could hear.

Felix didn't like the man. He was holding him in the air like a game bird, displaying him to the company. It wasn't an affectionate question; it was as if the man was taunting him. Felix began to panic. His face went red, his head pounded, and he couldn't breathe. He felt himself choking. The man dangled him in front of his father.

"What do you want to be when you grow up?"

Felix struggled to contain his tears. He didn't know what the man meant. The man kept repeating the question and his father was staring at him angrily.

Felix tried to speak but the words didn't come. He was choking and his father was looking at him as if he was a fool.

"Like my father."

The words were barely audible, and the man had to put his ear close to Felix's mouth to hear what he'd said. But it did the trick. The man bellowed his answer to the assembled company.

"He wants to be a scientist."

It was like magic. The man stopped asking questions, his father smiled, and his mother rescued him from the stranger. Everyone applauded, even the servants, as though he'd said something very clever.

And then everyone was saying it.

"Felix wants to be a scientist."

Felix had no idea what they meant. But it didn't matter. The words allowed him to breathe, and they pleased his father.

CHAPTER 1: FELIX, GENESIS OF A GENIUS

****

When he was eight, Felix discovered mother and father hated each other.

It was during the Easter holidays. Felix was at home with nanny and the servants, and mother and father were in London at the town house. It was a happy time. Felix was still attending the local village school, and his school friends were allowed to come to the castle and play with him. His closest friend was the daughter of a neighbouring banker. The others were the children of local trades' people, the sons and daughters of grocers, chemists and wine merchants. Felix wasn't a snob, but somehow he'd never become friendly with the servants' children. He instinctively knew it would create tensions within the household.

And then mother returned home unexpectedly. Felix was in the woods near the gates. He heard the honking of a car horn. He crept up through the long grass to see who'd arrived. Felix recognised the dark family Rolls, with the unfriendly chauffeur behind the driving wheel. His mother was leaning forward from the back seat slamming her hand on the horn, impatient and irritable, summoning the lodge keeper to open the gates. His heart was beating fast. He felt sick and unable to breathe properly. Mother was in a rage. He'd seen it once before, that look of wildness in her eyes. It was scary. It reminded him of the time when she'd had a row with father, and father had left the castle vowing never to return. He'd come back a couple of days later, but things had never been quite the same between them.

Mother kept the horn blaring the whole time, until the gatekeeper appeared.

The man was working in the kitchen garden, he hadn't expected mother home for another week, and he had to come limping down the half mile to the gates, summoned by the incessant horn. He hurried to open the wrought iron gates, and the black Rolls swept up the driveway.

Felix walked slowly back to the castle. He dreaded his meeting with mother. He was wheezing and choking, unable to catch his breath. Every few minutes he had to stop, it was almost as if he was forcing himself to delay the moment when he would have to face her.

She was waiting for him on the front terrace. As soon as she caught sight of him, she came running forward. Felix flinched. He thought she was going to strike him. But she swept him up in her arms and carried him into the air like a baby. Whatever had caused her anger had nothing to do with him. On the contrary, there was wildness in her passion. She hugged him and smothered him with kisses. The tightness in his chest lifted and he inhaled her breath into his lungs.

The next three days passed in a daze. He spent all his time with her; she wouldn't let him out of her sight, as if she might die if he wasn't there. At table she sat him on her lap, and they ate and drank from the same spoon and cup. At rest he slept in her bed and she cuddled him close to her in her sleep. She even insisted he sat beside her in the bathroom while she prepared her toilet. It was like a dream, Felix was the young knight courting and soothing his damsel in distress. He was Lancelot and she was Guinevere.

It was an idyll. On the fourth day, in the early morning, he woke early on purpose. He forced himself awake. It was like the holidays, when he'd set his alarm while it was still dark, for the pleasure of waking and knowing he didn't need to get up. It was the same now. The pleasure of lying in his mother's arms was too precious to waste in sleep.

She was lying on her back. He pulled back the blanket and sheets. Her body was covered by a light silk chiffon night gown trimmed with lace, her chestnut hair cascading to her waist. Felix lay on his side and stroked her, gently running his fingers through her hair, and circling her breasts with the palm of his hand. He noticed that they tightened under his touch, and she wriggled in her sleep with a sort of contentment.

He leaned forward and kissed her on the lips. She snuggled up to him, and cradled him in her arms.

And then the idyll ended.

There was a screeching of tires. A car came roaring up the drive. She woke. Her eyes were wide open, her pupils black, and she held on to him like a drowning woman. There was stomping of feet on the stairs, the door burst open. It was father. He stood at the doorway, screaming.

"Bitch!"

He kept shouting the word at her.

"Bitch!"

Mother was screaming back at him, but her words made no sense, they were just screeches and spit. Father stepped through the doorway. He came to the side of the bed, his arm raised as if to strike her. She gripped hold of Felix and held him above her. He was being used as a shield, a sort of talisman to ward off father.

It was the war of the worlds, a galactic explosion of the gods. They were fighting for possession... Of what?

His father took hold of Felix, and tried to tear him out of her hands. She was screaming, trying to hold on to Felix as if he was the only thing that could save her. But father was stronger, and Felix felt himself slipping out of her grasp. Father gave a final yank, and suddenly Felix felt himself flying through the air, flung out the doorway like a stray cat. He landed on the hard parquet floor with a thud and the door to the bedroom was slammed shut behind him.

The servants were there. They didn't know what to do, whether to intervene or leave their Lord and Lady to their own devices. Nanny was crying. She helped Felix to his feet and tried to lead him away. But Felix shook her free. He wanted to get back in the bedroom. But the door was locked; his father had bolted it from the inside.

He could hear his mother screaming behind the door. He rattled the door handle. The servants tried to calm him, but he wasn't upset. Whatever was going on between mother and father behind closed doors was a cause for fascination not terror. It was a battle of the gods. He wanted to get back inside the room not to defend mother but to see what was happening.

Suddenly mother gave a piercing scream, father a triumphant bellow, and then silence, silence except for panting.

The servants looked embarrassed and slipped away, quickly resuming whatever duties they did on an early Sunday morning. Nanny put her hands over Felix's ears to try and stop him hearing the panting sounds coming from behind the door. But even though she pressed her fingers tight into his ears, he could still hear a muffled noise, a sort of groaning and grunting. He imagined his father a bull, trampling Guinevere under foot.

Felix felt completely detached from what was going on inside. Whose side was he on? In a way he felt more akin to his father. He, too, wanted to conquer.

The noise subsided. Nanny took her hands from his ears. The door was unbolted. Nanny ran down the corridor, terrified of father. Father opened the door. Felix stretched out his hands in obeisance. Father looked down, but there was no solidarity. In father's eyes Felix was mother's ally, and father hated mother. As if to emphasise the point, father swung back his hand and gave Felix a stunning blow across the temple which sent him flying down the landing to the very edge of the stairwell.

Felix lay on the ground, his head throbbing with the pain of the blow. Father stepped over him and down the stairs. Felix tried to grab hold of his ankles. He wanted to hold on to him and tell him that whatever mother had done didn't involve him. But father was hurrying down the stairs, hurrying to get away from mother, and from him. Felix got to his feet and raced down the stairs trying to catch up with him, but father was much too fast. By the time Felix reached the entrance hall, father was already in the car. Felix heard the roar of the engine disappearing in the distance as he stumbled down the front steps.

Felix returned to his mother's room. Her night-dress had been torn from her body and she was lying, completely naked, across the bed. Her face was swollen, her arms bruised and she was sobbing. Felix lay down beside her. She hugged him, thinking he had come to comfort her. He lay in her arms. But he wasn't Lancelot. He buried his face in her breasts and slipped his hand between her legs. He rubbed the back of his hand against her hair. There was something sticky and moist, something that father had deposited between her legs.

"Bitch!" thought Felix.

****

Felix was twelve when mother and father divorced.

He was glad they'd finally separated. They'd given up speaking to each other in private. It wasn't speech, it was two wild animals hissing and screeching at each other. Yet in public they continued to appear the perfect couple, arm in arm to dinner, "my dear" this, "my dearest" that, it made Felix cringe. The worst was mother. She'd cling to father's side as though she adored him, and yet, as soon as the last of the guests had gone, she'd become a real bitch using Felix as the go between in all her transactions, including telling father that he was barred from her bed.

As for Felix, he'd become more and more detached. He'd ceased to exist since that day when father had come home and raped mother. He washed and brushed his teeth, he appeared at the dinner table, he spoke civilly when spoken to, he played with his friends and he did his schoolwork. But he didn't exist. He was outside his body looking in. And they didn't notice. Mother went on smothering him with affection, pretending she loved him, when all she really wanted was to use him against father. And father played into her hands by believing that Felix was actually siding with mother.

There was only one moment in the last four years when Felix had been truly happy. It was his last term at prep school. He was head boy, and been nominated for the Langsbridge Prize. The Langsbridge Prize was something special. It was only awarded occasionally, when a pupil displayed what Lord Langsbridge insisted upon, namely "intellectual eminence". There was considerable debate about whether Felix should be presented with the prize. The argument was political, whether it was seemly for the Honourable Felix Langsbridge to be awarded the Langsbridge Prize by his father Lord Langsbridge.

It was father who put an end to the discussion.

"If the boy deserves the prize he should get it."

Since Felix was the brightest pupil the school had ever had, nobody disputed that he deserved it. And so it was, on the last day of term, that Felix mounted the podium to be presented with the ribboned parchment by father. The audience applauded, father shook his hand. And then something quite extraordinary happened, something which hadn't happened since he'd been a small child. Father bent down and kissed him on the cheek.

"Well done son."

Father was proud of him.

For a brief moment, Felix re-entered his body.

The rest of the day was ruined by mother. She managed to make the union of father and son into a contest. She informed the headmaster, in earshot of father, that Felix was Wolfgang to father's Leopold.

When they returned to the Castle that evening, there was another savage row between mother and father, interrupted only by a terrible attack of asthma. It was the worst that Felix had ever experienced. He couldn't breath, not a breath. For a moment, from outside his own body, he watched himself choking to death. Mother was rushing around with inhalants and phoning doctors, and accusing father of wanting to kill his son out of jealousy. Father was white with rage, screaming that she was a bitch, and that she'd turned her son against his own father. Then, just before he passed out, Felix heard father slam the door behind him as he left the room, and the muffled shout.

"I hope he chokes to death!"

****

After mother and father divorced, Felix hadn't expected to leave the castle, and he certainly hadn't expected to spend all his time with mother. He'd taken it for granted he'd spend half his time with father. Instead, mother took Felix and set up home in London. Felix never saw father.

He tried to see him. Despite mother's protestations, he'd phone the castle from time to time and beg the servants to call father. But it didn't do any good. There was always an excuse why father was not available. Felix could sense that the servants were being told to lie by father. And when he put down the phone, mother would look triumphant, and she'd mouth the words, "I told you so", as if it was a joke.

Meanwhile Felix was growing up an unhappy young man. He was tall and gangly, with a long lantern jaw, and a Roman nose which was just too large to be elegant. He was uncomfortable in his body, and had little sense of fashion. He wore school uniform during term and frayed dark suits in the holidays. From time to time, mother would take him into town and fit him out in vivid colours and wonderfully tailored creations. Though Felix was excited at these excursions, joining with mother in imagining himself in his new guise, agreeing with her that the old Felix was too staid and dismal, when it came time to actually wear the new outfits, he lacked courage and continued in his habitual drab and dreary costume.

Felix accentuated the unease of his appearance by his social isolation. He had no natural charm. He didn't know how to conduct himself in company. Mother blossomed when she was with people, and the less she knew of them, the more she sparkled. Felix, on the other hand, was becoming more and more withdrawn. He had no friends, and when he was with others he departed his body and watched himself struggling to find an appropriate mode of being. His escape from his body was no relief. He was enraged by his futile attempts to cope with trivial and everyday social engagements. He just didn't know how to make his body work properly, and even the simplest encounters usually ended in a bout of asthma. Felix loathed his body and himself.

All in all, Felix was turning into a very strange young man, isolated from all passion and affection except for the image of his distant father.

What kept Felix sane was his master plan. As soon as he started at his new school, he developed a strategy to win back father's affection.

It was all so simple.

In two years time, there was to be the prize exam. The names of former prize winners were imprinted in gold leaf along the wooden panels of the great hall. And there was father's name, thirty years earlier, winner of the natural history prize. If father had been proud of him in prep school, how much more, here, at one of the premier public schools in England, where the brightest and the best were congregated, if Felix could equal his exploit and also win the prize?

Two years was a long way off, but so what? Felix was in no hurry. What mattered was to secure the goal. And in the meanwhile, Felix was kept going by just thinking about it. He spent hours each day fantasising about the occasion. A glorious summer's day, a cricket match on the school playing fields, father arriving in the Rolls, welcomed by Felix, shaking hands, Felix introducing father to the High Master who congratulates father on Felix's performance, the presentation of the prize, hurrahs from the assembly, Felix's name being engraved on the same panel with father's, father kissing him on the cheek, inviting him to ride back to the castle and spend the rest of the summer holidays with him, just the two of them, alone for the whole summer.

It would take hard work, but it could be done. In prep school, Felix had been by far the brightest pupil. But here the competition was much stiffer. There were probably four or five other boys who were on a par with Felix. All the same, by the end of the first term, Felix had worked so hard and so assiduously that he had edged himself into the lead. But only just. Close behind was Goldberg, a Jewish boy, who seemed to share the same maniacal need to excel as Felix.

And so it continued. During the next two years Felix stretched his lead over the rest of the class, with Goldberg just behind, a potential threat, a menace to all Felix's plans and hopes. Felix hated Goldberg. His fat Jewish presence threatened to ruin everything.

Without really being conscious of what he was doing, Felix devised a contingency plan. He became Goldberg's friend. He sensed that if he could wheedle his way into Goldberg's confidence he might discover a weakness which he could turn to his advantage.

But, more importantly, Felix discovered something about himself. He found that he could be at ease in the company of others if he despised them. He still remained outside his body, but now it was different. Instead of being a stumbling incoherent puppet, he was masterful. All that was needed was deceit. Felix was enthralled by his own performance. He watched himself talk animatedly to Goldberg about Goldberg's family, pretending an avid interest in their usurious exploits, complimenting Goldberg on his ghastly nouveau riche taste, even going so far as to express a desire to own a gold Rolex watch himself. It became a game. How far could Felix go in fake rapture before Goldberg realised it was phoney. The answer was... as far as he liked. There was no limit to Goldberg's vanity. And it didn't just apply to Goldberg. It was the same for everyone. So long as Felix kept a straight face, and expressed admiration, they ate out of his hands.

And so Felix learnt how to conduct himself in public. His demeanour changed. He stood upright and tall, his speech became fluent and articulate, he began to dress with style and flair, his asthma was a thing of the past. Everyone, particularly mother, commented with admiration on his transformation. And the trick? To despise the people you were addressing.

Thus it was with Goldberg. The more Felix despised internally, the more he pretended to admire outwardly; and the more Felix expressed fake admiration, the more Goldberg adored Felix and confided in him. Felix learnt the most private and precious things about Goldberg, the bank account in Switzerland, the brother in the mental home, the mother's affair with a non-Jew.

Unfortunately there was nothing in all this for Felix to use, nothing which could be used against Goldberg to halt his inexorable presence beside him in the prize exam. Even worse, Felix's tactics had begun to backfire. Goldberg considered it a measure of his affection for Felix to be his companion in academic excellence, and redoubled his efforts to keep up with Felix. In the final mock exam, in the term prior to the prize exam, Goldberg actually beat Felix in the calculus paper by writing an astonishingly erudite essay on the origins of calculus in relation to the philosophy of Leibnitz.

Felix became desperate. He began a charm offensive on the masters who were going to mark the prize exam. Mr Sturridge, the physics tutor, was particularly susceptible to Felix's approach. He was something of a snob and adored being courted by the "Honourable Felix Langsbridge", the future "Lord Langsbridge". Felix complimented Sturridge on his scholarship while secretly condemning him as an usher; he expressed amazement at Sturridge's familiarity with the ways of the world while privately cataloguing him as a gossip. In no time, Felix had Sturridge fawning on him. Even better, Sturridge was an anti-Semite, and Felix encouraged him in his righteous outrage that "Hebrews", like Goldberg, were being permitted access to the school, which was a "Christian Institution". Felix confided in Sturridge that Goldberg "sweated a lot" and didn't bath very often, that he "conveniently" forgot when he borrowed money, and that, like "all his race", he couldn't be trusted. It was a curious dialectic. Felix despised Goldberg. Yet, in denouncing Goldberg to Sturridge, Felix despised Sturridge for acquiescing in his denunciation of Goldberg.

But none of this really mattered. What mattered was the prize exam. If Goldberg produced a prize winning paper, it wouldn't matter a damn that the masters preferred Felix. Somehow or other Felix had to find a way to stop Goldberg.

In desperation he invited Goldberg to spend a week during the spring vacation with him and mother. Mother was outraged. She couldn't see what Felix saw in a fat, ugly, short sighted Jewish boy whose only saving grace was that he doted on Felix. Felix also wasn't altogether sure why he'd invited him. They spent a few days together in Monte Carlo, and Felix had an opportunity to push him out the window of the hotel. They were on the sixth floor; Goldberg was leaning out the window. But it was only a passing fancy. More concretely, Felix tried to corrupt Goldberg with drugs. He enticed him into a few puffs by telling him he smoked it all the time. Of course he didn't. He'd never tried it in his life, nor wanted to. But he knew where to find it; he'd long since learnt where mother hid it, in the red shoe stuffed with tissue paper. So one afternoon, in the hotel room in Monte Carlo, Felix initiated Goldberg into the joys of pot. As Felix rolled the cigarette paper, he had visions of Goldberg staggering into the prize exam, hands twitching, eyes red, pupils dilated, writing an incoherent drug crazed paper.

Nothing came of it. Felix and Goldberg returned to school at the beginning of the summer term, neck and neck in competition for the prize. For a while Felix thought of asking Goldberg to throw the exam in his favour. But that would have put a question mark on their relationship. Even stupid doting Goldberg might have realised that something wasn't quite right.

Then, in a moment of inspiration, with only a week to go, Felix knew how to do it. Like all good solutions it was simple and elegant.

The first step was to get Goldberg to revise with him.

The evening before the exam, he invited Goldberg to his study. Felix opened the standard three volume text book on theoretical physics and began dictating a complete list of all the key formulae and equations.

"But I know them all," Goldberg protested.

"It doesn't matter it's my way of revising," answered Felix imperiously.

Goldberg was too much in awe and admiration of Felix to thwart him at such a time. He began writing, and assumed that Felix's bizarre behaviour was due to exam stress.

The next step was to gain access to the exam room. At about one in the morning, Felix crept out of the dormitory, clutching the notes Goldberg had written down at his dictation. The other pupils were fast asleep. He went down the stairs, past matron's room, out through the quadrangle, in through the window of the dining room, and on to the examination hall. He made his way to the second desk on the right, his desk, and taped Goldberg's notes to the underside.

The rest was easy.

Next morning, he entered the examination hall with the other candidates. There were twelve students in all. They were the pick of the year, twelve from two hundred. But everyone knew that only two were in contention, Felix and Goldberg. The students went to their desks. Felix sat at the second desk on the right, with Goldberg immediately behind. Felix turned round to Goldberg.

"Good luck," he said.

"Thank you," Goldberg answered.

And then Goldberg stretched out his hand and shook Felix by the hand.

"I hope you win," he said.

Goldberg's face was screwed up with emotion. He actually wanted Felix to win.

Felix was disgusted. That someone should be so stupid as to believe in a fake friendship, that someone should be so sentimental as to let friendship take precedence over self interest, that someone should sacrifice his own interests for love! Felix's sense of contempt and disgust was renewed and reinforced. Instead of seeing the fat stupid face of Goldberg struggling to contain his feelings, Felix saw a maggot.

"Thank you. I very much appreciate it," Felix replied.

He looked Goldberg straight in the face, and watched himself mimicking Goldberg's passion, his lower lip trembling with emotion and tears welling in his eyes. And then Felix turned round rapidly, giving the impression he would break down if he faced his friend for a moment longer.

The invigilating master walked between the desks dealing out the morning exam paper. Felix fingered Goldberg's notes taped to the underside of his desk. The master laid the paper before him. Felix brought out his hand from under the desk, leaving Goldberg's notes in place. He opened the examination paper. It was a simple straightforward question on the mitochondrial respiratory system. Felix began writing his essay. There was a glow within him. Before the day was done the maggot would be crushed underfoot, and he would be rid of Goldberg once and for all.

The lunch break passed quickly. The atmosphere was fevered. The candidates were discussing the morning's session, some groaning in dejection as they discovered their errors and lacunae, others jubilant. Felix and Goldberg sat slightly apart from the rest, in recognition of their pre-eminent status and close friendship.

Towards the end of lunch, Felix made his excuses to Goldberg.

"I have to see a man about a dog."

They were eating rice pudding, Goldberg's favourite, so there was no chance he would try to follow.

Instead of going to the loo, Felix made his way to the examination hall. As he expected, Sturridge was already there, preparing for the afternoon session. Sturridge was delighted to see him, and complimented him on the morning's efforts, commenting that he'd only had a chance to glance at Felix's paper but that it looked first rate.

Felix put on a deeply troubled face.

"What's the matter?" asked Sturridge.

Felix played the scene where Iago pretends he has nothing to say and Othello has to coax it out of him, with Felix playing the part of Iago.

"There's nothing the matter."

"You look troubled."

"Troubled?"

Eventually, after a great deal of coaxing from Sturridge, Felix began to expound that there was a "delicate matter" which was distressing him. More coaxing from Sturridge, and Felix confessed to his "unease". Finally, with Sturridge almost begging him to be more precise, Felix vouchsafed his concern that Goldberg might be "cheating".

With many a pause, and with Sturridge leaning on his every word, Felix let slip that he'd caught Goldberg leaning forward, apparently copying from his paper.

Sturridge was outraged and wanted to inform the High Master at once. Felix begged him not to, it was only a suspicion, Felix could be wrong, was almost certainly wrong, should never have even mentioned it. Sturridge began to wax lyrical on the "nobility" of Felix, with an occasional outburst on the "loathsomeness" of Goldberg.

Time was running out, the students could be heard approaching down the corridor for the afternoon session. Felix begged Sturridge to put what he'd said out of his mind, that it was almost certainly a "misunderstanding".

Then, with the students congregating outside, Felix laid the trap. He suggested to Sturridge, "just to be on the safe side", and, "to remove all temptation", that Felix and Goldberg should swop desks, with Goldberg in front and Felix behind.

Goldberg entered the examination hall to be greeted by a scowling Mr Sturridge who ordered him to remove his things from his desk and to change places with the "Honourable" Felix Langsbridge. Sturridge was never particularly friendly towards Goldberg, but now he seemed positively deranged. Goldberg was baffled and looked towards Felix to see if he had an explanation. Felix gave him a friendly smile, and shrugged his shoulders as if to say "the whims of masters are beyond the comprehension of mere mortals".

The afternoon paper was the Physics essay. It turned out to be a difficult topic. Did Maxwell's Demon expend more energy in observing the molecules than it gained by sorting them? There was a general groan from the rest of the room. Only Felix and Goldberg set about the answer with gusto.

The afternoon rushed by in a fever of writing. Felix arranged it so that he finished his paper a couple of minutes early. He made a final correction and handed in his essay to Sturridge while the others were still putting the finishing touches to theirs. Then, just before leaving the examination hall, Felix bent forward and whispered in Sturridge's ear.

His last vision of Goldberg was a fat maggot face bent over its copy.

The other students told Felix what happened after he left, how Mr Sturridge had come charging up to Goldberg denouncing him as a cheat, how Mr Sturridge had found Goldberg's crib sheets stuck under his desk, how Goldberg had pretended he didn't know how they'd got there, how the High Master had been summoned, and how Goldberg had been expelled on the spot.

For the next few days, Felix was surrounded by kindness and consideration. Masters and students commiserated with him on the shameful deed, they were scandalised that his trust in Goldberg should have been so shamefully misused, and they encouraged him not to let the deceit of Goldberg mar his trust in others. As for Sturridge, he promised Felix that Felix's part in "unmasking the Jew" would be a secret between them, as "others", particularly the "Hebrews" in the school hierarchy, might misunderstand the "nobility" of Felix's act.

When it was announced in the great hall that Felix had won the prize, a cheer went up. There was spontaneous applause. It was an expression of genuine pleasure at a well deserved honour.

****

Far from things improving after the prize exam, they went from bad to worse.

There was the terrible day when Felix met father at church.

He'd tried to tell him the good news on the phone, but as usual the servants were ordered to block his call. Felix was so exasperated, he invoked every possible reason why father should be summoned. But nothing worked, not even a final recourse to "It's a matter of life or death!"

That's why Felix had to go to the castle and confront father with the news. He set out on the Sunday following the exam results. He got a school pass and took the early morning train. He still had it in his head that once the story of his success had sunk in, father's attitude would change. On the train journey, he fantasised about father's response. He saw father lifting him in the air and carrying him round the castle proclaiming his success to the servants. Or, even better, father dropping to his knees and begging Felix to forgive him, and Felix raising father from the ground, and kissing him on the cheek in sign of absolution. For Felix, time had stood still since he'd last seen father, and he couldn't conceive it would be any different for father. They were both waiting for the chance to be reconciled.

The journey took two hours. By the time Felix arrived at the castle station, the early morning chill had given way to a hot humid summer's day. Felix stepped onto the platform, the station master nodded his head in greeting, but he didn't recognise him. It was the first time Felix had been back for nearly four years, and he'd changed a great deal in that time.

Felix set off up the hill towards the village church. Father wasn't a believer, but he considered it his duty to set a good example to the servants, and therefore always attended Sunday mass. Felix had timed his arrival so that he could greet father as he left the church. Given father's reticence to communicate with Felix, it was better to meet him in public, on neutral territory.

Felix sat on a grave stone in front of the church. The sound of organ and choir spilled out from the porch and joined with the song of the birds in the garden. There wasn't a soul in the village, everyone was inside the church. Felix wiped the sweat from his brow. The climb up the hill had been tiring and he was still wearing his school uniform with its thick black jacket and starched white collar.

The service ended. The vicar was the first to leave the church. He stood at the portal and chatted to his parishioners as they filed past. Felix recognised some of them, like the local postmistress and the grocer. There were also new faces. Who was that lady in the primrose dress? She was the centre of attraction; everyone was gathered round her as though she was royalty. She was in her twenties, a strikingly beautiful young woman, exquisitely dressed, even Felix could recognise that, mother had taught him an appreciation of haute couture. She had her two children with her, a small boy of two or three, with curly blond hair, dressed in a velvet suit with a silk cravat. He looked like a miniature version of little Lord Fauntleroy. There was also a baby. It was in its pram alongside the woman in primrose. The pram was being pushed by nanny.

Suddenly Felix couldn't breath. The surrounding countryside poured out its pollen, spores, dust, every conceivable allergen. It was as though the air was thick with clogging particles. Felix's throat went into spasm, the bronchi in his lungs constricted and he wheezed and choked.

Father was standing alongside the young woman, his arm round her waist. The little boy was at his side, nanny and the baby just behind. They were a family group just like when Felix and mother stood beside father on Sundays after church.

Felix struggled to force the air from his chest. He couldn't breathe out. It was as if the air in his lungs refused to move.

The little boy was tugging at father's hand, trying to grab his attention. Father was talking to the vicar; the villagers were standing alongside listening to every word. It was the old days except that the woman in primrose had replaced mother, and the little boy, Felix.

Felix fought to push the air from his lungs. It was a losing battle. It was like trying to pump air into a tire which was already full. There was a gurgling, crackling, bubbling, noise from his lungs, and that was it. It was if he was being smothered inside an invisible air-tight bag.

The little boy went on tugging at father's sleeve. Father looked down at the little boy and smiled. The young woman bent down and picked up the little boy. She handed him over to father, who swept him up into the air. Father was beaming with pleasure as he held the little boy aloft. The villagers applauded. It was obvious, even for Felix, the little boy was father's son.

But father loved Felix.

Felix was his son and heir.

Felix made a supreme effort and staggered a few steps towards father. He was losing consciousness. What a catastrophe! He was going to pass out before he'd had the chance to tell father the news of his success.

The little boy shouted "Daddy!"

The little boy was pointing towards him. Father looked up. He'd seen him, father's face changed. Father recognised him. Felix stretched out his hand and made a desperate effort to keep upright as he fought his way towards father. Father shook his head, he was frowning, there was a look of disgust and contempt on his face. As Felix stumbled and fell, father turned his back on Felix and gathered his new family together to return to the castle.

Felix stopped struggling for breath. The air in his lungs gave up their last molecule of oxygen and he collapsed unconscious in the graveyard.

****

Felix survived. He never knew how. Perhaps it was nanny who'd carried the life saving drugs? Perhaps the emergency services came in time to save him from asphyxiation? At any event he went on living, if you could call it living.

Felix had no way of dealing with the catastrophe. Father had remarried three years earlier. No one had told him. Father had a new wife. No one had told him. Father had a new son and daughter, a brother and sister for Felix, and no one had told him.

Felix could have coped with that, probably. But what he couldn't accept was the image before he fell unconscious, father turning his back on him, and leaving him to choke to death.

Suddenly Felix was back where he'd started, only worse. He didn't know who he was, where he was, what he was. He stood outside his body unable to make any association between himself and it.

The body deteriorated. Felix took no care of it. He slept in his clothes at night and remained unwashed for weeks on end, until mother or the school authorities drove him into the showers. Worse, his asthma had returned more savagely than ever before. There wasn't a moment, day or night, when Felix wasn't struggling for breath. The only way to control the disease was ever increasing doses of steroids. The drugs didn't do much for his asthma, but his body began to puff up, with a layer of fat between his shoulder blades, giving him the appearance of a moon faced hunchback.

Felix didn't care. It had nothing to do with him. Nothing had anything to do with him. He watched himself day in and day out struggling for breath, and he didn't care. He didn't care if he choked to death.

Felix became mute, refusing to speak even in response to the simplest of questions. Mother became so worried she sent him to an analyst. But it didn't do any good. The analyst kept questioning Felix's body, but the body remained silent because Felix was somewhere else.

CHAPTER 1: FELIX, GENESIS OF A GENIUS

The trouble with Felix was that he didn't know where he was. He wasn't in his body, but he wasn't anywhere else. He was in a state of limbo, like a ghost hovering around outside of himself, waiting for somewhere to alight.

Felix left school. There was no point in being there. He didn't attend class, and when he did, he didn't speak or do any work. The school authorities suggested he take a year off. What they meant was, if he didn't get better within a year he wouldn't be taken back.

The analysts gave up, and Felix was passed on to the psychiatrists, who quickly tired of his mutism and sent him on to the neurologists. Eventually all the specialists were brought together, and there was a great debate about whether Felix's asthma was causing chronic asphyxia, leading to a neurological deficit of the central nervous system. In other words, they thought he was brain damaged. Felix watched from outside his body as the experts debated his case, and he agreed with them. He did feel brain dead.

Perhaps it was because he appeared an idiot that mother treated him as such. At any event when the news of father's action broke, she didn't try to hide it from him. On the contrary she took every opportunity to bring it up.

Father had begun legal proceedings to have Felix declared illegitimate.

Father's case was that mother had been having an affair with a groundsman at the time Felix was conceived. It became known as the "Lady Chatterley" case in the popular press. Father went to court so that Felix's title The Honourable Felix Langsbridge would pass instead to the little boy in the velvet suit who would become the future Lord Langsbridge. As mother put it, father wanted Felix to be known as The Bastard Felix Langsbridge.

The worst of it was that Felix believed father.

Mother was a bitch, a bitch on heat, and Felix could well imagine her having an affair with the groundsman. The photos of him in the papers showed him to be a handsome and husky young man, just the sort mother swooned over. Felix had no doubts. He was a bastard, and father had every right to reject and despise him.

The lawyers and doctors gathered for the great "blood taking" spectacle. Felix's arm was bared and a syringe full of blood taken from his vein to be analysed and compared with a similar sample from mother, father and groundsman. Science would decide if Felix was a bastard.

But science decided otherwise. The blood tests showed conclusively that Felix was indeed his father's legitimate son. Father's case collapsed, the court action was dropped, Felix returned to being The Honourable Felix Langsbridge, the future Lord Langsbridge. Everything was back to normal.

Except for Felix.

The discovery that father was wrong, that he had unjustly tried to deprive Felix of his rights, began to work away at Felix. It didn't happen right away. It wasn't a coup de théâtre. But, bit by bit, the old portrait of father was effaced. The man to be respected emulated and admired gave way to a more sinister figure. A new effigy of father began to form in Felix's mind, no longer the omnipotent, grandiose, admirable and unattainable goal of his life, but something quite different, an anti-being, someone who was trying to destroy Felix, who wasn't righteous and just, but monstrous and evil.

As the new image of father began to take shape in Felix's mind, so he began to recover. The step by step progression of Felix's detestation for his father was accompanied by the step by step recovery from his depression.

The first recovery was speech. Mother, who'd been right about father all along, was telling some acquaintance about father's vile behaviour. But she hadn't mentioned his loathsome language, so Felix intervened. The first words Felix spoke, for over a year, were...

"He used to call you a bitch."

****

The transformation of Felix was extraordinary. It was a veritable metamorphosis. Over a period of three months, the mute wheezing moon faced hunchback gave way to a fresh faced slim articulate young dandy.

The lessons of the past were applied with renewed vigour. Felix stood outside himself and manipulated his body like a puppet master. He decided to create himself as an instantly recognisable object. In his dress... expensively tailored clothes from Savile Row, but in a late Victorian cut, with flamboyant highly coloured silk linings, a bit like Oscar Wilde. In his speech... which came in rapid staccato bursts, like a muffled machine gun, a bit like Isaiah Berlin. In his name... he insisted on being called Felix, his first name, his last name, his only name was "Felix", a bit like Fernandel. In food... a gourmet, appreciative of la France Gourmande and deprecating the excesses of nouvelle cuisine, a bit like Robert Courtine. He also developed a mosaic of cultural tastes, representing an amalgam of overlapping critical currents, but which in their totality came to represent "Le Point de Vue de Felix". In art... ecstatic about Bonnard and Duchamps while despising Van Gogh and late Dali. In music... admirative of Handel and ambiguous about Wagner. In literature... damning the Levisites while admiring Lawrence. In the performing arts... extolling the virtues of Tennessee Williams against the deficiencies of Arthur Miller.

So Felix returned to school, and in no time he was a star. His style of dress, his manner of speech, his tastes were copied by others less gifted than himself, and gave rise to a movement "the Neo-Felixians". But where his followers were a subject of ridicule, Felix himself was never anything but a celebrity, one of the most gifted and charming students the school had ever produced. The opinion was universal. The boy had an amazing future. Some even went so far as to suggest that he was, perhaps, a genius.

And what was the trick? The same as before, namely an ability to look on while performing a part. It was a rerun of Goldberg taken to the nth degree. Felix had an intense contempt for everyone. The more he shone, the more he despised those who fell under his sway. And the more he despised those that adored him, the better he was at charming them. Everyone was subject to his charm and intelligence. And most of all, everyone was subject to his flattery.

To hone his skills, Felix practised on those who were the least likely to fall under his spell. There was, for example, the captain of the rugby fifteen, Mike Gibbon, a stupid boy who thought the world of himself by virtue of his brutish behaviour on the playing fields. He was aptly named, with an apish build, covered with body hair from the age of fourteen. At first sight it seemed impossible to win over such a lout, and Felix made mistakes. He learnt that you must not make your move while your adversary is otherwise engaged, i.e. don't disturb Gibbon during the rugby season. He learnt that you must enter their world rather than entice them into yours, i.e. dazzle Gibbon with an Arabian Nights on rugby, its history, its theory, its heroes. Finally he learnt that you must be careful about who you chose for practice, i.e. the ape man became his most slavish devotee and there was no way to get rid of him.

But what was going on inside Felix? While he stood outside himself, watching himself beguile others, was there anyone to seduce him? After all, Felix was a young man, seventeen years old, was there anyone he wanted?

Certainly not other boys. The covert affairs in the dormitories and the overt goings on behind the squash courts were not for Felix. But he wasn't keen on girls either. Mother arranged party after party, with the pick of the London debutantes, and Felix entered into the swing of it, choosing the belle of the ball and dancing till dawn. By the end of the season the prettiest girls in London were head over heels in love with him, but not him with them.

He wasn't interested in boys and he wasn't interested in girls. The strangest thing of all, he wasn't even drawn to himself. Of course he experimented, and from time to time he managed to get an erection, usually while soaping himself in the shower, but it stopped there. Try as he might, nothing came. He knew what was meant to happen, Felix wasn't ignorant about sex, but nothing came, probably because he had nobody to think about while he did it.

The only time anything came was at night, while he was asleep. There was a dream, about which he could remember nothing, and then the sticky stain on the bedclothes. He depended on his wet dreams. Sexual tension grew inside him over several days or weeks, there was no relief, frustration built up day on day, the need to discharge becoming more pressing. And then the joy of waking in the night to feel the stickiness around his groin, knowing that the tension would be gone, that he would be at peace.

And then the cycle started again. It never left him. He hated it. He hated the constant tension, the sexual need, the wait. He couldn't force the wet dream. It came when it came. And as for the need, the need for what? It had no object. And without an object he couldn't discharge it.

He began to envy the simple ridiculous passions of other boys, boys who liked girls, boys who liked boys, boys who liked goats! It didn't matter what it was, at least they knew what they wanted.

Then one night, it happened. Felix awoke during his dream, his hand between his legs, warm sperm cascading through his fingers and an image of Guinevere.

Maybe it was an idealisation, a romantic transformation of something more mundane. At any event it gave Felix the clue, an object began to form.

First, Felix needed a room, somewhere with privacy, not only privacy while he was doing it, but privacy from intruders when he wasn't there. Thank goodness he was now in the sixth form with his own personal study. Studies were inviolate, no one entered without permission. Nonetheless Felix took no chances, he fitted a padlock to the cupboard.

Next was the equipment. It was a complicated business, and it took several months of trial and error before he even began to understand what he was seeking. Then there were a couple of bungled experiments as he worked out exactly what was needed. But when he did, it all made sense. Some things were easy to acquire, the ropes and chains; some were more tricky, the women's stockings and undergarments. As for the most important item, the high heeled black leather boots, he stole them from Harrods. Bit by bit the locked cupboard was filled with treasure, like Aladdin's cave.

It was an evening in late autumn when Felix was finally ready to give it a try. The tension had been building up in him for days. Felix retired to his study and bolted the door. There was a thick swirling mist rising up against the dying sun. The wildly shaking branches of the trees alongside the playing fields were barely visible. The wind flung the dead leaves against the study window, and it sounded like the fluttering of moths struggling to get in. Felix lighted a candle, a black candle. There had to be a candle and it had to be black. He placed it on the mantelpiece above the fireplace and drew the curtains. The room was chilly and he lit the gas fire. He sat slouched in the massive green armchair and waited for the fire to warm the room. He was at peace, the flickering of candle and gas illuminating the room and bathing it in a glow of light and shade.

He unlocked the cupboard and pulled back the door. He looked at himself in the full length mirror that he'd attached to the back of the door. He stared at himself and smiled. He was savouring the moment, acknowledging the occasion, preparing to meet his first and only love.

He stripped off his clothes, and stood naked before the mirror. He was tall, already more than six foot, and slim and not bad looking. The Roman nose gave an air of haughtiness, and the massive jaw suggested profundity, but there was also a freshness and charm in the face to temper any heaviness. His skin was white like alabaster, with a soft down of jet black hair between his legs. It was the most striking feature of his appearance, the contrast between the pallor of his skin and the blackness of his hair, like an old print of Rudolph Valentino.

The first items of dress were the black silk stockings and lace garters. Felix perched himself on a stool in front of the mirror, and watched himself slip them on. He was like Marlene in the *Blue Angel.* He stroked his thighs and smiled at himself as he attached stocking to garter, swinging one long lanky leg over the other in an exaggerated gesture of seduction.

Next came the panties, again silk, but in a deep vermilion red. He stood up and slipped them on over the stockings. The panties were trimmed in lace and were open at their centre. He waved a greeting to himself as it grew from his groin, like a flagpole propelling itself through the hole in the centre.

Next came the corset, a whalebone and rubber affair that he'd managed to acquire at an Oxfam jumble sale. There were ties and belts and buckles and hooks. The corset was a delight. As Felix tightened the stays, the flagpole throbbed with pleasure at every squeeze and pinch.

Next came the bras. There were several to choose from, a skimpy see through from a sex shop, a fashionable half cup from a couturier, and an old fashioned heavily padded affair which he'd acquired at the same time as the corset. Only now did it become obvious. It had to be the heavy old fashioned rubber one. As he attached the hooks and eased it over his nipples, the flagpole grew another inch in appreciation, and a drop of moisture appeared at its tip.

He was nearly ready. He sat on the stool, legs wide apart, flagpole protruding erect from the central parting in the panties, catching the light from the candle and throwing a flickering shadow on the wall.

Felix took a box from the cupboard and began to apply his makeup. He had little idea of how it worked, there'd been no one to ask, but he managed to work it out from first principles and from what he could remember of mother when he'd watched her do it all those years ago. He started with foundation cream, applying it liberally, obliterating all trace of facial hair, then eyeliner, then rouge, then powder, then false eyelashes, and finally a deep vermilion lipstick to match the colour of the panties.

He looked wonderful. The object of his desire was being created before his very eyes. The flagpole secreted two drops from its tip in appreciation of the marvel standing before it.

Now came the wig. It had taken Felix weeks to track it down. Some shops had the right colour but the wrong style, some the right length but the wrong texture, it seemed impossible to get everything right, but it had to be, it was essential. Eventually Felix placed an ad in the personal columns of the Times. "Wanted: waist length auburn wig of finest quality". And here it was at last, the hair like silk, the colour a golden chestnut. He fitted it over his scalp, and shook his head. It cascaded down his back like a river. The reflection in the mirror was Guinevere, the demoiselle of his dreams.

Not quite. There was still one item. Felix reached into the cupboard and pulled out the boots. They were soft like puppy skin, with a smell of finest leather. The heels were long, like stilettos. He caressed the skin against his cheek, murmuring endearments, as if he were cradling a baby. Then he rubbed the black leather against the flagpole. It grew another inch, reared above his umbilicus, and shot two or three drops into space in jubilation.

Felix slipped on the boots and stood before his image in the mirror. He was now ready for the final act of consummation.

He stretched into the cupboard and brought out the rope and chains. He attached the rope to the heavy brass buckle he'd nailed to the wall, and knotted it to the chains. Next came the cellophane bag. He placed it over his head. It was transparent and he could see through it, watching himself in the mirror. He took the ties dangling from the cellophane bag and wound them round the chains. Last he slipped his wrists inside the chains. He gave a tug, he was firmly bound. Sure he could escape, but only from one position, the one he would use when he was done.

He looked at himself in the mirror. Guinevere bound and chained. He tugged at the ties and the cellophane bag tightened round his neck. He watched as Guinevere struggled for breath. He saw her begin to shake and gasp, the more she struggled the more she choked. The absence of oxygen was like a furnace for the flagpole. It rose ever higher, its tip stretching up to caress her breasts. She struggled, seeking to escape the flagpole. But it was like a snake rearing its head towards her, its ardour inflamed by her reticence. The cellophane bag was plastered against her face, there was not a breath of air, she was choking to death. As if in exultation the flagpole let loose a jet of liquid. It shot into the air like a firework, the drops glistening in the light of the candle. Guinevere moaned in ecstasy.

Felix slipped from his chains and removed the cellophane bag. The flagpole exhausted the last drops of its passion and shrivelled. Felix collapsed to the floor fighting for breath. It was alright. He'd judged it exactly, too soon and the thrill would have been lost, too late and she would have died.

Felix lay on the ground panting in satisfaction.

****

Felix was a strange and muddled young man. He despised those he pretended to admire, he turned passion into a grotesque and loveless fetish, he had no sense of his own identity. There was only one thing holding Felix together, hatred for his father. Day by day, week by week, month by month, his hatred for father deepened and intensified. It was his raison d'être, the abiding purpose of his life.

The destruction of father became the new masterplan, the sole mission of his being. Everything Felix did was geared to this one end.

Why did Felix become the most brilliant pupil at school? It wasn't for his own gratification. He had too little self esteem for that. He despised himself as much as he despised others. The reason was simple. It was a way of humiliating father. The greater Felix's success, the heavier father's defeat. It was a bizarre equation. Felix reversed the old masterplan. Instead of Felix seeking glory to win father's love, it was being used to engineer father's destruction.

To be a star at school was just the first stage. Father probably wouldn't even get to hear of it. And, even if he did, so what? Felix needed to go much further and reach much higher. He needed to excel in the real world, in the world where father lived and shone. Felix's star had to shine with such intensity that it would extinguish the light from father. There was only one place where that could happen, where Felix's success would embitter and humiliate father beyond endurance. That was in father's world, in the world of science. Felix's goal in life was set. He was determined to become a scientist of such rank, repute and renown, that it would cast a shadow of death over father.

****

Felix did well enough while he was at university. He was undoubtedly a bright young man, and with hard work he managed to keep ahead of his rivals. At any event he left Oxford University with First Class Honours. But, then, so did a lot of bright young men.

The next step was harder. The rules of the game for success at school and university were fairly straightforward. But success in the outside world was more problematic. He needed a Doctorate. But every research scientist, even the most commonplace, has a Doctorate. So, he had to get more than that, he had to get into the spotlight. His research had to be of sufficient distinction to be published. At the end of the day, publications were what counted. They counted so much that some people did just that, counted the number you had to your name. The more you had, the better you were. If you also managed to get your papers into the premier journals, such as *Nature* or *Science*, there could be no further doubt, you were the tops.

Felix found a scientist in London, at a neurological research unit, with tons of first class publications to his name. He seemed just right for sponsoring a bright young man like Felix. Felix set about reading up on his work. He was trying to identify the gene responsible for diabetic neuropathy, map it, sequence it, clone it, and create an animal model for experimenting on a cure. More important, Felix gained a pretty clear idea about the internal politics of the unit. The head man obviously didn't do any of the actual lab work; he supervised others and had his name on all the papers, his name coming last in the list of authors. Coming last signified you were number one. Then there were three chief underlings. They didn't appear on each other's papers. They did their own work where their name appeared first. Coming first signified you were number two. There were occasional exceptions to this rule. Sometimes, the underlings overlapped and their names appeared on each other's papers, and sometimes the work which was being reported was so important that the head man put his name first. Those were the ones in *Nature* or *Science*.

Felix wrote a flattering letter to the head of the London group, enclosing a brief resume of his school and university career, and asking for an opportunity to undertake his doctoral thesis with someone whose work he had "so much admired and respected" over the years. The interview followed. Everyone was there, the head man and his three number twos. Felix rattled off all he knew about their research until they were fired with enthusiasm at the thought of such a talented young man being their secret disciple.

Felix spent three uneventful years working in the lab of the London group. After the first interview he hardly saw the head man, who spent most of his time travelling the world reporting on the work of his assistants at international conferences. Felix was attached to one of his number twos, a sombre bearded Scotsman, who arrived early and left late, and who didn't enjoy idle conversation. Felix won over the Scotsman by arriving earlier and leaving later, and by being equally taciturn, speaking only when it was necessary to get some technical advice.

The Scotsman was surprisingly talented. Time and again, when experiments were getting nowhere, when Felix was faced with failure, the Scotsman would come up with the key piece of advice to get it all going again, altering the pH, substituting ion exchange chromatography, omitting enzyme inhibitor. Whatever the problem, somehow or other he had the knack for identifying it, and solving it.

At the end of three years Felix had his Ph.D. He also had six publications to his name, two as first author and four as secondary author. One of the publications was in *Nature*. Felix had achieved everything he could have wished.

But had he?

So what a PhD at 24? So what a paper in *Nature*? So what anything, if it didn't impress father?

Felix had to get to the top of the top. He had to be like Pasteur, Pauling, Salk, Crick, or Watson. Felix had to be a name so celebrated that he would be recorded in the annals of history.

Felix had achieved nothing so far which was going to overwhelm father. He needed more.

****

It was the sombre bearded Scotsman who gave Felix the way forward.

They were having tea and biscuits. The Scotsman was in a particularly bitter mood. He'd seen his boss on television the previous night, chairing a programme on biotechnology. The Scotsman began denouncing his boss, calling him a "media scientist", shaking his head in irritation as if it was something shameful.

"Who do you admire," asked Felix.

The Scotsman had a hero. His name was Sanger. Frederick Sanger had two Nobel prizes for chemistry, the first in the 1950s for sequencing proteins, the second in 1980 for sequencing DNA, and yet virtually no one, outside the world of science, had ever heard of him. For the Scotsman Sanger was his ideal virtue, excellence without vulgarity.

Felix was irritated. His time with the London group was coming to an end; he didn't know where he was going to go next, or what he wanted to do. He let down his guard and openly revealed his anxieties.

"I'd like to discover something important, and I'd like to be recognised for having done it."

Felix put emphasis on the word "and". It threw the Scotsman into a paroxysm of derision.

"You're no better than Watson."

Felix couldn't believe his ears. The idea that Watson should be criticised infuriated him.

"What's so bad about Watson?"

Felix's question set the Scotsman off on his hobby horse denouncing "fake" science. "True" science was done to advance "knowledge"; "fake" science was done for "self glorification". What the Scotsman meant was that "true" scientists were people like Sanger and himself, and "fake" scientists were people like Watson and his boss.

Watson was Felix's hero, the very model of who he wanted to be. When Watson had been a young research scientist, he'd decided that the only thing worth going after was the big prize. In his day it was the genetic code. Sure Watson was a bright scientist. But his genius, what made him one of the greats, was in identifying what was worth solving… and then solving it.

"Watson knew what to look for," said Felix. "You need genius to know what's worth doing."

"It doesn't take genius," said the Scotsman. "All you need is ambition."

"If you were ambitious, what would you be doing?"

"If I wanted to make a name for myself," said the Scotsman with a sneer, as though the very idea was anathema to him, "I'd go into something fashionable, into an area which the press and the public understand."

"Like what?"

"Probably medicine. Cure a disease and you're famous."

"Like diabetic neuropathy?"

"No! Something which everyone knows about, something where everyone's waiting for a cure."

"Like cancer."

"No. There are too many cancers. It'd have to be something simpler for the public to grasp."

"Like what?"

The Scotsman paused for an instant. He'd obviously never thought about anything as crass as this before. After a while he came up with the answer. And, like always, he was right.

"I'd go for AIDS," he said, as though it was the most obvious thing in the world. "Everyone has heard of AIDS. Everyone is scared of AIDS. The papers are full of AIDS. If I found the cure for AIDS I'd be the most famous scientist in the world."

The Scotsman uttered his reply disdainfully, as if he was describing something banal and reprehensible.

They collected together the tea things, and went back to work.

But Felix's path was decided, the final step in the masterplan was set.

Felix would discover the cure for AIDS... Felix triumphant...

Father destroyed!

****

Felix left the London group and set about his search.

He spent the next two years in frantic travel. He'd become a minor celebrity, and was made welcome in laboratories throughout the world. Why? Because it's a custom to welcome visiting scholars. The scientific community is one of the last bastions of an ancient tradition whereby strangers from foreign lands are offered hospitality. And? Because Felix was a young man who'd achieved a lot in a short time. The scientific community cherishes youth with a promising future. And? Because Felix was an "Honourable". The scientific community, like any community, is composed of snobs. Who can resist a Lord?

This meant that Felix could pick wherever he wished to go and be welcomed with open arms.

He chose the best of the best. He spent six months at NIH in Washington, sequencing Simian strains of the immunodeficiency virus. The result was another two papers to his name, and a lot of new friends. They were impressed by him as a scientist, he was good. They were enchanted by his speech; the soft staccato voice with the English accent was irresistible. They were enamoured of his manners, the clothes of a dandy and an old world culture. But most of all they loved the fact that he signed himself Felix. No one had ever dared give themselves an epithet. The scientific journals were furious. After all, how do you tell the difference between people in the literature if you don't use initials? But Felix held firm, and he was renowned for being the only scientist to be known by just one name.

Felix was less impressed by them. They worked in incredibly cramped spaces, tiny cubby holes with equipment stacked above their benches, everyone piled on top of everyone else, more like laboratory animals than laboratory scientists. But the worst of it was that they had nothing to offer. They were industrious, they were quick, but they were just another version of everyone else, easily flattered little people with small minds. There was no one with any genius, it was just hard work. If a cure for AIDS came from what they were doing, it wasn't going to be romantic, and it certainly wasn't going to do Felix any good.

No. He needed something outside the mainstream, something where people would say beforehand "You're mad!" and after "Why didn't I think of that?" So he went on his voyage from top lab to top lab on the lookout. For what? If he knew, he wouldn't have been looking.

After six months, he found himself at an INSERM lab in Paris. It was fun to be in France, and eating good food. Even the scientists seemed to be enjoying themselves. At any event they didn't have the deadly seriousness about their work which afflicted the Americans and the Japanese. But Felix's good humour only lasted a few weeks. He began to realise that the French were just as anxious and obsessed as everyone else, they just pretended not to be. They were working on a sensitive dipstick test for AIDS, and they were being super secretive in case the Americans got their hands on the technology before the patents were rock solid. In some ways their apparent *joie de vivre* was even more repellent than the intense sobriety of their competitors. Behind their good humour and relaxed manner, they were steadfast in defending the reputation of "La France", and their anti-Americanism was paranoid and idiotic.

Felix began to despair. It was late autumn, he was walking along the rue Serpente, and he began to feel his chest constrict and the polluted air of Paris clog his lungs. It didn't last long, barely five minutes, but it was the first time he'd had a recurrence of asthma since his recovery all those years ago. He knew why it was happening. It was a sign that things were going wrong. He was marking time. He hadn't got anywhere in his search for a cure. Worse, he had no idea about what to do next. Just thinking about it made him wheeze.

And then something happened.

Later, Felix came to believe it was predestined. Certainly, it was an amazing coincidence, the sort which makes you believe in fate. "There I was... walking along the rue Serpente... it was lunch time I was at the end of my tether... about to give up... when...!"

But it wasn't so extraordinary. After all, there are many more occasions when we are in deep despair and nothing happens to change our fate. Life is a roulette wheel; everyone's number is bound to come up once in a while. Destiny has nothing to do with it. What you do with your occasional good fortune is what matters.

Felix knew what to do.

He was walking along the rue Serpente, it was lunch time, he was downhearted and wheezing, when he saw him. *Him* was Joseph Stern. Felix had seen him before. He worked at the Institute in a lab down the corridor from Felix. Joseph Stern was a grubby little man who'd come to science late in the day, having converted from being a rabbi. At the Institute everyone treated him like a joke, finding his approach to science much too scholastic. Instead of getting on with experiments and publishing his data like everyone else, he would sit hunched over scientific journals, like a Talmudic scholar, rocking backwards and forwards, interpreting them as if they were biblical texts, and annotating them with a quasi-rabbinic commentary. He was known as the Yeshiva Boche, and it wasn't said affectionately.

Felix remembered what they'd told him about Joseph Stern.

"He's not stupid" said Guillaume. It was the day Felix arrived at the Institute. "He's just in the wrong métier; he doesn't accept the logic of science."

"Don't get into a discussion with him," said Pascal. They were having lunch in the canteen a week later, and Joseph Stern walked by to sit by himself at a corner table and eat his lunch alone. "He'll argue you into believing the world is flat."

But most of all, Felix remembered what Pierre had said only yesterday.

"I can't make up my mind. He's probably mad, but it's just possible he's a genius."

And there he was, alone as usual, walking ahead of Felix, his nose buried in a book, making his way to the Carrefour de l'Odeon. He was wearing a long black greasy coat with heavy boots and a shiny black Homburg, a shocking contrast to the students from the Sorbonne who were in jeans and T-shirts. Joseph Stern still looked every inch a rabbi. He stepped into the road paying no attention to the cars and motorbikes which were racing across in front of him. He probably couldn't see them. He wore thick pebble glasses, and he was straining to read the text in his book with the aid of a hand held lens. Cars were swerving to avoid hitting him. He walked straight through the traffic as if he was strolling along a mud path in a medieval Shtetl with passing oxcarts about him. A lorry came hurtling down the Boulevard Saint Germain. There was a screech of burning rubber, a scream of "Abyssinian!" from the distraught driver, and no sign of Joseph Stern. For a moment Felix thought Joseph Stern had gone for good. But then he emerged the other side, his head still buried in his book, oblivious to the commotion around him, continuing his way up the rue Monsieur-le-Prince.

Pierre's remark kept ringing in Felix's head

"He's probably mad, but it's just possible he's a genius."

Felix followed Joseph Stern.

Half way up the street, Joseph Stern stopped and peered into a doorway. He was reading the menu outside Polidor, an old established restaurant in the Latin quarter, which was the haunt of minor officials, struggling writers and unfashionable university lecturers. The ex-rabbi was peering through his lens mouthing the words as he read from the menu, and smacking his lips in anticipation.

Felix hurried up the street and followed Joseph into the restaurant. The tables were laid out in long rows. The customers, mostly men, mostly middle aged, and mostly alone, sat side by side studiously ignoring each other, reading books or marking papers or just staring into space between courses. Joseph Stern had sat himself down at the far end of the long table in the centre of the room, his hat to one side resting on his book, his face pushed into the menu, as if he could devour the food by just reading about it. A memory stirred inside Felix. He saw an ugly short sighted little creature, its mouth twitching in intense anticipation of gorging itself. Felix saw a maggot. Joseph Stern was a maggot.

Felix made his way down the restaurant between the tables, towards Joseph Stern, who was waving his menu in the air, gesticulating haphazardly at all and sundry, frantically trying to hail a waiter.

Felix stood next to him, about to introduce himself.

Joseph Stern looked at him and exclaimed, "Boudin!"

He thought Felix was the waiter.

Felix sat down, bringing his face up so close that even Joseph Stern's deficient eyes could see who he was. He stretched out his hand and presented himself. "My name is Felix. I work with you at the Institute."

Joseph Stern handed him the menu, and said again, even more emphatically, "Boudin!"

He seemed deaf as well as blind.

It took a further five minutes of fevered negotiation before Joseph Stern was reassured. First Felix summoned the waiter, and helped Joseph to choose his order. It consisted of dishes which were almost exclusively composed of pork. Joseph Stern was indulging himself in an orgy of unkosher food, revelling in blasphemous gluttony. Next Felix set about explaining who he was. Joseph Stern seemed to have no grasp on reality; he was convinced Felix was something to do with the restaurant! "Institute? What Institute?"... "Laboratory? What Laboratory?"

Then, suddenly, it clicked. Joseph Stern shot out his hand and said, "But of course! You are our friend from England. You are the redoubtable Felix."

They shook hands. There was an uncomfortable silence. Joseph Stern was unused to anyone seeking his company. He took out a large yellowing handkerchief and blew his nose. He buried his face inside the dirty handkerchief as if he was trying to find somewhere to hide. Felix decided that the way forward with Joseph was the same as for everyone else. He treated him to a dose of superabundant flattery, about how much he'd heard about Joseph, and how he was looking forward to this opportunity to talk with him, with someone who was a genuine scholar.

It worked. It always worked.

Joseph Stern clutched hold of Felix's sleeve and launched into a diatribe against his colleagues at the Institute. They had failed to understand the significance of what he was doing. He squeezed Felix's arm as he expounded his life's work. Felix had only the vaguest idea of what Joseph was talking about. He was speaking fast, and he was leaping about from topic to topic like a mountain goat, as if Felix knew all the main points and only needed the small print. It had something to do with "Homeostasis", and the fact that science has to seek an alternative theory for describing the workings of biology.

If only Joseph Stern hadn't been so un-prepossessing. All the while he was dribbling food out of a half open mouth, spilling gobs of fat onto his tie, and blowing his nose while talking and eating. Eventually the handkerchief was impregnated with a mixture of food and snot. Felix understood why others fled from Joseph Stern.

Joseph Stern spoke as rapidly as Felix himself, and there were few moments for pause. But, when they came, Felix laced his interjections with expressions of wonderment at the genius of Joseph Stern; and when Joseph was particularly heated about the attitude of some colleague, Felix muttered platitudes on how genius is misunderstood in its own age.

They were eating their dessert. Joseph had ordered a crème caramel and was adding large dollops of cream, as if in direct challenge to a hostile Jewish deity, glorying in the sin of following meat with milk.

Felix decided it was time to conclude his business. He launched into a hymn of praise to Joseph Stern, about how most scientists were just cartographers mapping out the known world, but Joseph was one of the elite with a mission to discover new worlds.

Joseph Stern sipped his coffee. He was content, content with his meal and content with the company. This nice young English scholar was clearly a clever and charming young man.

He turned to Felix and asked, "What about you?"

"Me?"

"Yes. What do you want to do with your life?"

This was Felix's moment. It was now that he would discover if Joseph Stern was truly a genius, the sort that mattered, a genius who would help Felix.

Felix leaned forward and said very distinctly, "I want to discover the cure for AIDS."

There was a long pause. Then, all of a sudden, Joseph Stern laughed.

"You're ambitious," he said, and laughed again.

Felix blushed. It was as if Joseph Stern had eavesdropped on his conversation with the bearded Scotsman. Felix began to talk rapidly, struggling to justify himself and show he had more noble pretensions.

"Stop!"

Joseph was waving his dirty handkerchief in the air, signalling Felix to stop talking.

"There's nothing wrong with ambition," he continued. "Don't be ashamed."

Felix blushed even deeper. He felt his face was on fire. He didn't like the feeling that someone else was able to see behind the mask.

"And do you have the cure?" Joseph asked. He was excited by the candour of Felix's confession.

Felix described his wanderings of the last year, travelling the world from lab to lab, and his increasing sense of futility.

"I'm at the end of the road," said Felix.

"And you think I can help?" asked Joseph.

"I saw you in the street, and I thought... maybe."

Joseph Stern was beaming. He enjoyed the challenge. He liked the idea that Felix had chosen him above all others to help him in his quest.

"Can you help?" asked Felix.

Joseph Stern began to chuckle. He was captivated and enchanted by the request.

"Of course!"

****

Joseph removed a sheet of paper from his coat pocket and laid it on the table. He chose a pen from the array stuck inside his chest pocket and began shaking it to get the ink to flow. Tiny green stains dappled the table cloth, and some even splattered over Felix's white shirt. The waiter, a portly elderly man, hobbled over protesting loudly. He removed the table cloth, laid down a paper lining and offered Joseph a ball point pen. Joseph accepted it graciously. He thought the waiter was just being friendly. He was oblivious of the damage he caused around him.

He raised his pen and asked,

"What is AIDS?"

Felix was dumbfounded. He suddenly felt sick at heart. This was ridiculous. Joseph Stern was no genius, he was a dolt. Felix began to mutter excuses about having no time, perhaps another day, and made ready to leave.

Joseph Stern grabbed hold of his sleeve.

"Don't be impetuous!"

The beady maggot eyes were looking up at Felix. But they weren't the eyes of a simpleton. There was a glint behind the pebble glasses, and it was steely hard. Joseph Stern spoke slowly and with great emphasis.

"I am a simple man. First I identify a problem... then I seek the solution. That is the way I work, I know no other way."

It was said with absolute conviction, and it was extraordinarily guileless. Felix suddenly had a resurgence of the feeling that he was in the presence of a genius.

"I'm sorry," said Felix.

He sat down again, facing Joseph Stern.

"What was your question?" he asked.

"What is AIDS?" repeated Joseph.

"It's a disease which destroys the immune system."

"No, no, no," said Joseph impatiently. "I am not interested in the consequence. What is the cause of the disease?"

"It is caused by the destruction of T4 lymphocytes... white cells."

"Ah!" exclaimed Joseph. And wrote it down on his piece of paper.

"And what destroys the T cells?" he asked.

"A virus."

"The HIV virus?"

"Yes," said Felix.

"Ah!" Joseph exclaimed again, and wrote down "HIV" on his piece of paper.

"The problem," he announced solemnly, "is a virus, called HIV, which destroys T cells."

"I think we knew this already," said Felix, unable to contain his sarcasm.

"We surely did," answered Joseph, ignoring the rebuke. "And so does everyone else. But we are returning to first principles. A solution can be missed if we forget first principles."

Joseph Stern tapped the paper, to show that as far as he was concerned the hard work was already over.

"Now we find the cure," said Joseph, as if it was the simplest thing in the world.

"Let's start at the beginning," he continued, looking towards Felix, encouraging him to speak.

"You mean the first way to treat AIDS?" asked Felix.

"No! Remember your first principles. I mean the first way to stop the virus destroying T cells."

"I suppose it's to stop the virus getting into the body."

"Excellent!" said Joseph, and began scribbling on his piece of paper.

"And what ways do we have for stopping the virus getting in the body?" Joseph Stern continued, looking at Felix, encouraging him to provide the answer.

"Avoid things which contain the virus... contaminated blood... contaminated sperm," said Felix.

"You mean no sex, or using condoms, and no needle sharing."

"That's the only way to be sure the virus doesn't get into the body."

"But it's not a cure," said Joseph.

"No. It's prevention."

Joseph pondered the point for a moment or two. He sighed, and drew a line on his piece of paper.

"Next?" He was looking at Felix, encouraging him.

"You mean the next way to stop the virus destroying T cells?"

"Yes."

"I suppose it's to destroy the virus before it gets a chance to destroy the T cells."

"Excellent," said Joseph, beginning to scribble under the line he'd drawn. "And what ways do we have for destroying the virus once it is in the body, but before it can destroy the T cells?"

The questions were following, one after the other, in perfect symmetry. Felix wasn't sure they were necessarily getting anywhere. But there was no faulting the logic of Joseph Stern's approach.

"We have to prepare our defences in advance... before the virus gets in... so that we destroy the virus as it enters the body."

"A vaccine?"

"Yes," said Felix. "There's a whole industry trying to develop vaccines. One jab with an effective vaccine and we'd be protected for years to come. An effective vaccine would inactivate the virus immediately it enters the body, whenever and however many times we contaminate ourselves."

"A possible solution?" said Joseph.

"Yes," said Felix.

"But one which does not please you." Joseph Stern had picked up the hesitation in Felix's answer.

"No."

"Because it carries no glory?"

Joseph Stern was dead right. Sure a vaccine would come along, but what credit to Felix if he worked on it. Thousands of researchers throughout the world were doing just that, here and now. It was going to be a long and slow business, certainly no way for a young man to forge a glorious reputation in the annals of science.

Joseph Stern was laughing. He was totally captivated by the ruthlessness behind Felix's ambition.

"So let us find a more glorious solution!" He drew a line across his paper, "... and let's find something which a talented scientist can achieve... alone... and in a short time!" He was chuckling; it was almost as if he was mocking Felix.

Felix blushed again, more furiously than before. He felt threatened. The knowledge that Joseph Stern was able to see what he was thinking and feeling was distinctly disturbing.

"Next?" Joseph Stern was tapping his pen on the piece of paper.

"You mean the next way to stop the virus destroying T cells?"

"Yes."

"Destroy the virus after it's inside the T cell."

"And how do we do that?"

"There's the problem! The virus splices itself into the human gene and becomes impregnable to attack."

"There's nothing we can do?"

"Not much. We can try and shoot at it when it comes out of hiding."

"When's that?"

"When it starts to replicate, using drugs like AZT. They attack the virus when it's trying to replicate itself."

"Not very effective?"

"Some are. But we don't know their long term effect. And you have to swallow them day in and day out for the rest of your life."

"Next?"

"The next step?"

"Yes."

"There is no next step."

Joseph Stern peered at the piece of paper. His face was screwed up in intense concentration. He was muttering to himself and rocking backwards and forwards as if in prayer.

"One. We stop the virus entering the body." He was reading from the paper.

"Two. We stop the virus infecting the T cells." He took out his hand lens and peered even more closely at his writing.

"Three. We attack the virus after it has infected the T cells."

Joseph thumped the table and the portly old waiter came hobbling up to rescue the water jug. It was about to topple off the edge on to the lap of a fat man, who looked a bit like Alfred Hitchcock, sitting on Joseph's right.

The waiter departed, and Felix watched Joseph rocking backwards and forwards. Joseph was like a chess grand master at the crucial moment in the game, the wrong move and it's over; the right move, the unexpected move, and everything changes.

"Let us return to first principles," Joseph Stern was speaking rapidly as if he was on to something.

"OK."

"AIDS is caused by a virus destroying T cells?"

"Yes."

"So what about four?" He was looking at Felix with a broad grin on his face.

"There is no four," said Felix

"Yes, there is!" Joseph was chuckling to himself, hugely satisfied.

"I don't understand," said Felix.

"You're thinking about it all wrong," said Joseph. "Forget about the virus. Forget about stopping it getting in. Forget about destroying it once it's inside."

"I still don't get it," said Felix.

"First principles!" Joseph screamed.

Joseph's voice rang round the restaurant. The fat man, who looked a bit like Alfred Hitchcock, was so startled he jumped out of his seat and dropped his fork. There was a shaking of heads from the surrounding diners, and the waiter came hobbling back.

"Monsieur! Un peu de calme s'il vous plait!"

Joseph paid him no attention, his mind was totally preoccupied with the problem in hand. The waiter left, shaking his head and patting the fat man on the shoulder to reassure him that he'd come back if Joseph gave any more trouble.

Joseph was tapping the paper with his pen.

"You," he said to Felix, "are obsessed with the cause of the disease. You want to destroy the virus!"

"Yes," said Felix.

"But there is another way... and it's staring you in the face."

He paused, hoping that Felix might be able to pick up on what he was saying.

"Remember what you told me," he said. "AIDS is caused by the destruction of T cells..."

"Yes," said Felix.

"Then the disease can be cured by providing more T cells," he exclaimed.

Felix felt a chill down his spine. Suddenly he got a feel for where Joseph was leading.

"You are so busy thinking up ways to destroy the virus," Joseph continued, "that you're forgetting something else. Why not make friends with it? Why not use it to your advantage?"

Joseph began writing on his piece of paper. He wrote four.

"Remind me," he asked Felix, "what destroys T cells?"

"The HIV virus."

"Good," said Joseph writing it under the new heading. "And is there a virus which will do the opposite... a virus which will increase T cells?"

Felix was breathing rapidly, his heart was racing. Now he knew exactly where Joseph was going!

"Yes."

"What's it called?"

"The T Cell Leukaemic virus... the HTLV virus."

"Ah!" exclaimed Joseph, and wrote it down.

He was looking at Felix. He saw that Felix had at last understood.

"You know what I am going to say," said Joseph. "That is good... you have imagination."

He looked down at his piece of paper.

"It's so simple!" He was chuckling at the very thought of the idea. "There's no need to cure AIDS by attacking the HIV virus. You cure AIDS by giving the patient another virus... the contrary virus... the opposite virus... the HTLV virus! Instead of having one disease which kills... you have two diseases which cancel each other out... you have two diseases which cure each other!"

Joseph jumped up and down in his seat in delight. The fat man, who looked a bit like Alfred Hitchcock, was knocked sideways. The waiter shook his head at the commotion, and winked at the fat man as if to say Joseph was just a harmless madman.

****

On his arrival in Paris, Felix had rented a shabby room in a little hotel off the rue St Andre des Arts. After his lunch with Joseph Stern, Felix went straight there. It was down the road from the restaurant, and he hurried back like a man rushing to get to the toilet before his bladder bursts. He pushed his way through the crowds of students and tourists who were jostling each other in the small cramped streets of the Latin Quarter, and bounded up the rickety wooden stairs to his room on the fifth floor.

It was as if Felix was on speed, his body tingling, an electric current applied to every nerve. He hurried to his room to discharge the energy before it consumed him.

It was brilliant. It was outrageous. It was exhilarating. It was everything Felix had been seeking, the simplest and most obvious solution, and yet no one had thought of it. No one except Felix and Joseph. Together they would pioneer the Felixian solution to the problem of AIDS. In years to come the "Neo-Felixians" would cite the Felixian message that disease was a friend, to be harnessed not destroyed. What a solution! Nobody would dare think like that, except a madman or a genius. But it wasn't mad. It made perfect sense. It was the sanest thing Felix had ever heard. Everything else was crude by comparison. Felix was a genius!

Felix bounded up the final flight of stairs. His hands were shaking so much, it took a full minute before he was able to get the key in the lock and enter his room. He bolted the door behind him and discharged the exhilaration that was overflowing within him. He shook hands with an imaginary King Carl Gustaf, and bowed to the ghostly audience in evening dress as they applauded. He stepped up to the intangible rostrum and delivered his acceptance speech. He spoke of that momentous day in Paris when he had sat down with Joseph and they had applied the Felixian method to the problem of AIDS. He was gracious, cultured and good humoured. And he was generous. He spoke of the debt he owed his father, without whom he would never have embarked on a career in science. Father was sitting in the audience. He was in the front row with his new son, the boy who'd replaced Felix in father's esteem. Felix looked directly at father while he spoke, and father squirmed in his seat. But Felix never said a harsh word. On the contrary, he was the epitome of filial devotion. Felix turned to King Carl Gustaf to accept his prize, and out the corner of his eye he saw father shamefacedly leave the chamber with his counterfeit son in tow.

Then he was in Hollywood to receive a special award. He was dubbed "the man of the century". The audience cheered and screamed as he came forward to accept the medal. Again he made a speech thanking father for all he'd done to encourage him. There was a special satellite link-up to England, with father on the big screen, sitting on the terrace in the castle. Father watched as Felix was born aloft by a phalanx of ex-patients, men who'd been in the last stages of the disease, literally dying of AIDS, until they'd been cured by Felix. They carried Felix into the crowd of screaming adoring fans. There was pandemonium, with people jostling each other to get close to Felix, just to touch him, the touch of divine grace. Above the hubbub, the commentator was trying to make himself heard. He was asking father a question; he was asking when father first knew Felix was a genius.

Then he was back in England. The Queen was unveiling the memorial plaque at the Felix Institute. Millions had been raised to honour Felix, and the funds had been used to build a scientific Institute in his name. Felix was standing side by side with the Queen. It was a warm summer's day. She pulled on the velvet rope and the silk coverlet dropped from the plaque. Even the journalists and photographers clapped. The Queen turned to Felix and shook him by the hand. The flashbulbs popped and those nearby heard her say that she was proud to shake his hand. It was a warm summer's day, just like it had been all those years ago when Felix had sat waiting outside the church. The Queen was in sparkling form, she was laughing and joking with him, she asked him why the Institute had been built on the outskirts of the village near the castle. Felix answered with complete truthfulness. So that father could see it from his window. The Queen commented that it must be a great joy for his father, to wake up in the morning and look out on an edifice which had been created to honour his son, the greatest scientist of the century.

Felix closed the windows of the hotel room and brought down the shutters. The murmur of the crowds in the narrow streets of the Latin Quarter was an approving backdrop to his dreams. He stripped off his clothes and lay naked on top of his bed. The fantasies rolled on, and with each new tableau he writhed and rolled on the bed in an ecstasy of delight. It continued throughout the afternoon, hour after hour, with never a repeat, always a fresh scene in the ascent of Felix and the humiliation of father.

Daylight faded, and Felix lit the black candle. It was time for ritual consummation. He sat himself in front of the mirror, legs wide apart, the Chestnut wig flowing down his back. He strapped himself into the corset, binding himself in the garters, ensheathing himself in the air tight polythene bag. And then the struggle... and the panic. The desperate fight for breath as Guinevere grapples and writhes in an agony of asphyxia. In the mirror Felix sees father. He is atop her, pulling at the cords around her neck, throttling her. Guinevere is expiring beneath him. With her dying breath comes release, and the cascade of fluid in the air splattering against the ceiling. The tug on the noose and release... release of sperm... release of air... breath and life.

****

Felix dubbed it the "Manhattan Project" and set up camp in Cambridge, England.

He rented space on the outskirts of the University in a science park. He recruited animal physiologists, cell culture experts, virologists, molecular biologists and administrators. Finally, when all was ready, he ferried Joseph, Joseph's wife, and Joseph's three children across the channel. They came with all their furniture and baggage like war time refugees. Felix rented them a charming cottage tucked away in the countryside, half a mile from the science park.

PART ONE: A TALE OF THREE LIVES

Felix converted the shed at the bottom of Joseph's garden into a book lined study. The rule was that Joseph was free to work there on anything he liked, for as long as he liked, except for an hour a day, after breakfast, when he would make himself available for Felix.

"AIDS is a human disease!" said Felix.

It was one such morning. Felix had been up most of the night organising the protocols for the HTLV transfections, and he was feeling tired and grumpy. He was sick of trying to explain the problem to Joseph. There were times when Joseph seemed incapable of understanding the simplest things. This time Felix couldn't get it into Joseph's head that they needed an animal species to experiment on.

Joseph blew his nose, and bits of half chewed bacon and egg flew out of his mouth. A particle landed on Felix's cheek. Felix didn't like Joseph. Indeed he was beginning to loathe him. Apart from his disgusting habits, his filth and untidiness, apart from his wretched family, his fawning fat wife and snivelling shrieking children, Joseph was becoming intellectually a pain. He took himself too seriously, and was beginning to give himself airs, as if he was some sort of genius. He didn't seem to realise that without Felix there was nothing.

"First principles!" Joseph proclaimed. And more bits of chewed up bacon shot across the shed.

He always said the same thing, like a demented parrot, and it was driving Felix mad. If he said it once more he'd kill him.

"First principles!" Joseph repeated.

Felix clenched his fists.

"Cats!" said Joseph.

"Cat's don't have Aids," said Felix with exaggerated patience. "... Aids is a human condition!"

"Cats get leukaemia!" Joseph exclaimed.

He had an idiot grin on his face and Felix began to wonder whether he was altogether sane.

"So what?"

Joseph was beaming with pleasure, his little maggot face triumphant.

"... we cure them by giving them AIDS!"

Felix left Joseph's cottage in a rage. His real reason for loathing Joseph was because he was right. Every time there was a dead end problem, Joseph had the answer. He was like the bearded Scotsman, only more so. Like now, Felix had been banging his head against a brick wall, incapable of forcing his way through, and suddenly Joseph was on the other side beckoning him to follow. It was infuriating. The sooner it was over the better.

CHAPTER 1: FELIX, GENESIS OF A GENIUS

Felix drove back to the science park. He weaved his old Triumph sports car around the winding country lanes, and vented his rage by churning up the mud and spraying it behind him. It was late autumn, the trees were bare of foliage and the thick morning mist was still in the air. As he approached the outskirts of the city, the mist began to lift and so did his mood.

He drove through the gates and headed up the main avenue, passing the newly opened facilities along the way. The science park was modelled on the American pattern, a meeting place for business and university, where risk taking entrepreneurs were encouraged to feed off the ideas generated on campus, and market oriented boffins were supposed to make millions by turning their theories into merchantable products. Felix passed the freshly painted sign, "Therapeutic Pathogens Ltd", and turned into the parking lot. There were spaces for about a hundred cars but this was Cambridge, and it was mostly bicycles. Felix parked his old Triumph in the space marked "President".

Harry was waiting for him in the front lobby. Harry was Felix's number two. Felix gave the orders and Harry made sure they were carried out. He was in his sixties, and his craggy creased face made him look even older. He was overweight, his stomach bursting through a shirt that was three sizes too small. His face was florid, as though anticipating an imminent heart attack. But he was dogged and meticulous in his work. His last job had been overseeing a planning division in the construction of the channel tunnel. When that job was done, he should have departed into the twilight world of retired managers, to drink himself into an early death and bore those around him with alcoholic reminiscences of bygone exploits. But Felix had given Harry a new lease of life. He'd chosen him over much younger rivals, and tough rough Harry was devoted to Felix.

Harry ushered Felix into the seminar room. It was the big monthly meeting and everyone was present. He introduced Felix to the new recruits, a dozen fresh faced young technicians in sparkling white lab coats. They were waiting in procession to meet Felix, nervous and excited, like a chorus line in a TV ad for a new washing powder.

Felix had read all the files and knew intimate personal details on all them. He greeted each one in turn, talking about them, never about himself or the project, and making it appear as if he was thrilled and honoured that they had joined the company. When the introductions were done, their rosy cheeks glowed with pleasure, and they beamed at Felix as at a new found blood brother.

The review meeting with Felix was the high point of the month. It was a time to reflect on the past, and plan for the future. Each of the section heads gave their reports. On the scientific front, the microbiologists were on target, with active cultures of all the principal strains of immunodeficiency and leukaemic viruses.

On the financial front, things were much more tricky, it was proving difficult to get funding. Felix had put a lot of his personal wealth into the project, but he wouldn't be able to sustain it all the way through to clinical trials. It was going to cost tens of millions and eventually he'd need a financial partner.

The section heads finished their reports and the room fell silent. It was time for Felix to speak. This was the moment they were all waiting for. Therapeutic Pathogens depended on Felix alone. He was their guide, motivator, and originator. He inspired everyone who worked there and everything they did.

Felix spoke rapidly and softly, and they craned forward to catch his voice. Some were taking notes, but Felix spoke so fast that only a stenographer could keep up. Those who'd been with the company a few weeks came prepared, with portable tape recorders, so that they could go over his instructions later.

Felix started by reminding them of the company mission, to rid the world of AIDS. He spoke of the disease as if it were a personal enemy. He described it as a scourge which had struck the youngest and finest, and which had wiped out a whole generation of intellectuals and artists. He reminded them of those who had already fallen. He recited the names of the great, Nureyev and Foucault, and the glitzy, Rock Hudson and Liberace. He spoke of his personal commitment to the struggle against AIDS, how he had made it his personal mission in life to rid the world of this evil pestilence once and for all.

It was a speech to fire the soul. His audience were spellbound. There wasn't a single employee who didn't share the conviction that they were involved in a crusade against evil. Even Harry, who in other circumstances might have dismissed AIDS as a disease of perverts and drug addicts, was won over by the fervour of Felix's conviction. Felix spoke softly and rapidly, with his characteristic clipped accent. But the rhythm came from the pulpit and those evangelical preachers Felix had watched on early morning American TV shows.

The next part of the speech turned from matters of the heart to those of the head. How Felix had struggled with the problem of finding a cure for AIDS. How he'd travelled the world and sought solutions in antiviral drugs and vaccines, all to no avail. How the idea had come to him, suddenly, unexpectedly, one day while riding a bus in Paris. How he saw a billboard, how it showed Asterix, the Gaul, clubbing his friend Obelix, and Obelix clubbing Asterix! How the vision of these two cartoon characters clubbing each other senseless had instantly awakened an idea in him. How he'd had a vision of the way forward, to use evil to fight evil. How Therapeutic Pathogens was started. How one pathogen equals disease, how one pathogen is an evil. But how two pathogens locked in mortal combat, two pathogens clubbing each other to death, are pathogens which heal... are... Therapeutic Pathogens!

There was a ripple of applause from the young technicians. completely bowled over by Felix. They were working for a man of high m and intellectual genius.

Felix turned from the general to the particular. He gave an expose AIDS virus and how it destroys the T cell, and on the leukaemic virus and h multiplies the T cell, and how their job at Therapeutic Pathogens was to bring th two viruses together so that they cancelled each other out.

The introductions over, Felix began on the work at hand.

"We need an animal model."

It was the problem they'd been struggling with for the last two months. There was no way of experimenting on the two viruses without an animal species to test them on.

"We can't use humans."

There was a look of anguish amongst the young technicians, and even Harry began to fidget. This was the crunch. Felix's vision was great, but if you couldn't test it.... What then?

"I thought of Asterix," said Felix.

Harry leaned forward. There was a look of anticipation on his florid face. Everyone in the room was silent. There was a feeling that Felix had found a solution.

"And I thought of Obelix."

They had stopped breathing. Felix sensed their anticipation, and he imagined that this was what it must have been like when Mao Tse Tung was about to promulgate an edict.

"If we can't use Asterix to club Obelix, we'll use Obelix to club Asterix!"

They didn't understand. Sometimes Felix wondered at the stupidity of his fellow men. He spelled it out, slowly and simply, syllable by syllable.

"Instead of infecting an animal with the AIDS virus, we'll infect it with the leukaemia virus. It'll be the same thing, only backwards."

They were still baffled. A young technician was smiling at Felix with immense intensity. He was so eager to please, and so obviously out of his depth. It was pitiable.

"We'll give an animal leukaemia, and then we'll see if we can cure its leukaemia by giving it the AIDS virus."

At last!

Harry snapped open his note book, and began writing. He didn't quite know what Felix was getting at, but he knew enough to know that something was starting, and there was work to be done.

still hadn't understood. He continued staring at
rin.

nt on the animal, change the dosages,
apy. If we learn how to cure an animal of
t will teach us how to cure humans of AIDS by

oops of pleasure. They'd all understood, even Harry and
be a scientist. All except the young technician. He was smiling
ely, vainly struggling to conceal his indomitable ignorance.

e'll use cats. There'll be three groups. Group one will be the negative
s... cats which haven't been infected with anything. Group two will be the
sitive controls... cats which have been infected with the feline leukaemic virus. And group three will be our experimental group... cats which have been infected with the feline leukaemic virus... and the AIDS virus."

The young technician's face was screwed up in intense concentration. He was battling to understand. It was like showing the Sistine Chapel to a blind man.

"The first group will be healthy. The second group will die of leukaemia. And... if we're right... the third group won't die of leukaemia... they'll be cured... they'll stay healthy."

The anguished smile crumbled. It was replaced by a crooked grin and the first flicker of understanding.

The meeting broke up. The microbiologists and animal physiologists went to a nearby computer and started searching the literature for FeLV and FIV. The young technician cornered an older colleague who re-explained it all to him. He was writing it down, step by step.

Harry was at Felix's side.

"I consider it an honour to be working with you", said Harry. "You may be right, you may be wrong, it doesn't really matter. Whichever way it goes I think you're a bloody genius!"

Felix shrugged his shoulders in diffident protest.

It was as if Joseph didn't exist.

****

The three months which followed were a time of intense activity and extraordinary success.

There was only one problem, and each day it hung heavier and heavier over Felix. It was Joseph. He hadn't intended to keep Joseph's existence a secret.

It just turned out that way. At the beginning, there'd been no need to talk about him. After all, Felix had set up the company and recruited its staff; it was natural that they thought he was the sole begetter and originator of the idea. Why tell them otherwise? But the longer it went on, the more difficult it became. "Harry I've something to tell you. I have a partner." It was preposterous. How could Felix have a partner? Somebody sitting with him on the bus when he spotted the billboard of Asterix and Obelix!

The easiest way was to go on acting as if Joseph didn't exist. And in many ways he didn't. Now that the experiments were under way, Felix had less need of Joseph. His daily visits to Joseph's cottage were delayed and postponed into weekly ones, and those only because Joseph was becoming suspicious.

He sensed it one day when he was showing Joseph the latest lab notes. The results were very promising. Great progress had been made. In one set of experiments a strain of the feline immunodeficiency virus had completely inhibited the feline leukaemic virus. T cell counts were normal, spleen histology was unchanged, and, most importantly, the animals were alive and thriving.

Joseph chuckled, pleased at this first concrete evidence that the theory was working. He pushed the notes aside.

"Soon you won't need me any more," he said, peering at Felix quizzically.

Felix was caught off guard. It took him the rest of the day to reassure Joseph, and it was uphill work. He had to go through the whole rigmarole of how much he admired Joseph's mind, how Joseph's work on homeostasis was going to open new vistas in science, how Felix was visiting less frequently only because he felt guilty about usurping Joseph's time and energy. He even tried a new tactic, complimenting Joseph's fat wife on anything that came to mind, her children, her sewing, her cooking. As a result she insisted he stay and have lunch with the family, pushing him to second helpings of roast pork and crackling. Even the whining snivelling children were won over by "Uncle Felix". They crowded round him while he ate, one even sitting on his lap.

Still Joseph was suspicious. The more Felix praised him, the more Joseph seemed to distrust him.

****

At the office, things were getting ever more complicated. A couple of days after the uncomfortable lunch with Joseph and his family, Harry came in to see Felix. He had an invoice in his hand.

"It's for a security system," Harry explained.

"For who?"

"That's just it. I don't know."

"Who authorised it?"

"You."

Felix took the invoice. Sure enough there was his signature on the order form.

Damn!

Joseph's cottage!

Joseph's wife was so panic stricken to be out in the country, she'd insisted on all sorts of alarms and video cameras and junketry. What did the stupid woman think was going to happen? She was more than a match for any burglar. She'd crush them to death.

"Sorry Harry. This one is personal, I shouldn't have billed it to the company."

"That's OK. We all make mistakes."

Harry was the epitome of discretion. If it was company business, he insisted on being informed. There was no such thing as a company secret. But if it was private, he had no need to know, nor did he want to. As far as Harry was concerned the incident was closed.

****

The experiments continued going well. Felix visited the animal house each day, and the cats were thriving. Sure, two or three from the first group eventually died. But the microbiologists modified the strain, altered the route of infection, and the next group were doing even better.

Felix decided to visit Joseph at his cottage more often. Joseph was right, Felix didn't need him any more. But he didn't want Joseph to know that, not yet, not until he'd worked out what exactly he was going to do with him.

They were discussing the next experiments.

"It'll soon be time to publish," said Joseph.

"I'd rather wait until we have more data," said Felix.

"Why?"

"I'd like a human cure before I go public."

He quickly changed it to "*we* go public," but he knew Joseph had picked up on his slip of the tongue.

"Do you think we're ready for a clinical trial?" asked Joseph.

"I'd like to make our first announcement next Spring, at the Cini Foundation AIDS Conference. We'll have all the cat experiments finished by then, and we'll have had time to try it on a human guinea pig to see if it works on humans."

Felix had been pondering on how to go public for months. He had two choices, go for lots of little publications, and build up his reputation bit by bit as the man with the cure for AIDS; or wait until he'd tested it on a human patient, and go for the big splash cure. Felix favoured the big splash. It corresponded with his sense of melodrama, and it was the opposite of what the bearded Scotsman would do.

"Is the Cini Conference the right place?" asked Joseph.

"Everyone will be there."

What he meant was that father would be there. The Cini Foundation assembled the elite. As soon as Felix had seen that his father was presiding the conference, he'd decided that this was the place and time for his revenge. There was no better moment. The conference was going to have only a couple of hundred delegates, but they represented the cream of the world's scientists. It was being held at the Cini Foundation conference centre in Venice, and already it was being hailed as the most prestigious scientific gathering of the decade.

"It sounds a good idea," said Joseph.

Joseph had no idea about the enmity between Felix and father. So much the better. Felix didn't want Joseph knowing anything more about him than he already did.

"I'll give the lecture on the principles behind our theory," Joseph continued, "and you can give the talk on our data."

Felix's heart stopped beating. He froze. It was the first time in weeks that Joseph had spoken about their working relationship. Felix had almost begun to believe that Joseph wanted no part in the glory of the cure. Now suddenly he was pushing himself forward, as though he had every right to be up there with Felix. It was even worse than Felix could have imagined. Joseph was pushing himself ahead of Felix, claiming the idea for himself, and relegating Felix to the role of a mere technician.

Felix began to choke. For a moment he was unable to breath. He made his excuses and left in a hurry.

He needed time to be by himself, time to breathe, and time to think.

****

Then Felix began having nightmares, the same scene repeated night after night, as if it was a rehearsal for the real thing. The dream starts with Felix in the seminar room, addressing the company. They are all there, the heads of section,

Harry, even the ridiculous young technician, smiling as idiotically as ever. Everything is normal, everyone is looking at Felix with trust and confidence, and then there's a knock at the door. Felix goes on talking, ignoring it, hoping it hasn't happened, hoping it will go away. The audience is unsettled, not knowing whether Felix has heard the knock, not knowing whether to open the door. Another knock. Felix goes on talking. The door opens behind him. Someone walks into the room. Everyone turns their eyes from Felix to whoever it is. It's standing there, behind him. Felix goes on talking, ignoring the thing behind him, knowing he mustn't stop talking, knowing he has to go on talking and talking to stop it from saying,

"Hello, Felix... I've come... It's me... Joseph."

But he can't go on talking. Something happens to his throat, he feels a tightening around his throat as if he's been paralysed. He struggles and struggles to go on talking, but his throat tightens and tightens and he starts gasping for breath. In the moment of silence, while he's battling for breath, the thing speaks. And it's saying,

"Hello, Felix. I've come. It's me... Joseph."

And then Joseph is in the middle of the room, his arms above his head as if in salutation. And he's saying,

"First principles... first principles."

He's saying it over and over again, like a war cry. And the others are looking at Felix and they're asking, "Who is this man?"

And then comes the worst. In his dream, Felix starts to sweat, it's pouring off him and soaking his clothes. They're so wet he has to take them off, and he's standing in the centre of the room, naked, with everybody staring at him. The young technician with the idiot grin is staring at him but the grin turns to contempt. The young technician is sneering at him. Only he isn't the young technician. It's father. Father is in the room, staring at him naked, and saying, "Tell them who he is... tell them... tell them!"

And then Felix wakes up. He starts from his bed, with his pyjamas soaked in sweat.

And he knows that one day it will happen. There is nothing he can do to stop everyone knowing about Joseph.

****

The fuse was lit when Joseph said, "I want to visit."

It was a month later, and Felix hadn't seen Joseph for two weeks.

He was greeted at the door to the cottage by Joseph's wife. She gave him a great big hug. Then the children clamoured round him demanding a kiss. The smallest one deposited a piece of snot on his cheek.

Joseph's wife gave him the grand tour of the cottage, pointing out the security devices which had been fitted the previous week, anti vibration sensors on the windows, video cameras in all the rooms, even electronic beams in the garden. There was something pathetic about her fears, as if she, or her wretched family, had anything that anybody could possibly want to steal.

She accompanied Felix down the path to the shed at the bottom of the garden.

The first thing Joseph said, as Felix came in, was,

"I want to visit the laboratory."

There was no budging him. Felix tried everything, appealing to Joseph's wife that Joseph should not venture out in an English winter, citing the Xmas holidays and how this or that person wouldn't be available to meet Joseph. But nothing worked. The more he found excuses the more Joseph became obdurate.

"I want to visit. I need to be involved with what's going on. I want to start preparing for my talk in Venice."

"But you've got months."

"It's what we do now that matters. If we aren't doing things properly now, it'll be too late to put them right in a couple of months."

Joseph spoke as though he was intending to take control of the company.

Felix changed his tactic.

"Sure... anytime."

"Do you mean that?"

"Sure. Any time you like."

"OK. Let's make it right now!"

Joseph ordered his wife to make ready. She rushed back to the house to get his pullover, his overcoat, his Homburg hat and umbrella.

"I'm sorry Joseph. I can't take you right now. I've got a meeting in London, I'm driving straight there. Let's make it some time next week."

"OK. It's time I met the staff. I particularly want to meet Harry. He sounds like a good chap."

"He is. He'll be thrilled to meet you. I've told him so much about you."

"Sometimes I wonder if you've told anybody about me. Do they know that I exist?"

They both laughed.

Joseph's eyes were twinkling as though he'd guessed the truth.

****

Felix didn't know exactly what he had in mind, or why he was doing what he was doing, but he spent the next few days making sure that there was nothing linking Therapeutic Pathogens to Joseph.

There wasn't much anyway. There were no contracts, no exchange of letters, no formal communications. The personal partnership between Felix and Joseph had not yet been converted into any sort of legal arrangement. Joseph's visit to the company next week was to be the first occasion for official recognition.

But there were lots of little things which needed tidying up.

For example, there was Dave. Dave was a carpenter. He'd been taken on by Harry to do odd jobs around the company, things like fitting lab benches, little things.

It was only natural that Felix should also ask him to do a few jobs for Joseph up in the cottage. Joseph's wife had been having a terrible time with the door to her fridge. It kept sticking against the dish washer. On one occasion the entire deep freeze had defrosted. A month ago Felix sent Dave up to the cottage to fix it. He'd done a good job and had been treated to a fine afternoon tea with crumpets and scones and double cream by Joseph's wife.

But Dave worked for the company, and it wouldn't do for a company employee to be working for someone who didn't exist.

Dave had to go.

The next day Felix's wallet went missing. It was a sad and upsetting time for everyone.

"Where did you last leave it?" asked Harry.

"Here, in my jacket pocket, hanging against the door."

"Was the office locked?"

"No. Dave was in here fixing the window frame."

"Do you think Dave took it?"

"Absolutely not!"

"I think we should check his locker."

"I forbid you to do that Harry. I trust Dave. It's probably me. I probably dropped it in the corridor."

"I trust him too, but we've got to check it out all the same."

"Let's forget the whole thing."

"We can't do that. There's a thief about."

"Let the matter drop. It's not important."

"It is important! It's important to me... and it's especially important to Dave! If I don't check, I'll always have that sneaking suspicion."

"OK If it's going to give you peace of mind... go ahead... have a look in his locker."

Everyone was shocked when Harry found Felix's wallet in Dave's locker, no one more than Felix.

Dave was sacked on the spot.

Felix was devastated. He refused to press charges, and told Harry he'd wished he'd never allowed him to look in Dave's locker.

Harry tried to comfort Felix, as did everyone else. They all agreed that the worst thing about the whole affair was the way Felix's trust had been abused.

It was like that time when Goldberg had been discovered cheating.

****

Then there was the incident with the fax machine.

Harry had been taking an inventory, and several things were found to be missing. There was nothing unusual about that, there were always things missing after an inventory. But Harry was a stickler for detail, and chased after them with dogged determination. The joke in the company was that the delay in completing the channel tunnel was because Harry had been taking an inventory.

Anyway everything was traced, eventually, except for the fax machine.

"It's been stolen!" said Harry.

"It'll turn up," said Felix.

Felix was hoping Harry would drop the investigation. But in his heart of hearts he knew he wouldn't. The affair of the fax machine would go on and on, until Harry had tracked down the culprit, or found it.

Felix knew exactly who the culprit was. It was him. He'd given the fax machine to Joseph. He'd done it weeks ago, long before he'd ever thought there might be a problem.

Felix had been using the fax to send Joseph the results of the experiments. Only yesterday he'd sent him the path results from last month's screening experiment. The lab had identified a strain of the leukaemia virus which killed the animals in a few days. Joseph wanted the histology report on the spleen, and Felix had faxed it to him.

Now what?

He could tell Harry. It would settle the issue of the fax machine. But then he would have to explain about Joseph.

No. The safest thing was to get the fax machine back.

But how to do it without raising Joseph's suspicion?

Simple.

Felix went into town and bought a new machine from a retail store. It was a combined answer machine and fax, with automatic dialling and staggered transmission facilities.

"Why do I need an answer machine?"

It was the next day, and Joseph was looking at his new machine. He was baffled. Felix muttered some reply about keeping Joseph up to date with the latest technology.

"But we're always here! There's always someone at home. Why do I need an answer machine?" He was looking at Felix as if he'd gone mad.

Felix set up the new machine, and packed up the old one to take back to the company.

"You're up to something," Joseph said to Felix as he was leaving. "I don't know what it is... but you're up to something!"

Felix stopped to give Joseph's wife a hug. Each of the three children gave him a sloppy kiss. He waved good-bye as he backed the Triumph down the driveway.

The trouble with Joseph was that he was always right. It was a dangerous thing to be always right.

"3533679/00603/00481"

Harry was reading out the serial number on the fax machine, and checking it against the one on the inventory list.

"It certainly matches!"

"Why shouldn't it?" said Felix.

"I don't know... there's something odd."

"How do you mean?"

"We've looked in the store room a dozen times... it wasn't there!"

"It is now... so why are you worrying."

"Something's odd. I can't put my finger on it... but something odd is going on in this place."

****

Next week came, and Felix still had no idea what he was going to do.

He became ill.

He spoke to Joseph on the phone from London. He explained how the doctors had found a polyp on the bowel, how it was bleeding, and how they were insisting on an immediate operation.

"I'll only be inside for a couple of days."

"Don't worry about it," said Joseph. "Martha sends her love... and Avram, Samuel and Izaac are blowing you get well kisses."

"I'll come and spend Xmas with you."

"Martha is already preparing the turkey!"

"And then afterwards... in the new year... we'll go to the company together."

"Don't worry about it. Just get yourself well."

"I'll arrange a special meeting just for you. It'll be better that way. Everyone will be there and they'll greet you in style."

"Don't worry about it. You know I trust you."

Joseph laughed.

Felix wasn't sure what the laugh meant.

Had Joseph guessed?

****

Felix waited until everyone had gone.

It was Xmas eve, and they were hurrying to finish their work.

Except the zealots.

Harry stayed until after eight, methodically checking all the reports. And the idiot young technician was the last to go, rushing around trying to complete his enzymo-immunoassay. He was in a sort of ecstasy of enthusiasm, and didn't finish until close on midnight. In the end, Felix had to push him out the door. He would have stayed and worked over Xmas if given half a chance.

Felix had the keys to all the rooms, to all the labs, and to all the cupboards. He knew exactly where to go. It was in the synthetic chemistry lab, in the safe marked poisons.

Felix unlocked the safe, and took out the vial. He carried it gingerly to the fume cupboard.

Cyanide was so toxic you could be killed by its vapour. Felix remembered that time in New York, during a hot humid summer, when the air conditioning had broken down for a few minutes, and his colleague, who'd been working at the bench next to him had collapsed. He'd shouted "cyanide" just before he'd crumpled to the floor. Thank goodness it happened with Felix right next to him. Felix had got hold of the antidote from the first aid box and injected him within a couple of minutes.

"You brought me back from the dead!"

If Felix hadn't been there he would surely have died. Five minutes and you were dead.

Felix opened the vial behind the hood of the fume cupboard. He spooned out a couple of crystals and placed them in a small test tube. He recapped the cyanide bottle, took it out from behind the hood of the fume cupboard and placed it back in the safe.

The log book was also in the safe. By rights, Felix should have entered the date and the new weight of the cyanide bottle. He didn't. It would just have to remain a mystery. Fortunately Harry wasn't involved with the lab inventory.

Felix locked the safe. He collected the small test tube with its two crystals of cyanide and took a vial of sodium nitrite and another of sodium thiosulphate from the first aid box.

He left the lab, locking the door behind him.

He went back to his office, and prepared to leave. He arranged the papers on his desk, collecting the last report from the animal lab. Joseph would be happy to see the latest results. There was no doubt about it; the evidence was startling, the data impregnable, and the facts unarguable. The cats with the leukaemic virus were dead or dying, but the cats with the AIDS and the leukaemic virus were thriving.

It would be a nice Xmas present for Joseph.

He put the report in his briefcase, together with the vials and the test tube containing the two crystals of cyanide.

****

Felix arrived at noon on Xmas day.

The cottage was festooned in a profusion of decoration. There were Yuletide garlands across the front door, and a Xmas tree emblazoned in the bay window, with coloured lights blinking all over the place. Joseph's wife had gone mad. She'd even attached a special "Merry Xmas" chime to the door bell.

The chime died away, and the children came running up with arms outstretched.

"Uncle Felix is here!"

He had to pick up each one in turn. The smallest, as usual, managed to deposit a stringy snotty globule on his collar.

Felix distributed his presents.

It was a scene from Dickens. There was a cook book for Martha. She almost wept with pleasure as she undid the wrapping. It was as if he'd given her a diamond tiara. After a lot of "ooing" and "aaing", and showing it around, and pointing to the pictures, especially one of a "feuilleté de homard" that she'd be incapable of making in a hundred years, she gave Felix a great big hug.

"You are our true friend."

There was a chemistry set for Avram.

"So that you can follow in the steps of your father..." said Felix.

"And in the steps of uncle Felix," added Joseph. "The greatest scientist of our age!"

Felix was unsure whether Joseph was being serious or sarcastic.

There was an electric train for Samuel, and an electric talking parrot for little snot faced Izaac. The parrot had a built in tape recorder so that it repeated the last thing which was said to it. Joseph was completely bowled over by the electronic parrot. Despite the tears and protestations of little Izaac, Joseph grabbed hold of it and examined it intently, peering at it through his thick pebble glasses, as though he still wasn't sure if it was real or not.

"First principles! First principles!" Joseph screamed.

"First principles! First principles!" replied the parrot.

Everyone fell about laughing, except Izaac, who was snivelling because his father wouldn't give him back his present. Joseph didn't care about Izaac. He had no intention of giving back the present until he was done with it.

"First principles! First principles!" screamed Joseph, again and again.

"First principles! First principles!" responded the parrot in the self same voice.

It was becoming a nightmare.

Finally Felix managed to draw Joseph away from Izaac's present by offering him his own. It was a vintage bottle of port, a Taylor's '63. Felix handed Joseph the bottle, and Izaac managed to grab back the parrot. Joseph peered at the bottle, examining it this way and that. He looked puzzled. The bottle of port was empty, except for a thick layer of sediment at the bottom.

Felix smiled and delved into his sack like a magician. He waited an instant to let the tension build up, then brought out a crystal decanter, filled with port.

"He thinks of everything!" exclaimed Joseph. "Not only a fine port... but already decanted... so that it isn't shaken up by the journey."

Felix had indeed thought of everything. Not only decanted... but already containing two crystals of cyanide.

****

The Xmas lunch was a combination of a French reveillon and traditional English fare. There was foie gras to start and buche de Noel to finish. In between, there was roast turkey, the skin basted by thick crispy bacon, the inside stuffed with chestnuts and sage and onion, and the whole accompanied by pork sausages, red cabbage and Brussels sprouts.

Joseph ate like the condemned man at his last supper. He had three helpings of foie gras, knifing great chunks of the pink creamy textured delicacy on to warm toast impregnated with melted goose fat. He munched his way through the main course, twice. First concentrating on breast and wing, second specialising in brown meat, particularly the thigh bone. On both occasions he loaded his plate with an abundance of crispy bacon and pork sausages.

There was something extraordinarily incongruous about the scene. Joseph's wife was a great fat nervous woman, and yet she was barely eating anything. Instead she was obsessed by the need to serve others, constantly on the move, changing plates, replenishing dishes, clucking over Felix and her children, and most of all watching over Joseph, as if he was some frail invalid in need of nursing. Joseph was just the opposite. He was a small thin man, focused only on food, peering at the dishes through his thick pebble glasses, gorging himself like the Emperor Nero, and totally self absorbed, indifferent to anyone but himself.

The meal drew to a close. Joseph daubed huge spoonfuls of crème fraiche into his mouth. He was stuffing in so much that it began oozing and dribbling from the sides. The image was startling. Felix was looking at a maggot.

Joseph sat back in his chair, replete. He pulled out a luxurious cigar from its metal tube, another present from Felix, and let Avram light it for him. Izaac was on his lap, and Samuel was playing with his presents at Joseph's feet. Martha was rushing about clearing the table and laying out the fruit and nuts. Joseph was the very picture of the paterfamilias.

Martha carried the decanter of port from the sideboard and placed it at the centre of the dining table. Joseph reached forward to take out the glass stopper.

"Stop!" shouted Felix.

Joseph jumped. He was startled by the imperious tone of Felix's command. Even Martha stopped in her tracks and looked at Felix, wondering what was happening.

"Hold it a second," said Felix, smiling broadly, anxious that he had spoken too loudly, and keen to calm everyone down.

"I want to make a toast..." he said.

Joseph smiled and settled back in his chair. Martha gathered the children, somewhat awed by the formality of Felix's announcement.

"But first... the needs of nature."

Felix hurried to the bathroom. There was no time to spare. Joseph was so self centred, he might pour himself a glass before Felix got back. That wouldn't do. It was absolutely essential that Felix drink a glass of port before Joseph.

He took the ampoule of sodium nitrite from his jacket. It was the antidote to cyanide, as effective if given before exposure as after. He took out a small plastic syringe and drew the liquid up from the ampoule into the syringe. He put a tourniquet above his elbow, straightened his arm and felt for the cubital vein. It began to swell like a fat worm. He slid the syringe needle into it, and drew back a few drops of blood. There! The needle was firmly in position, centred in the vein. He released the tourniquet and injected the contents of the syringe into his arm. The sodium nitrite coursed through his blood rendering it impregnable to attack by cyanide.

The antidote would be effective for another five minutes. And he had the sodium thiosulphate in reserve, if he needed to come back for more.

Felix hurried back to the Xmas table.

"I want us to toast..." said Felix, pausing for maximum effect, "... us! First a toast to Martha, for being a wonderful wife... mother... cook... and hostess."

He stretched forward and took the glass stopper out of the decanter.

"A toast to Avram, Samuel and Izaac for being who they are."

Even Felix found it difficult to conjure up anything complimentary to say about the children.

"A toast to Joseph for being the best friend and colleague anyone could ever wish."

He filled his own and Joseph's glass with port, the liquid trickling thickly down the side like treacle.

"And a toast to me... for having the good fortune to be a guest in your home."

He took a large bottle of Coke and filled glasses for Martha and the children. Thank God she didn't touch alcohol. And the children were too young.

He raised his glass.

"To us!"

He gulped down the poisoned port in one draught.

"To us!" said Martha and downed her coke.

"To us!" said Avram, Samuel and Izaac, and they slurped at their glasses of coke.

"To us!" said Joseph.

But instead of putting the glass to his lips he offered it to Avram to have a sip.

Felix watched as if it was in slow motion. Joseph beckoning to Avram. Avram putting down his glass of coke and coming round to stand next to his father. Joseph handing Avram the poisoned glass. Avram taking hold of it. Avram holding it to the light. Avram putting the glass to his lips!

Avram screamed.

He screamed because Felix grabbed the glass from his hand.

Martha screamed.

She screamed because Felix hurled the glass out of the window smashing a pane and setting off one of Martha's infernal security devices which started a high pitched wailing siren.

Felix screamed.

He screamed as he took hold of the decanter and hurled it out the window to join the poisoned glass.

The rest of the day was subdued. Nobody really understood what had possessed Felix. His statement that the port was corked and unfit for human consumption was seen to be an inadequate explanation for such extreme behaviour.

Joseph was the most subdued.

It was as if he at last knew the awful truth about Felix.

****

Felix was no master criminal. He'd acted on instinct. He hadn't thought it through. It was the chance of Xmas dinner and the bringing of presents which had created the opportunity. Why would anyone suspect poisoning? Everyone had eaten the same things. Why would anyone suspect murder? There was no motive. At least, not a motive that any ordinary person could understand.

And Felix might have got away with it. He would have telephoned a local doctor who would have diagnosed a heart attack.

"It always happens at Xmas. People eat too much."

Why would anyone think anything else?

But of course it could have turned extremely nasty.

"It's probably a heart attack... all the same... it is a suspicious death... we'll have to have a post mortem."

And then what?

And now what?

Now things were becoming a true nightmare. The staff were back at work on Monday, and Joseph insisted on meeting them. He was preparing a speech, he'd been preparing it ever since the awful Xmas dinner.

What was he going to say?

"My friends... let me introduce myself... Asterix is garbage! It's all my idea. Felix had nothing to do with it. He was so keen to keep me a secret... he even tried to kill me!"

****

It was Monday morning, and the time bomb was ticking.

Felix drove along the ice covered country roads. The sports car was slipping and swerving. He was on his way to pick up Joseph.

A bend came up in front of him, and he purposefully accelerated. The car went into a vicious skid, and Felix accelerated even harder. It was as if he was willing himself to have a crash, even kill himself. Anything was better than have the day proceed towards its inevitable conclusion.

He was heading for the ditch.

The back wheels suddenly got a grip on a solid surface, and the Triumph hurtled round the corner. Felix eased back the peddle. He was still in one piece.

It was like being in a dream, the sort where you can see an inevitable disastrous end, an escalator sliding you into a furnace, a lift hurtling you down a shaft. You know you should do something, but you're paralysed, and the catastrophe looms closer and closer.

And you wake up.

But he wasn't asleep. He was on his way to pick up Joseph, and to take him to a supposedly rousing reception at the company. Felix had told Joseph that Harry had organised a catered function so that the staff and their families would have a chance to chat with Joseph. How had he ever allowed it to get this far? What was going to happen when Joseph arrived and no one had ever heard of him?

What was going to happen?

Something was going to happen. Something had to happen!

Joseph's cottage sprang into view. God how he loathed Joseph. How he wished he'd never met the maggot.

There was poor fat stupid Martha on the steps to greet him. She still believed he was their greatest friend. And there were the children, running out to welcome him, the awful snivelling ghastly children who believed that Uncle Felix was the nicest Uncle any little boy could possibly have.

The only one who wasn't waiting to greet him was Joseph. He was in the shed, poring over the notes for his speech, working until the last possible moment, refining and elaborating his denunciation of Felix. Joseph was the only one in that idiot family who had any inkling of what Felix was up to.

What was Felix going to do? How was he going to get rid of Joseph? Drive him to the airport and bundle him on to a plane? Drive him to a lonely spot along the roadside and strangle him? Felix had no plan. It was a nightmare. The lift was hurtling down the shaft and Felix was paralysed.

He parked the car and jumped out. He gave Martha a big hug.

"Today's the day. Make sure you dress Joseph warm. We don't want him catching a cold."

Martha went back into the house to get ready Joseph's thick woollen coat, his Homburg hat, his mittens.

Felix walked down the path to the bottom of the garden. He could see Joseph through the window, bent over his table, scribbling away making the final notes for his speech. There was a large plate of half eaten bacon and scrambled eggs beside him. Every time he paused, he stuffed his mouth with another forkful.

Felix opened the door and let himself in.

"I thought this day would never come," said Joseph, dribbling bits of half chewed bacon out the side of his mouth.

"What do you mean?"

"I thought you were keeping my existence a secret."

"Why should I do that?"

"To keep it all for yourself!"

"How could I do that? Even if I wanted... how could I do that?"

"By getting rid of me."

"Get rid of you?"

"Yes."

"How?"

"By killing me."

It was true. He had guessed.

"What?"

"I thought you tried to poison me the other day. I thought you'd put poison in the port."

"Poison in the port?"

"Yes."

Felix had gone bright red. He couldn't control it. His face was blushing furiously, admitting his guilt by its very colour. Joseph was peering at him through his thick pebble glasses. Even he must see the redness.

"You did try to kill me!"

Joseph had jumped from his chair and was standing close to Felix, peering at him, certain at last.

"Don't be ridiculous!" But Felix could not control the blush. It was as if his face was on fire.

Joseph began to chuckle.

"You're so ambitious, you'd kill for it?"

Felix's face reddened even further. If it had been dark it would have glowed like a furnace.

Joseph stuffed some more food in his mouth. He was jubilant, enjoying his discovery, mocking Felix.

He blew his nose with his filthy handkerchief, and bits of half chewed bacon and scrambled egg flew across the room splattering against Felix's face like spit.

Felix heard a gurgling sound. Something had gone down the wrong way.

Joseph was choking!

Felix came up to him to pat him on the back.

Joseph flinched.

He was choking. But he didn't trust Felix.

Felix put his hand over Joseph's handkerchief and squeezed.

Joseph was choking, panic appearing in the little maggot eyes.

Felix held the handkerchief against Joseph's face, pressing it against Joseph's mouth and nose.

Joseph was struggling, writhing this way and that. He was like a snake, desperate to escape.

Felix held tight. It was a maggot, and he had it in his grasp.

Joseph was kicking and lashing about, his thick boots kicking viciously against Felix's shins.

Felix felt nothing. Nothing hurt him. There was only one thing to do, kill the maggot.

A strange racking sound came from Joseph's chest, and an ooze of frothy blood stained spittle seeped into the handkerchief, and began to drip from Felix's fingers.

Felix held the handkerchief firmly against the face, allowing not a breath of air to be taken.

Joseph's chest was making burbling and gurgling sounds. His eyes were flickering. It was a death rattle.

Felix held on tight as Joseph slumped to the ground.

Felix held the handkerchief tight over the maggot's mouth and nose as it lay on the ground and gave a final twitch.

He held it tight until he heard Martha coming down the path.

By that time the maggot was long dead. Dead from its own gluttony.

Good riddance!

****

The following day Felix was back in the office with his mind clear and free.

Yesterday couldn't have gone better. Martha came bursting through the door to try and revive her inert husband. Felix called the doctor. The doctor pronounced Joseph dead from inhaled food. And then poor Martha blamed herself. She told the doctor she should have served Joseph's breakfast earlier and given him more time to eat it at his leisure. Nobody suspected Felix. Why should they? Felix was Joseph's friend and benefactor.

And that was that.

Exit Joseph.

Felix asked Harry to assemble the staff.

"I have an important announcement," he told Harry, "and I want everyone to hear what I have to say."

Harry set off to gather the staff into the seminar room.

"They're waiting," Harry announced.

Felix entered the seminar room. The babble of voices died down as he stood to speak. They were looking at him expectantly. They sensed he was about to deliver a momentous message.

"It's time to move forward," Felix spoke softly.

There was not a sound in the room. All heads were craning forward eager to catch his every word.

"The time has come to try our therapy on a human patient."

There was a gasp of pleasure and a ripple of applause.

"Somewhere out there," Felix pointed to a map pinned to the wall, "someone is waiting."

Joseph was gone, and Felix was free to pursue his vengeance against father.

All he needed was a human guinea pig.

"We will find someone who is dying from AIDS," Felix continued, "and we will offer a cure."

There were cheers and stamping of feet.

Harry opened up a bottle of champagne to celebrate the new phase in their operation.

"I wonder who our guinea pig will be?" Harry asked, as he filled Felix's glass.

CHAPTER TWO

DARIUS
LIFE WITH MOM

Felix's guinea pig was Darius.

Darius was born and brought up in a small suburb outside of Chicago. He was as different from Felix as any two humans can be. Where Felix was cultured, urbane and manipulative; Darius was crude, wild and guileless. Felix was obsessed by his father; Darius was tormented by his mother. She was the bane of his life. His formative years were spent in perpetual dispute with her. It started when he was very young, with little things, for example what musical instrument he should bring to school.

"You can lay there on your back like an evil turtle until the cows come home, young man, but we are not buying you a xylophone and that is final, you can just scream to your little heart's content."

Darius and his mother disagreed on just about everything. When he was ten years old they had a fight about his education.

"You are not going to any special music school and that's final! I'm sorry now I ever opted for those piano lessons, but who knew you'd just run it into the ground? They were just supposed to be so you'd know how to play a nice tune or two for a guest. God! That's all we need! You going to a special school and getting more swollen headed than you are already!"

The crux of the dispute was that Darius was wanting to make a name for himself, while his mother thought he was overambitious.

"If you'd stuck to the piano like we begged, you might've stood a chance; but who's going to pick you with that guitar thing? Even a solo trumpet performance - and God knows who'd give their child a trumpet - stands a better chance of winning than the noise you make!"

And she was ungenerous even when he did succeed.

"Alright now, Swollen Head; different people like different things on different days. The next day you'll just as easily find the judges not in the mood at all to give the award to something Kooky and'll give it to something normal and think you're just terrible."

And so it went on, a perpetual argument between mother and son, right throughout Darius' schooldays. Eventually, when Darius told his mother he was leaving home to make his fortune, she tried to discourage him.

"You haven't made a single cent since you graduated. You are just stupid thinking you're going to earn any more money with a band than you did on your own. And another thing; don't think I'm going to be supporting you when that Darius and His Dopes… or whatever it is thing you're doing comes to nothing."

Nor did she understand why he wanted to change his name.

"*Bernard Hubert Plank*, no matter how much you want to pretend - remember it's on your birth certificate!"

And when Darius became a big star, his mother still treated him like a child.

"Young Man, what is this funny looking red sports-car thing that's just been delivered and plunked down in the middle of the drive way? What have you done now, gone off and thrown away more money on some foreign thing that won't run well and'll start falling apart the first week you have it. If I were you, instead of going roaring through the few decent States of the Union that are left, disrupting and alienating decent people with your nasty car and personality, I'd be getting my head out of the clouds and starting to think about preparing for a rainy day. You know, when all this is over and no one wants you on the covers of their magazines any more and they stop buying your albums and coming to your concerts and your money's gone because you've wasted it, everybody's just going to hate you for being so show-offy. You were plenty well disliked around the neighbourhood before with the way your Attitude is, but now it'll be HATE, because I was asking your father, and we think the general consensus when it's all over is going to be that you were just a fad, like that Bobby Darin, a flash in the pan, and that you got what you deserved by strutting around acting and spending like you were an Elvis Presily or a Duke Ellington who was going to last..."

Nothing seemed to please his mother, not even when Darius brought his fiancée to meet her.

"Persimmon? Persimmon?! After the globular fruit whose seeds make you abort? That's almost as stupid as calling yourself Darius."

And she suspected his motives.

"And by the way, just what is your game here anyway with this big fat girl, may I ask? I mean really, there's overweight and then there's just plain being a big fat slob. What is it you're after? Marrying yourself into a place on the board of the family's drug company? Showing off to your druggie friends? Serving them up unlimited gold platters full of that pure pharmaceutical cocaine that's supposed to be such a status symbol amongst your sick set? - I know how that warped mind of yours works."

When Darius got AIDS, his mother came straight to his bedside. But, as usual, she wasn't any comfort,

"Well, I hate to say it, Bernard, but I told you so! But then, you know what they say, 'No use crying over spilt milk'. I suppose now that you've gone and gotten this disease and you're here in the hospital and there's nothing in the world you can do about it, you'd just better try and make the best of it with what little time you've got left... Well, your father sends his regards and hopes you'll be feeling better soon; you know how he is, always the ostrich."

Fortunately, Darius' mother was completely wrong about one thing.

"There's no hope for you, Bernard, so the best thing for you would be to just spend the time you do have left facing that and stop wasting it pining for pie-in-the-sky. I mean, sure, they'll find a cure someday, but I'm afraid, Bernard - and as a mother I hate to say it - not in time for you. Not that I wish you any harm...."

She had no way of knowing about Henry.

CHAPTER THREE

HENRY
CALVARY IN CALIFORNIA

Henry introduced Darius to Felix.

But only after he died.

It happened one Autumn day in San Diego.

Henry couldn't sleep and woke early. He pulled aside the blinds to let the misty light of morning into his room. Henry lived in the cheap district, between the freeway and the naval dockyard, on the southern part of town near the Mexican border. The mist was so thick, he couldn't see the buildings opposite. The trouble with San Diego was the mist, not just in the fall but all year round. Sure enough, by about mid-day, the sun would be shining, the temperature would be in the 80s, the air would be clean, and the tourists would be saying 'another day in paradise'. But first you had to get through the morning, and every morning the ocean mist was there to dampen Henry's spirit.

He pulled off his pyjamas and stood naked in front of the cupboard mirror. He wasn't much to look at, five foot six, skimpy arms and legs, a thin bony chest, and a sagging pot belly. He was thirty five, but could have been fifty. He touched the protruding ribs on his chest and the ginger hair round his scrotum. His own image didn't excite him.

He crossed the thin faded carpet and selected a video. There were five, HANK HITCHES A RIDE, JEFF SCORES FROM BEHIND, RANDY HEADS IT HOME, BRAD GOES DOWN and JASON EATS IT UP.

Big boy likes Daddy. Big boy likes to swallow his Daddy. Big boy likes to gobble and gobble and gobble and SWALLOW.

A dribble of sperm trickled over Henry's fingers. He watched the video as the boy with tattoos stuck a pin in the buttock of a short redhead, who was squirting a torrent of creamy liquid into the mouth of a tall blond. JASON was Henry's favourite. Jason reminded him of the platinum blond.

Henry rinsed his hands at the sink. He'd met the kid five years ago. He was a dream come true, a six foot, slim, twenty year old platinum blond. The boy had come up to him in the store. Henry hadn't said anything, hadn't even looked in his direction, boys like that just aren't interested in men like Henry. But this one was. For some wonderful magical reason Henry was Mr Right, just the person the boy had been looking for. They spent three weeks together, and for the first time in his life Henry was loved. Or he thought he was, until the boy was arrested for breaking into the store with Henry's keys.

The boy was jailed and Henry was sacked. The worst of it was that the boy accused Henry of planning the whole thing, and the police were about to bring charges against Henry until they discovered the boy had done the same thing with three other older men.

Henry made himself a cup of tea. Why did he have to dwell on the rotten things that had happened in his life? Anyway he'd been lucky. The police dropped the case against him.

Henry sipped his tea and remembered the last time he'd seen the boy. It was just before they'd taken him off to jail.

"I thought you loved me," Henry said to him.

"You're such a dope," was all the boy had replied.

After the platinum blond disappeared from his life, Henry looked for others. He went to the gay bars, but it was a disaster. There were plenty of gorgeous boys, but they were only interested in each other. They snubbed him. They were just plain nasty, acting as if he had no right to be there.

Henry stayed away from the scene after that, and his only friends were the two bitchy queens who lived in the rented apartment next door. They weren't really friends, just two lonely old men who had no one else to talk to. As for sex, Henry paid for it. At least that way he could be sure of having someone, of getting something. He used to joke with his friends next door, "What's worse than sex without love?", and they'd answer, "No sex without love." But Henry couldn't afford to pay very much, and the boys he bought didn't try too hard. His friends suggested he should use videos, and they lent him a couple of their own. It was an improvement; the boys didn't have to look at Henry and were able to get off with the action on screen.

Henry put the cassette of JASON back with the others. He opened his wardrobe and set about dressing himself with care. He flicked through the sombre coloured suits which he wore to work. None of them would do, they were too drab and tatty and made him look like a clerk. He lingered over the leather and rubber gear, trying it on for fun. He was almost tempted, but he knew it wouldn't do. Today might be special, but not that special. He would regret it as soon as he stepped into the street. There would be catcalls and jeers. One of his boys had called him "Batman gone wrong" when he'd first dressed up, so he could imagine what others might say when he wasn't paying.

Henry was a bit of a coward, and he wasn't going to change just because he was doing something brave. He put on a T shirt, denim jacket and frayed jeans. As a finishing touch he trimmed his ginger moustache, and put a smart red leather cap over his bald patch. He looked like a clone, and that suited him just fine. He didn't want to stand out in the crowd.

On his way down the stairs the two bitchy friends came out of their apartment to wish him good luck.

"You look great," said one.

"You'll be the talk of the town," said the other.

It was meaningless but Henry was grateful all the same. Few people ever said anything kind. It didn't matter that his two friends would laugh and joke about him behind his back; it was comforting that they didn't do it to his face.

Henry walked down the road and on to the main boulevard. He stood at the tram stop waiting for the tramcar. It would be along by eight AM. The young doctor had told him to be at the clinic by nine. The journey took half an hour. But Henry didn't want to be rushed. Better to be sitting for half an hour in the waiting room than be late.

Henry yawned. He was tired. He'd had a sleepless night. The more he'd struggled to get to sleep, the worse it had been. The trouble with nights is that everything gets blown up out of all proportion and you start fretting about the littlest things. At first Henry hadn't settled because he was worried about the shop. He hated taking time off, he imagined all sorts of catastrophes. Maybe the lady from last Tuesday would come back with a complaint. Henry could imagine her denouncing him, bringing a doctor's certificate attesting that he'd assaulted her little boy.

It was ridiculous. That's always the trouble with sleepless nights. The ridiculous becomes reality.

The tramcar came clattering down the road. It was on time. He boarded the car and found himself a seat near the front. It was crowded, mostly with Mexicans on their way to their cleaning jobs in the city. There was a smartly dressed woman in her fifties, sitting all alone. She probably worked as a secretary for a slave driver boss. Towards the back of the tramcar was a much younger girl, perhaps a student on her way to early class. She had her arms round her boyfriend, a stunning blond.

Daddy wants Jason naked. Daddy wants Jason to dance in front of Daddy. Jason is Daddy's big boy and Daddy will swallow and gobble.

The boy caught Henry staring at him, and the girl giggled. Henry thought he saw the boy mouthing the word "faggot!"

Henry arrived at the clinic at eight thirty on the dot. As usual, nurse was in a bad mood, not even bothering to greet him. Ever since he'd been coming she'd been like that. It wasn't personal. It was her attitude with everyone. Henry had hoped that today would be different, that some of the excitement he was feeling would be shared by her. But she didn't give an inch. She snapped at him when he rested his feet on a chair and ignored him when he asked if she was going join him on the march.

Henry wanted so much to be a nurse himself. All through his childhood he'd dreamed of becoming a theatre nurse. There was something magical about being camouflaged in a gown and mask, standing alongside a surgeon, with the operating lights beaming down, illuminating you like lovers in a spotlight. And there was a special thrill to the dialogue! Words like 'scalpel' and 'forceps' carried messages of endearment way beyond anything obvious and trivial like 'I love you'. It had been a burning ambition, and he'd struggled through school to try and make the grade. It hadn't been easy. He wasn't cut out for studying. He spent months grappling with text books that ordinary average students were able to master in a day or two. But he didn't care. The fact that he had to toil harder than the others made the goal even more desirable. It took him six years, with lots of repeated classes en route, but he finally graduated. And then came his debut as a theatre nurse. He had gone to work so excited, he'd half expected the doctors to be as excited as he. But they paid him no attention. He scrubbed and gowned and they talked amongst themselves. No one welcomed him. No one even asked his name. Together they passed through into the operating theatre. The patient was already on the table. It was a complicated bowel resection. Henry stumbled on a couple of occasions, he was a bit slow handing over a swab and he'd forgotten to connect the vacuum to the sucker, but these were teething troubles and Henry was sure he'd soon get into the swing of things. Then the surgeon asked him for the "Lloyd-Davis". Henry knew it was either the long dagger like knife or the curved scissors. He handed over the scissors. Wrong! The surgeon didn't say anything, he didn't bother to correct him. Instead he flung the instrument to the floor and asked the second doctor to take over at the nursing station. Henry stood back while someone else did his job. He stood behind the two doctors, and he listened in silence while they talked about him. They knew all about him, and they talked about him as if he was the village idiot. They'd been dreading his coming. He listened in silence. He didn't dare say a word. He was only grateful that they couldn't see the tears which were streaming down his face. As the operation drew to its close, they began laughing. They didn't try to hide it. They were giggling about the hospital lottery with Henry as the booby prize. The surgeon with his back to Henry was the loser. At last the operation was over. The surgeon completed his final stitch and offered his concluding remark. "I wonder how long it will take him to know he isn't wanted here?" Then they all trooped out to the changing rooms and nobody spoke to him, or about him, again. Henry went home and threw away all his notes and nursing books. He never came back. And he struggled never to think of it, except at times like this, when he was tired and over excited.

Another guy came into the waiting room. He'd been there last time getting an AIDS test, and Henry guessed he must be back for a repeat. Henry remembered his own test. It was after the platinum blond had been arrested and Henry suddenly realised the danger. Henry wasn't the platinum blond's first lover, more like the thousand and first.

Daddy likes it when big boy's inside him.... to be squashed and stuffed by his big boy.... until he bursts!

The platinum blond had deposited his sperm, loaded with HIV, night after night in Henry's rectum, and the virus had wriggled its way through the mucosal lining to find a home in Henry's T cells. When he went for his first AIDS test it came back HIV negative, and Henry celebrated with his bitchy friends who'd always feared the worst about the platinum blond. But the doctors told him not to read too much into the first test. The AIDS test detected the antibodies against HIV and not HIV itself. If Henry had the virus, it would take several weeks before the antibodies would develop against it. So Henry went back for his second test three months later and sure enough it was positive. His bitchy friends expressed sorrow and grief. Secretly they were jubilant; they couldn't bear the thought that Henry might have had his moment of pleasure without having to pay for it.

"Hi!" said the young doctor.

It was the strikingly handsome black doctor who'd been looking after him for the last few months. Henry had liked him from their very first meeting. He didn't want to sleep with him, the young doctor wasn't his type, too dark, Henry wasn't attracted to black skin. But he liked him. In fact, over the months, without really being aware of it, Henry had fallen in love with the young doctor.

"Hi!" said Henry.

Doctor Kwanza went through into his office and Henry waited to be called. It was strange how Henry enjoyed coming to the clinic. Most people loathed it. The rich gays went to their private physicians, and only those who couldn't afford the private health schemes frequented the city funded service. But Henry liked it all the same, he felt a sense of camaraderie, as if they all belonged to a community where people cared for each other. Of course it wasn't true; Henry was an incorrigible romanticiser who mistook indifference for affection.

The clinic became busier as guys streamed in to be checked before the big parade, and the nurse became sourer. When it was Henry's turn to be called she gestured to him with a flick of her hand as if he was an animal. He didn't mind, it was all part of the big day, and it would give him something to laugh about when he told his two friends later.

"I'm glad you could make it."

Doctor Kwanza shook his hand and smiled at him. Henry was so happy he began to swell. Nothing in the world would have induced him to go on the march if it hadn't been that Doctor Kwanza had personally invited him. Henry had accepted to please him, and now he felt the young doctor was proud of him.

Daddy doesn't want to rub a dark chest! Daddy doesn't want to touch a black tummy!

As he undressed, Henry fought to control his erection. But the bloody thing had a mind of its own, and when Doctor Kwanza turned to examine him it was standing bolt upright.

"I'll leave you to cool down a bit."

The young doctor smiled but he wasn't pleased, and he left the room in a hurry. Henry covered himself with a towel, and lay on the couch feeling guilty and ashamed. It was the first time anything like that had ever happened to him. Normally it was the other way round, the boys used to complain that he took too long. Yet here he was making a fool of himself in front of Doctor Kwanza, and he wasn't even attracted to him.

As he lay on the couch he began to think back to another time, to the memory of the last boy two years ago. He was an eighteen year old and his name was Robbie. Henry had picked him up on the meat rack, near the entrance to the bus terminal. Henry had taken him home and fed him and fussed over him. When Robbie was undressed he was gorgeous. He had a beautiful slender waist with smooth pale skin and long blond hair falling over powerful shoulders. Robbie's chest was massive, like a body builder.

Daddy will kiss Robbie's breasts.... Daddy will squeeze Robbie's bottom.... Daddy will bite Robbie's neck.... Robbie is so happy to have his Daddy beside him.

Henry got undressed, and Robbie stared at him. At first Henry thought it was because Robbie liked him. Then he realised that Robbie was staring at a mark on his back. Suddenly Robbie's face turned black and ugly and he pointed at the mark screaming "Get away from me you faggot! You've got AIDS!" Henry didn't know what had got into him but Robbie was wild, pointing at Henry's back, hurling abuse, cursing and demanding money. Henry wasn't going to pay him, he hadn't done anything yet! But Robbie got crazier and crazier, and in the end Henry was glad to pay him just to get him out of the apartment.

Doctor Kwanza explained it to Henry the next day. The HIV virus, which had been living and breeding in Henry's T cells ever since the platinum blond had put it there, was at last doing some damage. Henry's T cells were dying and they could no longer do their job, which was to protect Henry from being invaded by disease. Doctor Kwanza pointed to the scarlet mark on Henry's back and explained that what

Robbie had seen was a Kaposi Sarcoma, a skin cancer. It was an extremely rare cancer only ever seen on AIDS patients. Robbie must have seen it before on someone he knew which was why he'd got so excited. Doctor Kwanza was very reassuring, explaining to Henry that because his T cells couldn't defend him from disease any more, he, Doctor Kwanza, was going to do the job instead and give Henry whatever drugs were needed to kill the diseases as they struck. It was probably at that moment that Henry fell in love with the young doctor. Robbie had seen the mark of death, and been repelled by it, but Doctor Kwanza had consoled Henry, and was prepared to guide him on the hazardous journey through what was left of his life.

There had been two occasions since the incident with Robbie when Henry had nearly died. The first was a pneumonia. It was about three months ago. Henry hadn't realised how ill he was, he'd thought he'd got a bad cold, that's all. It was only when he began to find it difficult to breathe that he plucked up the courage to go to the clinic and see the young doctor. Doctor Kwanza began by scolding him for leaving it so late, but when he listened to Henry's chest there was no time for anything else except getting Henry straight into hospital and pumping him full of antibiotics. It took ten days before Henry was out of danger. The second occasion was only three weeks ago. Henry had a blinding headache which started quite suddenly one evening. This time Henry had learnt his lesson and he went to see the young doctor straight away. Again he was rushed into hospital with a fulminating meningitis. It took until last week to get him right and Henry's memory was still not quite normal.

It was when Henry was leaving the hospital after his meningitis that Doctor Kwanza had told him of the parade and asked him if he'd join. Henry would do anything for the young doctor. He agreed immediately, and had been looking forward to it ever since.

"Are we respectable?"

Doctor Kwanza was back in the room. He peaked under the towel and gave a relieved grin when he saw that Henry's erection had melted.

He began the routine examination. First the lymph nodes, prodding and palpating the swellings under Henry's chin and down his neck.

"They're fine, no changes that I can feel."

Then under his arm tickling Henry as he pushed his fingers into the pit, and finally in the groin between Henry's stomach and thigh. Henry felt him pushing on the right side and knew what he was going to say, Henry had felt it there himself earlier that day.

"I think there's a new one here."

Hold Daddy tight. Don't let Daddy go. Daddy wants his little boy to hug him and stay close to him. Don't leave Daddy alone.

The young doctor saw the fright in Henry's eyes.

"It's not too bad. I'd say you're doing very well."

Henry knew he was lying. But he was curiously uplifted by the fact that the young doctor was even bothering to protect him.

Doctor Kwanza listened to his chest, thumped his back, squeezed his tummy and measured the marks on his skin. Finally he weighed him and looked disappointed when he saw that Henry had lost another pound.

"When I lose my fat tummy I'll start to worry," Henry said jokingly. He felt it was now his turn to reassure the young doctor.

In fact Henry was well on his way to losing his pot belly, the rest of him had wasted away and loose skin folds were beginning to appear around his middle. Another two or three months and he would take on the look of the concentration camp victim which signalled the last stage of the disease. Doctor Kwanza called it "cachexia". Henry called it the final solution.

Henry dressed himself while Doctor Kwanza washed his hands at the sink. The young doctor was chattering away, telling Henry about the day's events. The main parade was happening upstate in San Francisco, but San Diego was not going to be left out of the picture. Doctor Kwanza was the principal co-ordinator for San Diego county, he'd arranged for a picket outside the drug company, and a TV crew were set to cover the main rally outside City Hall. It was certainly going to make the local news and maybe even get a few seconds on national TV. The young doctor was gossiping with Henry as if they were the best of friends. Henry felt himself swelling again. This time he let his body have its way, and harden in secret.

Doctor Kwanza led Henry by the arm out into the hallway. The organisers were handing out arm bands and banners. Some marchers were wearing pink triangles; others were brandishing slogans DEMOCRATS DON'T CARE - REPUBLICANS CARE LESS. Doctor Kwanza took a bright yellow banner CURE NOT COSMETICS - SHAME ON TRUST, and unfurled it. He asked Henry to hold the other end and they posed for photos. The flashlights popped in Henry's eyes as he shook the banner above his head and shouted the march slogan GIVE US A CURE!

When the photos were done and the banner was put back on the table, the young doctor put his arms around Henry and gave him a hug.

Hug Daddy forever. Let Daddy rest in your arms. Let me be loved by you forever and ever.

Henry was ready to die. It was all worth it, the years of neglect disease and suffering, just to arrive here and now, at this moment of love.

Henry put his hands to his eyes. He was beginning to cry with joy, and he wanted to hide his happiness.

Then things started to go wrong.

First Henry found himself separated from the young doctor. Doctor Kwanza led the main march to City Hall with the TV cameras following. Henry tried to accompany him, but Doctor Kwanza was most insistent that Henry should go instead with the small group heading for Trust Pharmaceuticals. Doctor Kwanza told Henry that it made better use of their resources to divide the march this way. But Henry didn't understand. Why couldn't he stay next to the young doctor?

Henry sat on the steps of the clinic as Doctor Kwanza's group disappeared round the corner. All the razzmatazz disappeared with them. The young guys, the good looking guys, the celebrities, the politicians, the journalists, the medics and paramedics had all followed Doctor Kwanza. Henry was left with the scummy crowd. Even Henry could see that. Henry's group consisted of nonentities like himself, and a scattering of punks and winos, street people who didn't look good at the best of times and looked even worse with AIDS. The only decent looking people were the two young women, nurses at a private hospital for rich patients, who'd been left behind to lead them. And even they looked disgruntled, as if they would rather be followers in the main march than leaders of the second division.

For a while Henry felt let down. But his faith in the young doctor was unshakeable and he created a reassuring fantasy to ease his mind. He decided that Doctor Kwanza trusted him, and needed him to look after things when Doctor Kwanza wasn't there to do it himself. Henry always sought virtue in the actions of others, unless their actions were manifestly evil.

The two young nurses rallied the troops, and set off in a procession heading North. Henry began to feel terribly tired after about half an hour. Their destination was much further than City Hall. Even if he'd been feeling well, it was too far to expect someone to walk. Also nobody wanted to walk with him. Every time he tried to come alongside they seemed to shy away. Henry supposed it was because they wanted to stay with their friends. All the same it made for a long lonely walk, and it wasn't helped by insults from spectators along the rout. Passers-by seemed to single Henry out, maybe because he looked so ill, or maybe because he looked alone and defenceless. At any event the comments weren't nice, "Fuck off Faggot" was favourite. Henry was really surprised when a nice old lady walking her dog suddenly screamed at him "I hope it kills you!" He tried to talk to her, but she just spat in his face.

Henry was beginning to regret that he'd ever come and was even thinking of slipping away. As far as he could see no one would notice if he left. The march was three quarters of the way to the Trust headquarters and the only thing that stopped Henry taking off was that he didn't know how to get home. They were walking down a wide tree lined avenue with small high tech businesses behind the driveways, "Molecular Biology Inc.", "Gen Probe Tec Inc", "DNA Code Constructs Inc", but no sign of public transport. Henry didn't fancy going into one of the entrances and asking to use their telephone to call a cab. So he kept walking. But he was breathing hard, and he had this strange pain in his chest.

He was not feeling well and he didn't know what to do. The two young nurses were leading the march, but they were keeping themselves apart from the main body of demonstrators, forcing the pace, and turning from time to time to shout a slogan and encourage their followers to march faster. They didn't seem to realise that they were leading a group of sick people. Henry decided to catch up with them and ask for help. One of the girls was a friend of the young doctor. Henry had seen her laughing and joking with the young doctor before the two groups had separated. Someone had said that the young doctor fancied her. Henry didn't really believe it, she wasn't the sort of person to attract the young doctor. Henry was sure the young doctor preferred people who were mature and responsible. She was too flighty. Henry guessed that she was throwing herself at the young doctor and that he was too much of a gentleman to know how to deal with her.

Anyway she seemed to be the group leader, and Henry increased his pace to catch up with her. It was a real struggle, she was walking so fast, and Henry was having more and more trouble breathing. When he was just a couple of yards from her he had to stop, he just couldn't go on. He sat on the kerb, the pain in his chest was making him nauseous and he was fighting for breath. The file of demonstrators marched past him without even a glance. Nobody said anything, nobody asked how he was, or stopped to see if he needed help. Henry began to feel frightened. They were going to leave him behind in the middle of nowhere. He pulled himself to his feet and tried to catch up with the tail of the procession.

He was breathing easier now. It was as if he'd caught his second wind. Suddenly things didn't seem so bad. He was positively light headed and was racing forward, almost running. In five minutes he'd caught up with the procession and in another two he was just behind the girls.

They were talking and laughing with each other. They seemed so cheerful. Henry was infected with their good humour. He was happy for them, happy that they were going to live, happy that they had their youth, and happy that they found life so joyful. Henry never resented the pleasure of others.

Henry came right behind them. He could hear every word they were saying. The young doctor's girl friend was doing the talking and the other girl was in fits of laughter. The young doctor's girl friend was telling her companion about the young doctor's patient. Apparently a patient had tried to seduce the young doctor. The young doctor's girl friend told how the patient had exposed his tiny prick to the young doctor. The other girl shrieked as she heard how the young doctor had to flee into the side room to stop himself laughing.

Henry was walking like an automaton, his face pale, his skin cold. The young doctor's girl friend caught sight of him. She stopped talking and whispered in the ear of her companion. The other girl looked at him and went into shrieks of suppressed laughter. They'd been talking about him! The young doctor had told his girl friend about what had happened at the examination.

Don't let Daddy go. Don't leave Daddy alone. You're hurting your Daddy. Please don't hurt Daddy.

It was the nightmare of the operating theatre.

"I wonder how long it will take him to know he isn't wanted?"

Henry slowed his pace and slipped into the midst of the crowd of marchers. His mind was a blank, there was nothing there, no substance, not even pain, just blank with a feeling of great blackness all round him. He didn't know why, but tears were welling in his eyes, and he covered his face to hide his embarrassment. He kept on walking, there was no reason not to. Henry didn't want to let the young doctor down. The young doctor was relying on Henry. But the tears kept coming and the blackness gathered about him.

At last the procession arrived at Trust Pharmaceuticals. Henry was stumbling. He couldn't have gone on another minute. The pain inside his chest had come back worse than ever and he couldn't breathe. He stood gasping for breath in the middle of the crowd. His head was bowed and he clutched at his chest trying to ease the pain. He could hear the chanting "GIVE US A CURE... GIVE US A CURE" but he couldn't see anyone. He was in the middle of a black cloud, completely surrounded by darkness.

It was all a blur. He heard the hooting of a horn, and cries and curses all round him. The crowd had melted away leaving him alone. He was abandoned in the middle of a black cloud. But something was trying to push him aside, it was a car and it had come out of the black cloud. It was gently pushing itself against him. The car had come to rescue him. In the back seat was a face, it looked worried and anxious. Henry reached out and opened the door. He wanted to comfort the face. The face was in front of him, it began to scream. Henry tried to stroke the face but it was filled with detestation and loathing. The face hated Henry. The face spat at him.

Why?

What had he done to the face?

Why did the face hate him?

The pain in his chest was so intense that Henry was lifted by it. It propelled him forward. He wanted to kiss the face and comfort it. He wanted to cover the face with his embrace.

He chased after the face. He followed it, urging it to stop, telling it there was nothing to fear.

The face turned on him.

It raised a wooden bat.

Henry stretched out his hands to embrace the face. Everything was going to be all right.

The face began beating him about the head with the wooden bat.

It was caressing him. It was soothing him to sleep and whispering that it loved him.

And Daddy loves you too. Daddy will always love you.

PART TWO

CRIME AND PUNISHMENT

CHAPTER FOUR

CAUSE OF DEATH

"Why did you do it?"

Bismarck Trust was sitting upright in front of a large wooden desk. He was in police headquarters near the mayor's office in down town San Diego.

"Why did you do it?"

It was the fiftieth or five hundredth time they'd asked him the same question.

What was the use of asking the same question over and over again?

The policeman asking the question was a fat man. He looked stupid. He had no subtlety or refinement.

"Why did you do it?"

It was typical of a stupid man to go on banging his head against a brick wall. Bismarck noticed that every time he asked the question a bead of sweat dripped from his bald scalp onto the bridge of his nose. Bismarck didn't like fat people. His daughter was fat. Fat people had no discipline. If they couldn't control their eating, they were hardly likely to be able to control anything else in their lives.

There were three policemen sitting opposite him. The fat stupid one seemed to be in charge. The other two were his assistants. Adler was sitting by his side, ready to advise him. So far he hadn't needed his help. They'd been interrogating him for three hours and he'd told them nothing.

He'd told them his name.

"Bismarck Trust."

He'd told them his job.

"President and principal shareholder of Trust Pharmaceuticals."

He'd told them about the party.

"It was father's birthday."

"But your father's dead."

The fat policeman was incorrigibly stupid.

Bismarck spelt it out in words of one syllable. He explained how in the old days Papa invited the family to gather round and celebrate his birthday. Bismarck kept the ceremony going after he died, making the day into a sort of memorial to Papa and a symbol of family unity.

All the Trusts who mattered had been there, Bismarck's four sisters, his two brothers in law, the third was divorced and banished, and the fourth had died of cancer. Bismarck didn't like to think of him. Disease emanated from the inner man.

His daughter had also been there. She'd arrived late, as usual, with yet another of her awful boyfriends. She was breathless and sweating. Bismarck could not forgive Persimmon for being so overweight. She was even fatter than the policeman who was interviewing him. It was hardly surprising that she only attracted gigolos. Nobody respectable would want to be seen with anyone as fat as her.

There were also eight nieces and five nephews. The grand nieces and nephews had not been invited. They were children or babies. Bismarck wasn't fond of babies. *Trust Day* was only open to adults. It was also an unwritten rule that if you were sick you didn't come.

"Did you know about the march?"

The fat policeman's question was vague. Bismarck made it a rule never to answer an imprecise question. He wasn't going to change now, just because he was in custody.

He said nothing, and the fat policeman just went on sweating.

Bismarck could have answered him easily enough. He remembered exactly when he'd learnt about the march. His wife, Isabel, had been at his side. The entrance to the office was festooned with jolly signs 'Trust welcomes the Trusts'. There was a drinks table near the door, and the main reception was out the back on the secluded covered patio with its view towards the hills. A local catering company had laid out a feast of Californian fruit and salads with wines from the Napa valley and the finest Colorado beef for the barbecue. There was also a giant birthday cake with 98 candles for Papa Trust as though he were still alive. In the front of the building, forming part of the reception committee with Bismarck and Isabel, were Bismarck's principal executives.

He'd been in a genial mood. He put his arm round Isabel's waist and posed for the group photo. Bismarck and Isabel at the centre, surrounded by sisters and their spouses, and flanked by the senior company staff. The photo would be used to illustrate the annual report. Fortunately Persimmon had stayed out the back, gorging herself, with her latest boyfriend in tow.

And then his PR man had come running up with news that a march was coming their way.

"They've been keeping their route secret, sir", his PR man had told him, as if that was an excuse for not knowing.

"Who's responsible?"

"A committee called AIDS Concern."

"Why don't you stop them?"

"It's a political campaign, sir."

"Give them a donation, and keep them away."

He remembered Isabel taking hold of his hand and stroking it in an effort to calm him. She thought he was irritated by the news of a demonstration coming to spoil his day. But it wasn't that. He couldn't have cared less if the place was picketed by demonstrators. It had happened to him before, when he deunionised the Chicago facility, and he hadn't been in the least discomfited by shouting and screaming syndicalists. What was worrying him were the people who were coming.

"Did you know there was going to be a march?" The fat sweating policeman repeated his idiotic question.

Bismarck said nothing. The policeman probably thought he was trying to hide something. But he didn't care. Of course he knew there was going to be a march. The question was 'When did he know?' If the stupid policeman asked him that, he'd give him the answer. But how was he expected to answer something which made no sense? They must learn to ask precise questions.

The door opened and a woman police officer came in with drinks and sandwiches. She placed them on the desk in front of Bismarck. He could smell her odour as she stepped in front of him. There was a nauseous stench of cheap perfume. He held his breath until she left.

She'd also brought the early edition of the morning paper.

There it was, a front page headline.

Bismarck Trust Scandal!

His photo was splashed across the front page. It was a picture of him at the races, taken two years ago, when he'd been at Ascot. He was in full morning dress with his top hat by his side. He was standing next to the queen. She was looking up at him. It gave the impression she was besotted by him. The photo was flattering but misleading.

Underneath the photo was a short bio, a hastily written piece of journalistic illiteracy.

Bismarck Trust has everything! Six foot four, slim, handsome, and silver haired Bismarck was destined for greatness...

The newspaper pretended he had inherited a billion dollars and then tripled it. They always got their facts wrong.

There was a smaller picture on the inside page. It was a smudged photograph, and you could barely make out the body. The caption read; *Henry Meadows, shop assistant, lies in a pool of his own blood after being battered to death by Fortune 400 industrialist Bismarck Trust.*

The fat stupid policeman picked up the sandwich. His fingers were dirty. Bismarck could see black rings of encrusted dirt under his nails.

He gestured for Bismarck to take a bite.

Bismarck shook his head.

Another policeman offered him a drink. Bismarck asked for tea. The policeman poured it into a mug. He placed it in front of Bismarck. The mug was unclean, there was a trace of lipstick round the rim. Bismarck pushed the tea away.

The fat sweating policeman pointed at the newspaper. His podgy dirty finger was pointing at the question headlining the second page.

Why did he do it?

It was Adler who eventually brought the proceedings to a close. He informed the fat stupid policeman that his time was up. He had to make up his mind whether to charge Bismarck or not. Adler's ultimatum caused pandemonium. Everyone in police headquarters began crowding into the interview room, and everyone had something to say. Adler was adamant. 'Charge my client, or let him go.' Eventually they were left with no choice and Bismarck was charged with murder.

Adler left, telling Bismarck he'd be back first thing in the morning to arrange bail.

It was three AM. The police were tired. The fat policeman handed Bismarck over to the woman police officer. She led him down a series of corridors. On each side were black steel doors armed with great bolts and locks. Bismarck kept several paces behind in an effort to put a safe distance between him and her cheap perfume.

The place was old fashioned. It looked as though it had been designed to depress the inmates rather than enforce security. As if to emphasise the point, the woman police officer took out a large rusty key and unlocked the door to Bismarck's cell.

He stepped into a bare room with whitewashed brick walls. There was no window. The light came from a single feeble bulb dangling from the black ceiling. There were no furnishings, just a washstand and a flimsy iron bed.

The policewoman bade him good night and locked the door behind her.

Bismarck sat on the bed. It was hard.

He didn't mind. He preferred it hard. Bismarck was a man of the North. He liked cold rather than hot, blond rather than dark, Luther rather than the Vatican, cleanliness rather than dirt, and control rather than passion.

So why the passion?

Why had he done it?

Everything had been under control, until he'd heard about the march.

Isabel noticed straight away that something was the matter. He must have turned white. He'd begun to shake. His whole body was trembling. She looked at him as though he'd gone mad.

In his mind's eye Bismarck had seen the demonstrators marching towards him. He couldn't contain himself. There was no disease more loathsome than AIDS. Everything about it was hateful. Starting with the way you caught it, the disgusting idea of two men having sex together, and one of them putting his filthy thing into the backside of the other. It was the activity of degenerates. The very idea made him writhe in disgust. And the consequence! The virus entering the body, invading the cells, multiplying secretly, destroying all capacity to resist. There could be no more terrible disease than a disease which gave you all other diseases. He had an image of the virus people, enveloped in a mist of bacteria, fungus and yeast, gathering their force, marching towards him and preparing to attack.

He had to get away, to get out of there before they infected him.

He summoned George and told him to prepare the Mercedes. The party was a disaster. He'd leave Isabel to sort it out. All that mattered was to get away.

Then he'd heard them. They were outside. They were shouting their idiotic slogans. Every time they shouted he trembled. He lost all restraint. He had to get out. He had to get away from them. He felt the germs all round creeping up on him.

He jumped in the car and ordered George to force a path through the demonstrators.

They were almost through. There was just one man barring the way.

Bismarck ordered George to drive straight on. But the man grabbed hold of the door. In his panic, Bismarck had forgotten to lock it. The man was climbing in the car struggling to get close to Bismarck. He wanted to infect him.

Bismarck stumbled out of the car pushed the man aside and raced back to the office building. He was looking for Isabel. She'd protect him.

But the disease followed him, trying to catch him. It wouldn't leave him alone. It wanted to destroy him.

He ran through the building and out to the back patio.

Persimmon was standing by the birthday cake, her mouth wide open ready to accept another mouthful of food. She also looked at him as if he'd gone mad.

Then Bismarck felt a touch on his shoulder.

He turned round.

And there it was. The disease. It had caught up with him.

It was pouring blood, infecting and contaminating everything in its path. It reached out its corrupt and defiled hands. It wanted to smother him in its contagion.

Bismarck grabbed hold of a wooden croquet mallet.

He struck the disease with the mallet. He hit it, again and again, stopping it dead in its tracks.

The disease lay on the ground, seeping its infected blood into the soil.

The family gathered round.

Isabel took hold of Bismarck and led him away from the body. She sat him down and wiped the sweat from his brow.

The police came. The investigation was brief, the evidence indisputable. Bismarck had killed one of the demonstrators. He'd battered him to death.

Why did he do it?

It was so obvious. Why did they need to ask?

It was self defence.

****

"No it wasn't," said Adler.

It was the next day. Bismarck was on his way home. He was in the back seat of the Mercedes. Adler was sitting beside him. George was up front driving. It was late afternoon. Adler had managed to get him bail despite the outcry of the liberal press and the gay militant organisations.

"It won't do!"

Adler was contradicting Bismarck.

As soon as they'd left police headquarters and were safely away from all the hidden microphones and listening devices, Bismarck explained what had happened. He told Adler about how Henry had followed him. How all Bismarck had done was to try and get away from him. How it wasn't Bismarck's fault.

But Adler didn't seem to understand. He was meant to be the best criminal lawyer in the business, but he just wasn't interested in Bismarck's explanation. Why wasn't it self defence? Why wouldn't self defence do?

"He was chasing me!" Bismarck insisted. "How was I meant to defend myself?"

"He didn't attack you", Adler replied.

"He was trying to contaminate me."

"You don't get contaminated by someone touching you."

"He was bleeding!"

"Only because you struck him."

"He had AIDS!"

"So what?"

Adler was a tall elegant man, the image of an old world Eastern seaboard patrician. You'd never know he was a Jew. But he was a Jew, Adler was a Jewish name. Bismarck wasn't an anti-Semite. He didn't mind Jews in their place, as scientists or lawyers or accountants, where a smart brain was an advantage. But he didn't like Jews pretending to come from the same sort of background as himself. And he wasn't comfortable sitting side by side with one in the back seat of his car. He certainly didn't like Adler telling him what he could or couldn't do.

"Right now Mr Trust," Adler continued undaunted, "you're cast in the role of a monster. The American people see you as rich powerful and privileged..."

He gestured towards George up front behind the wheel. He was dressed in an immaculate blue uniform and peaked cap.

"... and they see your victim," Adler emphasised the word victim, "as a poor sick and defenceless little man."

He paused, giving Bismarck an opportunity to question the premise.

"Do you want me to tell a jury," he was speaking slowly, measuring his words, "that they've got it wrong? Do you expect me to persuade them that you're the victim, and that the man you slaughtered was an aggressor?"

Bismarck didn't like his tone. It wasn't really a question, it was more like an insult. Bismarck had a fleeting impression that Adler would prefer to prosecute him.

They were driving up Interstate Five towards La Jolla. On the left was Pacific Beach.

Bismarck thought of his daughter. She lived there with her boyfriend, some sort of pop star, in a brightly painted pink and yellow wooden house on the boardwalk. It was more like a beach hut. Persimmon had visited him in police headquarters earlier in the day. She'd brought the late editions of the papers with her. Adler was right about one thing. The press were after his blood. Page after page was devoted to the incident. The gay community loathed Bismarck. They were demanding the right to be represented at the trial, and were already denouncing him as a homophobic assassin. There was even a group of militants, the Remember Henry Brigade, who were talking about direct action. They were planning to boycott Trust products and picket department stores which carried the Trust line.

The Mercedes sped up the hill towards the promontory. For the first time Bismarck had a sense of unease. He hadn't really had time to digest what was happening. It had all happened so fast. Why had he been so intemperate? Why hadn't he just shut himself up in his office until the demonstrators had gone away? He'd demeaned himself. He'd become one of them.

And now there was going to be a trial. There was no getting away from it. Bismarck had half hoped the police would just drop the case. But they were treating him like a common criminal, and Adler was already talking as if he was guilty.

Bismarck had lived his life on the basis of being in total control. This was a new situation for him. What if he was found guilty? His body began to shake as he tried to force the thought from his head.

They rounded a bend near the top of the hill, and drove through the steel gates and up the drive to the house. Isabel was waiting at the top of the steps. She began fussing as soon as he got out of the car. She was distressed at the thought of his night in police headquarters. She imagined he'd missed the luxuries of home.

They'd been married thirty three years and she still didn't understand him. She managed to confuse his insistence on high standards with a need for opulence. Nothing could be further from the truth. Last month, when they'd had dinner at the Ritz in Paris, Bismarck had pushed away the dessert trolley and denounced it as barely worthy of a second rate Italian restaurant. The waiters ran about like scalded cats seeking a dessert to please him. Isabel had left the table to go to a nearby patisserie to find something suitable. They hadn't understood. He didn't mind eating the desserts they were offering, not in the least. It was just a question of standards. The Ritz had failed to fulfil its standard.

"My poor darling," Isabel was cooing, "was it dreadful?"

It hadn't been. He'd slept comparatively well. It had been primitive but clean.

Bismarck took Adler through to the green room while Isabel organised the servants to bring tea and cakes. The green room was Bismarck's favourite spot in the whole house. It stood on the very tip of the promontory and its huge windows gave a spectacular view over the Ocean. The sun was setting, a glowing orange ball disappearing beneath the sea on the horizon.

"Mr Adler," Bismarck said, "Do you wish to defend me?"

"Certainly."

"But, not with a plea of self defence?"

"No."

"What then?"

Adler didn't answer.

Isabel ushered in the servants. The tea trolley was rolled across the carpet to the sideboard near the window. The last trace of the setting sun sank below the ocean leaving just a puff of cloud to mark the spot.

Isabel poured the tea. She offered a cup to Adler. He took it without even a thank you. He sipped the tea, slumped deep in his chair, ruminating on the question Bismarck had put to him.

Bismarck was becoming increasingly irritated by his lawyer. He seemed so sure of himself, so comfortable in giving advice to Bismarck, to someone who was his social superior. That was the trouble with Jews, they didn't know their place. They thought they belonged simply because they were needed.

"If it wasn't self defence", Bismarck asked, "why did I do it?"

"I have no idea why you did it Mr Trust", Adler replied, "and I don't care."

Isabel frowned at the abruptness of Adler's reply. It was almost rude. Bismarck wondered if he should dismiss Adler and find someone more amenable.

"I know what the prosecution will say", Adler continued, following his train of thought. "They'll have no trouble telling us why you did it. They'll enjoy spelling it out in court."

Again, Bismarck had the impression that Adler was more at ease in the role of a prosecutor.

"They'll say you're an arrogant, selfish, self centred man. They'll argue you're a neurotic who is so terrified of disease and so obsessed with your own well being that you're prepared to kill rather than be contaminated."

Adler was staring directly at Bismarck, as if daring him to contradict what he was saying.

Bismarck's hand began to tremble, and some tea spilled into the saucer.

"They'll say", Adler continued, warming to his theme, "that you battered Henry to death because you didn't want him to come anywhere near you."

Bismarck found he couldn't hold the cup. His hand was trembling so hard that the tea was spilling onto the carpet.

"They'll say", Adler continued as if addressing a jury, "that you killed a sick and defenceless human being because you were scared of him."

Isabel came and sat beside Bismarck. She took his cup and put it on the table. The tea was slopping out of the saucer. She wiped the sweat from his brow with a napkin.

Adler got up to leave.

"I'm sorry if I distressed you Mr Trust", he said as he shook his hand. "But I need you to understand that my job isn't to explain why you did what you did."

Bismarck felt the firm hand of his lawyer gripping him. He struggled to tear his hand away. The more he pulled, the more Adler held his hand tight.

"I don't care why you did it", Adler insisted, still gripping hold of Bismarck's hand, "because if we go along that route you're a condemned man."

"What other defence do I have?"

"Perhaps you didn't do it."

He released Bismarck's hand, and left the room.

Bismarck had no idea what he meant. Was Adler going to bring Henry back from the dead?

****

Bismarck loved his wife. Isabel had mothered his child and she was a plump homely woman who brought comfort and warmth into his household. But, as far as sex was concerned, she had never really attracted him, and after Persimmon was born he had not thought it necessary to sleep with her again. It didn't mean he didn't love her. Sex wasn't love; it had nothing to do with love. Sex was a bodily need which required satisfying from time to time.

Bismarck didn't understand sex. It lay outside his control. He tried to make it as separate as possible from everyday life, something to pacify when the urge arose, and to get over with as quickly as possible.

The trauma of the last two days, his violence against Henry, his panic in front of Adler, were all signs of lack of control. Bismarck felt an overwhelming need to regain control over his feelings.

After Adler left, Bismarck picked up the phone and called Trudy. He told her to get herself ready.

Trudy had been employed by Bismarck for the last two years. He paid her rent and all her day to day expenses. She also received a comfortable salary which she was able to save, and a promise from Bismarck for a final lump sum of $100,000 when he grew tired of her. Bismarck was an honourable man and would keep to his bargain so long as she kept to hers. In return, she had to be ready to pacify Bismarck whenever he called, and, even more important, she had to guarantee him that she would take no other lover while she was working for him.

Bismarck was not a suspicious man, he was just cautious. So he employed a private detective agency to keep a watch on Trudy and make sure she was seeing no one but him. The agency reported regularly to Bismarck and up till now Trudy had been as good as her word. The agency assumed that Bismarck was a jealous client who could not bear the thought of a rival. If they had known him better, they would have realised that he didn't care about such things. The only thing that worried Bismarck was that Trudy might be seeing someone who was dirty or diseased, and thereby contaminate him.

Bismarck summoned George and told him to get the car ready.

He pecked Isabel on the cheek.

"I'll be back in a couple of hours, and then we'll have dinner."

Isabel hurried off into the kitchen to oversee cook.

Bismarck knew dinner would be ready and waiting by the time he got back. Isabel was highly effective as a housekeeper. It was one of the reasons Bismarck loved her. It gave him an appetite just to see the house running smoothly again.

He sat in the back of the car.

George asked where he wished to go.

"Carlsbad."

They set off North on Interstate Five, skirting Del Mar, Solana Beach and Cardiff-by-the-Sea. It took about thirty minutes to reach Carlsbad. Bismarck had bought Trudy a small ocean view apartment there. It was perfectly situated, not so close to home as to be indelicate, and not so far away as to be impractical.

George drew up alongside the entrance to the apartment building. He jumped out and opened the back door for Bismarck. Bismarck left the car without saying a word. George knew he would be inside for an hour. It was never more, and never less.

Bismarck let himself into Trudy's apartment. He didn't say a word, there was no need to speak, that was part of the agreement. He went straight to the bathroom and stripped. When he was naked, he began to scrub up, just like a surgeon, a quick wash with soap and water, then scouring his fingers and nails for several minutes with a brush and one of Trust's own yellow staining disinfectants, a final rinse under fast flowing water, and then off with the taps using his elbows to keep his hands clean.

Bismarck dried his hands on the sterile towels that Trudy had already laid out for him. He powdered his palms with talc and slipped on the thin surgical rubber gloves. He placed the surgical mask over his nose and mouth, and the surgical bonnet over his hair. Bismarck was ready. He looked just like a surgeon preparing to operate, except for the fact that he was naked.

He went through to the living room. Trudy had cleared the central area to make space for the couch, which was covered like an operating table with green sterile linen.

Trudy was lying naked on top of it. She was nineteen years old and gorgeous. Her long blond hair trailed over the back of the couch and on to the floor. Her bust was firm and round. Her hips were wide. She had naturally rosy cheeks. She looked like a country girl from a hill farm in Austria, the sort that city men dream about.

She lay perfectly still on the couch with her arms and legs spread apart. Bismarck stood over her and began his investigation.

You loathsome bitch!

Bismarck was inspecting under her arms, looking for signs of dirt, and sniffing to test if he could detect any odour.

After he was finished with her upper body, he examined the folds between her thighs. He pressed and prodded, squeezing the skin between his gloved fingers, probing between the creases. He stood astride her and wiped his index finger around the entrance to the vagina, scrutinising it afterwards for signs of secretion. All the while he was swelling, not an abrupt sudden erection but something which grew as he probed and prodded.

You foul filthy stinking whore!

Trudy was pulling the cheeks apart while Bismarck rocked backwards and forwards above her, about an inch away, not touching, but thrusting towards it.

Open it up! Let me see inside your blackness!

When his sperm came, Trudy positioned herself to catch it.

Wider you evil cow!

"Thank you, my dear."

They were the first words he said to her after he dressed.

Bismarck liked to think of himself as a man of impeccable courtesy, no matter who he was dealing with. He always treated Trudy with good manners and respect.

She thanked him for his visit.

Bismarck returned home feeling cleansed. The nagging urge in his groin had gone and he could give his full attention to life at home, and to things that really mattered.

****

It took six months before the case came to court.

Bismarck left the preparation of his defence to Adler. Everyone told him that Adler was the best in the business. Anyway Bismarck couldn't bear to think about it. The hopelessness of the situation was too much to handle. Whenever he was asked to comment on this or that aspect of the case, he just shook uncontrollably. He was embarrassed by his own pusillanimity. Adler quickly realised that Bismarck was no help and just got on with his job.

Bismarck turned his mind to business, where there was plenty to do. Trust sales were plummeting. The gay community was treating the trial as a cause célèbre, a way of outing the homophobia that was prevalent in the highest echelons of society. The militants, the Remember Henry Brigade, were on the news each day spelling out their message; *Avenge Henry*! They were a force to be reckoned with. They had organised the boycott of Trust products, their members were called Warriors and they were painting crossed fists, the so called *Sign of Henry*, on shopfronts which carried Trust goods. There'd even been a couple of bomb attacks on stores which ignored their warning and continued stocking the Trust line. They were more like fire crackers than bombs, but the public panicked and the Trust stock shed millions.

The Remember Henry Brigade was led by an ugly brute of a man. His name was Tiger. He was young, about thirty. He was constantly on TV telling how he and his fellow Warriors were going to exact revenge on Bismarck for Henry's death. Tiger was squat and heavily muscled, with a shaven head and the crossed fist *Sign of Henry* tattooed on his scalp. It made for a great visual, and the TV companies loved getting Tiger on air to show a close up of the tattoo.

The worst of the waiting was that it put Bismarck in a sort of limbo where he had no real control of anything that was happening around him. Isabel, for example, had become positively deranged with her reliance on psychics and faith healers. She was convinced that Bismarck's problems were due to a malevolent force invading Bismarck's aura. She had employed a white robed charlatan to come to the house and exorcise it. In the normal course of events Bismarck would have sent the man packing. But he didn't seem possessed of any of his old authority. Despite his orders, the white robed charlatan doused him with holy water and Isabel interpreted his protestations as the voice of Beelzebub.

Persimmon was nearly as bad. She decided that he needed comforting, and every day she sat her fat sweaty body in front of him and talked inane rubbish about what her analyst had been telling her. Apparently the root of her eating problems had nothing to do with the fact that she stuffed herself full with food, it was all caused by the absence of parental bonding.

Persimmon also insisted on introducing her awful boyfriend. She brought him to the house one day. Darius turned out to be everything Bismarck loathed, a shallow vainglorious young man who thought he was doing Bismarck a favour by becoming his son in law, as though a pop star was something to be admired. After a morning of being exposed to young Darius' opinion of himself, and how he was willing to help Bismarck should Bismarck fall on hard times, Bismarck decided on a radical remedy. He went to the sports cupboard and brought back a croquet mallet. Darius fled, and Persimmon reduced her daughterly visitations.

The day of the trial arrived. It came as a relief. Whatever the verdict and whatever the consequence, Bismarck was glad that the waiting and worrying were over. In a strange way he felt better suited to dealing with the certainty of disaster than the uncertainties of waiting.

On the morning of the opening day, Adler came to the house to fetch him. Bismarck waited in the green room, the same room where six months earlier Adler had spelled out the hopelessness of Bismarck's situation. Bismarck had learnt a lot in those six months. He knew that he himself was Adler's biggest problem. He oozed wealth and privilege, and he gave the appearance of being supercilious and disdainful. But Bismarck couldn't do anything about it. It was the truth, and nothing can change the truth. He had to accept that public opinion was set firmly against him, and that there was a sense of relish at the anticipation that he was going to get what he deserved.

Isabel led Adler into the green room. Bismarck rose to greet him.

"Good morning Mr Trust."

Adler didn't stretch out his hand. He knew Bismarck didn't like touching people and he had become considerate, even solicitous, of Bismarck's needs as the trial approached.

Isabel served tea and toast while they watched the early morning TV news. Bismarck was once again the top story, and once again Tiger was there promising hell fire and brimstone. Tiger was asked about the symbolic meaning of the vivid pink tattoo of two crossed fists emblazoned across the crown of his head. Tiger told the interviewer that it was the *Sign of Henry*. The colour was pink to indicate that the bearer was gay, and the clenched fists symbolised that the gays were fighting back. Those who bore the *Sign of Henry* were Warriors in the Remember Henry Brigade. They were the crème de la crème. The Warriors had taken a vow to *Avenge Henry*.

In normal circumstances Bismarck would have treated a spokesman like Tiger with disdain. He was ill educated and uncultured, and just mouthed a stream of catch phrases and political jargon. His favourite phrase was "the Warriors demand justice." There was no substance to anything he said, it was pure rhetoric. Also he was dirty. He never changed his clothes. He always wore the same outfit. It was a sort of uniform consisting of faded heavy duty blue jeans, thick leather boots and a sweat stained T shirt. He never washed. He was pitiful and contemptible. And yet Tiger had become Bismarck's nightmare. He had formed a fantasy that if he was sent to jail, Tiger would find a way to join him.

"You mustn't mind him," said Adler.

"He speaks for the public."

"He's just a loud mouthed publicity seeker. He isn't involved in the trial. He's nothing."

"He can influence the jury."

"The jury are picked and they're being kept away from all TV and newspaper reporting. The only thing they will see and hear from now on is what goes on in court."

Bismarck remembered the jury selection process a couple of weeks earlier. It had been so patent. Adler had tried to exclude anyone who sympathised with gays or AIDS sufferers, and the DA had tried to do the opposite. Adler rejected the young, the radicals, and the artists; and the DA rejected the elderly, the conservatives and the hard hats. In the end the jury seemed to have been picked from people who didn't have an opinion about anything.

As the trial approached, Bismarck noticed the change in Adler. He was like a sportsman preparing for the Olympics. The only thing that mattered was gold, which in Adler's case was getting a verdict. It was almost as if Adler enjoyed the odds stacked against him, it made the possibility of Bismarck's acquittal even more of a personal triumph. Bismarck didn't like Adler. He wasn't Bismarck's sort of person. Bismarck preferred men who acquired their position by title rather than merit. They were less ambitious and less full of themselves. But Bismarck respected Adler, and he appreciated the daring of his defence strategy. He understood why Adler had the reputation of being the best criminal defence lawyer in the world.

****

Isabel set a cup of tea in front of Adler. Tiger disappeared from the TV screen to be replaced by a series of so called legal experts. Adler sat in his chair, sipping at his tea, chuckling as he watched them give their opinion on Bismarck's defence. Adler had refused to announce his tactics publicly. All he'd say was that Bismarck had a complete defence, and that he was not guilty. This led to enormous speculation. One of the experts was convinced that Adler was going to play the psychiatric card, and he'd try and prove Bismarck was temporarily insane at the time he did it. Another was banking on a self defence plea, the sort of thing that Bismarck had argued the day after he did it. This second expert was convinced Adler would make out that Henry was the aggressor. The third expert was having none of it. He said the others were being fanciful. Adler might be the greatest lawyer in the world but he couldn't turn black into white and vice versa. He thought the whole thing was going to end in a giant anti-climax with Adler pleading for clemency on the grounds of Bismarck's remorse.

Adler's chuckle turned into a laugh. He nearly spilled his tea. Bismarck knew Adler was tickled by the idea of Bismarck having a sense of remorse. Bismarck regretted killing Henry, but there was no point in pretending anything else. He wasn't ashamed of what he'd done. Henry had brought it on himself. He was diseased. He should have stayed at home or in hospital. He had no right to be out and about contaminating others.

The commentators were being thanked. Not one of them had come close to guessing Adler's real defence strategy.

"It's time to go Mr Trust," said Adler.

There was an air of excitement in his voice. Adler was eager to be on his way. He was being paid a fortune to defend Bismarck, but he was also being paid to do what he most enjoyed in life.

Bismarck summoned George. Isabel waved goodbye from the porch. She'd go to the court house later with Persimmon. Darius had hired a vulgar stretch limousine to take them there each day.

George drove the Mercedes along the coast road. They passed Pacific Beach on their right. Persimmon was living there in her beach house on the boardwalk with Darius. The three girls in his group, the absurdly named *Darius and the Dolls*, shared a house at the end of the row. Persimmon spent her time snivelling and worrying about whether Darius truly loved her. If Bismarck hadn't been so preoccupied with the trial, he'd have found a way to get rid of Darius by now. Instead Persimmon was totally besotted, and it was going to be a struggle to prise her away.

They arrived early at the court house, but the journalists and photographers were already there, gathered on the steps, flashlights popping, screaming questions, jostling and pushing. The Remember Henry Brigade were across the road, held back by a police barrier. They were brandishing placards.

Tiger was standing under a banner proclaiming "Warriors demand justice". He caught sight of Bismarck, let out a bellow, and charged forward across the road. The police chased after him. He was trying to push his way forward and barge through the crowd to get to Bismarck. Bismarck was engulfed by the crowd. It was like being capsized at sea, blown here and there, sometimes carried close to Tiger, sometimes far. At one moment they nearly touched. It was the first time Bismarck had seen Tiger in the flesh. He was even more ominous than on screen. He hadn't shaved for a couple of days, and the scars and pockmarks on his face were half covered with bristle. He looked like Bluto in the Popeye cartoon, except for the pink crossed fists tattooed on his head. Bismarck caught his stench before they were parted, and the smell of Tiger lingered in his nostrils as he was jostled into the court house.

CHAPTER 4: CAUSE OF DEATH

****

The trial began.

There were opening statements, and then the prosecution case, starting with testimony about the victim. Everyone seemed to have liked Henry. The two girls who led the demonstration told how he had kept up their spirits during the long march; Doctor Kwanza told of his commitment towards those less fortunate than himself; and the gay couple who lived next door to him told of his neighbourliness and good humour. No one had a bad word to say about Henry.

As the week progressed things got worse and worse. The DA began calling witnesses to the killing. He even subpoenaed George, and treated him as a hostile witness. George was asked about what Bismarck said as they drove through the demonstrators.

"What were Mr Trust's words?"

"He asked me to make my way through the crowd."

"What were his words?"

"I can't remember."

"Did he shout *run him down?*."

"I can't remember."

"I have witnesses who heard him shout *run him down*."

"I can't remember."

"What happened when he got out of the car?"

"He pushed the man aside and went back to the main building."

"Did he strike Henry?"

"I didn't see."

"Did he punch Henry in the face and draw blood?"

"I didn't see."

"I have witnesses who saw him punch Henry in the face."

"I didn't see anything except Mr Trust pushing him aside and returning to the main building."

George's testimony didn't sound right. He was evasive and defensive. He'd given nothing away, but it left a bad impression. And he was sweating. It was the first time Bismarck had seen George looking uncomfortable. Usually he was as calm and self assured as his master.

The next witnesses were devastating. The first was a young man who'd been standing next to Henry when Bismarck's car had tried to push its way through.

"What did you hear?"

"Mister Trust was in the back seat screaming."

"What was he shouting?"

"He was screaming at George... *Run them down! Run them down!...* he was like a madman."

"What did George say?"

"He said he couldn't go on any further, he might hurt us."

"What did Mister Trust say?"

"He said... *I don't care if you kill them!*"

"Are you sure he said that?"

"Yes."

There was a babble of outrage from the public gallery, and the judge had to call for order.

Adler sat unperturbed. He let it pass, as if it didn't matter.

The DA called his next witness.

"Where were you standing?"

"Towards the back of the car."

"What happened?"

"Henry opened the back door."

"Why did he do that?"

"He was trying to calm Mr Trust, to let him know he had nothing to be scared of."

Adler rose to his feet. He objected on the grounds that the witness's evidence was conjecture. Adler's intervention was unenthusiastic, and his voice was tired. He was going through the motions, and didn't really care about the consequence. He was preparing for battle on a different day and in a different war.

The judge agreed with Adler's objection and the witness's answer was struck from the record.

"Describe what you saw, and what was said," the DA tried.

"Henry just stood there. He was doing nothing, just standing and looking at Mr Trust. He wasn't saying anything."

"What did Mr Trust say?"

"He was screaming at Henry. I can't remember his exact words, but they were rude. Words like *scum* and *filth*."

"What did Mr Trust do?"

"Henry was standing near the door and Mr Trust screamed for him to move away. When he didn't... Henry was just standing there doing nothing, just standing still... Mr Trust leapt out of the car and lashed at Henry with his fist. He hit Henry above his eye. Then Mr Trust ran away as if he was frightened of Henry."

Adler made another tired objection, and the remark about Bismarck being frightened of Henry was struck from the record.

The journalists and commentators couldn't fathom what Adler was up to. He seemed to be letting the evidence build up, encouraging the DA to create an invincible case against Bismarck. It was almost as if Adler wanted the prosecution to have a head start so that Adler's ultimate victory would be all the more glorious.

The last witness was a member of the catering staff. He'd been grilling the steaks on the back patio.

"Can you identify the man who struck Henry?"

"Yes sir. It was Mr Trust."

"Can you point to him?"

The witness pointed at Bismarck.

"What happened?"

"He ran towards the big table... the one with the birthday cake... he looked crazy, as if he was trying to find somewhere to hide."

Adler got to his feet and made another tired objection. The DA got into an argument with the judge which went on for about five minutes about whether Bismarck was or wasn't looking crazy and whether he was or wasn't trying to hide. The judge eventually decided that *crazy* was out but *hide* was in.

The DA continued his examination, and asked the witness about Henry's last minutes alive.

"Mr Trust grabbed a croquet mallet."

"And what did Henry do?"

"He just kept on coming... He was moving slowly like he was in a trance. But he kept on coming towards Mr Trust."

"Was he threatening Mr Trust?"

"No sir. He wasn't doing or saying anything just coming towards him."

"What did Mr Trust do?"

"He was screaming at Henry, telling him to keep away."

"What did Mr Trust say?"

"He was using bad language."

"Tell me the words he used."

"Words like *scum* and *filth* and ..."

"And what?"

"Words you use against gays... words like *faggot*."

"What else was he screaming?"

"It was strange... He kept on shouting *you filthy whore... you filthy bitch*."

"What did Henry do?"

"He didn't seem to mind... He just kept on coming... As he got near to Mr Trust he held out his arms."

"Was he trying to hurt Mr Trust?"

"Oh no sir. He was stretching his arms out to him as if he wanted to hold him."

"What did Mr Trust do?"

"He raised the mallet and brought it down on Henry's head. He smashed his head in."

"How many times did he hit him?"

"Six or seven. I didn't keep count. He was smashing the mallet into Henry's scalp. Blood and brains and bones were flying all over the place."

"When did he stop?"

"He didn't stop. Mr Trust's daughter, Miss Persimmon, and her friend, Mr Darius, got hold of him and dragged him away."

There was a bubble of excitement as the witness pointed to Persimmon and Darius sitting in court next to Isabel. Darius waved back to the crowd like he was at a rock concert.

The day was almost over when Adler started his cross examination.

Bismarck tensed.

There was a hubbub of noise in the court. The DA was leaning over and discussing a document with his assistant and barely paying any attention to Adler who was rising to his feet. Bismarck knew this was the moment. No one could see it coming. It was as Adler had predicted. They were totally unprepared.

"When Mr Trust struck Henry with the croquet mallet," Adler asked, "where was Henry?"

"Henry was right in front of Mr Trust."

"I want you to be more precise."

The DA looked up from his papers. He'd caught the sharp tone in Adler's question.

"I don't understand," said the witness.

"Was Henry standing in front of Mr Trust, or was he kneeling in front of him, or was he at his feet."

The DA looked puzzled by Adler's line of questioning. He hadn't yet fathomed what Adler was up to.

"After Mr Trust hit him, he was lying at his feet."

"No. I'm asking about before he hit him."

"He was standing in front of him."

"Are you sure?"

"I think so."

"Thinking won't do. You have to be sure."

Adler was a different man. He was wide awake. These questions mattered, and Adler had no intention of letting his witness off the hook.

"Everything happened so fast."

"I have witnesses who will say that Henry was at Mr Trust's feet when Mr Trust hit him."

"Henry was stretching out his hands to Mr Trust. He could have been kneeling when Mr Trust hit him. I don't remember."

"You don't remember?"

"No."

"Ah!"

Adler let out an exclamation of triumph, and the judge adjourned until the next day.

****

Bismarck watched the TV news that night as he lay in bed unable to sleep. It was all about the trial and the breaking story of Adler's astonishing tactics.

Henry's doctor was being interviewed, and he was telling about Henry's state of health on the day he died. Kwanza explained how AIDS produces all sorts of diseases, and how you'll eventually die from one of them. But he couldn't say for certain when Henry was going to die.

"He was a sick man."

That was as far as he was prepared to go. The TV reporter pressed him. But Kwanza stuck to his guns. He couldn't say if Henry was dead before Bismarck hit him. How could he? Only the autopsy evidence would clear that one up.

Next the TV news switched to an interview with Adler. At last he was speaking freely. He spelled it out. Bismarck hadn't murdered Henry because Henry was already dead.

"You can't kill a dead man."

That was the sentence Adler kept repeating.

Adler was a genius. He'd outmanoeuvred the prosecution. The battle was going to be fought on Adler's terms and conditions. Adler had focused on only one issue. He wasn't interested in making Bismarck look good. He didn't care about Bismarck's murderous intent. If Henry was already dead, it didn't matter whether Bismarck had intended to murder him or not.

It was clever, but it was also dangerous. It all depended on whether Henry had died before Bismarck hit him. As far as Bismarck could remember, and

Adler had quizzed him on this time and time again, Henry had collapsed at his feet before he ever struck him with the mallet. But did that mean he was already dead? There was no way Bismarck could answer that question. It all depended on the autopsy evidence, and Adler's ability to get the medics to testify to a cause of death before Bismarck ever had a chance to touch him.

The TV news switched to an interview with Tiger. Tiger wasn't interested by Adler's defence. The reporter tried to question him about it, but Tiger obviously hadn't understood. Instead Tiger was telling the interviewer about the Warriors and their Shadows. He was obviously living in his own fantasy world. The Remember Henry Brigade had been set up like a medieval order of chivalry. The Warriors were the knights of old; they were the macho gays who rode out on their chargers to take direct action against their enemies. The Shadows were the more timid gays. They were like the squires of old, standing alongside their Masters, assisting them in their preparations for war. Tiger introduced his Shadow. He was a thin nondescript young man called Mark. Every time Tiger talked about him, Mark writhed and wriggled in front of the TV camera. He was shy and a bit effeminate. But you could tell he adored Tiger. He kept batting his eyes at Tiger, like a young girl out on her first date.

Bismarck stared at the screen, fascinated and repelled by what he saw. Tiger and his Shadow were alien to everything in Bismarck's world. It was like watching a freak show.

"Do you think Mister Trust killed Henry," the interviewer asked yet again.

It was extraordinary that a man who Bismarck despised and abhorred should be invited to pass judgement on him.

"Of course he did," Tiger replied.

Bismarck didn't care about Tiger's opinions. But maybe the jury were going to think like Tiger.

It was all or nothing. Either Bismarck killed Henry, or Henry was dead before he hit him. There was no fall back.

Bismarck lay in bed trembling. For Adler it was a game. For Bismarck it was a nightmare. The remembered stench of Tiger infiltrated his fitful sleep.

****

It took three weeks before battle was really joined over the cause of Henry's death.

First there was a rumpus about a juror. The DA had discovered that he'd signed a deal to publish a book about the trial. The judge ordered an investigation. There was a delay of three days before he was replaced by an alternate.

Then there was the concluding testimony by those who'd seen Bismarck hit Henry. There were no surprises. All the witnesses told the same story, they'd all seen Bismarck batter Henry to smithereens. No one could swear that Henry was on his feet before the assault began. All they knew for certain was that he was a crumpled bleeding mess by the end.

Eventually the big day came.

The DA called his first expert witness.

Doctor Patterson was the chief Medical Examiner. He'd done the autopsy on Henry the day he'd died. Patterson gave his evidence quietly and competently. After describing the state of the body, Patterson concluded that Henry had died from injuries to the brain.

"I want to be quite clear on this," said the DA, "in your opinion, Henry Meadows died from blows to the head?"

"Yes."

"There is no other reason why he died?"

"None."

"There is no possibility Henry could have died before Mr Trust hit him?"

"No."

Patterson was a tall lanky man. He wore an ill fitting crumpled brown suit. He wasn't seeking media attention. He had nothing to gain by lying or exaggerating. Bismarck couldn't see how Adler was going to rattle him.

Adler rose to his feet.

You told us that Henry Meadows died from a combined injury to the head. What's that?"

Adler had gone through an astonishing transformation. In private he was every bit as arrogant and supercilious as Bismarck, but in court he was intent on creating a different image. He'd taken off his jacket and was pacing the floor in shirt and suspenders, like one of the boys you can trust on Larry King Live.

"It's an injury to scalp, skull, meninges and brain."

"Was Henry Meadows killed because of the injuries to his scalp?"

"There were abrasions, contusions and lacerations of the scalp."

"Did they kill him?"

Adler's tone was hostile. He'd made a choice, either get Patterson on his side or destroy him, and Adler had decided on destruction.

"No... abrasions are scratches... contusions are bruises... and lacerations are cuts. They won't kill anyone. Scalp lacerations can cause a severe bleed, but there's no evidence that Henry Meadows bled to death."

"Why?"

"There just wasn't enough blood at the scene of the crime."

"Stick to the facts Doctor Patterson."

Adler's tone was deadly. Patterson seemed shocked by his aggression.

"I don't understand."

"Who said anything about a crime?"

Adler was not going to allow Patterson to get away with the presumption that Bismarck had killed Henry.

"There wasn't enough blood at the scene of the..."

Patterson was having trouble thinking up a suitable alternative description.

"... incident?" Adler suggested.

"If you say so," Patterson agreed.

"Then why not say so?" asked Adler.

"... incident," Patterson repeated. He sounded feeble.

"Thank you," said Adler.

Adler had identified a weakness in Patterson. Patterson didn't like confrontation. He didn't stand up for himself. He was easily bullied. Adler was exploiting Patterson's cowardice under fire.

"We agree Henry Meadows didn't die from the injuries to his scalp..." Adler continued. "... Did he die from the injuries to his skull?"

"The injuries to the skull were severe. There was a simple fracture of the left temporal bone, and an open compound fracture and a comminuted depressed fracture to the occipital area."

Patterson was taking refuge in jargon.

"Please describe the injuries so that an ordinary man like myself can understand?"

Adler snapped at his suspenders. He was putting himself on the side of the layman against the pretensions of the expert.

"On the left side of the victim's head the bone was broken but it remained in place. It didn't break into bits, and none of it was showing through the scalp."

"That's the simple fracture?"

"Yes."

"What about the others?"

"There was a severe compound fracture with jagged ends of bone protruding through the scalp... and a comminuted depressed fracture with the bone smashed into several pieces. I found some small pieces embedded in the brain."

"And these injuries were around the bones on the back of the skull?"

"Yes... the occipital bone."

Patterson was still trying to hide behind technical jargon. It wasn't endearing him to the jury. And it wasn't going to protect him from Adler.

"So what about the answer to my question."

"What question?"

"Did Henry Meadows die from fractures to his skull?"

"Not directly... You don't die from fractures you die from their consequence."

"What consequence?"

"Damage to the brain."

"We'll come to that. In the meanwhile, answer my question."

"What question?"

"Did Henry Meadows die from fractures to his skull?"

"I've already said... not directly."

"Don't be evasive Doctor Patterson. It's a simple question, and it requires a simple answer. Yes or no? Did Henry Meadows die from fractures to his skull?"

"No."

"Thank you."

Now Patterson was beginning to sweat. He wasn't the accused, he had nothing to lose, and yet he found himself on trial. It was obvious he hadn't bargained for this. It must have all seemed so simple to him when he did the autopsy. There'd been no doubt about how the victim had died. When a body has been battered to death, and the police have arrested the man who's done the battering, you don't expect the facts to be in dispute.

"You testified that Henry Meadows died from a combined injury?"

"Yes."

"A combined injury to scalp, skull, meninges and brain?"

"Yes."

"We've established Henry Meadows did not die from the injury to his scalp and skull?"

"Not directly."

"OK. Let's see if we can find what he did die from..." Adler paused, "... directly!"

Adler gave another snap to his suspenders.

There was laughter in the court, even some members of the jury were smiling. Adler was mocking Patterson, making him appear evasive and defensive.

The DA objected that Adler was bullying and badgering the witness. But the judge didn't agree. Adler was managing to keep just within the bounds of propriety.

"Did Henry Meadows die from the injury to his meninges?" Adler continued.

"It depends which meninges."

"Explain it to a simple man like me."

Adler was being openly sarcastic, underlining Patterson's pomposity.

"The meninges are membranes which line the surface of the brain."

"I don't need a lesson in anatomy!"

The DA objected. But before the judge could give a ruling, Adler withdrew his remark and apologised.

There was no way Patterson could win. Whatever he said, however he said it, Adler was going to make him look ridiculous. But Adler mustn't become too arrogant. The jury might start sympathising with Patterson.

"The outer membrane is the dura," Patterson continued. He was wriggling uncomfortably. Adler had undermined his self confidence. "If it's torn it can bleed profusely and can cause death."

"Was it torn?"

"Yes."

"Did it cause the death of Henry Meadows?"

"Not on its own."

"Explain yourself."

"If it's torn, it bleeds into the brain... it's called a subdural haemorrhage... it compresses the brain.... and it kills."

"A subdural haemorrhage!"

Adler was beaming with pleasure. He wasn't sarcastic, he appeared genuinely excited. The tone had changed. Adler was smiling at Patterson, as if they were on the same side, as if all the antagonism up to now had been the result of a misunderstanding.

"At last we have an answer to my question," Adler continued. "My client struck Henry Meadows a blow on his head..."

Adler was inviting Patterson to join him in an explanation of Henry's death.

"As a result of the blow, a bone in Henry Meadows' skull was fractured. As a result of the fracture, the dura was torn."

Patterson was nodding, following every word, relieved that the pressure was off.

"As a result of the tear, there was a bleed. As a result of the bleed, the brain was compressed."

Patterson was fidgeting.

"As a result of the compression, Henry Meadows died!"

Adler snapped his suspenders and looked at Patterson, seeking his approval. Here was a simple straightforward cause of death that everyone could understand.

Patterson hesitated. He was weighing up his options. If he accepted what Adler said, it would all be over and he could leave the stand.

"I'm asking you Doctor Patterson..." said Adler smiling and encouraging him as he spoke, "... is it possible Henry Meadows died from a subdural haemorrhage?"

Patterson was being invited to say yes.

"Yes."

As soon as Patterson spoke, Adler stopped smiling. He lowered his eyes. He hunched his back. He was like a matador getting ready for the kill.

"Forgive me... a simple layman...." Adler was looking towards the jury, associating them with his predicament. "... Doesn't it take several hours... or even days... before a subdural haemorrhage can do enough damage to kill a patient?"

It was a trap. Adler had led Patterson down a blind alley. He'd judged Patterson perfectly. Patterson had agreed to something for a quiet life, and Adler was going to make him pay for it.

Adler looked Patterson straight in the eyes, defying him to go on lying.

"I would be grateful if you would answer my question Doctor."

"What question?"

"Does it take hours or even days for a subdural haemorrhage to kill someone?"

"Yes."

"Bear with me a moment Doctor...." Adler was emphasising the word Doctor as if Patterson had usurped the title. "... Isn't it true, that Henry Meadows died immediately?"

"Yes."

"It therefore follows he couldn't have died from a subdural haemorrhage."

Patterson was writhing in the witness box, literally lost for words.

"Would you mind answering my question?"

"What question?"

"Did Henry Meadows die from a subdural haemorrhage?"

"No."

"And yet a minute ago you said he did."

Patterson was silent.

Adler didn't press him to answer. There was a long pause. Adler let the silence sink in.

"I have no further questions."

****

Bismarck sat in the green room with Isabel and Adler watching the TV news. The curtains were open and the sun was setting over the Pacific. The experts were agreed that Adler had done a great job. But they were also agreed that nothing much had changed. Maybe the jury had lost confidence in Patterson, but that didn't mean they thought Bismarck was innocent.

"Patterson's been discredited," said one expert, "but Adler hasn't established that Henry died from anything other than blows to the head. He'll have to do better than that if he's going to sway the jury."

They were all agreed that tomorrow was going to be different. Tomorrow Adler was up against Kopp. Doctor Kopp was a formidable opponent. He was a teacher at Harvard Medical School, and Adler was going to meet his match with Kopp.

The TV news switched to a clip of Kopp arriving at San Diego airport. Kopp was quickly besieged by reporters. He seemed matter of fact and untroubled. He answered their questions briefly and succinctly. Bismarck noticed Adler watching the screen intently, as though he was trying to pick up a clue about his opponent. It was strange. Kopp and Adler were very alike. They were both tall and elegant, and they were both concealing their Jewishness. Bismarck couldn't help wondering whether Kopp mightn't have been his lawyer if he'd chosen a different profession.

"Do you know how Henry died," a reporter asked Kopp.

"Yes," said Kopp.

"How?"

"Blows to the head."

The TV news ended. Adler got to his feet. He bade Bismarck goodnight. Bismarck walked him to the door. Adler was silent, and Bismarck had a suspicion that Adler might be thinking he'd taken on too much, even for him.

****

The DA put his final question. Kopp answered. In his opinion, the cause of death was brain damage caused by blows to the head.

Adler rose to his feet to begin the cross examination.

"Was Henry Meadows a homosexual?"

"I have no idea."

The question seemed to take Kopp by surprise. It wasn't relevant.

"You mean, Doctor Kopp, that you are unable to determine if someone was a passive homosexual from your autopsy?"

Adler's voice was incredulous. It was intended as a reproach, as if Kopp had been inept by not discovering evidence of homosexuality.

"It used to be thought that you could discover these things," said Kopp.

"But no longer?"

"No."

"Tell me what the experts used to think."

Adler was snapping his suspenders, taunting him, encouraging him to make the fatal error of appearing superior.

"In the old days it was thought that a general examination of the anus would reveal if someone was a passive homosexual."

"Why?"

"On the basis that the passive partner was repeatedly..."

Kopp hesitated trying to choose an appropriate word.

"Buggered?"

There was something brutal about Adler's interjection, as if he was trying to shock the court.

"Yes. It was thought that an experienced passive partner would no longer have the normal folds at the anal margin... There might also be white linear scars from healed fissures."

"Fissures?"

"Skin tears."

"But that's not what we think today?"

"No."

"You mean that homosexuals are not being buggered any more?"

Adler's question was outrageous. There was a loud guffaw from the back of the court, the jury looked embarrassed, and the judge called for order.

Adler stood his ground, and waited for Kopp to answer.

"No, I don't."

"Homosexuals are being buggered?"

"Yes."

"Then please explain what you meant."

"I mean that you cannot determine at autopsy whether someone's been..."

"Buggered?"

Adler seemed to take a delight in repeating the word. Bismarck was astonished at the crudity of Adler's cross examination. It was so unlike him, he wasn't a vulgar man, either privately or publicly.

"... the repeated recipient of anal penetration," said Kopp. He'd finally found the words to finish his sentence, and they sounded prissy alongside Adler's earthy interjections.

"Why?"

"Because the cadaver does not behave like a living body."

"We're still talking about the anus?"

"Yes. In life, there is a sphincter with a firm spasmic grip."

"What does spasmic mean?"

"A sphincter is something which contracts against pressure."

"So if you put your finger into the anus it will grip it?"

"In life... yes."

"But not in a homosexual?"

"If someone is repeatedly penetrated, the sphincter tone is said to deteriorate."

"Tone?"

"Contractility."

"Did you test the sphincter tone of Henry Meadows?"

"No."

"Why not?"

"Because he wasn't alive."

"What difference does that make?"

"The cadaver is not alive... it has no sphincter tone."

"So you cannot tell that Henry Meadows was a homosexual?"

"No."

"But he was a homosexual!"

"It makes no difference. We're all the same when we're dead."

"I'm surprised. Let me quote from a text book on Forensic Pathology."

Adler thumbed through a large red volume. Kopp was looking uneasy. He was bemused by Adler's line of investigation. The questions were salacious. They had nothing to do with Henry's death.

"*A widely open patulous anus is often seen post mortem...*"

Adler was reading from his text book. He paused and looked at Kopp.

"We're not medical in this court house. Can you explain, Doctor Kopp, what patulous means?"

"It's another word for open."

"A sort of gaping hole?"

"Yes."

Adler continued reading.

"*A widely open patulous anus is often seen post mortem due to the flaccidity of the sphincter...*"

He paused.

"Flaccidity?"

"Floppy."

"Floppy?"

"Yes."

"Thank you."

He continued reading from the book.

"*In extreme cases...*"

He emphasised the word extreme, and looked at the jury.

"*In extreme cases the entry to the anus is funnelled...*"

He paused at the word funnelled, and again looked at the jury.

"Tell me, Doctor Kopp, did Henry Meadows have a funnel shaped anus?"

"You're reading a very old text book."

"You mean that passive homosexuals don't have a funnel shaped anus?"

"No."

"You mean that passive homosexuals don't have a widely open patulous anus?"

"No."

"The anus isn't floppy?"

"No."

"Passive homosexuals don't have..."

He started reading from the book again.

"*... shiny silvery hyper keratinized skin around the anal margin*?"

"No."

"Passive homosexuals don't have... *mucocutaneous eversion at the anal sphincter*?"

"No."

"So you can't tell from the autopsy that Henry Meadows was a passive homosexual?"

"No."

"I'm surprised."

Adler put down his book. He'd finished the first stage of the cross examination.

"Why?" asked Kopp.

"Because he was! Henry Meadows was a passive homosexual, and everybody knew it!"

****

That night on TV, the experts were busy explaining Adler's tactics. Adler's cross examination of Kopp was being compared to a prize fight.

"Adler's pacing himself," said one expert. "At each round he'll work at a different part of the body. This is the round where he tries to get the jury to stop identifying with Henry. Adler wants the jury to see Henry from Bismarck Trust's point of view."

The expert explained how before round one, Henry Meadows was a nice little guy who'd been mercilessly slaughtered by Bismarck. Now, after round one, Henry Meadows was nothing more than a dead anus, and not a nice one either, an anus which gripped your finger between its sphincter, an anus which lay open and patulous when replete, an anus surrounded by sores and fissures. All in all a disgusting and disagreeable object.

The experts were right. Bismarck had noticed the effect of Adler's questions on the jury. It was dramatic. The old lady fidgeted with her bag. She always did that when she was nervous. The respectable accountant unwrapped a candy to get an ugly taste out of his mouth. And the intense young man, the one Adler thought might be a closet gay, slid around in his seat during the entire cross examination, sweating and red faced.

"Adler's task," the expert concluded, "is to make the jury think that Bismarck Trust didn't kill a man. He's put it into their heads that Bismarck Trust protected them from a predatory anus."

For the first time, since his arrest, Bismarck felt that his actions had been understood. He turned off the TV and slept soundly.

****

"Death was caused by injuries to the brain?"

"Yes."

"Can you describe them?"

It was the next day. Adler had resumed his cross examination of Kopp. Adler's question wasn't sarcastic or aggressive. It was as if Adler genuinely wanted to know Kopp's opinion.

"There were several sorts of injury.... what we call coup and contrecoup... and injuries due to haemorrhage."

"Let's start with what you call a coup."

"A coup is a blow to the brain. It originates from the great public debate in Paris in 1766, with the experts of the day arguing between the rival theories of coup and contrecoup."

"Contrecoup?"

"I'll try and explain. In the case of Henry Meadows there were extensive fractures to the occipital bone. With a coup injury, the brain underneath is damaged."

"The broken skull at the back of the head damages the brain underneath?"

"Exactly. That's a coup injury. But in Henry Meadows case, that didn't happen.

Instead there were extensive injuries to the frontal and temporal poles of the brain... on the opposite side from where the skull was damaged. We call that a contrecoup."

"Why on the opposite side?"

"Think of the brain as soft... able to move about... not much, but a little. The skull is hard and immobile. If you strike someone on the back of the head, the brain is propelled forward. The real damage is done when it hits the opposite end. That's a contrecoup."

"And that's what happened in Henry Meadows case?"

"Yes. The major injuries are contrecoup injuries to the front of the brain."

"And that's due to the brain banging itself against the frontal bone."

"Yes... partly. It's also due to tearing itself away again. It's a bit like a tennis ball. You throw it against a wall... the damage is done as it strikes... and as it rebounds."

The questions were straightforward, honest and genuine. It was as if Adler wanted the jury to understand. But it didn't really make sense. The more the jury understood, the more they'd realise that Bismarck had killed Henry.

"Did the contrecoup injuries at the front kill Henry Meadows?"

"No."

Kopp was on his guard. After what had happened to Patterson, Kopp wasn't going to let himself be led into a false explanation as to how Henry might have died.

"Why?"

"The contrecoup injuries did a lot of damage. The victim might have been in a coma for days or weeks. He might even have been killed by them... but not immediately. They're not a cause of sudden death. Henry Meadows died immediately after being struck."

"So... what killed Henry Meadows?"

"The other sort of injury to the brain."

"Which is...?"

"Haemorrhage."

"Haemorrhage?"

"Bleeding."

"Where from?"

"The membranes."

"We're back to a subdural haemorrhage?"

"No! Henry Meadows had a dural tear... but it didn't kill him. It might have, if he'd lived long enough. But he didn't live long enough."

"So what killed him?"

"A subarachnoid haemorrhage."

"What's that?"

"It's a bleed from another membrane... the arachnoid membrane."

"What's the difference?"

"Arachnoid is the Greek for cobweb. The arachnoid membrane covers the brain like a spider's web. It clings to the brain. A subarachnoid haemorrhage is a bleed under the arachnoid membrane. It's extremely dangerous because it bleeds directly into brain tissue."

"But people can survive for years with brain damage?"

"Yes. It depends on where it bleeds."

"Some places are more dangerous than others?"

"Exactly. In the case of Henry Meadows there was a subarachnoid bleed in the Circle of Willis."

"You'll have to explain!"

Kopp was being led through his evidence with courtesy and respect. Even the DA hadn't got him into this much detail. Yet here was Adler encouraging him to spell out the precise technical means by which Bismarck killed Henry.

"The Circle of Willis is a network of blood vessels under the arachnoid membrane. A bleed from these vessels can cause sudden death."

"Why?"

"We're not absolutely sure. One explanation is that the leakage of blood irritates the cardio respiratory centres of the medulla... the part of the brain which controls the heart and breathing. The patient suddenly stops breathing... and the heart suddenly stops pumping."

"And the other explanation?"

"The leakage of blood is so irritant that there is generalised vascular spasm within the brain... a sort of total shutdown."

"Vascular spasm?"

"All the arteries constrict... and the blood supply to the brain closes down."

"Whatever the reason, a subarachnoid haemorrhage can cause sudden death?"

"Yes."

"I think I've heard of this condition."

There was something odd about Adler's remark. It wasn't a question, it was a comment. And his tone was sharper, an indication that battle was about to begin. Kopp caught the signal. He seemed to stiffen.

"Didn't I read the other day..." Adler continued, "that a young man collapsed and died at the Beverly Wilshire from just such a complaint?"

"You may have done. I don't know. It's certainly something which can happen."

"You mean it can happen to anyone?"

"Unfortunately, yes."

"Without being struck on the head?"

"Yes. There are two ways of having a subarachnoid haemorrhage. One is like Henry Meadows... You're hit on the head and the injury causes the bleed."

"And the second...?"

"It occurs naturally... you've got an aneurysm... a weakness in the wall of your blood vessel... and it suddenly ruptures."

"Ruptures?"

"Breaks... the blood vessel breaks and the blood leaks."

"And this can happen naturally."

"Yes."

"Is there any way of knowing if you've got this aneurysm... weakness... before it happens."

"Usually not. There are no symptoms or signs before it ruptures."

"How can you be sure Henry Meadows didn't have one?"

Adler snapped his suspenders. There it was, the question Adler had been stalking all the while. Kopp tensed. This was the front line of battle. The cause of death was not in dispute. Adler was prepared to accept that it was a subarachnoid haemorrhage. The issue was what caused the haemorrhage. Bismarck or a pre-existing aneurysm?

"I looked for it."

Adler looked rattled. He wasn't expecting such a definite answer.

"You can find evidence of an aneurysm, even after it's burst?"

"Yes, at autopsy."

"What did you do?"

"I dissected the tissue surrounding the haemorrhage and examined it microscopically."

"And you found no evidence of an aneurysm?"

"None."

Adler had dug a hole for himself. And he wasn't making it any better by going on with this line of questioning.

"Does that mean there wasn't one?"

Kopp paused before answering. He seemed to be remembering what had happened to Patterson.

"No."

He was keeping his answers short and accurate.

"You mean, even if Meadows had an aneurysm, you wouldn't necessarily find it?"

"Yes."

"So how can you be so certain he didn't?"

"Two reasons. It's very unusual... not impossible but unusual... not to find it at autopsy."

"And the second?"

"It would be an extraordinary coincidence that an aneurysm would burst just at the same time as someone was being hit over the head!"

"Or before."

"I don't understand."

"Or before he was hit over the head."

There it was again, the Adler defence. Henry had a naturally occurring aneurysm which burst before Bismarck ever touched him.

"It would be an extraordinary coincidence."

"So extraordinary that you've ruled it out as a possible cause of death?"

"Yes."

"Which is why you say that Bismarck Trust killed Henry Meadows?"

"Yes."

"But if I was able to persuade you that it's not such an extraordinary coincidence, you'd be prepared to change your mind?"

The offer seemed to be made in good faith. But there was something about the way Adler was holding himself which Bismarck recognised. Adler had spotted a weakness in Kopp. It was just like when he'd realised that Patterson was a coward. He'd got Kopp in his sights.

"Yes."

"Yes what?"

"Yes I'd be prepared to change my mind if you persuaded me it wasn't an extraordinary coincidence."

"You're a fair man."

That was it. Kopp's weakness was that he was a fair man. Adler wasn't going to destroy him. He was going to ensnare him, and force him over to Bismarck's side.

"Let's suppose I had an aneurysm," said Adler.

"God forbid."

"Thank you. But let's suppose I did."

"OK."

"What would you recommend that I do?"

"Have it repaired."

"Surgically?"

"Yes."

"Let's suppose I refuse surgery."

"Then you're in the hands of the gods."

"You mean there's nothing you'd recommend?"

"It can burst at any time. Just try and stay cool."

"Exactly!"

Adler's voice was crisp. He snapped his suspenders and leant forward, looking directly at Kopp. He was looking him right in the eyes, forcing him to follow through on his argument.

"... and why would you recommend I stay cool?"

Kopp was bound to give a truthful answer. His weakness was that he was a fair man.

"So that you don't get excited."

"Why shouldn't I get excited?"

"So that your blood pressure and heart rate don't rise."

"Why shouldn't my blood pressure and heart rate rise?"

"So that you don't blow a blood vessel."

"That's what I thought."

Adler paused. He reached down to his desk and pulled out a large leather bound book.

"This is a text book of Neurology. I'd like to quote a sentence... "

He shuffled through the pages and began to read.

"... *a raised internal blood pressure is a far more potent reason for rupture than a blow on the head*."

He looked at Kopp.

"Would you agree?"

"With reference to a subarachnoid haemorrhage?"

"Yes."

"Only if there's a pre-existing aneurysm."

"That's what I'm asking."

"What?"

"If Henry Meadows had a pre-existing aneurysm, would a rise in blood pressure be a more potent reason for its rupture than a blow on the head?"

"Possibly."

"Possibly?"

"Probably."

"Thank you. Let me go on reading; *someone with a spontaneously leaking aneurysm rapidly develops behavioural abnormalities leading him into conflict with another person*. Do you agree?"

"Yes, that's often the case. Sometimes people with a subarachnoid haemorrhage are thrown into police cells because they seem drunk and violent."

"Thank you. So let's sum up the evidence. Henry Meadows died from a subarachnoid haemorrhage."

"Yes."

"The subarachnoid haemorrhage may have been caused by the blows to his head."

"Yes."

"Alternatively, Henry Meadows may have had a pre-existing aneurysm... "

Kopp said nothing.

"Let us suppose Henry Meadows had a pre-existing aneurysm... "

"OK."

"Thank you. His strange behaviour in pursuing Mr Trust could be considered... *a behavioural abnormality leading him into conflict with another person*?"

Adler paused and waited for Kopp's reply.

"Maybe."

"Maybe yes?"

"Yes."

"Thank you. His state of excitement and the general commotion surrounding his altercation with Bismarck Trust would have raised his blood pressure and increased his heart rate?"

"Yes."

"In such circumstances it wouldn't be a coincidence that his aneurysm burst?"

"If he had one."

"Exactly! If he had an aneurysm it may have burst before Bismarck Trust hit him?"

Kopp said nothing.

"I'd be grateful if you'd answer my question."

"What question?"

"If Henry Meadows had an aneurysm, would it have been a coincidence that it burst before Bismarck Trust hit him?"

"No."

"No, what?"

"No, it wouldn't have been a coincidence."

"Thank you. So you're ready to change your mind?"

Kopp said nothing.

"You remember you said you'd change your mind if I persuaded you it wasn't an extraordinary coincidence?"

"Yes."

"And, I have persuaded you it wasn't an extraordinary coincidence?"

"Yes."

"So you're ready?"

"Yes."

"You're ready to change your mind?"

"Yes."

"You agree that Henry Meadows may have had an aneurysm which burst spontaneously."

"Yes."

"You agree that Bismarck Trust may not have killed Henry Meadows?"

"Yes."

"Thank you. You're a fair man."

****

Round two had been a battle of substance. Round two was Henry's head, not his anus. And round two was won by Adler.

By a knockout?

Maybe?

What does the jury think? Do they understand? The old lady with the hand bag is puzzled... Who persuaded who about what? The accountant is concerned with the premise... Who says Henry had a pre-existing aneurysm? The intense young man is flustered. He's got a look on his face which says... The bastard hit him over the head... Guilty! Who knows what the jury is thinking?

A good lawyer would leave it alone. But a great lawyer doesn't trust the jury. A great lawyer goes for the kill.

Round three. Seconds out.

****

"Henry Meadows had AIDS?"

"Yes."

"Can you explain to the jury what it is?"

"It's caused by a viral infection."

"A virus?"

"A small living particle."

"What do you mean living?"

"It's a small particle which lives in someone's body and reproduces there. It's like a guest in your house, and you're the host."

"An unwanted guest?"

"Absolutely. And an unwilling host!"

"What happens if it's outside the body?"

"It dies."

"But after you die... how does it survive?"

"By getting itself into someone else's body. It does that before you die... it makes sure its offspring have somewhere else to live before you die."

Kopp was comfortable about giving this little lesson on AIDS. Adler seemed to be going off the boil.

"How does it get from body to body?"

"It doesn't find it easy. It's not like a cold virus or a flu virus which can be breathed into the air and inhaled."

"It can't jump from body to body?"

"No. It's got to be put into the body."

"How?"

"A blood transfusion. If you're given infected blood, you become infected."

"That wasn't how Henry Meadows got AIDS?"

"No. He got it from infected semen."

"Someone with AIDS buggered him?"

Again, Adler was being purposely crude. But he was going backwards. He'd been through all this before.

"Will you answer my question?"

"What question?"

"Henry Meadows got AIDS, because someone with AIDS buggered him?"

"I guess so."

"Have you any reason to doubt it?"

"No."

"Someone who was already infected with the AIDS virus penetrated Henry Meadows... through his patulous anus... and deposited infected sperm in his rectum?"

"Yes."

This wasn't the stuff to worry Kopp. Adler was in danger of staging an anti climax.

"And then what happens?"

"What do you mean?"

"What happens when the virus enters his body?"

"It finds its home."

"Where?"

"In the white cells."

"White?"

"Blood is made of red cells and white cells. The virus invades a special white cell. It's called the T cell."

"The T cell is the unwilling host?"

"Yes."

"How quickly does it happen?"

"In a few days... straight away."

"But Henry Meadows didn't have AIDS immediately after he was buggered?"

"No. The first stage of the infection is silent."

"Silent?"

"The virus is in the T cell but it doesn't do any damage."

"So how do we know it's there?"

Bismarck couldn't understand what Adler was up to? The questions were getting nowhere. Apart from the cheap jibes about Henry's sex life, there didn't seem to be any point to the cross examination.

"I don't follow?"

"If the infection is silent, how can you tell you've got it?"

"There's a test."

"The AIDS test?"

"Yes. It's not strictly an AIDS test... you haven't got the disease... you've just got the virus."

"What's it called?"

"The virus?"

"Yes."

"HIV."

"That's the name of the AIDS virus... HIV?"

"Yes. The Human Immunodeficiency Virus."

"So after Henry Meadows was buggered, he became HIV positive?"

"Not immediately."

"I thought you said it happened straight away?"

"He became infected straight away... but it takes a few weeks... even months... before the test can pick it up."

"He became infected immediately... he tested positive after a few weeks... when did he get sick?"

"I don't understand."

"How long did it take before the virus started to do any damage?"

"It varies. It can be a year or two... it can be much longer. In Henry Meadows case, it was about 18 months."

"What were the first signs?"

"A persistent generalised lymphadenopathy. It's called PGL... the glands in the neck... groin... under the arms... are swollen and sore."

"But PGL isn't AIDS?"

"No. It's a sort of precursor... you can have PGL for years without having AIDS."

"And then what happened?"

"He got sicker and sicker."

"What in particular?"

"Two years ago he developed Kaposi's sarcoma."

"What's that?"

"It's a rare tumour... a sort of cancer of the skin... patches of dark red black nodules on the trunk and limbs."

"Does it kill?"

"Not if it's treated."

"How?"

"Radiotherapy and chemotherapy."

"Did it kill Henry Meadows?"

"Did what kill Henry Meadows?"

"Kaposi's sarcoma?"

Adler was back to what killed Henry.

Kopp was dumbfounded. He thought they'd already decided Henry died from a subarachnoid haemorrhage. He didn't understand Adler's change of tack.

"You're asking me if Henry Meadows died from Kaposi's sarcoma?"

"You sound surprised?"

"I am."

"You're surprised that AIDS can kill?"

"Of course not! But we agreed he died from a subarachnoid haemorrhage, which certainly wasn't caused by AIDS."

"We didn't agree anything of the sort."

****

Adler snapped at his suspenders. The truce was over. Adler wasn't accepting Kopp's version of events. He had his own idea how Henry died. It had nothing to do with injuries to the head. Adler was going to prove it was AIDS.

It was all out war.

"I'd like an answer."

"To what?"

"Did Henry Meadows die from Kaposi's sarcoma?"

"No."

"Why?"

"Why what?"

"Why didn't he die from Kaposi's sarcoma?"

"Because he died from a subarachnoid haemorrhage!"

"Don't play games with me."

Adler stopped snapping at his suspenders. His voice was steely hard. He pointed his finger at Kopp in admonition. His attitude was one of menace and attack.

The DA jumped to his feet. The judge ruled against Adler.

"Let me rephrase my question..." said Adler.

He wasn't apologising, he was just getting on with it.

"I didn't think I'd need to explain to an expert," he said the word expert with a mixture of sarcasm and disgust, "... to an expert like yourself, that people die from AIDS."

"Of course I know people die from AIDS," Kopp replied. He was confused and rattled by the change in Adler's line of questioning. "But Henry Meadows didn't."

"Didn't what?" asked Adler.

"He didn't die from AIDS!" Kopp shouted his answer.

There was a long pause. Adler was looking into Kopp's eyes. He was like a tiger getting ready to pounce. He took a deep breath and said, almost under his breath.

"Prove it."

"I don't have to. I don't have to prove what didn't happen. Henry Meadows didn't die from AIDS. He died from a brain injury."

Adler moved from behind his desk, and began to pace up and down in front of Kopp, his head lowered his brows furrowed. At last he spoke.

"I'm a fair man," he was addressing Kopp, "and I believe you are as well. I'm prepared to concede that you don't have to prove anything you don't want to."

He was pacing up and down, faster and faster, looking towards the jury from time to time, shaking his head as if he was wrestling with some great dilemma.

"But there is a problem which troubles me." Adler pointed towards the jury. "And which I guess troubles my colleagues on the jury bench as well. After all we're simple people. We're not experts." Again he spoke the word expert with disdain. "But if we're told that Henry Meadows is riddled with AIDS, and if we're told Henry Meadows is dead, we're likely to ask the question didn't Henry Meadows die from AIDS?"

He stretched out his hands towards the jury to envelop them in a common goal. He walked up to them, turned round and faced Kopp. It was a shoulder to shoulder alliance of plain honest citizens against the snares and charms of a city sophisticate.

"So I'm asking you to bear with us, and help free us of our," he paused, searching for the right words, "... simplistic misapprehensions."

Adler was smiling, an honest open smile, but his voice was dripping with sarcasm.

"I'll do my best." Kopp's answer was flat. He was under attack, and he'd decided the best form of defence wasn't to fight back, but just stick to the facts.

Adler walked away from the jury bench and resumed his position behind his desk, with his notes before him on the table. He began to fire questions at Kopp, giving no opportunity for a pause between answers.

"When someone dies from AIDS, what kills them?"

"Usually an infection."

"What sort?"

"They're called opportunistic infections."

"Why opportunistic?"

"Because they have an opportunity which doesn't exist in non AIDS people."

"Explain."

"Someone with AIDS has got no natural immunity against disease... that's what the T cells are for... to help your immune system to resist disease. Someone with AIDS has lost this natural immunity... the HIV virus kills the T cells... giving an opportunity for all sorts of infections to strike which normally wouldn't have a chance of hurting you."

"Such as?"

"Pneumocystis carinii."

"What's that?"

"A protozoan organism which normally never hurts us."

"Why?"

"Because we're immune... but in the case of AIDS patients... it takes hold and produces a dangerous form of pneumonia."

"What's pneumonia?"

"An infection of the lungs."

"Why dangerous?"

"It can kill."

"Did Henry Meadows have Pneumocystis carinii pneumonia?"

"Yes."

"Did it kill him?"

"No."

"Why?"

"He had it a year ago... he received treatment... and he was cured."

"Can it recur?"

"Yes."

"Did it recur?"

"Not as far as I can tell."

"How can you tell?"

"At autopsy there were signs of healed disease... but no evidence of active pneumonia."

"Active?"

"The lungs were not infected."

"What other diseases are caused by AIDS?"

"Cachexia."

"What's that?"

"A general wasting away... a tremendous drop in weight... the patient looks as though he's starved."

"But he's not?"

"No. Sometimes the patient doesn't eat much... because he doesn't feel like it... but that's not the reason for the profound loss of weight. It may be due to chronic diarrhoea. More often than not there's no explanation... it just happens."

"Can it kill?"

"Weight loss?"

"Yes."

"In a way. It's so debilitating... the body wastes away... you become so weak that almost anything can kill you."

"... a bit like the way very old people die... they just waste away?"

"In a way."

"Did Henry Meadows have cachexia?"

"Yes."

"Did it kill him?"

"No."

"Why?"

"It hadn't reached that stage."

"How do you know?"

"He'd just taken part in strenuous exercise... he'd marched nearly five miles. He wouldn't have been able to do that if he was in the last stages of a debilitating disease."

"Exactly!"

Adler shouted the word and thumped the table at the same time. He looked towards the jury as though they were sharing in his triumph. This was it. Wherever Adler was leading, this was it, the final assault.

Before Kopp had time to marshal his thoughts or prepare himself for the onslaught, Adler was firing questions at him, rushing him towards a conclusion of which he was only dimly aware.

"Henry Meadows had AIDS?"

"Yes."

"Henry Meadows was going to die?"

"Yes."

"When?"

"When what?"

"If he hadn't gone on the march, when would he have died?"

"I've no idea."

"Why not?"

"I'm not God!"

"You're an expert." Again the word expert was spat at him like a curse. "You've an opinion on everything else."

"I can't say exactly when he would have died."

"Who said anything about exactly... give me an estimate."

"He was in the final stages of the disease."

"So?"

"So... I suppose he had another two or three months."

"Exactly!"

Adler shouted the word. It was like he was striking a gong every time he scored a point.

"What was going to kill him?"

"Another infection."

"Or...?"

"Or?"

"Or... what else was going to kill him?"

"General debilitation."

"Causing...?"

"... causing his heart to give up the ghost."

"Exactly!"

Adler walked towards the jury bench. He stood in front, his back to the jury. He gave the impression that the final questions were coming from them, as if Adler was just their mouthpiece.

"Why would his heart have given up the ghost?"

"It's difficult to give an exact cause."

"Who said anything about exact. Just give me some reasons why the heart stops in the final stages of AIDS?"

"Myocardial infarction."

"A heart attack?"

"Yes."

"Did Meadows have a heart attack?"

"No."

"How do you know?"

"There was no evidence of coronary occlusion."

"Blocked arteries?"

"Yes."

"What else can stop his heart?"

"Cardiomyopathy... "

"What's that?"

"A disease of the muscles of the heart."

"Did he have a cardiomyopathy?"

"Not that I can tell."

"How can you tell?"

"The heart is bigger than expected."

"What was the size of his heart?"

"Two hundred and eighty grams."

"You weighed it?"

"Yes."

"How much did Meadows weigh?"

"One hundred and ten pounds."

"You weighed him?"

"Yes."

"What heart size do you expect a hundred and ten pound man to have?"

"About two hundred and fifteen grams."

"Exactly!"

"Yes. But..."

"No buts! Answer my question. He could have had a cardiomyopathy?"

"Could?"

"Could he?"

"Yes he could. But..."

"No buts. Just answer my question. What else could stop his heart?"

"Apart from a myopathy?"

"Yes."

"A myocarditis."

"What's that?"

"An infection of the heart muscles."

"What causes the infection?"

"Bacteria... viruses."

"Did Meadows have myocarditis?"

"I can't say."

"Why not?"

"It's a difficult diagnosis... you're looking for interstitial fibrosis... and for pockets of lymphocytes... everyone has signs of myocarditis."

"You found evidence of myocarditis in Henry Meadows heart!"

"Yes. But... "

"No buts. Answer my question. You found evidence of myocarditis!"

"Yes."

"Remind me... Meadows had AIDS?"

"Yes."

"... Meadows had a few days to live?"

"Days... weeks... perhaps months."

"... perhaps hours!"

"Perhaps."

"Exactly!"

"He went on a march?"

"Yes."

"A long gruelling march?"

"Yes."

"A man riddled with AIDS... his lungs diseased... his heart failing... a march which could have killed him?"

"Could?"

"Could it?"

"It could. But..."

"No buts. Just answer my question. Could it?"

"I suppose so."

"Exactly!"

Adler was an engine gathering speed. He was hurtling towards his conclusion, question after question exploding like pistons.

"At autopsy you found injuries to Meadows head?"
"Yes."
"Did you look for injuries elsewhere?"
"Yes."
"Did you find them?"
"No."
"Exactly! He wasn't injured on his arms?"
"No."
"Why not?"
"Why not... what?"
"Why weren't his arms injured?"
"Why should they be?"
"To protect him!"
Adler was almost screaming.
"... a man who is being hit on the head will bring up his arms to protect himself!"
"Yes. But..."
"No buts. A man dying of AIDS... at the end of a march... a march which could have killed him... who can say he didn't die from AIDS?"
Kopp said nothing
"... a man who collapses before he is touched... a man who makes no attempt to defend himself... who can say he didn't die from AIDS?"
Kopp remained silent.
"I insist on an answer!"
"What's the question?"
"Who can say he didn't die from AIDS? Is it possible Henry Meadows died from AIDS?"
"Anything's possible."
"Exactly!"

The questions hammered in on Kopp until he was submerged under the deluge. It was like watching chess being played against the clock. The faster Kopp answered the faster the riposte. And with each answer Kopp opened up yet new ways for Henry Meadows to die.

Eventually Adler slowed down. He began resuming Kopp's evidence. One by one he recapped the various ways that Henry Meadows had died. And with each possibility it became less and less certain that Bismarck had killed him.

Finally Adler looked towards Kopp and asked if he agreed.
Kopp was a broken man.
He nodded his head in silence.
"Thank you Doctor Kopp," Adler said, "you've been a fair man."

CHAPTER FIVE

TIGER'S DREAM

It was Monday morning when Tiger heard the news.

The jury had been deliberating since the Wednesday before. On Saturday, they were hopelessly deadlocked. They'd come back to court asking to be dismissed. Tiger wouldn't have minded that, the idea of Bismarck Trust having to face a second trial, it was just what he deserved, and would make it twice as bad when he finally went to prison. But late on Sunday, rumours began to fly. Tiger didn't understand, a jury should be secret, but the gossip in the press was that it was only one juror who was holding out against all the others. The judge ordered them to come to a decision, threatening that if they didn't, they'd be there till the end of time. Early on Monday, when it was still dark, at about three in the morning, while Tiger was back home and asleep, the jury filed back into court.

Not guilty!

The lone voice of defiance had capitulated. The jury was unanimous. Trust had got away with it. Scot-free.

Mark had come round straight away. He'd knocked at the door. It was a timid knock, typical of Mark. Tiger shouted for him to come in. Mark poked his head round the door. His lips were thin and tense, his hands were shaking. Tiger could see the relief on his face when he saw Tiger watching TV. Mark wouldn't have wanted to be the first to tell Tiger.

The early morning news was full of the story. Trust acquitted, yet another brilliant defence by Adler, victim dead before the accused touched him. Legal experts were wheeled out to discuss whether Trust could be tried on other counts. The consensus was that nothing could be done, couldn't even get him on assault, you can't assault a dead body.

Tiger lay on the bed and Mark sat beside him. He let Mark take his hand and stroke it. They watched TV together and they didn't speak. Everything was Trust... Trust's family... Trust's looks... Trust's business. Nobody talked about Henry. Henry was one of life's losers, a loser even after death.

At about midday Tiger was summoned to the local news studio for an interview. He told the reporter that the acquittal didn't change anything. He cried during the interview. It was like watching King Kong, chained and mocked, with every thing he lives for slipping away. Tiger bared his soul. He was freed of jargon, and he talked simply and from the heart. He was carried along by his passion, and the words flowed from him. He'd never spoken like this in public before, the injustice of what was happening was moving him to tears.

"It's enough we're going to die, it's enough there's no cure, it's enough no one gives a shit. It's enough! But when the murderer blames the corpse it's too much!"

He spoke of the horror of AIDS, how people like him were despised and ignored, how the trial was important because for once in their lives there was a chance that justice would be on their side, how he didn't care if Henry was dead before Bismarck hit him, what mattered was that Bismarck was a murderer.

The reporter didn't seem interested. The interview was cut to less than two minutes, and he was driven home.

Mark was still waiting for him. The room was stifling. It was a scorching hot day, condensation was forming on the ceiling and dripping down on Tiger's shaven head to join the beads of sweat on his forehead. From time to time Mark wiped him down, whispering as he did so, trying to calm and soothe. Tiger said nothing. In the early afternoon Trust's acquittal became stale news, and reports began to centre on a minor earthquake which had hit the coast just north of Malibu. Tiger stopped looking at the TV. He left it on, and just stared at the wall behind. They stayed like that the whole day, a sort of vigil for Henry.

When the light began to fail, Tiger stretched out on the bed and took Mark into his arms. They lay together throughout the night. The TV was on, flickering out inconsequential bulletins on the weather and Michael Jackson and the San Diego Padres. Tiger and Mark lay in each other's arms. There was no sex, not even affection, just two people comforting each other.

****

During the night Tiger had a dream.

He dreamt he was waiting for Mark at the Chain Saw.

The Chain Saw was Tiger's favourite bar. It had a strict dress code and nobody was let through unless they were in full leather. Even that wasn't enough. If you didn't look the part, even if the clothes were right, you were shown the door. There was a rumour that Henry had once tried to get in and been refused.

There was a cheer as Mark came into the bar. The guys shook his hand as he passed between them. It was a crazy scene. Mark wasn't dressed right, he was in a sort of wild west outfit, and Marlboro man was not the Chain Saw look. Also Mark was skinny and a little bit effeminate. But Mark was being treated like a hero. Tiger felt exhilarated. This was what the gay movement should be like. Butch leather men applauding a queen, and all working for a single cause.

The reason for the uproar was the trial, and Tiger's appearance as a spokesman for the Remember Henry Brigade. Tiger was speaking on behalf of the gay movement, and the world could now see that gays were not to be treated like shit. The Henry Brigade was again front page news, and guys were queuing up to become Warriors.

"If you respect a Warrior, you respect his Shadow."

Mark was Tiger's Shadow, so Mark was entitled to just as much respect as Tiger.

And he was getting it. Mark had to push his way through the throng of well-wishers into Tiger's outstretched arms. There was a cheer as they embraced. Some of the guys began to sing "We shall not be moved". Tiger hoisted Mark onto his shoulders and did a lap of honour round the bar, with guys slapping him on the back and others blowing kisses to Mark up in the sky.

The next moments were spent in celebration, congratulation and planning. Guys formed up in line to talk to them. Before he knew it, Tiger had a whole état-major, a chief of staff, an external relations advisor, a private secretary, and a group of guys who offered themselves as a "war cabinet". They were egg heads who wanted to give Tiger the tactics to convert words into deeds. Tiger felt like a new President. Everyone wanted to help, not for money or ambition, but because they wanted to do good. Tiger had become the focus of the gay movement's outrage.

The music was getting louder and the lights lower when one of the guys suggested Tiger invite Mark to the dark room. Tiger hoisted Mark onto his shoulders, and carried him to the back. There was a cheer as they disappeared into the blackness.

Tiger walked slowly down the steps. At the bottom, he let Mark slip down his shoulders to stand beside him. He held Mark by the hand. It was pitch black except for the faint glow of light coming from the large screen with the porno movie. He could feel Mark's hand shaking, but it wasn't fear, it was excitement. The dark room at the Chain Saw was the most famous back room in San Diego, and what happened there was reported with hushed awe in other gay clubs and bars. Its reputation had even reached San Francisco. By inviting Mark to the dark room the Chain Saw was doing him an honour, and Mark would dine out on it for the rest of his life.

Tiger stood still, letting Mark adjust to the dark and giving him the opportunity to savour the smell. It wasn't a dirty smell, most guys showered before they came to the Chain Saw, but it was free of deodorant and perfume. It was the smell of guys, and there was no greater smell in the world. Tiger breathed it in through his nose. It was heady like dope. The first impression was at the front, a healthy masculine sharp body smell. Behind, at the back of the nose, was the fainter syrupy pungent smell of drying sperm.

Tiger led Mark into the centre of the room. They were surrounded by shapes and heat. Tiger held Mark tight as the dance of the dark room began. Fingers working their way down the front of pants, tongues welcoming it out of its home, mouths gobbling as it surged into the open, and all the while a mass of amorphous anonymous bodies pressing to replace those that had gone before.

There was no sound except for the creaking of leather and stifled groans and grunts. The light from the porno movie gave just enough flickering glow to suffuse the indistinct shapes looming up out of the darkness. All the while Tiger was holding on to Mark, not to protect or reassure him, but as a sign of solidarity. Good times or bad, a Warrior stood alongside his Shadow.

And these were good times. The guys were really making a fuss of Mark. Tiger felt Mark shaking as time after time guys came against him. He was beginning to make whimpering sounds as the excitement mounted. Suddenly Mark turned and dropped to his knees in front of Tiger. He put Tiger in his mouth. This was it. Mark was about to come and he wanted Tiger to come with him.

It was like a marriage ceremony. The guys gathered round to cheer on Tiger and Mark as they consummated their alliance. Someone switched on the TV. The porno movie was replaced by a recording of the evening news. There he was. Tiger! On the big screen, telling the world that Henry would be avenged.

Tiger was reaching further and further into the back of Mark's throat. The guys formed a circle around them. It was like a maypole, with Tiger and Mark humping and pumping at the centre, and the guys forming a guard of honour, saluting with their erections.

Tiger was emblazoned on TV, his impassioned words proclaiming the solidarity of gays throughout the world. Mark swallowed faster and faster, and the guys stroked themselves in unison as if they were all trying to come at the same time.

The TV showed the final image. Tiger lowering his head and charging towards the camera. The crossed fists tattooed on Tiger's scalp were captured in close up. The *Sign of Henry* filled the room.

Mark groaned. He was coming. Tiger pushed as far as he could into his mouth and let it spurt. The guys were roaring, it was like the sound of an oncoming tidal wave. Mark's body shook with convulsions as he swallowed every drop of Tiger into his being.

A picture of Bismarck Trust suddenly filled the screen.

There were shouts of abuse. The guys came, all of them, a jet of liquid shot into the sky and splashed against the screen. Bismarck Trust's face turned from prissy disapproval to horrified revulsion.

Tiger turned his face upward, and drank in the stream of life.

****

The next morning Tiger woke with renewed zeal. He was a man with a mission. He was up by six, showering and cleaning. Mark ran around, clucking like a chicken, trying to take over the domestic chores, tut tutting at Tiger's misdemeanours, scrubbing the floor after Tiger had given it a quick wipe, re-laundering the T shirts after Tiger had dropped coffee over them, scraping off the egg stains that Tiger had left behind on the dishes, and all the while chattering away to Tiger about his friends and their peccadilloes. Normally Tiger would have been infuriated with a queen like Mark fussing around him. But today there was something fitting about their partnership, as though they were part of a gay machine working in harmony to achieve a common end.

Tiger arrived at the Brigade office to find it empty. Throughout the trial the phones had been manned and there were always at least four or five Warriors on hand to issue press statements and organise press briefings. The acquittal had demoralised them, like it had Tiger. But Tiger's disappointment was behind him, and now it was time to rally the faithful. While Mark opened windows and dusted down desks, Tiger was on the phone summoning Warriors and announcing the new catch phrase which was to be their slogan in the coming campaign: "A DAY OF GRIEF, A YEAR OF ACTION!"

Randy and Dell were the first to arrive. They'd been in Los Angeles over the weekend at a fund raising reception for the Remember Henry Brigade. It hadn't gone as well as expected. They'd barely raised a thousand dollars, and only half of it in ready cash, the rest promised. Tiger tried calling a rich gay in San Diego. He'd been very generous. Tiger didn't like him, but he was a ready source of cash. He wasn't home. The manservant said he'd left the country. The manservant wouldn't give Tiger a forwarding address. It felt like rats leaving a sinking ship.

But Tiger was not put off. He set Dell to work organising a public meeting of protest in Balboa Park for the following Saturday, and Randy to chase up press and TV for the event. As the day wore on, other Warriors drifted into the

Brigade headquarters. Tiger's enthusiasm and commitment began to lift them from their dejection.

By the end of the day they had a flag flying from the front window with the newly painted slogan, "A DAY OF GRIEF, A YEAR OF ACTION!"

Tiger spent a feverish week organising the day of mass protest. He was on the phone to Brigade offices throughout the country summoning them to the event. He placed ads in the gay press, and had articles by sympathetic reporters in the National Press announcing the rally. All the same, he didn't get the same feel of excitement that there'd been during the trial. It was as if people were reluctant to continue the battle, as if somehow the judicial process had drawn a line under the affair and settled it once and for all. Tiger was almost single-handedly having to raise morale with the war cry "A DAY OF GRIEF, A YEAR OF ACTION!"

Mark was at Tiger's side throughout the week, running errands, cooking meals, typing letters. Tiger came to rely on him more and more, especially as some Warriors drifted away, making lame excuses about responsibilities at work or family troubles.

****

On Saturday morning, Tiger and Mark were the first to arrive at Balboa. They got there at dawn. Tiger set to work. He was like a military commander staking out the battle plan, the podium for speakers on the hill, an assembly area near the road, an information booth at the intersection, and most important of all, the recruitment centre at the strategic location near the bus stop. For Tiger this was the key to the day's event, capturing the outrage of the public at the result of the trial by recruiting fresh volunteers for the "YEAR OF ACTION!"

Randy and Dell turned up with the truck at 8 AM and set to work erecting stands and tents. A further ten or twelve Warriors with half a dozen Shadows were on hand an hour later, and everything was ready by 11 AM. The rally was due to start at midday, and the Warriors and their Shadows lay on the grass taking their few minutes relaxation with cool cans of Pepsi and Soda. The day was getting hotter and hotter, brush fires were reported in the hills around San Diego. Tiger lay in the sun, Mark by his side, and surveyed the scene.

Despite the heat, despite the sun's rays beating down on him, Tiger felt a chill. There it was, tents, flags, microphones, stewards and welcoming music, but something was wrong. The more he looked the more he froze. Something was desperately wrong. There was no one there! Sure there were about a hundred, but there should be ten thousand. Where were the volunteers from Seattle? Their plane had landed an hour ago. Where were the Warriors from Phoenix? They said they'd drive down overnight. And where were the people of San Diego?

Over the next hour, they drifted in, not in their tens of thousands, not in their thousands, just a couple of hundred committed citizens, mostly college kids. As Tiger looked on with increasing distress, Mark gossiped about everything and nothing, telling Tiger of the guys he fancied, the clothes he liked, sparing no detail, no matter how trivial, about who was courting who, and why it would or wouldn't last. As Mark chattered, Tiger saw the TV news crew draw up. Randy ran up to welcome them. But they didn't stop. Tiger saw the young reporter shake his head and signal the crew to drive off again.

It was a disaster. The day of action, which was meant to consecrate the renewed struggle for justice, was a complete and total disaster. Most of the public drifted away during the speeches. There were some half hearted resolutions about continuing the boycott of Trust products, and that was it.

The crowd went home knowing it was over, and knowing they would never meet again.

Henry was dead, and buried, and forgotten.

It was an outrage.

"Fuck Trust!"

CHAPTER SIX

RETRIBUTION

"Tea?"

Trudy hurried into the kitchen, hoping he would wait for her in the lounge. But he didn't. He followed her. The change in Bismarck was unbelievable. He wouldn't leave her alone, he followed her everywhere, like a nervous lapdog. But the worst of it was that he didn't stop talking. He went on and on, and always about the same thing, about what would have happened if he'd been found guilty, about how he would have gone to jail and had to share a cell with other prisoners, about how these men were dirty and degenerate, about how he would have had no escape, about how they would have molested him. He went on and on and on, until she felt like screaming.

"Sugar?"

One day he took sugar the next not. One day one spoonful the next three. Nothing he did made any sense any more. Trudy preferred him the way he'd been, the courteous, refined, wise old gentleman, reticent and discreet, someone she'd respected. He'd been like her own father. But now he was puffing and blowing and sweating and worrying. For the first time, Trudy felt she was entitled to the money. Her life with Bismarck had become a burden, and she was really earning her keep. The irony was that he didn't want sex any more. He just wanted to be close to her... and talk and talk and talk!

"Milk?"

He was going on about gang rape, about how prisoners gather in the shower room to choose their victim, how they jump him, how they hold him down with legs apart and take turns to attack and rape. It was all so frenzied and incongruous, stories of torture and defilement coming from such a proper person.

"Biscuits?"

His appetite was gargantuan. Every time he visited, he spent his time guzzling her food as well as talking. This afternoon he'd already got through a packet of peanuts and two cans of almonds. Before he left, she'd have to make him sandwiches. It was beginning to show. His fine upright posture had the outlines of a pot belly.

"Cake?"

He was telling her about the AIDS epidemic in prison. She'd heard it all before, about how most criminals were already HIV positive before they got to prison, about how they spread it to the other inmates through sex and dirty needles, about how the authorities didn't give a damn. And about how he, Bismarck, could have been exposed to these horrors. He'd told her all this... twice... twenty times already! And each time he'd start trembling, sweat pouring from his brow. Every time it was the same, the same fantasies, the same obsessions, an unending nightmare.

"Another cup?"

He didn't answer. He'd stopped talking. He was looking out the window, his mouth half open, cut off in mid sentence, his face white as if he'd seen a ghost. But the startling thing was his hair.

It was standing on end.

Trudy thought it was just a manner of speech. But no. Bismarck's hair had risen from his scalp and was standing straight upright.

****

Tiger ducked behind a bush. Trust was staring down from the top floor window.

He'd seen him.

Tiger kept his head down and inched himself to the right. He was in a small garden at the back of an apartment building, outside of Carlsbad. Trust had arrived an hour ago. He was visiting his whore. She lived there. Trust had bought her a small ocean view apartment and he kept her there for his convenience. Carlsbad was a thirty minute drive North of La Jolla. It was a perfect location for Trust. He could spend the evening fucking his whore, watch the sun set over the Pacific, and still be back in time to have dinner with his wife and guests at the Trust mansion.

Tiger crawled towards the edge of the bush. There wasn't much cover, a couple more bushes, a tree and that was it. Trust had seen him. He was sure of it. He'd be watching the garden, waiting for him to make a run for it. What the hell? It was too late to try and hide.

Tiger sprinted across the open grass.

He reached the kerb and looked up. There he was. Trust was watching him. There was no doubt about it. He was looking out the back window from the top floor. Tiger could see the expression on his face. He looked crazed.

Tiger raced round the corner and out of Trust's line of sight.

Randy was waiting for him in the car. Tiger jumped into the driving seat, started the engine, and screeched away from the building.

"What happened?"

"He saw me!"

They didn't stop until they got to the slip road near the freeway. Dell and Mark were there, sitting on the grass verge next to Dell's truck.

Tiger drew up and parked alongside them. He turned off the engine.

"What happened?" asked Mark.

Tiger got out of his car and sat next to them on the grass by the roadside. He called for Randy to come and join him. It was time for a war conference.

Mark, Dell and Randy sat cross legged in front of him, the last survivors of the Remember Henry Brigade, the only ones left. Tiger's Three Musketeers.

"What happened?" asked Mark again.

"Tiger thinks Trust spotted him," said Randy.

"Are you sure?" asked Dell.

"Certain!"

Tiger was trying to gather his thoughts. He'd just wanted to reconnoitre and now he'd blown it.

Dell seemed almost relieved. "Let's go home," he said. "We'll try again another day."

Dell was a chubby amiable man in his forties, with his own clothes store in a fashionable part of down town San Diego. But he was nervous and tense, his plump face screwed up in anxiety. He'd become a Warrior because he'd been outraged by the death of Henry. But he was a timid Warrior and he didn't enjoy the prospect of real action.

"We can't..." said Randy. "It's now or never."

Randy took hold of Dell's hand, trying to give him strength. Randy was Dell's business partner. They'd been lovers ten years ago, when Randy was a tough blond teenager fresh out of Arkansas. Now they were good mature friends who trusted each other. Randy had his own clothes store financed by Dell. It was Randy who'd persuaded Dell to become a Warrior, and it was Randy who'd given him the courage to stay in the movement till the very last.

"Later," said Dell. It was almost as if he was pleading with Randy.

"There's no later," said Tiger. "He's seen me. He knows I'm after him. He won't sit still."

"What'll he do?"

"He'll clear out! He'll get the hell out of here. He'll go home, pack up his bags, and take a nice long holiday where I can't get at him, in Monte Carlo or somewhere."

"We have to stop him," said Randy, joining in on Tiger's side.

Dell was trembling. He looked as though he was about to cry. Mark was sitting opposite. He was pale and the tears were starting in his eyes as well. Dell's fear was infectious.

"We have to grab him now..." Tiger insisted, "... before he has time to think what to do."

Dell's podgy face was wobbling like a jelly. His eyes were screwed up. He was trying to hold in his tears. As for Mark, he'd become rigid, petrified with fear.

Randy put his arm round Dell's shoulder, and whispered something in his ear. He was hoping to calm him down. It didn't work. The tears began to pour down Dell's face. He was unable to control his panic.

Tiger didn't know what it was like to be scared. Tiger was carefree, audacious and reckless, and he guessed Randy was much the same. But there was no special virtue in being brave. It was only brave to be brave if you were a coward. Dell and Mark were natural cowards. It took courage for them to be doing what they were doing. They were the real heroes.

"Do you want to quit?" Tiger asked.

If Dell and Mark didn't want to go on with it, Tiger was ready to call it a day. He didn't want to force them.

Dell dabbed his eyes with a handkerchief. He shook his head.

"Let's get the bastard!" he said through his tears.

"What about you?" Tiger asked Mark.

Mark squeezed Tiger's hand. He too was ready to go on with the struggle. He was with Tiger, right to the end.

Tiger cuddled Mark, and Randy cuddled Dell. Now they all began to cry, except that they were laughing too. They were rolling around in the grass like school kids.

A car slowed down on its way into the freeway. The driver stared at them disapprovingly. The woman sitting in the back tried to cover up the eyes of her child. She didn't want her little boy seeing something nasty.

Tiger called them to order. They stopped laughing and horsing around. Dell and Randy went back into Dell's truck. Tiger and Mark got into Tiger's car.

Tiger started up his car.

"Get ready and stay close behind," he shouted to Randy.

"What's he driving?" asked Mark.

"He'll be in the Mercedes, with the chauffeur driving."

"When will he come?"

"He'll be panicking. He'll be here any minute."

Tiger heard Randy starting up the truck. He gave a thumbs up. Dell leaned out the window and shouted "Let's get the bastard." His tears had dried.

They were ready for action.

Tiger was proud of them. He didn't mind they were only three. What mattered was they were the best.

****

Trudy laid out her dresses on the bed.

She wasn't sure if Bismarck had finally flipped or if there was something in it. He'd said he'd seen the man with the tattoo on his head. He'd said he'd seen him lurking outside in the bushes. Maybe he had. Trudy didn't know. But it could just as easily have been an hallucination. Bismarck was so crazy at the moment she didn't know what to believe. Anyway he'd left the apartment in a blind panic.

Trudy began to sort her clothes.

Bismarck had told her they were leaving the country and they were doing it right now. He'd gone back home to pack some bags, and she was to meet him at the airport. Trudy had the impression she'd be flying somewhere far away from everything she knew and loved.

Trudy closed the case. It was the fourth and last. She'd packed everything. There was no point in trying to choose. She didn't know where she was going, hot climate or cold, wet weather or dry. And she didn't know for how long, a few days, or, God Forbid, a few years.

Trudy sighed. This was not going to be a fun trip.

****

The Mercedes came shooting round the corner, and down the slip road. Tiger just had time to spot the chauffeur sitting in front with the figure of a hunched man in the back before the Mercedes was gone.

Tiger set off in pursuit. The wheels of the car spun on the grass for a second and then gripped the surface. He took off with such a lurch that Mark was hurled off his seat. Tiger saw Mark grabbing at the door handle to steady himself. Tiger swung out onto the freeway, and Mark's knuckles turned white as he held on.

There was a roar from behind. Randy and Dell were following in the truck.

Tiger was onto the freeway, weaving his way through the traffic, switching lanes, accelerating all the while. Mark pulled himself upright. He was struggling to overcome his fright, and was craning his head forward trying to join with Tiger in spotting the Mercedes. Tiger patted him on the hand. He was proud of him.

They chased down the freeway. Tiger overtook a massive red diesel truck, and Mark began jumping up and down in his seat. He was pointing ahead. There it was! The Mercedes was a few hundred yards in front speeding South on its way into town.

Where was it going? Was Trust going straight to the airport? Was he going home?

For all Tiger's determination and firm words, he didn't have the least idea. He hadn't worked out anything except that he had to get hold of Trust right now.

There was a honk from behind. Randy and Dell had also spotted the Mercedes. Tiger put his hand out the window and gave a thumbs up.

Tiger slowed down, and kept the Mercedes in his sights. There was no way he could take Trust on the freeway. He'd have to wait until the Mercedes stopped, wherever or whenever that might be.

They'd been on the road about fifteen minutes and were approaching the exit road to La Jolla. The Mercedes switched onto the near side lane. Thank God! Trust was going home. It would be much easier getting him in his house. Tiger dreaded the idea of snatching him at the airport. It was too public, too many security guards and they were likely to be trigger happy.

Not that it was going to be a piece of cake at the Trust mansion. Tiger had been watching it off and on for days. There were thick steel doors at the entrance, and at least two armed men standing behind.

Fuck them! Tiger wasn't going to be stopped. Not now.

The Mercedes turned right and off onto the slip road. Tiger followed. He noticed Mark was gripping the door handle again. Poor Mark. He knew the crunch was coming. Tiger saw his face. It was pale. His body was stiff. Tiger squeezed his thigh. He loved Mark. He loved him because he was scared and because he was still prepared to fight.

They wound their way up the hill towards the promontory, only three cars on the road, the Mercedes leading the way, Tiger and Mark about a hundred yards behind, and Randy and Dell on Tiger's tail. Tiger could see Trust in the back seat. He'd turned round and was looking straight at him.

It looked as though Trust's hair was standing on end.

The Mercedes screeched round the bends hurrying to get up the hill and into the safety of its home. Tiger was having trouble keeping up. Little by little the Mercedes increased its lead. By the time they got near the top of the promontory, the Mercedes was out of sight. It had disappeared round the final bend just before the entrance to the Trust mansion.

Tiger imagined the Mercedes approaching the front of the house. He could hear the horn in the distance, honking furiously, summoning the guards to open the steel gates. Trust would be screaming for them to open quickly.

Tiger kept his foot flat on the accelerator. He was catching up. He heard the honking much louder as he came round the bend. There it was! The Mercedes had stopped in front of the gates. It was still waiting for them to open. Trust was leaping up and down in the back seat. The gates were still firmly shut. The chauffeur was honking desperately as though the noise would blow them open.

Tiger was two hundred yards away when the gates began to swing apart. He pressed his foot down hard on the accelerator, and pushed forward in his seat trying to urge the car to greater speed. The gates were opening, but it was taking time. Tiger was catching up. The Mercedes inched itself forward. The gap in the gates widened. Tiger was a hundred yards away. The Mercedes slipped through the opening and roared up the drive.

Trust was home.

Tiger kept his foot flat on the accelerator. The security men were now struggling to close the gates. Tiger was fifty yards away. The security men were pushing at each gate and the gap was narrowing. Tiger kept his foot flat on the accelerator. They were heaving with all their might. The gates were closing before his eyes.

Mark began whimpering. His body had slipped down in his seat his hands were clutching hold of the door handle.

Tiger kept his foot down hard on the accelerator. The gates were almost closed but he kept going. He was ten yards away. The security men gave a final heave.

Tiger kept his foot on the accelerator and he hit the steel gates.

There was a grinding crash. Bits of car went flying into the air. Tiger hit his head against the windscreen. Mark was upside down on his seat. But they were through! The steel gates were flung apart by the force of the impact.

Tiger fought to keep control of the car. One of the wheels was damaged and the car was lurching madly from one side to the other. It didn't matter. They were through!

Tiger nursed the car as it zigzagged its way up the driveway towards the front of the house.

Randy and Dell were right behind. Randy stopped the truck at the damaged gateway. The security guards were lying flat on their backs. They'd been knocked senseless by the gates exploding in their faces.

Randy was out of the truck in a flash. Tiger watched from his rear view mirror as Randy took the handcuffs from the guards' belts, and cuffed them.

Randy waved at Tiger. He was sending a victory salute. They'd done it!

Tiger drove slowly up the driveway. The car was swerving from one side to the other, but it was advancing remorselessly towards Trust.

The Mercedes had pulled up at the entrance to the house.

Trust got out from the back seat and was standing on the steps leading up to the porch. He'd seen what had happened. He watched Tiger coming up the driveway and his hair was standing on end.

****

Trudy sat on the couch in her living room. She'd finished her packing, and now she wasn't sure what to do. She didn't want to leave with Bismarck. She was pondering if he'd really mind if she didn't turn up at the airport.

But Trudy was a loyal girl. Until the stress of the last few days, Bismarck had been a polite and gentle man. He'd been the epitome of good manners. She was lucky to have a client who was so clean, so punctual, and so courteous.

And considerate. He'd not seen her for nearly two months during the trial, and yet he'd made sure she received her regular allowance. Some clients wouldn't have bothered. If they weren't able to benefit from the service they'd have forgotten all about it.

Some people thought Bismarck was a bit cold. It didn't trouble Trudy. She wasn't interested in passionate sex. She appreciated his distant tone. She found it a sign of breeding and good manners. She certainly didn't feel degraded by it.

Trudy liked her work and she had no time for those who didn't. There were so many choices in life, why bother doing something you dislike? Trudy saw herself as offering a service, no different from being a cook or a cleaner, and she enjoyed doing it.

With Bismarck she got the impression that she was satisfying a need rather than providing a pleasure. So what? If that's what he wanted, she was content.

As she sat and pondered, her mind drifted back to when she was a child, and to the other man in her life.

She remembered her father. Of course he wasn't really her father, he'd been the man mother saw from time to time. But ever since she'd been a little girl she'd called him Daddy. And he behaved like a real Daddy. Every time he came to visit, he'd bring her presents. And he'd send special presents on her birthday and Xmas. He never forgot. He was a kind man, just like Bismarck.

Her mother died when she was only twelve, and Daddy, who wasn't really Daddy, continued to look after her. He turned out to be as good a Daddy as any girl could want. He moved her from Chicago, where she'd lived with her mother, to the West Coast to be nearer to him. He put her in a smart apartment and hired a nice lady to look after her. And he sent her to a fine school.

She found out what Daddy did. He was a banker. He was President of one of San Diego's principal banks.

When she was about thirteen or fourteen their relationship changed. It became more physical. Daddy had always been close with her, hugging and kissing on meetings and partings. But one day it was more. He spoke of her mother, how much he missed her, what they used to do together, and it seemed only natural that Trudy should step into mother's shoes.

After that she stopped calling him Daddy. It didn't seem right. But it didn't stop her from thinking of him as her father. He was father and husband, and she was daughter and wife. It was a muddling situation.

It became even more muddled after he died. It happened suddenly one Sunday afternoon. They'd spent the day together. He'd turned up as usual in the morning, after the nice lady who looked after her had gone out for the day. Daddy did his thing. They spent the rest of their time in Balboa Park, visiting the museum and galleries. Daddy had a passion for painting and loved to teach her about art and artists. It was a lovely day. In the late afternoon he'd accompanied her home. He did his thing again. Then, when he was getting ready to leave, putting on his shirt, he died. Suddenly, without warning, he grabbed hold of his chest and keeled over.

That was when everything went wrong. Daddy's real family denied any knowledge of Trudy. Worst of all, Daddy hadn't made any provision for her in his will.

The nice lady left. The apartment was repossessed. Trudy found herself on the street.

A girl of sixteen, very good looking, no family, no skills, on her own, there wasn't much choice about what she should do to keep herself together. Fortunately, Trudy came across Miss April. Miss April took her in hand. Miss April introduced her to only the best sort of client. If Trudy didn't like someone, she wasn't forced. That was how she'd met Bismarck. She'd liked him as soon as she'd seen him. He reminded her of Daddy.

****

Tiger raced up the front steps. He wasn't sure, but he thought he could hear Trust whimpering as he closed the gap on him.

Randy and Dell came roaring up the drive in the truck. Randy jumped out and grabbed hold of the Trust chauffeur who was still sitting in the Mercedes. He hadn't moved. He was like a petrified mute. Randy took hold of his hands and cuffed them to the steering wheel.

"There! He won't give us any more trouble." It was a bit of an overstatement. The man was frozen with fear anyway.

Randy was brandishing his supply of cuffs. He'd raided the security guards' lodge and had taken away a stack of them. Randy seemed ready and eager to cuff an army.

Just at that moment a tall man with a long white beard came out the front door. He was clothed in a long flowing white robe. He stood at the top of the stairs, brandishing a crucifix.

He looked like Rasputin.

The next instant, a dumpy little lady was at his side, clutching at his robe. Tiger recognised her. It was Trust's wife.

"Destroy them Alexei!" she shrieked.

The man in white held his crucifix aloft and started to babble.

"What the fuck?" said Randy

"Who the hell?" said Dell.

Mark didn't say anything. He just grabbed hold of Tiger's shirt and held tight.

Tiger stared at the man in white at the top of the stairs. He knew exactly who he was. Trust's wife had been giving interviews to the papers after the trial. She'd been telling everyone Trust had been saved by the prayers of her guru. The man in white, the guru, Alexei, was cashing in on it. He was lapping it up, and every crazed housewife in San Diego was opening a Circle in his honour.

Tiger didn't like the man in white.

Tiger advanced up the stairs. Mark was still at his side, clutching at his shirt. He was too scared to let go. The man in white began babbling more and more feverishly. Tiger didn't stop. He wasn't going to be thwarted by a phoney swami.

As Tiger got close, the man in white dangled his crucifix in front of him, trying to ward off Tiger, treating Tiger like a vampire or something.

Mark let go of Tiger's shirt. Tiger took the last step. The man in white uttered some sort of weird curse. Tiger socked him in the jaw. The man in white gurgled, and dropped to his knees. Tiger socked him again. The man in white lay on the ground senseless.

Trust's wife ran screaming into the house.

Randy came up the stairs and cuffed the comatose guru.

Tiger followed the shrieking cries of Trust's wife as she disappeared into the house. She was yelling for her husband to call the police.

Tiger caught up with her in a room with a huge panoramic window looking out on the Pacific. The room was painted all in green. Trust's wife was standing by a thick oak beam door. She was barring his way. Trust was behind the door. He had to be. Trust's wife was standing with her back to the door her arms outspread. There was a green glow from the paint. It made her look like a witch.

"Keep him away! For God's sake keep him away!"

Tiger could hear Trust whimpering behind the door.

Trust's wife stiffened as Tiger approached.

"Get out the way," said Tiger.

"You will not pass," she said.

"Keep him away!" came the gurgled scream from inside.

Randy and the others had joined Tiger. Randy took hold of Trust's wife. She tried to bite him. He had the cuffs on her before she could do any damage.

Tiger slammed his shoulder against the massive oak door. It didn't move an inch. It was one of those fancy heavy framed doors, typical of a millionaire's house, designed to give the appearance of substance and solidity.

Tiger cursed, stepped back, and charged again.

Thud!

The pain ran up his arm, through his shoulder and into the small of his back. Still it didn't move.

"He's in there! I can see him!" shouted Mark.

Mark was perched on top of a table, peering in through a small fan light above the door.

"He's hiding under his desk!"

"Fucking coward" thought Tiger, and stepped back for another charge.

Randy grabbed hold of him.

"You'll never do it," he said. "Let's ram it."

There was nothing. Just a large table, too big to use, a few chairs, too flimsy, and a sideboard, too unwieldy. Time was pressing. God alone knew if Trust had called for help. They had to act quickly.

To hell with pain. Tiger stepped back, beat his chest, gave a roar, and charged. Thwack! The great hinge creaked and a piece of wood split.

Tiger felt no pain. He was jubilant. This was it. One more heave and he'd have him!

He walked back. He took slow even steps, breathing deeply, concentrating his mind on the one and only task in front of him. Smash the door to bits.

Tiger turned, focused on the crack in the wood, and charged. Crash! Tiger fell through the opening, Randy Dell and Mark tumbling over him in the follow through.

Trust was lying under his desk, writhing, as if in agony. He looked directly at Tiger and let out a low lingering wail.

It was the sound of a wounded animal about to be savaged by beasts of the jungle.

****

Trudy was woken from her reverie by the phone ringing. It was Bismarck. He was calling from his home. He was screaming and ranting that the man with the tattoo was in the building, coming after him. He was completely out of control, sobbing and pleading for her to come quickly before it was too late.

Too late for what? What was going on? Trudy tried to soothe him over the phone but it was no good. He just went on whimpering, pleading for her to get to him quickly.

"It's OK. I'm on my way," she said.

"It's too late," was all he replied.

She heard a crashing sound in the background.

She put down the telephone, picked up her bags and hurried down to the car.

It was a pretty little French car, a yellow Renault Clio. She loved it. She called it 'Cleo'. She hated the idea of having to leave it behind. She wondered if Bismarck would let her ship it to wherever they were going. He probably wouldn't. He'd say it wasn't worth it, and buy her another instead. But that wasn't the point. She loved this one. It wasn't exchangeable.

She stuffed her bags in the trunk, and set off for the airport.

As she drove down the freeway she thought of Bismarck's last words. He'd said it was too late.

"Too late for what?" Trudy wondered.

She approached the junction to La Jolla and turned off. Maybe something had gone wrong. She'd better check at his home. Maybe he hadn't left for the airport.

In her heart of hearts Trudy was hoping something had gone wrong. She was happy where she was. She didn't want to go off with Bismarck and leave her yellow Cleo behind.

****

Tiger dragged Trust out from under the table and picked him up off the floor. He was limp and unconscious with fear. Tiger carried him out of the green room. Randy and Dell went ahead, keeping their eyes open for anyone who might be lying in wait. Mark brought up the rear.

Tiger carried Trust out the front door and over the man in white who was still lying crumpled on the top step. He carried him down the steps. Trust didn't stir. He was like a rag doll in Tiger's arms.

Tiger's car was a mess. Randy uncuffed the chauffeur from the steering wheel of the Mercedes, and pushed him out onto the driveway.

"Get in the back," said Randy.

Tiger stepped into the back of the Mercedes with Trust still in his arms.

Randy got in the driving seat and started the car.

Mark and Dell went to the truck.

They set off down the driveway.

They passed the shattered gates and swept out onto the open road.

Tiger patted Trust on his cheeks.

Trust opened his eyes.

Tiger felt his erection pushing against Trust.

Trust gave a yelp and fainted again.

****

Trudy approached the last bend on the road leading up the hill. She glanced at the view over the promontory onto the ocean. Suddenly the Mercedes came swerving round the corner. She tried to avoid it by pulling to her right, but the Mercedes gave a glancing blow to her front wing. There was a grinding scratching scraping sound as the two cars slid against each other. The Mercedes didn't stop. It picked up speed and roared off down the road, closely followed by a truck which nearly hit her too.

Trudy experienced a gamut of emotions in quick succession. She was shocked by the collision. She was troubled by her own lack of concentration. She wondered who was driving the Mercedes. It didn't look like George. Anyway it was being driven too fast for it to be George. She wondered if Bismarck was in the Mercedes, and if he was in any sort of danger. But, most of all, she was in despair. Cleo was damaged! She was as distressed as if a child had been knocked down. And she felt guilty. She should have been looking after her little friend more carefully.

Trudy got out of her car and stroked the damaged yellow paintwork.

"I'm sorry Cleo."

"He's been kidnapped!" George came running round the bend. He was puffing and blowing. Sweat was pouring down his brow. His tie was dishevelled. He'd lost his cap. And his hands were handcuffed.

He gave a weird story about how they'd been followed on the way back from her apartment. He told how a platoon of armed men had stormed the house and spirited Bismarck away in a commando raid.

"Where's Bismarck now?" asked Trudy.

George pointed his handcuffed hands in the direction of the disappearing Mercedes.

"Let's get the police," said Trudy.

George shook his head. He told her there was no time. God knows what the men were intending to do with Bismarck. It was vital to follow and find out where they were taking him.

"Let's go after them...." said George. "... While they're still in our sights."

Trudy didn't argue. George knew about these things better than her. Perhaps there wasn't enough time. Time for what? Anyway, it wasn't for her to meddle. Let George do whatever he thought best.

Trudy got back in Cleo. She sat in the driving seat and told George to sit next to her. She wasn't going to let George drive. He was still handcuffed. The armed men had gone off with the keys. Anyway no one drove Cleo except Trudy.

She set off. In a way she was pleased to be chasing after the Mercedes. It was a way for Cleo to exact her revenge. The Mercedes was a bully, picking on a little car. She put her foot down and manipulated the twists and turns in the road with great skill. The Renault cornered extremely well. It wasn't difficult to keep up with the Mercedes.

They went back to the freeway, and on into downtown San Diego. The Mercedes and the truck slowed right down. They were obviously worried about alerting a speed cop. Little Cleo kept about fifty yards behind. She followed them all the way to Delancey Street.

The Mercedes and the truck pulled up outside an office which was closed, its windows shuttered.

"It's the headquarters of the Remember Henry Brigade," said George.

Trudy watched as two men got out of the truck and unlocked the door of the office.

Then out came a man from the rear door of the Mercedes. Trudy recognised him. It was the man with the tattoo on his head. He was reaching back into the car trying to pull something out. It was Bismarck! The man with the tattoo took Bismarck in his arms, and carried him into the office.

Trudy heard George gasp.

Trudy was baffled. San Diego didn't have terrorists. The Henry Brigade weren't going to kill Bismarck. Surely not? So what was it all about?

The four men disappeared into the office, the four men and Bismarck.

There wasn't a soul about, the street was empty except for the two deserted vehicles outside the office.

"What are we going to do?" said George, biting his lip, and pondering on their next move.

Trudy was surprised by her reaction.

She didn't care. Everyone else seemed agitated, but she was out of it. In a way she felt strangely elated. She was glad she wasn't going abroad with Bismarck. She was happy to know that she'd be staying home with Cleo. All she could think about was when and where she'd have Cleo repaired and restored.

****

Tiger carried Trust into Brigade headquarters and through into the back office.

Mark bolted the front door and shuttered the windows. Randy brought in chairs, and Dell laid out a rug and sheets.

Tiger placed Trust on a chair. He was like a puppet, no tone to his muscles, no resistance in his joints. He was just a sad limp rag doll, giving an occasional whimper.

Dell sat himself behind the office desk and got out his knitting. Dell took to knitting whenever he was preoccupied. He said the sound of the needles soothed him.

Click click click.

Tiger brought out a piece of paper.

"Look at this," he said.

Trust didn't move, his head lolled on his neck as if he'd been hanged.

"I said look at this!"

Tiger brought his face right up against Trust and tugged him by the hair. Trust sat bolt upright.

"Read it."

Trust was looking at the paper but his eyes weren't focusing.

"I want you to read it," said Tiger again.

The menace in Tiger's voice got through to Trust. He looked at the paper and tried to decipher what was on it.

"It's a photo of you," he said at last.

Trust's words were dry and strangled. It was difficult to hear what he was saying.

"What's written, under my photo?"

Trust looked at the paper.

"It's a medical report," he said.

"That's right. And what does it say?"

Trust's head was jerking and twitching. He was unable to keep still.

Randy grabbed hold of Trust's ears, held them tight, and dragged Trust's face towards the paper.

"What written on the paper?" Randy asked.

He kept repeating the question, pulling on Trust's ears, stretching them apart.

"It says you're ill!" Trust squealed.

"With what?" Randy and Tiger asked in unison.

"I don't know."

"Look again," said Randy, and gave a vicious pull.

Trust screeched. When the pain eased, he looked at the paper. He read it, and gave another little screech.

"What does it say?" said Tiger.

Tiger was smiling at Trust.

"What does it say? said Randy.

"What does it say... what does it say?" said Mark, taking up the chant, mocking and scoffing.

Click click click went Dell's needles.

Tiger took hold of Trust's ears from Randy, and pulled on them until he got the answer.

"It says you've got AIDS!"

Trust's voice was a whisper.

Click click click.

"I'm sorry... " said Trust, "... I really am sorry."

Tiger smiled. He pulled on Trust's ears. He pulled and pulled until Trust was shrieking and screaming in pain.

"You're right!" shouted Tiger above Trust's screams. "... I've got AIDS... and you'll be sorry."

Click click click.

Tiger released Trust's ears and left him to sit and sob. He was like a baby blubbing.

When Trust was quiet Tiger stepped forward and picked him up off the chair. Trust tried to struggle. But it was ineffectual. He was like a tiny kitten wriggling and writhing in the palm of a giant.

Tiger strode across the room with Trust in his arms, displaying him to each member of the audience in turn, to Mark, who ruffled his hair and tweaked his nose, to Randy who made the sign of the cross and kissed him on the forehead as if he were about to die, and finally to Dell, sitting on his chair behind the desk. Dell just knitted more furiously as Trust was displayed before him.

Click click click.

Tiger stepped into the middle of the room and lay Trust on a sheet, on top of the rug.

"Are you comfortable?"

The gentleness of Tiger's question was chilling. Trust lay on the sheet, rigid with fear, like a condemned man being offered his last meal.

"He's comfortable!" Randy answered on his behalf, and chuckled.

Click click click went Dell's needles.

"Let me make you more comfortable," said Tiger.

He reached down and very gently began to undress him.

Trust didn't resist. He just trembled and twitched each time Tiger touched him.

Tiger was gentle, as if he were changing the nappy on a baby. He took off Trust's tie, his shirt, his vest. He also took off his wrist watch and the gold pendant chain, so that Trust was completely naked from the waist up.

"He's much more comfortable now," said Randy.

Click click click, went Dell's needles in assent.

"I want you completely comfortable," said Tiger.

He untied his laces. He took off his shoes, his garters, his socks. He loosened his belt, and undid the buttons round his waist. Then one, the trousers were off, and two, the underpants gone.

Trust lay on the sheet in the middle of the room with nothing to cover him. He was stark naked. The audience clapped and laughed as he tried to hide himself with his hands. Mark whooped, Randy wolf whistled, and Dell's needles went click click click.

Trust shivered in the centre of the room. There were goose pimples on his flesh.

The room grew silent. His trembling and shivering made little knocking noises through the rug onto the wooden floor.

Trust lay naked on the sheet and waited.

There was no other sound, except for the noise of muffled knocking, and the click click click of the needles.

****

Trudy sat in her little yellow Renault with George by her side. They were still in Delancey Street. George was biting his lip, undecided what to do.

Trudy wanted to go home. But there wasn't much chance of that. They'd have to do something. They couldn't just leave Bismarck in the Brigade headquarters and hope for the best. All the same, she didn't understand what the fuss was all about. Bismarck wasn't in any real danger, not here, not in down town San Diego. Why didn't they just go to the police and leave it to them?

"Let's get the cops," she said.

"I'm not sure," said George. "These people..."

George was gesturing towards the office building, his face screwed up in distaste. He couldn't bring himself to spell out in words the contempt he felt for the people who'd kidnapped Bismarck. He was so like Bismarck. Trudy admired a gentleman who was a gentleman, but she didn't have time for someone who wasn't a gentleman pretending to be one. As far as Trudy was concerned, George was a fake.

"... These people..." continued George, "... want a scandal. They know about Mr Trust and you."

Trudy didn't like the way he said you. Now he was trying to lump her in with them. It was just like him to try and blame her for what had happened.

"Perhaps that's their plan..." George persisted. "They want us to call the police so as to embarrass Mr Trust."

"More likely embarrass you... you fathead," thought Trudy. George was such a pompous prude. He made it so obvious he didn't approve of her.

"So what do we do?" she asked curtly.

As far as Trudy was concerned, she just wanted to forget about all of them, George, Bismarck, the man with the tattoo, even Henry. Let them fight it out between themselves, and leave her alone. She wanted to take Cleo to a repair shop. She had more affinity for her little injured friend than the lot of them put together.

George seemed to guess at her irritation. At any event he came to a decision, and asked her to set off down the road. At first Trudy thought he was going to take her advice and get the cops. But he told her to veer North along the highway. After a couple of miles he told her to turn left towards Pacific Beach.

Trudy realised where they were heading. They were going to the beach house where Bismarck's daughter lived. It was typical of George. Don't cause a fuss, keep it in the family.

Trudy parked Cleo at the edge of the boardwalk. Before George got out of the car, he asked her for something to cover his hands. He didn't want people to see his handcuffs, he was fearful they might think he'd escaped from jail. Trudy couldn't think of anyone less likely to be a dangerous prisoner than George. Anyway, the real reason was because he was embarrassed to show himself in public with handcuffs. For George maintaining appearances was all important. Trudy went to the trunk. She took out a jumper from her bags, not a very good one, and gave it to him to wrap round his wrists.

They hurried along the boardwalk between the sand and the brightly painted houses facing the Pacific Ocean, heading for Bismarck's daughter's house. The beach houses were mostly made of wood and mostly rented to holidaying families or college kids. Trudy knew Bismarck's girl, Persimmon, from pictures in the papers and from seeing her in the court house. She was a fat girl. Trudy admired her for that. It took courage to buck fashion and be your own person. Anyway Persimmon always looked stylish, wearing haute couture from Paris, and conducting herself like a lady. She wondered if Persimmon knew about her. Bismarck never talked about Persimmon with her, and she guessed that he was even less likely to talk about her with Persimmon.

Persimmon's beach house was situated at the end of the boardwalk, and it was like going through an obstacle course to reach it. The boardwalk was packed with sightseers and the sights they'd come to see, frightened old ladies tottering along arm in arm with their companions struggling to avoid the clumsy clattering teenage skateboarders, rubber wheeled roller skaters whooshing silently by at high speed, weaving and wending their way between the pedestrians with skill and grace, Jack Russells demanding right of way to catch a frisbee on the wing, and a tall blond girl in yellow and black wet suit with a green scaled iguana on a lead. The boardwalk was a world of its own where the sun shone above and the ocean beckoned to the West. It was on the edge of the universe, a million miles from catastrophe and carnage.

Trudy knocked at the door. The door opened. It was Persimmon. Trudy left it to George to explain what was going on. What a strange way to meet Bismarck's family. Trudy could see the surprise on Persimmon's face as she struggled to make sense of George's innuendoes. When Persimmon finally realised what he was talking about, she just laughed and took Trudy in her arms and embraced her like a long lost sister.

"We've got to save old Dad," said Persimmon.

Persimmon took charge. She was giggling. It sounded as if she was enjoying the whole thing. Trudy liked her more and more. She was full of fun, energetic and sharp. She summoned her boyfriend, up on the balcony sunning himself. Trudy knew him too. It was Darius, of *Darius and the Dolls* He'd just made a big hit at a charity concert. Trudy wondered if she could ask for his autograph. Maybe later?

Darius was fun too. He caught sight of George's handcuffs and made a song and dance of George being into bondage. George was furious. He went purple with embarrassment. Trudy could tell he was sorry he'd ever come to ask Persimmon for help.

Serve him right.

Darius went down the boardwalk summoning assistance from all his friends and neighbours. He brought along The Dolls. They were living at the end of the row.

They were three gorgeous girls, a redhead, a raven, and a blond. In about fifteen minutes Darius had gathered together a posse of a dozen tough looking guys, and a handful of sexy women to encourage them.

Trudy felt as if she was in the movies, part of a cavalry charge storming to the rescue.

She wondered if Bismarck was having as much fun.

****

Tiger stripped off his T shirt.

He was standing above Trust, who was lying curled and huddled between his feet.

"Look at me!" said Tiger.

It was no good. Trust just curled himself up tighter, a silver haired naked ball, shivering furiously under foot.

Tiger snapped his fingers and summoned Randy and Mark. Randy took hold of Trust's hands, Mark his feet. They pulled him apart. He screamed as they forced him to uncurl.

Trust was stretched out under Tiger, like on a rack, naked and defenceless. But he wouldn't look at Tiger. His eyes were tight shut.

"Look at me!" said Tiger.

It was no good. No matter how hard they pulled and stretched, he kept his eyes tight closed.

Eventually Randy had had enough. With Randy there was no nonsense. Randy let go of Trust's arms and grabbed hold of his ears. He pulled them outwards with all his force, as if he was trying to tear them from his head.

Trust let out a piercing scream of pain.

"Tiger asked you to look at him," Randy whispered.

Trust opened his eyes and looked at Tiger.

Tiger stripped off his pants. Trust shut his eyes. Randy tugged at his ears. Trust screamed and opened his eyes.

Tiger stripped off his shorts and straddled him. He was naked. They were both naked. Trust looked at Tiger and shivered furiously.

Tiger began to rub himself, up and down, up and down, and he stroked and squeezed, and said over and over again, again and again.

"I've got AIDS... and... you'll be sorry!"

The click click clicking of the needles kept time to the rhythm of Tiger's motion.

Slowly Tiger grew, swelling larger at each pull.

Trust's eyes were wide open as Tiger reared above him.

"I've got AIDS... and... you'll be sorry!"

Tiger was breathing harder. It was like a piston in his hands, the click click clicking of the needles urging him on.

Little drops began to seep from the end.

He was straddling Trust, and a drop fell from him. He watched it plummet towards Trust. Trust saw it coming and screamed. It was a scream to wake the dead.

Trust closed his eyes and no matter how hard Randy pulled at his ears, his eyes stayed shut.

****

It was fun.

Trudy was driving Cleo with Persimmon by her side. Darius was just ahead in his red Lamborghini with the redhead. She was a stunning girl, and Darius was one heck of a good looking guy.

Darius had Heavy Metal cranked high, and the redhead was shrieking and boogying in her seat. The sound carried back, and Persimmon was rocking to the rhythm. Trudy had the impression that even Cleo was enjoying herself.

Sour faced George was up ahead with the two other girls, the raven and the blond.

Behind was a convoy of about a dozen cars. The guys from the beach were honking their horns and riding along as if they were in a wedding procession.

Persimmon was jamming to the music. Every now and then she'd shout, "We're coming Dad! We're on our way!"

It was party time!

****

Tiger was ready. It was ready. Ten inches long, three inches wide, and throbbing.

Randy and Mark rolled Trust on to his stomach.

He began to scream.

"Please don't... I'll do anything... please don't!"

Randy opened a tube of KY jelly and squeezed. He rubbed the ointment into Trust's bottom. Trust's screams became a gurgle. He was vomiting.

"Please... I'll do anything... please don't!"

His cries were choked by the trickle of green vomit coming from his mouth.

Tiger dropped down on one knee.

"I've got AIDS... and... you'll be sorry!"

Trust vomited again. Randy stepped aside to prevent it splashing on him.

Tiger dropped down on both knees, straddling Trust's bottom.

"I've got AIDS... and... you'll be sorry!"

Trust began to fight like a demented being. He had nothing to lose. He cursed and spat and tugged and writhed and squirmed. Tiger sat on his bottom pinning him to the ground. Mark pulled at his legs, keeping them apart. Randy tugged at his ears.

Click click click went Dell's needles.

After a minute the pain in his ears got through to Trust. He stopped struggling and lay stretched out and limp, groaning.

Randy gave a final vicious pull, and Trust gave a yell of such pain that the sound must have reached into hell.

Tiger lay on top of him, and began to rub himself between the cleft of his cheeks.

The click click clicking of the needles were urging Tiger towards the final act.

****

The convoy arrived at Delancey Street. The cars piled up one after the other in front of the boarded up offices, the guys honking their horns as they pulled up.

Darius jumped out of the Lamborghini, and began dancing with the redhead and the blond on the sidewalk. The other guys gathered round and laughed and cheered.

It was like a street party.

Suddenly there was a scream. Above the noise of the music and laughing and honking and shouting, there was a scream.

Trudy heard it. She recognised the sound. It was Bismarck.

The guys stopped honking and shouting, the girls stopped dancing, the street became silent.

They heard it again. Another scream, more terrible than the first. It was coming from behind the boarded up offices.

The guys started battering down the door.

There was a third scream. It was a terrible sound, like a death cry.

They were too late.

Too late for what?

****

Tiger pushed. Trust screamed. Tiger was inside.

He began to pump. Up and down, pushing harder at each thrust, deeper and deeper.

The click click clicking of the needles kept time to the rhythm of his motion.

Tiger began to sweat. It dripped off him onto Trust's back.

There was knocking and banging at the door. A rescue party had arrived.

Tiger pumped harder. The click click click of the needles urged him on.

There was a sound of breaking windows.

He pumped harder and deeper. Suddenly, in his mind, he saw the face of Henry. There he was. He was standing before Tiger, suffused with love.

He pumped harder and deeper. Henry was standing before him, his arms outstretched to receive his love.

Hug Daddy forever. Don't let Daddy go... let Daddy be loved by you forever and ever.

It gushed. From the inside of his being it poured from him, washing its way through Trust, bathing Henry in its passion.

Trust screamed.

There was no cause to scream.

It was an act of love.

PART THREE

DEATH IN VENICE

CHAPTER SEVEN

LAZARUS

Eldridge Kwanza was a man apart, a black doctor practising within a predominantly white fraternity. Even amongst his black colleagues, Eldridge didn't feel at home. His roots were in Africa, not in the USA.

Eldridge's ancestors originated from Portuguese West Africa. They were a ruling family within the indigenous population who were favoured by their colonisers and given the privileges of honorary whites. Many settled in mainland Portugal, to become lawyers, teachers, doctors and churchmen. Some rose to the very pinnacle of their profession, for example Eldridge's great uncle had become cardinal archbishop of Lisbon. Eldridge's own parents were tenured professors at the University of Oporto when the struggle for liberation in the overseas province of West Africa took hold. They immediately sided with the militants, and became freedom fighters for an independent Angola. Because of their background, they were recruited into the highest ranks of the liberation movement and became roving ambassadors, raising funds and preaching propaganda on behalf of their guerrilla comrades in the bush.

It was while his parents were on a diplomatic mission to the United Nations that Eldridge was born. His father wanted to call him Frantz, in honour of Frantz Fanon, the African revolutionary author of the *Wretched of the Earth*. His mother preferred Aimé, in honour Aimé Césaire, the poet and politician from Martinique, one of the founding fathers of the négritude movement. They finally settled on Eldridge, as a homage to Eldridge Cleaver, the American leader of the Black Panthers who at that time had fled the US and taken up exile in Algiers.

His parents made sure that Eldridge took advantage of his place of birth and acquired US citizenship. They also gave him a first rate education. Eldridge attended the very best schools in Rome, Paris and London. When he was ready for university his parents urged him to study economics; they saw him as a potential Minister of Finance, even President, of the new independent Angola. But Eldridge had become increasingly disenchanted with politics… and his parents. They talked socialism and distribution of wealth while they holidayed in ultra chic hotels and dined in exquisite restaurants. But what most distressed him was their inability to accept that their words no longer matched their deeds. Eldridge would have been more at ease if they'd been honestly corrupt, a pair of con artists who acknowledged they were stealing from the pot of gold. What he couldn't abide was their self deception, their continued belief in themselves as champions of the oppressed long after they had become the oppressor.

So Eldridge abandoned politics and opted instead for medicine. It was a way of protecting himself from the route his parents had trod. He wanted a career which would shield him from corruption, a clear sign that he didn't altogether trust himself. He loved his parents, he despised what they had become and he feared that he might repeat their trajectory. By entering medicine, Eldridge was attempting to isolate himself from temptation.

He was in his final year of med school at Harvard when he received the news that his parents had died. The official report spoke of an unfortunate car crash near Strasbourg, but Eldridge guessed they'd been assassinated. His mother had been hysterical on the phone the day before, obviously scared out of her wits by something or someone, and she'd made no mention of car trips to Strasbourg. The liberation movement was in its final death throe and had degenerated into a collection of mafia style gangs fighting over the spoils of war. His parents must have become involved in a scam over secret funds and paid the price.

They left no will, no assets, no bank accounts, no pension. Eldridge was an American citizen, and the Angolan government had no interest in assisting him. He was totally alone, a highly educated African in the land of the free without a penny to his name. After the first shock of his abandonment, he felt a surge of exhilaration, a stripping away of the past with its lies and deceit. Eldridge was free to create his own destiny.

He quickly formulated a plan. First, he scraped together a loan to complete his medical studies. Then, after graduating from Harvard, he travelled West to the University of San Diego to specialise in infectious diseases. His aim was to work his way through his post-grad training before relocating to where he was needed most, back in Africa. There he could work as a humble doctor amongst his own people to fight the greatest menace to confront them since colonisation. Eldridge would become a freedom fighter in the battle against AIDS.

It was while Eldridge was doing his post grad training in San Diego that he found himself called as a witness at Bismarck's trial. It was inevitable, he was Henry's doctor, and the court wanted to know about Henry's sickness. What wasn't inevitable was what followed.

CHAPTER 7: LAZARUS

****

During a lull in the trial, when one of the jurors had to be replaced, Eldridge got an invitation from Adler to meet Bismarck at his home in La Jolla. The invitation was puzzling. Eldridge could not conceive why Bismarck would want to talk with him. Clearly it had something to do with the trial. It was curiosity more than anything, which made Eldridge accept.

Bismarck sent his chauffeur, George, to pick him up from outside the clinic after his day's shift. He was driven to La Jolla, and up the hill to Bismarck's mansion on the promontory. He found himself before a spectacular home, nothing gaudy or flashy, just old world opulence. A butler escorted him through the hallway into a green room. Bismarck was standing at an enormous window looking out to sea. Adler was there plus Bismarck's wife.

There were the usual courtesies, the offer of tea and cakes, milk and sugar, even cucumber sandwiches. Then Adler got to the point. He suggested Eldridge head up a committee to find a cure for AIDS. It was to be funded by Bismarck, and Eldridge was to have ten million dollars as a starter.

"You expect me, Henry's doctor, to tell the world that Bismarck cares about people with AIDS!"

Eldridge was astonished at the grossness of the proposal. It was a crude PR manoeuvre to make Bismarck look good for the jury and public opinion, as obscene as a cigarette company offering money to fight lung cancer. Adler must have taken a poll which showed that Bismarck was universally detested and was trying to turn things round and improve Bismarck's public image by getting Eldridge on their side.

But they'd chosen the wrong man. Eldridge hadn't become a doctor to be corrupted like his parents. The proposal represented everything he loathed and detested. He told Adler he'd consider the offer after the trial was over, when Bismarck had nothing to gain by being so generous.

****

The trial ended. Bismarck was acquitted. Naturally, Adler didn't renew the offer about the AIDS charity, and Eldridge never expected to hear from Bismarck again.

Then, out of the blue, about three months later, Eldridge got a call from Persimmon. She was Darius' girl friend and Eldridge had met her on several occasions while attending Darius in an expensive private AIDS clinic where Eldridge worked weekends. Persimmon was calling to tell him there'd been some sort of accident. She sounded terribly upset. At first Eldridge thought something had happened to Darius. Then he realised she was talking about her father. She was pleading for Eldridge to come quickly to a building in Delancey street, something about Bismarck being assaulted and needing a doctor urgently.

Eldridge was there in five minutes. There were a crowd of youngsters outside, the guys and girls were dancing in the street. It was like walking through a beach party except it was the middle of down town San Diego on a quiet Sunday morning. George, was at the door. He beckoned for Eldridge to come in quickly.

George took Eldridge through to the back room. Bismarck was lying on the floor. He was naked. He was in a terrible state, a shrivelled trembling naked wreck of a man spread-eagled on the floor like a broken puppet. He just lay there whimpering. It took Eldridge an age to get him to his feet. The thing Eldridge most noticed about him was the colour. His body was yellow, as though his liver had been pouring out bile. And his eyes were shrunken.

It was obvious what had happened. Bismarck had been raped. Eldridge did a quick examination. Apart from the tears and the blood there was no physical damage. Eldridge went to the sink and washed him down. He was like a corpse. Eldridge got a towel and dried him. He put him into his clothes. It took a time. It was like putting clothes on a dead man.

When he was decent, George drove Bismarck back home in the Mercedes. The police were never called. Eldridge guessed Adler had arranged everything, probably no prosecution in return for silence and cover up.

A month later Eldridge was summoned once more to Bismarck's mansion on the hill overlooking La Jolla. This time the invitation came directly from Bismarck. Eldridge was ushered into the green room overlooking the Ocean where Bismarck and his wife were waiting for him. They made small talk while Isabel busied herself with tea and crumpets. It was all very old world and English. Isabel even spoke about the weather, and there's absolutely nothing to say about the weather in San Diego. It never changes.

Eldridge was astonished at the change in Bismarck. Though he seemed to have completely recovered his physical composure, just as if the rape had never occurred, he was altered inside. He'd developed a terrible stutter, and just couldn't get his words out. It was the strangest thing, as if the trauma of the rape had been concentrated and condensed into this one infirmity, a constant reminder of what he'd endured.

After a while, Bismarck told Isabel to leave.

"I would like to ta.. talk to Doc.. Doctor K.. K.. Kwanza in pri.. private."

Isabel waited for him to complete his sentence and then scuttled out of the room like an obedient puppy.

Eldridge was left alone with Bismarck. He was a tall man, six foot three or four, handsome, with a Gregory Peck face and silver hair. His hair was his own, which isn't the case with most sixty year olds. He was cultured and cultivated. He was rich and intelligent. All in all he should have been an attractive man. But he wasn't. There was something dreadfully damaged about him and the stutter just made it all the more obvious.

The conversation had nothing to do with the rape. He never mentioned it once. Instead it was a curious rambling stuttering monologue, all about Bismarck. How he was misunderstood. How his only interest in life was to serve others and maintain standards. How he saw his life as a duty. It was self serving and pompous, a mixture of self pity and glorification.

"A.. AIDS is a ter.. terrible disease. Af... Africa is be.. being ra.. ravaged by this dre.. dreadful condition...."

His hand began to shake. His face was yellow. Maybe it was the light bouncing off the walls of the strange green room? He rose from his chair and began pacing up and down. Eldridge had the impression he was struggling to hide his trembling hand from view.

"... We have a re.. re.. responsibility and a du.. duty to hu.. humanity..."

He hid his shaking hand behind his back, but there was no way of camouflaging the terrible stutter. He was having more and more trouble getting the words out. His shoulders were stooped and his cheeks sunken. Bit by bit he trickled out his request. He wanted Eldridge to find the cure for AIDS. It was the old Adler proposition but with a difference. Through all his pretence about helping the sick and dying in Africa, Eldridge got the message. The rape had infected Bismarck with the HIV virus. Now Bismarck needed the cure for AIDS to save himself.

****

Find the cure for AIDS! Total carte blanche. Money no object. All the resources of Trust Pharmaceuticals at his disposal. The old Adler proposal would have been cut short as soon as its PR mission had been accomplished. This one was for real, Bismarck needed the cure. And so did Africa.

What to do? It was exactly the sort of dilemma Eldridge had hoped to avoid by becoming a doctor. The choice was excruciating. If he accepted, he'd be just like his parents a pretend saviour of the sick and needy while actually serving the rich and selfish. If he said no, he'd be a coward, a self-serving prima donna sacrificing the needs of millions to save his own soul.

It took Eldridge days to come to his decision. First he had to grapple with his dislike of Bismarck, a mean man with no insight into his own meanness. Eldridge found it difficult to think of anybody he liked less, or anybody he'd less like to work for. But in the end he realised the problem wasn't with Bismarck, it was himself. The only reason he was hesitating was because he didn't trust himself. He feared the power that was being offered him, he feared his tainted roots and his own propensity for corruption. He decided to accept Bismarck's offer. By doing so, Eldridge would learn who he was.

The decision taken, he resigned from his position at the public clinic, the one Henry had attended, but insisted that Bismarck provide a large donation to employ three new doctors in his place. He decided to spend the next few months in travel. There was no point in starting from scratch. If there was to be any chance of finding a cure, he had to find the people who were already half way there, and give them a push to the finish line.

He started at NIH. The place was packed with top notch scientists. But they were mostly working on vaccines. All well and good if you hadn't got the disease, but useless if you were already infected and needed a cure.

He spent a couple of months in Kyoto. They were industrious to the point of madness, and they fawned over Eldridge as if he was the Emperor himself. There was nothing wrong with their work. It was the best in the world for what it was, a factory turning out genetic probes instead of Toyotas. But it was all to do with new diagnostic tests. What's the point in knowing you've got a disease if you can't do anything about it?

Eldridge decided to check out an elderly semi-retired scientist working from a private clinic in Buenos Aires. He was an eminent old fellow who'd got the Nobel Prize for his work on Complement Fixation in the early fifties. Now he was pushing a bizarre theory that AIDS was the result of Manganese deficiency. His work was being reported in the popular press, and ignored by the scientific journals. It sounded mad, but you never know. When Eldridge met him, he was treated to a convoluted theory that Manganese had been rendered unabsorbable due to some contaminant from the plastics industry, and that everyone needed to consume vast quantities of a concoction the old man had created with so called "Organic Manganese". Everything was curable thanks to this potion. Cancer, heart disease, ulcers, the old man had the panacea for all the world's ills. AIDS was just one of the diseases he could cure. He took Eldridge on a visit to some of his patients. As far as Eldridge could tell, they were still dying. It was just they didn't think they were. Then the old man started telling Eldridge how Manganese deficiency had affected Hitler and Stalin. Eldridge decided it was time to leave.

CHAPTER 7: LAZARUS

Eldridge visited some prestige laboratories in Europe, and even found himself at a Mafia financed company in Rome which was marketing a fake cure for AIDS as a way of laundering its cash.

The next stop was a lab on the outskirts of Cambridge in England, a strange set up in a science park, and an even stranger guy, an English Lord, a scientist called Felix. There were rumours that he was working on something top secret.

Eldridge arrived in London on an Alitalia flight from Rome. On the way over he read the research documents Felix had sent over to prepare for the meeting. Eldridge had been asked to sign a pile of papers before Felix agreed to release them. Felix had no intention of confiding his discovery to anyone without water tight confidentiality agreements.

There was a long queue through immigration for non EU citizens. The Brits just couldn't make up their mind about Europe. On the Continent nobody cared about passport checks, but at Heathrow, treaty or no treaty, Eldridge had to wait in line. It took forty minutes before immigration were satisfied he was fit to enter.

Eldridge came out from the blue channel and stood with his back to the wall. He was trying to spot Felix. He didn't know what he looked like. He knew he was young and dark and tall, but not much else.

"Doctor Kwanza?"

Eldridge was approached by a small sixty year old man. He looked a bit like W.C. Fields, overweight, with the blotchy face of an alcoholic. It was Harry, Felix's number two. He was nothing like the sort of executive Eldridge had been dealing with these last few months. They were thrusting aggressive young men with perfectly manicured nails and buttoned down shirts. They reeked of cologne and were selling their cure for AIDS like charlatan medicine men of the nineteenth century. Harry was a welcome relief.

"I'm sorry Felix isn't here to greet you," said Harry.

He took hold of Eldridge's case and guided him towards the car park. They made small talk on the way. Harry chatted about the weather, a typical chilly grey English winter, and Eldridge spoke about his flight, and how Alitalia had diverted him to Milan for no apparent reason.

They were on their way to Cambridge when Harry began telling Eldridge about Therapeutic Pathogens. Eldridge already knew quite a bit about its founder, the Honourable Felix Langsbridge, who called himself Felix like it was a title, like calling yourself "Excellence". Eldridge wasn't at all sure he was going to like Felix. He sounded a bit too snooty, a bit too precious, for Eldridge's taste.

Harry obviously adored Felix, and in a way the man did sound quite remarkable. His idea was astonishing. Eldridge hadn't come across anything quite like it. It was probably rubbish. The odds were if you give a dying man a second disease, you don't cure the first, you just die quicker. But, who knows? It was worth a look.

"He was riding on a bus in Paris..."

Harry was telling Eldridge about how the idea came to Felix.

"He saw a picture of Asterix."

Eldridge had a sense of deja vu. The story rang a bell. He'd heard it before.

"Asterix was clubbing Obelix."

Not quite, but similar. Eldridge remembered a class at Harvard, his first year at med school, and the teacher was telling the story of Kekule, and how he'd discovered the structure of the benzene ring. Kekule had been riding a tram. Where? Prague? Heidelberg? Vienna? Eldridge couldn't remember. It didn't matter. What mattered was that Kekule had been riding a tram. He'd dreamed the structure of the benzene ring on a tram.

"He was riding the bus when he had the vision! Why not fight disease with disease?"

Harry went on to tell Eldridge about the latest results, and how the cats with immunodeficiency and leukaemic virus had survived as long as the controls. Eldridge was suspicious. There was something fishy about the company, especially Felix. One thing was for sure, nothing should be taken on trust. Eldridge had learnt his lesson these last few months. Forget about what they tell you, look at the evidence for yourself.

Harry sensed Eldridge's scepticism.

"The HTLV virus will multiply T cells as fast as the HIV virus destroys them... we leave the two of them to slug it out...We watch them batter each other senseless!"

Harry had instinctively supposed that a black man would be more susceptible to a boxing analogy, and he finished by giving a quick one two against the windscreen, followed by an uppercut to an imaginary opponent.

"Wow! It sounds exciting," Eldridge was humouring the old man. It was a harmless piece of racism, less offensive than his Jewish liberal friends who were all over him just because he was black. Eldridge was often courted by white liberals. They liked him because he was young and attractive, but most of all they liked him because he was an educated black. It was a form of inverted racism to which he'd grown accustomed. Their pleasure in befriending him was in direct proportion to their barely concealed surprise at the extent of his culture.

"So, when can I meet Felix?" Eldridge asked.

"Tomorrow."

There was a pause.

"Felix wanted to pick you up at the airport himself," Harry continued, "unfortunately he was called away. He had to go to a funeral."

****

Eldridge's meeting with Felix next day was something of an anti-climax. He'd expected a more flamboyant figure, someone extravagant and histrionic, someone struggling to create an effect. Instead he was confronted with a man who seemed subdued, even depressed.

"I'm sorry I wasn't able to meet you at the airport," Felix said.

"I gather you had an unexpected engagement."

It was a question rather than a statement, but Felix didn't comment. He made no reference to the funeral. Instead he asked about Eldridge, his needs and requirements. It was curious the way in which he offered no information about himself.

Eldridge tried quizzing him on the origins of the idea.

"It came to you while you were working in Paris?"

Felix didn't take the bait. There was no reference to buses or cartoon characters. Instead he shrugged it off as if it was nothing, as if anyone could have come up with a similar idea.

Felix remained hunched over his desk. He was a tall gangly young man, ill at ease, unsure of himself. Harry was at his side, stepping in to provide the answers when Felix ran out of steam. Harry was like a father, protecting a gifted but vulnerable child.

Eldridge began to change his ideas about Felix. He obviously wasn't a con man. He was doing nothing to sell his business. On the contrary, it was Eldridge and Harry who were making all the running. They were having to push Felix to say something positive about himself. Felix was not the sort of person to inspire confidence in the venture capital community, which pleased Eldridge.

Eldridge spent the rest of the day touring the facility. Felix introduced him to everyone, making sure he had an opportunity to talk to whomever he wished. There seemed to be no secrets with Felix.

It was extraordinary how Felix had his pulse on what was going on. He knew everybody in the organisation, and exactly what they were doing. It was as if everybody was important, except Felix.

Eldridge particularly remembered the smiling young technician who squirmed with pleasure when Felix described how he'd worked until nearly midnight on

Xmas eve. What nobody seemed to recognise was that Felix must have worked even harder to have noticed the young man.

It was the end of the day, and they were sitting together in Felix's office alone. Even Harry had left.

There was no getting away from it, Felix was a phenomenon. He treated everyone with genuine respect and consideration, and his own enterprise with a matter of factness and a modesty which was totally endearing. It was almost as if he didn't understand the significance of his own discovery. Yet he must have done. Otherwise why would he have set up the business?

"If your theory is right, you'll be very famous," Eldridge said.

Felix just shrugged his shoulders, as if the thought didn't interest him.

They spent the rest of the evening going through the scientific data. Felix showed everything, executive summaries, weekly reports, even lab books. He concealed nothing. It was the first time, in all Eldridge's travels, that he became truly excited. It began to look as though Felix's idea might work.

"What do you need from Trust?" Eldridge asked.

"Finance."

"To do what?"

"To pay for the next stage. It'll cost a fortune to move from the pilot experiments to full stage clinical trials. If I don't get a financial partner I'll have to stop."

That night, in his hotel, Eldridge drafted his report to Bismarck.

"My preliminary finding is that we should support Therapeutic Pathogens. It is the only company I have encountered where there is a possibility for an immediate breakthrough in AIDS treatment. I believe the idea is strikingly original, and that Felix, the founder of the company, is possibly a genius."

****

Bismarck gave the go ahead, and in no time the little office which Harry had opened for Eldridge in the science park was being expanded to accommodate the extra secretaries, accountants and lawyers who were drafted in to prepare the paperwork for Trust's participation in Therapeutic Pathogens.

The next few weeks were taken up with meetings to work through the details for the investment. But whenever Felix was present, it was if he didn't belong. It was eerie. Here was a young man, not yet twenty five, about to sign a deal which valued his company at well over ten million dollars, discoverer of what could be one of the greatest scientific breakthroughs of the century, and he behaved as if he didn't count.

He seemed to latch on to people, it didn't matter who they were, and endow them with exaggerated qualities. Sometimes it was farcical, as with the lawyer Bismarck had sent over from one of the big law firms out of Los Angeles, a vain lean man without quality. Sure, he had a good grasp of company law, he knew how to maximise tax concessions in an R & D partnership, and he was pretty good at negotiating escape clauses, the sort of thing which deals with events like Trust going bust or Felix dying or whatever. But outside of that, he was nothing special, constantly puffing himself up, pretending to be some sort of wunderkind. Which is why Felix's behaviour was so odd. Everyone, including Harry, saw through him. Everyone realised that outside of his work the lawyer was a wretched creature. Everyone knew he was a bore, everyone except Felix.

Felix inhabited a different world. He lapped up the lawyer's stories, plying him with questions about his early career, gasping in astonishment over his discovering a new tax dodge. It was preposterous. Felix was treating this commonplace west coast lawyer as if he was Alexander the Great. It might have been OK if Felix had been a young lawyer struggling to get himself a position in his firm. But Felix was much more impressive than the person impressing him. So what was the angle?

Eldridge was confused. There was something hollow about Felix. He should have had everything going for him. He had youth. He had looks, except for the oversize jaw, and even that gave him a certain distinction. He had a personal fortune, which would become immense at the death of his father making him one of the richest men in England. He had breeding, charm, and, most of all, intelligence. He was on his way to the Nobel Prize. Who could ask for anything more? And yet something was missing. And it was the most important thing of all, a centre. Eldridge wondered whether Felix knew who he was. Perhaps that's why he fawned on people? It took the attention off of himself.

The only thing on which Felix held firm and where Eldridge couldn't move him, was his insistence about trying the cure on a human volunteer. Eldridge warned him of the dangers of doing this too quickly, explaining that they must continue with animal experiments before starting on humans. If they ignored the statutory regulations on drug development and something went wrong, they'd be crucified by the FDA. But Felix was adamant. He insisted they try it on a human, and soon.

"Why?" Eldridge insisted.

"I want to present it at the AIDS conference in Venice."

Eldridge didn't get it. It seemed a tacky sort of reason. But there was no budging Felix.

****

The day finally arrived for the official signing. Bismarck was so high on the news coming out of England that he decided to come and sign personally. He flew in to the UK and asked Eldridge to meet him at the Savoy Hotel for breakfast.

Eldridge drove up to London early and joined Bismarck in the Riverside restaurant. Bismarck was sitting at a table near the window. He had a companion with him. Eldridge recognised her immediately. He'd seen her the day of the rape. Her name was Trudy, she was Bismarck's mistress. Bismarck would never have shown himself in public with her back home. But now that he was out of the country, he didn't seem to care. The man had his own code of conduct, and it reeked of double standards.

Bismarck wiped his mouth and stood up to greet Eldridge.

"You know Miss Tru.. Tru.. Trudy," he stuttered.

It was a shock hearing him again. Eldridge just couldn't get used to the idea of his rape induced stutter. It must be so embarrassing for him, as if he was constantly confessing to the humiliation he'd received at the hands of Tiger.

Trudy was dressed in a neat outfit, very prim and proper, looking more like a secretary than a hooker. She was exquisite. As usual Bismarck had purchased the best.

Once the introductions were over, Bismarck ignored Trudy and set about quizzing Eldridge on the latest developments in Cambridge. Eldridge showed Bismarck the amendment to the partnership deal he had negotiated with Felix the previous evening. Bismarck seemed satisfied.

"There's one catch," Eldridge said.

"What's that?" Bismarck stammered.

"Felix insists we try the cure on a human volunteer."

"How soon?"

"He wants to do it right now. He's got a thing about presenting it as a show stopper for the Venice AIDS conference."

"What's the catch?"

"If it works it'll be fine. If it doesn't we'll go to jail. We have to go through statutory procedures. We can't just jump from cats to humans."

"How about a will.. willing vo.. volunteer who's pre.. prepared to keep it co.. confidential?"

Bismarck was stuttering more than usual, and Eldridge thought he was about to suggest himself.

"Felix wants somebody at death's door," Eldridge added hastily. "He wants to bring someone back from the dead and hit the headlines."

Breakfast was over, the table was cleared, and Bismarck left to clean up in his room. He was constantly cleaning up. He had a sort of mania about cleanliness. He wouldn't touch people. At first Eldridge thought Bismarck refused to touch him because he was black. Then he realised it wasn't racism, Bismarck went through contortions to avoid shaking hands with anyone.

While Bismarck was off scrubbing himself clean, Eldridge was left alone with Trudy at the breakfast table. It was the first time they'd been alone together. They were a perfect couple, young beautiful and a striking contrast of black and white. Customers were turning to peer at them, off duty waiters were being summoned to take a peek.

Trudy seemed unaware of the buzz of interest around her. She was silent, uneasy in his presence. Maybe she was uncomfortable about being left alone with a black man, a blonde trophy in the hands of a savage. Or maybe she just didn't know how to handle herself with anyone who wasn't a client.

Bismarck came back. He'd been busy on the phone.

"You say Felix is insisting we try it on a volunteer right now?" Bismarck asked, taking about thirty seconds to splutter through his sentence.

"He's got a thing about this conference in Venice," Eldridge replied. "He's obsessed by it."

"I've a suggestion." Bismarck continued. He paused for a moment to collect his thoughts. "While I was up.. upstairs I made a few ca.. calls. I've got the pe.. perfect volunteer waiting for you in Lo.. Los Angeles. You can bring him back, and Felix can cu.. cure him or ki.. ki.. ki.. ," Bismarck went into total arrest for about ten seconds, and then spat it out, " ... kill him."

****

The volunteer was to be Darius.

While Bismarck was busy at the signing ceremony in Cambridge, Eldridge was on the next day's flight to LA to check out whether it made sense. The world seemed to have gone crazy, everyone linked to everyone else in a sort of HIV carousel, like a Schnitzler play from old Vienna.

Eldridge landed at LAX and there was Persimmon waiting for him. She was hopelessly overweight, five foot eight and weighing at least 200 pounds. But she dressed right, which wasn't easy for someone her size. All her clothes were designer from Paris and she looked good in them, even with the extra pounds. Also she was bright. She could have made a career for herself if she hadn't been stuck with being a billionaire's daughter with no need to work.

She threw herself into Eldridge's arms and immediately began sobbing.

"I wish you'd never left," she whispered between her tears. "He was alright while you were looking after him."

Persimmon was being unfair. Once the disease takes hold it destroys the patient, whoever the doctor. If Darius was dying it had nothing to do with Eldridge's absence.

Persimmon rushed Eldridge to the waiting taxi.

"He's lost a ton of weight and he keeps getting infections. He can't last much longer."

They were heading to Pasadena to the hospital where Eldridge used to treat Darius. The taxi picked up speed as they left the heavy smog laden city centre. The day was sunny. They passed the Dodgers Stadium and headed for the hills. In Alhambra they skirted a park packed with joggers and sun bathers. Eldridge felt good to be back on the West Coast, and away from the dreadful tedium of an English winter.

They entered the hospital grounds, towards a neat modern building set in a garden surrounded by lakes and woods. They passed through an elaborate security check before being allowed through the main doors. Eldridge had to show his ID, Persimmon had to produce a letter of authorisation, and everything was put through X ray cameras. It was just like boarding a plane, only the security guards weren't seeking out terrorists but reporters and photographers. The hospital had a lot of important patients, and the press were looking for ways to break in and take ghoulish shots of celebrities on their death beds. The security was particularly tight because the hospital had a reputation for catering for AIDS cases. There was nothing the press liked more than ferreting out the rich and famous with AIDS.

They went up to the third floor, and came out of the elevator into a sort of space ship of high technology. Nurses were whizzing around in aluminium suits, doctors were scurrying up and down the corridor with test tubes, charts and mobile phones. Portable scanners were being pushed in and out the private rooms like dodgems. It was obviously costing a bomb. Darius could afford it. His last album had sold ten million. The place was designed to cater for the rich, the rich and dying.

Persimmon entered Darius' room first.

"Hi! I've brought someone to see you."

Eldridge followed. Darius was lying on his bed, drips attached to both arms. His head was propped up by a pile of pillows. He was as near dead as anybody alive can possibly be. He looked like a cadaver, like those concentration camp victims when the allies first came through the gates of Belsen. His ribs were showing through his scrawny chest, his cheekbones were covered by skin, no flesh, just skin. And his eyes were sockets.

Darius struggled to rouse himself from his torpor. He stretched out his hand to Persimmon. She sat beside the bed and took his hand in hers. She began stroking his fingers, making soothing clucking noises, like a mother bird to a dying fledgling. It was an incongruous scene, the fat girl comforting the thin man. He'd been such a good looking young man, and now he'd aged fifty years in as many days.

Persimmon was telling Darius Eldridge had come to help. Darius looked at Eldridge and tried to speak, he was trying to say "glad to see you", but it was more like a croak. He gave up trying and just raised his hand and gave a little wave of greeting, a "Hi" from his death bed.

Persimmon told him Eldridge had a cure and was going to save him. Darius pretended to believe her, whispering words like "great" and "terrific". But his eyes were resigned to death. He probably thought she was lying, that she was just trying to encourage him. And he, in his turn, was doing all he could to encourage her.

"Tell him what you're planning to do," urged Persimmon.

Eldridge explained to Darius how he was experimenting the cure in England, and how it hadn't been tried out on anyone yet. Darius's expression didn't change. He went on saying "great" and "terrific", but he didn't seem to understand. He was so far gone he probably didn't take in what was happening around him.

Eldridge took hold of Darius' hand and gave it a squeeze. Darius looked so vulnerable, as though his life could be blown away by a breeze. Eldridge wasn't sure he'd make it across the Atlantic. He thought of Felix and how hollow he was behind the facade. It was the strangest sensation. If the cure worked, they'd both get what they most wanted. Felix would receive the accolade of the world's scientists, and Darius would regain his health, his life, his looks, and his youth. If it didn't, Darius would fade away and die, and maybe Felix too.

****

Eldridge went into action. He called up the charter airline companies. There were dozens to choose from, with planes ranging from little propeller craft which wouldn't make it more than a few hundred miles, to mid range executive jets that could do a thousand miles or so, to the long range executive jets, like the Gulf Stream, seating about a dozen passengers, that could cross the Atlantic in one go. Darius was so ill, Eldridge wasn't taking any chances. John Wayne Airport in Orange County and Long Beach Municipal Airport were too far away. He decided on a company operating out of Burbank Glendale Pasadena airport which was right next door to the hospital. They operated a Falcon 900 which was already fitted out to take a stretcher case. They promised to fly straight into Stansted airport which was only a few minutes drive from Cambridge.

Eldridge called Felix. He'd just signed the partnership deal with Bismarck. Bismarck and Harry were still with him in the office celebrating. Eldridge told Felix about Darius, and that he was bringing him back with him. Harry took hold of the phone to get the details of the flight and to make arrangements for a private ambulance to be waiting at Stansted as soon as they landed. The ambulance would take Darius to a cottage Felix had recently bought in the countryside near the Science Park.

It was late afternoon, and Eldridge invited Persimmon to have dinner with him before the flight next morning. Persimmon declined, she didn't want to move from Darius' side.

"Why don't you give Trudy a call?" she suggested.

Eldridge sensed Persimmon was doing a bit of mischief making, but the idea appealed to him. Trudy had been dispatched back to the States by Bismarck and would be languishing on her own. Eldridge remembered the effect they'd had as a couple at the Savoy and quite fancied the idea of taking her out on a date without Bismarck uglying it up. He was also intrigued to know how her behaviour towards him might change if he was her client.

Persimmon gave Eldridge Trudy's number.

Eldridge hired a car and headed towards National Five. It was the route South from LA. It led to Carlsbad and Trudy's home.

He gave her a call, he wasn't sure how she'd respond. Did she take other clients apart from Bismarck? She seemed delighted to hear from him and jumped at the idea of joining him for dinner. They didn't discuss money. Eldridge supposed this would be settled before sex. Eldridge had no problems about using a hooker, it was no different from eating a meal. Dinner for one… masturbation; dinner at home… mutual sex; dinner in town… prostitution. He couldn't see why the act of paying for something carried such a stigma, nor why the job of a prostitute should be so different from that of a waiter.

He headed on towards Carlsbad. It lay on the shore of the Pacific Ocean, far from the bustle of a major city, with charming old houses, painted in pretty colours. But there was an enormous black concrete power station towering on the edge, blighting the town and its residents.

Eldridge also had no criticism of Bismarck employing Trudy for sex. What he loathed was his hypocrisy, pretending to be the defender of family values while sneaking a prostitute on the sly. Worst of all was Bismarck's inability to face up to who he was. Why couldn't he acknowledge that his actions didn't match his words?

For Eldridge, the greatest crime was lying to yourself.

Trudy was ready and waiting for him. She'd put on the Versace gown she'd picked up in London. It changed her look completely. The vibrant yellows and golds hugged the line of her figure, proclaiming rather than shrouding what she had on offer.

Eldridge decided to take her to the Hotel del Coronado. They drove down along the coast and in through the city and out over suicide bridge. Eldridge loved the Coronado. Ever since he'd seen *Some Like It Hot,* he'd fantasised about the marvellous beach hotel where Marilyn Monroe had been looking to marry her millionaire. It was only when he'd come to San Diego that he discovered the hotel wasn't a studio set, and it wasn't in Florida, but on his own doorstep.

Now that he was her client, Trudy plied him with questions and pretended to lap up everything he had to say. She explained how she'd never been to the Coronado. Eldridge didn't believe her. It was her way to make him feel important, to allow him to show off to her. He played along. He told her of the magnificent dining room with its marvellous wooden ceiling. He explained how the hotel had been a point of assignation for eminent people in the twenties and thirties.

"The grill room is named after the Prince of Wales."

She listened to him in a pretence of rapt attention while he gave her a potted history of the pre-war years, how Edward was the most popular Prince of all time, how shocked the British were at the thought of their Prince Charming falling for an American hussy, how Mrs Simpson was married, and how, worst of all, she was a commoner.

They were driving over the bridge as he was telling her all this, passing the signs which give the emergency numbers to dial if you were contemplating jumping off. Trudy was leaning on his every word like an eager little school kid. He admired her professionalism, he felt he was in the presence of a world class hooker, make the client feel interesting, pretend he's the most fascinating man in the world, and inwardly yawn and dream of the large tip.

They pulled into the driveway, he handed the keys of the car to the boy at the entrance and watched Trudy walking up the steps. The gown was delicious. With her swaying hips and wiggling yellow peach bottom, she could have been Marilyn. All that was missing was "Zowie!" from a row of massed millionaires in their bath chairs.

They sat in the bar and again they were the focus of attention, even more than at the Savoy. The strikingly handsome young black man with the gorgeous blonde, a Hollywood couple if ever there was one.

Eldridge expounded on Billy Wilder and the venetian blinds in *Double Indemnity.* From there he got onto other exiles, Lang and Sternberg, then Murnau and his lament about the demise of the silent movies. Trudy continued to lap it up. She pretended she was fascinated. It didn't matter what the topic, she treated his every word as a judgement from Mount Olympus.

They went down the steps to the grill room. The other diners stopped talking as they came in, their knives and forks suspended in mid air. The men were envious, the women jealous, and everyone wondering who they were.

They sat at their table and she listened attentively as Eldridge took her through the items on the menu. She pretended she wanted to know the translation for every dish, what was in it, and how it was cooked. She ooed and aahed as Eldridge described some of the fancier concoctions. Eldridge explained how the Coronado had the old fashioned idea that fine cooking equalled dousing everything in alcohol and setting fire to it.

"Thermidor is a dish designed for those who hate lobster!"

She laughed. She hadn't the faintest idea what he was talking about, but she guessed he was being sarcastic about something or other. She had a go at saying it herself, repeating the sentence until she felt she'd got the tone just right.

Eldridge was being encouraged to show off to his heart's content. The more obscure he became, the more she lapped it up. He gave her a culinary history on the origins of Nouvelle Cuisine, pontificating on Ferdinand Point and his disciples, Bocuse, Guerard...

"... and the late, much lamented, Alain Chapel."

What a preposterous thing to say. But she just nodded and looked suitably subdued, mourning the loss of someone she'd first heard about a moment earlier. He rushed her through a crash course on twentieth century gastronomy. She hardly had time to enjoy the delights of Escoffier when he was ditched in favour of Maximin and Robuchon. Eldridge was dropping names like confetti. It was like shedding clothes... stark naked... any position... any way.

The meal was coming to an end. Foreplay over... time for bed.

"I've booked us a room."

He wasn't quite sure how to handle the money situation. He decided to leave it to her to name a price.

Instead she looked at him with misty eyes and said.

"I can't... It wouldn't be fair."

She wasn't for sale! She began to explain about Bismarck, about how she saw no one but him. She had her own rules, and she couldn't betray them or him. Eldridge felt distinctly uncomfortable, he'd completely misjudged what she was about.

"I know what you think of me", she continued. "You think I'm a nobody... worse than nobody... scum. Bismarck thinks the same. But it doesn't matter. I don't

mind. What matters is that he teach me things... teache
learn... I can learn how to be someone."

He realised that her responses to him all evening hac
folding her in his arms to apologise. But he held back. He dic
was just another ploy to get her into bed.

"I'm no better than you," Eldridge said. It was inadequate, h
didn't know how to answer her.

"That's what people who are better..." she paused, and Eldrid
was coming next, "... say to their inferiors."

At just that moment, one of the diners came up to their table and asked fo autographs. It broke the embarrassment of the moment. They laughed and tried to explain that they weren't anybody famous. The evening came to an end and Eldridge drove her home. She gave him a chaste kiss on her doorstep. Eldridge waved goodbye. He wished he could have stayed.

****

He drove back to LA and next morning rode in the ambulance with Persimmon and Darius out to the airport. He was still unsettled by his evening with Trudy. He kept replaying the scenes in his mind, and cursed himself for having been so dim-witted and disparaging.

Persimmon soothed and stroked Darius's head while Eldridge tended the drip and injections. Darius was on a cocktail of antibiotics to keep infection at bay. He stayed asleep the whole of the journey. It was more like a coma. He didn't stir when he was loaded aboard the plane and he didn't wake during the entire flight to England.

The arrival at Stansted was almost surreal. It was still dark on a cold English Spring morning, and there was mist in the air. It felt like they were smuggling a dying man into the country. Standing beside the runway as a sort of official greeting party were Felix and Bismarck. Bismarck was waiting to board the charter and fly straight back to LA. Bismarck didn't even bother to look at Darius as he was wheeled past him. Persimmon blew her dad a kiss, she wanted to thank him for giving Darius this last chance for survival. But Bismarck avoided any physical contact with her and hurried on to the plane.

Eldridge joined Darius and Persimmon in the ambulance following Felix in his little red Triumph sports car leading the way through the winding country lanes. Ten minutes later, they drew into a driveway. It curved between immaculate green lawns, with ice crystals layering the grass. As they rounded the bend, the building ew. It was a charming country cottage, with a gnarled Wisteria stretching s across the white plaster walls. Eldridge wondered at the coincidence of ving a place ready and waiting for use as a sanatorium for Darius.

Harry was standing at the front steps. He supervised the unloading of Darius n the ambulance and had him stretchered straight up to the master bedroom on e first floor. Harry had organised round the clock nursing and there were also a couple of junior doctors to watch over things when Eldridge wasn't there.

Persimmon tucked Darius up in bed, and Eldridge explained the care procedures to the nurses and young medics.

Felix began plying Eldridge with questions about Darius' condition, like a young student with a revered teacher, treating Eldridge with exaggerated respect. There was something chilling about the way he fussed and fawned over Eldridge while totally ignoring Darius who was lying comatose in the bed. There wasn't a shadow of sympathy for Darius. He was just another experimental animal as far as Felix was concerned.

"Why is he so thin?" Felix asked.

"It's called HIV Wasting Syndrome," Eldridge told him.

Eldridge reeled off the criteria that the Centre for Disease Control in Atlanta had laid down. There were three. First the patient had to be HIV positive. That was pretty obvious, it was hardly likely to be "HIV Wasting Syndrome", if you didn't have HIV. Second the patient had to have lost more than 10% of his body weight.

"We've got Darius's medical records from a couple of years ago," Eldridge said. "He weighed a hundred and fifty five pounds. Now it's one hundred and five. He's lost more than 30% of his body weight."

"And the third criteria?" asked Felix. His questions seemed tailored to show off Eldridge's knowledge.

"The patient should have either chronic diarrhoea or chronic weakness and fever."

"How do they define diarrhoea?"

"More than two loose stools a day for more than thirty days."

"And chronic weakness?"

"Bedridden for more than 50% of the day for more than thirty days."

"The CDC obviously believes in tight definitions," said Felix admiringly.

"They have to..." Eldridge replied. "... We have to agree on what we mean. We'll never learn unless we know where we're starting from."

Eldridge pointed to Darius's chart where all this information had been recorded in minute detail. He'd been spiking a temperature ever since he'd been admitted to the hospital in Pasadena. The diarrhoea had started three months ago. And the weakness had been increasing bit by bit. The chart showed he'd been 100% bedridden for well over a month.

"What's the cause?" Felix asked.

"Of what?"

"Why he's losing weight."

"It's a mixture of reasons..." Eldridge replied. "... In Darius's case I guess it's anorexia. He's got no appetite. We're partly responsible."

"You?"

"Doctors. Because of the drugs we give him. It kills his appetite. But the real problem is diarrhoea."

"What's the reason?"

"Sometimes there's a cause... like CMV or herpes or protozoan or helminthic infestations. We can treat them. Sometimes it's cryptosporidiosis... which we can't treat. In Darius's case it's nothing in particular... just the enteropathogenic effects of HIV itself."

"Enteropathogenic?"

"A fancy way of saying that HIV causes diarrhoea."

Darius was lying on the bed, his eyes were closed. Was he conscious? Could he hear them? They were talking about him as if he didn't exist. Eldridge was uncomfortable. Darius had ceased to be a person, he'd become a disease.

"The CDC has even got a system for predicting survival with the HIV Wasting Syndrome," Eldridge continued. "Patients are at most risk when their serum albumin drops below two grams per decilitre."

"What's Darius's?"

Eldridge showed Felix the lab tests. He flipped through the reports. Darius's albumin had been low ever since he'd been admitted. Two weeks ago it had fallen to 2.5. As of yesterday, it was 2.1.

Suddenly Felix stopped questioning Eldridge. He was looking at Darius with alarm. Darius was as near dead as any live person can be. Maybe Darius was the wrong person. Maybe they should try it on someone with more of a chance.

"When will the virus be ready for inoculation?" Eldridge asked.

"Tomorrow," Felix replied.

"I'll start him on parenteral feeding."

"Parenteral?"

"I'll put up a line and pour food straight into his blood stream."

"Will it work?"

He meant, would it keep Darius alive long enough for them to test the cure.

Eldridge shrugged his shoulders in reply.

Just then Persimmon came into the room. She'd brought a bunch of fresh flowers. She'd gone out with Harry to the local florist in the village and she'd come back with a splendid bouquet of yellow daffodils. She said she'd buy fresh flowers every day. Each day fresh flowers, each day life.

****

It was the strangest set up. It was like something out of one of those war time movies, where the good guys set up their headquarters in a safe house in the heart of enemy territory. The FDA and the British committee for the safety of medicines would have gone berserk if they'd known about an experiment on a human volunteer without authorisation. Everything had to be kept top secret. Only those with a need to know were kept informed, and Harry personally vetted the nurses and young medics before he recruited them.

The cottage itself had an extraordinarily sophisticated security system. Every door was alarmed, and you had to punch a series of code numbers into a monstrously complicated security device to go from one room to the other. Outside there were floodlit illuminations, with security cameras looking at you from every vantage point. Harry gave Eldridge a tour round the cottage and took him into the attic where the video cameras were activated automatically and everything was stored on tape. It was the sort of security system that would have been suitable for guarding a President.

"You've done a wonderful job," Eldridge complimented Harry.

"It's got nothing to do with me," Harry confided. "It was already installed before we came. The cottage was occupied by a French couple, friends of Felix, and they put in the security system."

It seemed an astonishing coincidence. Eldridge wondered what had happened to the French couple and how Felix had been able to buy the cottage from them just when he needed it.

They met next morning in a downstairs room that had been converted into a sort of briefing centre. However late they'd been working the night before, whatever else they'd been doing, the daily meetings were a must. Felix insisted that everyone who was part of the inner sanctum should know what was going on. It was all part of his need to make the people around him feel important.

Most of the meeting was taken up with the practical problems of the day, especially how to transport the viruses. It wasn't as simple as it sounded. The damned things thrived in their own humid little universe, but dropped dead as soon as they hit the outside world. Harry organised a transporter with temperature controlled incubators and gas supplies, a sort of ambulance for viruses, to get them safely from the Science Park to Darius's bedside.

The HTLV leukemic virus vials arrived, and Felix Harry and Eldridge marched up to the sick room. The others had been told to stay away, even Persimmon. Harry was nervous. He was carrying the vials like a bomb, avoiding contact with anyone, shielding them from knocks and bumps. He was acting as if the tiniest jolt and the whole thing would explode.

Eldridge led the way, then Harry, then Felix putting himself, as usual, last and least in line. They were like the three wise men bearing gifts, celebrating the new born child. In a way that's what it was all about. Not so much a birth as a resurrection, bringing Darius back from the dead.

Darius was propped up in bed, wearing a Hawaiian shirt with a flowered lei round his neck. Persimmon had been in before the meeting and got him decked up in preparation. She was into the flower symbol for life. Even Darius seemed more animated. Up to now, Eldridge had felt that Darius was going along with it all because he thought it was a way of sustaining Persimmon, as if he knew he was doomed but wanted to give her something to hold on to. But now he seemed wide awake, almost cheerful. He'd even eaten a little breakfast. There was a bowl of half eaten cereal by his bedside table.

Darius tried joking with Eldridge. Darius's sense of humour wasn't Eldridge's cup of tea. He seemed to think that if you swore at someone and called him an "asshole" you were being affectionate.

Eldridge rolled up the sleeve of Darius' Hawaiian shirt, cleaned the side of his arm with an alcohol swab, and took hold of a vial from Harry. Harry gave an audible sigh of relief as he handed it over. Eldridge uncorked it, inserted a needle, and scratched Darius's skin with the inoculum. That's all there was to it.

Next day, Eldridge joined Felix for their visit to Darius. Darius was sitting up in bed as cheerful as could be, a fresh lei around his neck. Persimmon was insisting on the Hawaiian motif throughout the early stages of treatment. Darius proceeded to inform them that when the history of these days came to be written, it wasn't going to be about medical research, or a cure for AIDS, or anything so mundane, it was going to be about the saving of Darius. They were lucky that he was ill, because if he hadn't been ill their lives would have gone nowhere.

The worst of it was that Darius wasn't intending to be rude. In his own idiotic self centred way, he thought he was being friendly, even encouraging. Darius was just telling it the way Darius saw it.

Felix paid Darius no attention whatsoever. Felix was only interested in Darius's body and seemed to have tuned out anything to do with Darius' personality. In his own way Felix was just as much an egoist as Darius.

After Eldridge was done with the examination, he took Felix across the corridor to the nurse's station to have a look at Darius's latest lab reports. Persimmon brought Darius a fresh lei. Her flower symbolism was becoming positively fetishist.

"He seems to be improving," Felix said.

Eldridge was looking at the notes. He didn't answer.

Persimmon came to join them. She was elated, thrilled at Darius's high spirits.

"It must be working," Persimmon said, "I've never seen him so good... not for months."

Eldridge continued reviewing the lab results.

Persimmon's expression became more and more crestfallen as Eldridge failed to respond, refusing to smile or to share in her elation. Felix bent forward to peer at the notes. He was also looking tense and nervous.

"You don't think he's better?" Persimmon asked, almost pleading.

"He feels better," Eldridge said. "Most patients feel better when you tell them they're better. It's called a placebo."

"You mean he's suggestible."

"Sort of... except it really works. If you think you're getting better, something happens in the body which makes you better. The problem about a placebo is that it doesn't last. It's just a temporary blip on a downward spiral."

"He isn't getting better?" She just couldn't believe what Eldridge had told her.

Eldridge paused for a moment, reflecting on what he was going to say. When it came, the answer was brutal and short.

"No."

He showed her the morning's path report. Darius's albumin was down a point. He pointed to the weight chart. Darius's weight was also down, not by much, but it was dropping, and every ounce was a matter of life and death.

"The worst is the CD4 cell count." Eldridge pulled out the haematology report. "Normally there are more than 800 CD4 cells per millilitre of blood. You get AIDS proper when it drops below 200. Death is round the corner when it reaches 50."

"What's Darius's?" Persimmon asked in a whisper.

"Yesterday it was 80. This morning it's 45."

He pointed to the number on the report.

"What about those other numbers?" Persimmon was barely audible.

"We measure the CD4 to CD8 ratio, or in this case the CD4 percentage. It's the percentage of CD4 cells compared to the other white cells in the circulation.

Normally 40% of the lymphocytes are CD4 cells. You start to get really worried when the CD4 cells drop below 15% of the total."

"What's Darius's?"

Persimmon was barely audible. It was a murmur more than a question.

"Yesterday it was 12%. Today it's 8%."

Persimmon didn't bother to look where Eldridge was pointing. She wouldn't have seen anyway. Tears were welling in her eyes.

She gave an excuse about having to get more flowers and left the room. Eldridge didn't see what else he could do except tell her the truth. Either Darius was going to live or he was going to die. Right now the odds were stacked against him, and Persimmon might as well know. He wasn't doing her any favours by pretending otherwise.

"What about the HTLV?" Felix asked.

"I don't think it's taken."

They looked at the path reports on the presence of HTLV protein. There was no sign of it.

"How long should we wait?"

"We've got no time," Eldridge answered. "If we don't get a response in the next few hours he's finished."

"What do you suggest?"

"Let's re-inoculate. A higher titre... a different strain. Let's give him all the strains! We've got nothing to lose."

The rest of the day was taken up in feverish activity. The virus ambulance ferried its passengers between the Science Park and the cottage. Harry became less nervous after two or three trips. He began carrying the vials as if they were ordinary samples, and stopped behaving like they were going to produce a mushroom cloud over the UK.

Darius was puzzled by the first inoculation. He became alarmed when they were repeated. He began to sense their panic. He realised they were becoming desperate. Persimmon changing his lei every few hours didn't help. The placebo effect wore off. He no longer joked when they came into the room. He hadn't the energy to tell them what an important patient he was. He slipped into a dim world of delusional fantasy and inertia. By the time the last inoculation was given in the late afternoon, he didn't stir.

That night Felix dropped Eldridge off at his apartment in the city. Eldridge was exhausted. He went straight to bed. But he couldn't sleep. He tossed and turned. He was anxious about Darius. This time, more than ever, he didn't think he'd see him alive again. He was even more worried about Persimmon, his last vision was her placing yet another fresh lei round Darius' neck, it looked like she was garlanding a corpse. He wondered what would happen to her once Darius disappeared from her life. He wanted Darius to survive for her sake more than anything else.

****

"I've got the latest path report."
"What's it say?"
"It's positive."
"HTLV?"
"Yes."
At last.
The HTLV leukemic virus had taken. It was producing its own proteins. It was replicating inside Darius. They'd given Darius leukaemia. Darius had leukaemia as well as AIDS. Would it do him any good? Or was he going to die twice as fast?
The next six days were the most exciting Eldridge had ever spent in his life.

DAY ONE:

Darius was awake. That was a good sign. He'd been in a virtual coma since the last of the inoculations.
He was abusive. That was a another good sign. It meant he was feeling better.
He was feeling so much better that he was almost rude to Persimmon, not quite, but nearly. She came into the room to replace the lei and he said the usual "dear" and "darling" and he kissed her on the cheek. But he let fly a muttered "more fucking flowers!" which she pretended not to hear.
His high spirits could have been a false alarm, another placebo effect. But when Eldridge got to the office and started reviewing his chemistry, he had the first intimation that something real was happening. His albumin had stopped falling, it had even increased a fraction... back up to 2.1.
"Don't jump to any conclusions..." Eldridge warned. "... It's within the

limits of variability. It doesn't mean anything... one way or the other."

But it did.

DAY TWO

Darius was feeling so much better, he'd become positively hateful. He began screaming abuse as soon as Eldridge entered his room. He needed a pen. He wanted to write to his fans.

The "little people", as he liked to refer to his adoring public, were "pining" for news of him.

The albumin was creeping up. It was now a definite improvement, up to 2.4.

"It's early days," was Eldridge's only comment to Felix, but his hands were trembling with excitement as he said it.

DAY THREE

There'd been a panic in the night. Eldridge had been summoned from his apartment in Cambridge by the young medic on duty. He'd been told Darius was having a massive heart attack.

It turned out to be a false alarm. It was just Darius being Darius.

He'd been shouting at one of the nurses, telling her he wanted to get out of bed and watch a TV programme that was on a late night British TV show. It was showing one of his concerts from last year. During his tantrum he managed to tear out one of his chest leads. Not unnaturally, the computer thought he'd died, and the young medic believed the computer.

Eldridge calmed everyone down. The computer was put back to work. It gave a bleep of protest and then settled down to its task. Eldridge went back to bed, relieved. He felt sorry for the computer left alone with Darius.

Next morning, there was no doubt about the progress. The CD4 count had leapt to 180. There was no change in his weight but the albumin was up above 3.

Persimmon was doubling the rows of flowers on the lei.

Eldridge was still cautious. "Mustn't count our chickens before they're hatched," he said, but he could definitely hear a distant tweeting.

DAY FOUR

This was the day he knew they were winning.

The CD4 count had gone above 200. They were making history.

Felix allowed himself a moment of celebration. He organised a lunch in the city. They were all there, Eldridge, Felix, Harry, Persimmon and Bismarck.

Bismarck had flown in that morning on the charter. The news coming out of Cambridge was too good for him to stay in California. He wanted to be in on the action.

It was Bismarck who monopolised the conversation at the restaurant. He was jubilant, he wasn't stuttering as badly. It was as if Darius' improvement was already bringing him benefit. He regaled them with an account of his "vision", how he'd accepted the responsibilities fate had thrust upon him, and put principle before personal benefit. Felix was lapping up every sanctimonious sentiment like a puppy.

Eldridge was fed up with Bismarck and Felix. He decided to prick Bismarck where it hurt. Eldridge asked him why he'd got involved in AIDS research.

"I've always sided with the untouchables," he replied.

"Before you killed Henry?"

Bismarck's lips disappeared. He was furious. No one had ever challenged him on Henry since the court case.

"I didn't ki.. ki.. ki.. kill him. The un.. un.. unfor.. for.. fortunate young man died from na.. na.. na.. na.. na.. natural causes."

Bismarck suddenly remembered he had an appointment. He called for a cab and left the table.

The atmosphere eased.

Persimmon got up as Bismarck was going out the door. For a moment Eldridge thought she was going to side with her father against him. But she didn't follow Bismarck. Instead she came round the table and gave Eldridge a kiss, smack on his lips. It was partly a way of letting him know she was on his side. It was mostly to say thank you for what he was doing for Darius.

DAY FIVE

Darius was staying true to form. The healthier he became, the more obnoxious his behaviour. He'd got a TV set installed in his room, but that wasn't what he wanted. He wanted to see the old videos of his concerts.

He had a video recorder installed but it was the wrong sort, it showed PAL instead of whatever, and he nearly went berserk.

Darius's weight was up, a hundred and seven pounds, and he was eating like a horse.

Eldridge decided to take down the parenteral feeding line.

"We can always put it up again if..."

He just didn't want to admit they were winning. He was frightened to acknowledge success in case he was being premature. He was terrified of Darius having a relapse.

DAY SIX

They'd won!

Darius's CD4 count had shot up to nearly 400. The CD4 cells were now over 20% of the total. He'd not had a sign of diarrhoea for more than twenty four hours. There was no fever. His albumin was 4.6. And his weight nearly one hundred and ten pounds.

Darius was in such good health he was ranting. He was still going on about his video recorder and how he needed to start practising in front of the cameras again to see how he looked. Eldridge tried to calm him down, to tell him that he shouldn't rush things too much.

When they left his room, Felix looked nervous.

"Is it AIDS dementia?" he asked.

"No."

Eldridge was categorical. He'd done extensive neurological tests, and Darius's brain was untouched by the disease. Eldridge had seen plenty of real AIDS dementia. Darius wasn't demented just agitated and anxious.

"He's on the mend... he knows he is... and he's thinking of the future."

Felix didn't seem reassured.

"He's vain. He used to be a very good looking young man," Eldridge explained. "He doesn't want his public to see him looking like a concentration camp victim. He wants to work on his looks... humour him... and his agitation will disappear. Just give it time."

Famous last words.

DAY SEVEN

And on the seventh day God rested.

It was about three in the morning.

The young doctor tending Darius telephoned Eldridge and told him to come quickly.

Was it another false alarm?

Eldridge rushed to the cottage.

"Give it time," Eldridge had said.

There was no time.

He'd gone.

Darius had disappeared.

CHAPTER EIGHT

LOST TO FOLLOW UP

Felix and Harry were already at the cottage, and were searching up and down and in all the rooms.

The alarm had been raised by the duty nurse. She'd visited Darius at midnight when he'd been asleep, and again at one in the morning when he was awake and in good spirits. He'd even signed one of his albums for the nurse's kid who was a Darius fan. She came back at 2.00 AM and taken his temperature. He'd told her he couldn't sleep and was going to watch some of his old tapes up in the attic where the security system was installed. He'd discovered it had a multistandard video and it could play his US tapes. The nurse thought nothing of it, Darius had done the same thing the night before. Over the last couple of days, as he'd recovered his strength, he'd been encouraged to get out of bed whenever he felt like it. They wanted him back on his feet as quickly as possible. Eldridge had even taken him for a short walk in the gardens the previous afternoon. They'd chatted about the big conference coming up in Venice and how Darius was going to be the star attraction. Darius was keen to co-operate. He'd got it into his head that if he made a personal appearance in Venice he'd end up sharing the Nobel prize with Felix.

Anyway, after the nurse had taken his temperature, she'd gone back to her leisure room to listen to music on the radio. An hour later she went back to his room to give him his shot and take a blood sample. He wasn't there, so she went up the stairs to the attic. The video machine was playing a tape of one of his concerts but he wasn't there. She looked in all the rooms but he wasn't anywhere. At this point she'd begun to panic. She woke up the other nurse and the duty medic and they began a hurried search of the cottage and the grounds. After half an hour with no sign of Darius they decided to summon help. Felix and Harry had arrived just a few minutes before Eldridge.

They spent the next few hours going over every inch of the cottage. Eldridge undertook a search of every shrub and bush in the gardens. Harry rummaged through the study outhouse. Felix organised the others to search through every room, drawer and cupboard in the cottage. Darius was nowhere to be found. He'd vanished into thin air.

Harry sent the two nurses and the young medic home, and joined Eldridge and Felix in the breakfast room. It was about five in the morning. Harry made the coffee. It was just the three of them trying to work out what could have happened.

Felix had a theory that Darius had wandered off into the countryside.

"He's been acting strangely," said Felix, "maybe he forgot where he was and what's been happening. Maybe he's disorientated. He's probably been picked up on the roadside, and right now he's in a local police station or hospital."

Harry put a call through to all the local hospitals and police stations to check up on Felix's theory. He gave a cock and bull story about a young American friend not turning up at a meeting and being concerned in case there'd been an accident. But he drew a blank, nobody matching Darius' description had been brought in.

"I'm sure he'll turn up before the day is out," Felix said, still sticking to his guns.

Harry thought Darius might have gone off to visit Persimmon. Persimmon had stayed with Darius most of the previous evening. She'd left shortly after the nurses changed their watch at about 11.15.

Eldridge phoned her. She was staying at a small hotel in a nearby village. He woke her. She was alarmed.

"Is it Darius?"

"He's fine," Eldridge said, "or at least I think he is."

"Why? What's the trouble?"

"Is he with you?"

"No! Of course not. What's happened?"

She got in her car and was at the cottage in five minutes. She was on the verge of hysteria by the time she reached them.

"He was fine," she said. "He was happy. We'd been talking about his next tour, and how the story of him beating AIDS was going to make it the biggest draw of all time. He wasn't acting up-tight or strange. I just don't believe he suddenly forgot where he was."

"So what do you think has happened to him?" Felix asked.

"He's been kidnapped!"

Persimmon echoed Eldridge's own thoughts. It was exactly what he was thinking. The whole thing sounded fishy. Eldridge didn't buy Felix's theory of Darius suddenly wandering off into the countryside. Eldridge asked Harry if he was absolutely sure of the nurses and the young medic.

"I'm not going to swear to anything," said Harry, "but it just doesn't make any sense. One of the nurses is a mother with three kids, she lives locally. She's lived here for the last twenty years. The other is a friend of my daughter, she's lodging with me while she's doing this job. I've known the young doctor since he was a little kid, my only criticism is that he's a bit of a stick in the mud. None of them fit the bill for being a criminal. Anyway what have they got to gain? Why would they want to kidnap Darius?"

"For a ransom," said Persimmon.

Harry shook his head.

"Nobody's asked for a ransom," said Felix.

It just didn't seem to make any sort of sense.

Their last hope was Bismarck. For the life of him Eldridge couldn't conceive what Darius would be doing with Bismarck, but phoned him just in case at his smart hotel in the centre of Cambridge.

"He's go.. go.. gone?"

Bismarck spluttered out his astonishment at the end of the line. He ordered a cab and joined them at the cottage within the hour.

They were all sitting in the breakfast room. It was seven in the morning. It was like one of those Agatha Christie whodunits where the suspects are gathered before the denouement. But where was Hercule Poirot? More to the point, where was Darius?

One by one, Eldridge reviewed the list of suspects. Cogito ergo sum. It wasn't the narrator. This wasn't a book where the reader can be tricked by a literary device like *The Murder of Roger Ackroyd.* It wasn't Eldridge.

Was it the victim? Was it Darius, like in *Ten Little Indians*, pretending to be dead? Not a chance. Darius was uncomplicated. You get what you see with Darius. His disappearance wasn't of his choosing. He'd been abducted by someone.

But who?

It wasn't Persimmon. She loved Darius. She was hysterical with worry, rummaging through the kitchen gorging herself on anything she could find to solace her anxiety. She wasn't acting.

Harry? Harry was a man of old fashioned virtues. He was honest, truthful, and loyal. He was shocked by Darius' disappearance. He was taking it personally, as though he'd let them all down. It wasn't Harry.

Was it Bismarck?

Bismarck didn't like Darius. He didn't approve of him as a son-in-law. Also, Bismarck was a bona fide killer. Jury or no jury, Bismarck had murdered Henry. But Bismarck had killed Henry because of panic. Bismarck wasn't a cold blooded psychopath. The more Eldridge thought about it the less he liked the idea. Why would Bismarck abduct Darius? Why would he have anything to do with it? Darius didn't matter to Bismarck. Bismarck was too much of an egoist to care about what happened to Darius.

As if to prove his point, Bismarck stopped pretending to show any interest in Darius' whereabouts. After the first few minutes of shock, after the news sank in that Darius had disappeared, he ceased to be concerned. Between occasional bouts of criticising Persimmon for overeating, he spent his time deliberating on how Felix could still go to the Venice Conference.

Bismarck was determined not to let Darius' disappearance spoil their progress. He still wanted Felix to make the announcement about the cure. He didn't want anything so trivial as the disappearance of the principal piece of evidence to hold back their research. He insisted that Felix present Darius' medical records, with or without Darius.

"I can't talk about Darius' condition if I don't know what's become of him," Felix objected.

Felix was totally dejected. The consequence of Darius' disappearance had finally begun to sink in. Felix wasn't in a mood to accept Bismarck's reassurances.

"Doctors don't always know what happens to their patients after they leave their surgery," Eldridge said, supporting Bismarck.

"But I can't use Darius' case records, if I don't know where he is," Felix insisted. "It will look as though he died and I'm covering up."

Was it Felix? Felix was the last person in the world to want Darius out of the way. Darius was living proof of Felix's success. Without Darius, Felix was back to his cats, without any evidence that his cure worked on humans.

"You can say he's been lost to follow up," Eldridge replied.

"Lost to follow up..." Felix echoed his words, weighing them up, not sure about what they meant.

Eldridge caught the barest glimmer of a smile flicker across Felix's face. It lasted hardly a fraction of a second. But in that brief moment it was like a mask slipping, and Eldridge knew he'd said exactly what Felix had planned for him to say. He'd spoken the words like a ventriloquist's dummy. Felix was just pretending that it was Eldridge's idea.

"That's right," Eldridge went on, completing what Felix wanted him to say. "It happens all the time. When doctors don't know what's become of their patients they say they've been lost to follow up..."

"Lost to follow up..."

Felix was repeating Eldridge's words, but Felix didn't need prompting. He knew that you couldn't always trace your patients. There was nothing unusual about doctors having patients who didn't come back. Lost to follow up was how doctors described patients they never saw again. It wasn't unusual. Felix knew it as well as Eldridge. He just wanted Eldridge to say it first.

Felix was pretending to come round to Eldridge's idea, and yet it was Felix who'd planted it. He was manipulating Eldridge, controlling him, plotting and scheming to get him to do his bidding.

Suddenly it became clear as daylight to Eldridge. Felix was mad. Everything was being masterminded by Felix, the cottage, the security system, the French couple. Felix was stark staring raving mad.

It had to be Felix.

Felix had abducted Darius. And Felix was going to kill Darius if he hadn't already done so.

****

Eldridge watched Felix hunch himself ever deeper into the chair opposite Bismarck, pretending to be the very picture of misery. The disappearance of Darius had become Felix's own personal misfortune and he was determined that everyone should know it. Eldridge didn't know the why, the how, or the where of it, but he knew Felix was a killer.

Bismarck was buying Felix's act, hook line and sinker. Even Harry had given up chasing the leads on Darius' whereabouts, and was joining with Bismarck to console Felix. The contrast with Persimmon next door was preposterous. While Bismarck and Harry fussed over Felix, she was in the kitchen cracking eggs, frying bacon, popping toast, hurling herself into a delirium of gluttony in an attempt to assuage her grief. Nobody cared about her. She was just a fat silly girl. The attention was all on Felix.

But for Eldridge the mask had gone, Felix was just a second rate actor. He could see right through him. It was all phoney. He was giving a rotten performance. Now that Eldridge knew he was acting, he could spot the defects. Felix was too miserable, too self effacing. If Eldridge had been directing, he'd have told him to rein it in, it was amateurish and melodramatic. It hardly seemed possible that anyone could be taken in by it, yet Bismarck and Harry were lapping it up, responding to Felix's hammy despair, trying every argument at their disposal to persuade him to go to Venice. Couldn't they see Felix was leading them on?

Eldridge began to piece it together. Felix must have come back to the cottage last night. He'd have no problem getting in. Everyone was asleep or busy in their own rooms. Felix had the codes to all the security devices, he could slip in and out of all the doors and corridors without disturbing anyone. Maybe he'd got to the cottage early enough to spy on the nurse on her last visit to Darius. Maybe he'd overheard

Darius telling the nurse he was going up to watch his video. Perhaps Felix waited until the nurse went back to her room and then followed Darius up to the attic. Then what? Felix waits outside the door to the attic until Darius is settled in front of the TV... Felix opens the door... Felix comes up behind Darius. Perhaps Darius had his headphones on? Perhaps Darius didn't hear Felix stealing into the room behind him?

But why? It was no good speculating, it was time for some amateur sleuthing.

While Persimmon was in the kitchen finishing her gigantic breakfast, and while Felix continued his wretched play acting with Bismarck and Harry, Eldridge made an excuse to leave the room. If Felix did it, there had to be some evidence in the attic.

Eldridge went into the hallway and up the stairs to the landing on the first floor. It was the first time he'd been to the top of the cottage since Darius disappeared. He hurried past Darius' bedroom. He knew he had to act quickly. Maybe Felix had hidden Darius upstairs? While Eldridge had been out looking for Darius in the garden, and Harry had been searching for him in the outhouse study, Felix had had the cottage virtually to himself. He was the only person who'd spent any time in the attic. Darius could be concealed up there with nobody knowing except Felix.

Eldridge punched in the security number to the door that separated the main section of the cottage from the upper floor. He waited for the click, then pushed the door open and stepped up on to the winding stairs that led to the top landing under the thatched roof. The steps were made of old timbered wood. Half way up, there was a loud creak. One of the planks was springy, and creaked under his weight.

He made his way forward, as he imagined Felix had done the previous night. Cautious step after cautious step he climbed the rest of the winding stairs. There were no more creaks. He was able to advance silently. Near the top he bent low. The roof was timbered and sloped down at the sides. The winding stairs came out near the side of the sloping roof so there was barely enough room to pass. He stepped up on to the top landing and the corridor that ran towards the attic room. Two steps forward and he was able to stand upright again. Ahead lay the attic room. Its door was closed. He made his way forward inch by inch. He was moving ever more slowly. He'd become anxious and scared. He dreaded the thought of opening the door, he had a vision of carnage, in his mind's eye he saw a frenzy of butchery, a weird ceremonial, a kind of ritualised death. He imagined Darius' body impaled on a pole, his torso slit from top to bottom, his head skinned bare, two bleeding sockets for his eyes, a skull-like grimace for a smile, his face upturned towards the rafters where his scalped hair lay dangling like a trophy.

Eldridge placed his hand on the handle, pulled it down and pushed. The door swung forward without a sound. He stepped into the attic room.

It was empty. There was no one there.

He calmed himself. He began to breathe more easily. Sun was streaming in through the gabled window in front of him, illuminating the space, chasing away the ghosts. The room was neat and tidy. It was even cosy. It had wall to wall carpeting, with an extra rug, a small North African kilim, between the sofa and the fireplace. There was an armchair next to the sofa, and a long wide sturdy wooden table running the length of the bare red bricked side wall. Stacked on top of the table, along its entire length, lay the paraphernalia for the video security.

Eldridge undertook a systematic search. He looked in all the cupboards and drawers. He still had it in mind that Felix might have killed Darius and stuffed the body in some nook or cranny. He looked behind the bookcase near the door, he opened two old crates which were lying beside the wooden table. He even punched out a hole in the plaster ceiling and pushed his head into the space between the timbered rafters and the thatch, disturbing a family of field mice who scampered off into the thatch. There was nothing except dead leaves and dust and droppings.

Darius wasn't in the attic. Felix had spirited him down stairs and out the cottage. He couldn't have done it in the morning, while everyone was milling around looking for Darius. He must have done it in the night. But how? Did he bash Darius over the head and bundle him out unconscious? Did he kill him? Maybe he'd stabbed him, or strangled him, and carried him out already dead?

Eldridge began a new examination, inspecting everything like he imagined a police forensic scientist would do. He was no longer looking for Darius, just for some hint of violence. He put his head close to the fabric of the sofa and ran his hand along every inch of the cloth feeling for any change in texture. He removed the cushions and the linen coverings of the armchair. He crawled across the carpet with his face inches from the surface. There was no sign of blood. He lifted the kilim rug. The carpet underneath was unmarked. He examined the walls to see if there was anything stuck to the paintwork. He drew another blank. There wasn't even a trace of anything having been cleaned. There was nothing to suggest there'd been a struggle, let alone a murder.

But there was something strange. Everything was much too tidy. Even Darius' headphones were neatly folded away on the bookcase. Felix had been busy while Eldridge and Harry had been out in the garden. He'd had plenty of time to clean up the place and hide away the evidence.

Eldridge sat on the wooden stool and looked at the equipment on the table. Why was it there? Maybe it had something to do with Darius? It was a weird coincidence that Darius should have disappeared just when he was fiddling around with the security video.

Eldridge plugged in the mains supply and turned the system on. There was a large master TV in the centre of the table, and a bank of smaller screens each side of it. Bit by bit the screens came flickering to life. Each small screen was linked to individual TV cameras placed at strategic points in the cottage or the grounds. There was a camera in virtually every room and corridor. Eldridge manipulated the master control, bringing pictures from the small screens on to the main monitor. There was a camera in Darius' bedroom. It showed an empty room and an empty bed. There was a camera in the kitchen. Eldridge watched as Persimmon cleaned up her plates and put them in the dishwasher. The image was so clear he could even see the tears in her eyes as she plopped herself down at the kitchen table and started on a Danish she'd discovered in one of the cupboards.

Eldridge switched to the camera overlooking the front drive. He was able to sweep it from side to side, covering every angle. He saw Felix's red Triumph sports car parked at the base of the Wisteria. Eldridge's own car, a little rented two-door saloon, was right behind. Harry's car was slewed across the middle of the driveway. Harry had been in such a hurry he hadn't parked with his usual care and attention.

Eldridge turned to the cameras at the back of the cottage. He brought up the picture from the outhouse. It showed the entry door, the writing table, and every detail of the study. He could even read the writing on one of the letters on the desk. He surveyed the garden area. He imagined Felix, earlier in the morning, sitting right where he was sitting and watching Eldridge on the monitor. He'd have seen everything that Eldridge was doing out in the garden.

Now it was Eldridge's turn to watch Felix. He switched to the camera in the living room. The large monitor filled with an image of Felix slumped deep in his seat. Harry was sitting on the arm rest beside him, his hand on Felix's shoulder, like a father comforting a son. Bismarck was standing over them, gesticulating wildly. Eldridge fiddled with the knobs on the master control. He found the audio input button and suddenly Bismarck's stuttering voice came through. Bismarck was still trying to persuade Felix to go to Venice. He kept repeating Eldridge's argument that it was not unusual for patients to be lost to follow up. He was repeating it like a mantra, as if he was trying to hypnotise Felix into going. The irony was that Felix had mesmerised him.

Eldridge was sure Darius' disappearance had something to do with the security system. Darius had come to this same exact spot last night to play his video cassette. Maybe that was it? Maybe it had something to do with Darius' cassette? Eldridge turned on the video recorder and pressed the eject button. Nothing came out. The nurse said the video had been left on when she'd come looking for Darius last night. Where was Darius' tape? Why wasn't it in the video?

Eldridge remembered Darius' headphones placed neatly on the bookcase near the door. Had Felix also tidied away Darius' tape? Eldridge looked round the room. There was a row of video cassettes lined up along the top shelf of the bookcase. He took the wooden stool and put it by the bookcase. He stood on it to get up to eye level with the top shelf. The cassettes were numbered and dated, all except one which had no marking. He took the unmarked cassette down and slipped it into the video recorder. Suddenly the big screen was filled with Darius rocking and rolling at his open air concert in Atlanta the year before. It was Darius' tape, the one he'd come up to play. Eldridge turned down the sound. Darius' music wasn't really to his taste.

So that was it. Everything accounted for, everything in its place, and Eldridge no nearer to knowing what had happened.

Or why?

Why did Felix want Darius out of the way? It wasn't blood lust. Felix didn't want Darius dead for dead's sake. On the contrary, Darius' disappearance complicated things terribly for Felix. Darius must have done something awful for Felix to want to get rid of him.

Maybe it had something to do with Darius' tape? Eldridge turned the sound back on and watched Darius and the Dolls gyrating in front of the camera. He scrutinised the backing band and searched through the audience. He was convinced that the concert in Atlanta held the key. Somewhere in this tape was a record of why Felix had to get rid of Darius.

Eldridge scrutinised it for a good half hour. He replayed certain parts. There was a moment when he thought he spotted Felix in the audience. He played the section again and again. He freeze framed the shot. But it wasn't Felix, just a tall lanky Georgian who looked a bit like Felix. Eldridge gave up. There was nothing in the cassette to link Felix and Darius. It was worse than nothing. There was no possible relationship between a Darius concert and Felix. They led different lives. Eldridge was barking up the wrong tree. It couldn't be the Atlanta concert. It had to be something else. Something was staring him in the face and yet he couldn't get it.

As he sat on the wooden stool by the table with the security monitoring device spread out in front of him, an idea began to form in his head. Why all the equipment? Who were the French couple? Why did they have the system installed? Maybe Darius' disappearance had something to do with them?

If it wasn't the Darius tape, maybe it was the other tapes, the tapes stacked up on the top shelf of the bookcase.

Eldridge scrambled back to the bookcase, climbed on the stool, and looked through the cassettes on the top shelf. There were thirty in all, each one dated and timed. They were the security recordings from the time when the French couple had lived in the cottage. That was why the video recorder was there. It recorded from all the cameras and kept a continuous record of what was going on in the cottage. Harry hadn't bothered to use it. He'd told Eldridge he couldn't see any need to keep a video recording of what was happening, he found the whole idea invasive and distasteful. But not the French couple. They'd kept the video recorder going on a daily basis. The dates on the cassettes showed that each tape was a recording lasting 24 hours.

Eldridge took down the tapes and began to play them. It was incredible, it was a chronicle of daily happenings in the cottage. The recordings were recycled on a monthly basis. The thirty cassettes were a record of the last month of the French couple's stay.

Eldridge discovered it wasn't a French couple, it was a whole French family. There were hours and hours of recordings giving minute details of their domestic life. Most of the images were time lapse recordings, but those in the lounge and dining room were in real time with audio input. Eldridge went hurrying through the tapes trying to glean what it was all about. The parents were called Joseph and Martha. They were obviously Jewish, sometimes they spoke French, sometimes Yiddish. Joseph was a small grubby little man who ordered his family around like a patriarch. Martha was a warm round cuddly woman who seemed perpetually in a dither choosing between the demands of her husband and her children. There were three kids, all boys, the youngest with a name like "Yitzach", who was a sweety, and his two brothers, Avram and Samuel.

There was absolutely nothing odd or weird about the family except for one thing. Felix was their only contact with the outside world. Every week or so the camera picked up Felix's sports car turning into the drive, Martha and the kids were there to greet him on the steps. Felix gave them all a kiss. It wasn't in character for Felix to do anything so human as kiss anyone. Was it another bit of play acting by Felix? Anyway after the greetings were over, the camera followed Felix through the cottage, out the back, and down the path of the garden to the study outhouse. It was there that he met with Joseph.

Eldridge wasn't sure what Felix and Joseph were meeting about. There was no audio installed in the study outhouse. He guessed it had something to do with Felix's AIDS research. One time they met in the lounge and Eldridge heard Joseph use the word "SIDA", which he knew was French for AIDS.

There was a specially interesting tape dated Xmas day. Felix had come to lunch. He'd brought presents. There was a talking parrot for Yitzach which Joseph immediately purloined. It kept repeating "First Principles... First Principles" in English throughout the meal. Every time it squawked, Joseph laughed and spluttered over his food. He seemed a charmless boorish sort of man. Eldridge felt sorry for Martha who deserved better. Felix pretended to be amused by it all, but he was play acting. It was obvious he loathed Joseph. But it didn't stop him giving Joseph a present. At the end of the meal Felix presented Joseph with a gift of wine. Then something went wrong, and Felix hurled the wine out the window, smashing the dining room window panes to smithereens. It was as if Felix had gone crazy. Eldridge replayed the scene trying to work out what it was all about. Bit by bit, an idea began to form in his head. It was slow in coming but by the end everything began to make sense.

The wine was poisoned. Felix had intended to kill Joseph.

Eldridge played the scene again and again to be absolutely certain. He watched the part where Felix gave Joseph his present. The wine was already decanted, which meant that Felix had an opportunity to put something in it before he ever came to the cottage. Martha said something about red wine being bad for her stomach. Felix would have known all about that before he came. As for the children, they were too young to drink alcohol and anyway preferred Coke. The wine was going to be drunk only by Joseph and Felix. That was the bit that threw Eldridge. How could the wine be poisoned if Felix drank it? But then he realised it was all part of Felix's scheming, and that he'd managed to protect himself against the poison. Just before he was about to drink the wine, Felix left the dining room and went to the bathroom. The camera didn't follow him. Even the security people had enough propriety not to stick a camera in the toilet. So Eldridge couldn't see what Felix was up to in the bathroom. But he guessed it. Felix had taken an antidote. He obviously thought that if he drank the wine and nothing happened, nobody would suspect his gift was poisoned. And that's what he did. He came back from the bathroom, toasted Joseph, swigged a mouthful of the wine, and waited for Joseph to do the same. And then everything went wrong. Instead of Joseph drinking the wine, he passed it over to Avram to have a sip. That's why Felix had to hurl the wine out the window. He had to get rid of it before Avram touched it. If Avram had been poisoned, the police would have been swarming around investigating everything. So Felix decided to cut his losses and terminate the operation.

Eldridge gave the scene a final play. It was all there. Everything pieced together. He'd watched a murder that had gone wrong.

Eldridge was becoming more tense and more excited. At last everything was beginning to make sense. If Felix had aborted his Xmas day murder, maybe he'd tried again later? Eldridge skipped through the remaining tapes and went straight to the last.

It was a chronicle of pandemonium. All Eldridge could see was Martha rushing round the cottage sobbing and screaming. Felix was there, running after her trying to comfort her. Martha was in black. So were the kids. They were in mourning. Joseph was nowhere to be seen. He must be dead.

Eldridge looked at the date on the last tape. It was two days before he'd flown into London. Now he knew why Felix hadn't been able to meet him. Felix had been at a funeral all right, the funeral of Joseph, the funeral of the man he'd murdered.

Eldridge skipped back to the second last tape. This had to be it. This had to have the scene where Felix killed Joseph.

It was just an ordinary day. There was no sign of Felix. It was the usual scene of the family, Martha in the kitchen and Joseph scribbling away at his desk in the outhouse at the bottom of the garden.

Eldridge didn't understand. The tapes were a continuous record. Joseph couldn't have just vaporised into thin air. Eldridge looked at the date on the tape. There was a day missing.

Suddenly it came blindingly in on him. A missing day meant a missing tape, a tape with a murder, a tape which showed Felix killing Joseph.

And now the pieces were all in place. The jigsaw was complete.

Darius must have stumbled across the missing tape while he was up in the attic. He must have played it and witnessed the scene where Felix kills Joseph. Darius had become a witness to murder.

And Felix must have found out about Darius and the missing tape. That's why he'd disposed of both of them.

Eldridge's heart was beating more and more rapidly, ideas were rushing through his mind. He was barely able to keep track of his own thoughts.

Everything was happening so fast, he didn't hear the creak.

****

There'd been a creak.

In the background of Eldridge's mind it registered that someone had put their weight on the step which creaked.

It came from the winding stairs. Someone was coming up the stairs to the attic.

Eldridge switched on the security cameras. He scanned the kitchen. Persimmon was no longer there. He tuned to the sitting room. She was standing by the fireplace, tears streaming down her face. Bismarck was scolding her from the armchair. There was no sign of Harry or Felix. He tuned to the front drive. Harry was out there in his car, parking it carefully by the side of the kitchen. He scanned the drive to see if Felix's sports car was still there. It was. It was still parked under the Wisteria.

Where was Felix?

Eldridge scanned the garden, the outhouse, the first floor. Felix was nowhere to be seen.

Where was Felix?

But he knew where he was, he didn't need to look.

It was his foot that had stepped on to the creaking step. He'd crept up the attic stairs. He was standing in back of Eldridge, just like he'd stood behind Darius last night.

The hairs on Eldridge's neck bristled. He could feel Felix right behind him.

He heard a slight movement. A knife being drawn?

Eldridge turned.

It was Felix. He was towering over Eldridge, a poker in his hand, he'd picked it up from the fireplace in the dining room. Felix was blushing. His face was bright red, it was almost glowing. He knew Eldridge knew. Felix tightened his grip on the poker, his arm half raised, ready to kill.

Eldridge didn't make a move, just stared at him, like a cat waiting for the other to pounce.

Felix froze. He was weighing up what to do. Even with the poker in his hand, he wasn't sure. Eldridge was stronger than him. Maybe he'd get the poker away from him?

Eldridge let him think. Eldridge wanted to give him time to ask some questions. Even if he bludgeoned Eldridge to smithereens, how was he going to dispose of the corpse?

Felix blushed more furiously.

Eldridge wanted Felix's tortured mind to weigh things up, to realise Eldridge didn't know anything for sure, didn't have any proof, couldn't do him any harm... not yet.

Eldridge saw his grasp on the poker easing, his arm begin to drop.

Bit by bit Felix's arm came down and rested by his side.

It was like the Xmas party with Joseph. Felix had decided to abort the murder, to save it for another day.

Felix turned to leave.

"I've accepted your idea," he said from the doorway. "I've decided to go to Venice."

And he walked out the attic room and down the stairs as if nothing had happened.

****

Eldridge heard the creak as he went down the winding stairs. The security camera picked him up striding past Darius' bedroom. It followed him as he went along the landing and down the next flight of stairs. The camera in the dining room swivelled as he crossed in front of it, and it zoomed in on him as he stooped in front of the fireplace to put the poker back in the grate. The camera in the hallway tracked him as he made his way to the living room. The camera in the living room caught him as he came through the door.

Eldridge panned the camera across the living room. Persimmon was sitting on the sofa. Harry was standing by the patio windows. He'd got back from parking his car and was standing next to Bismarck. They were listening to Felix. Eldridge turned the camera back to Felix, fiddled with the audio and picked up his final remark.

"Kwanza insists I go to Venice."

Eldridge caught him glancing at the camera. He knew Eldridge was watching. Was it nervousness? Was it defiance?

Bismarck crossed the room and slapped Felix on the shoulder. It was the first time Eldridge had seen him touch anybody. Harry shook his hand, Harry still believed everything Felix told him. They followed him out to his car, leaving Persimmon alone in the living room, still sobbing, all by herself.

Eldridge switched to the camera in the driveway and watched Felix get into his sports car. Bismarck joined Harry in his car. Felix started up his engine and swept out the driveway. Bismarck and Harry followed close behind.

It was just Persimmon and Eldridge alone in the cottage.

Eldridge turned off the security cameras and went down the stairs to join her.

She was in the living room. She hadn't moved. She was sitting on the sofa like a crumpled sack, abandoned by father and friends.

Eldridge sat beside her and gave her a great big hug. She fell into his arms sobbing and wailing. She just couldn't contain her grief. She clung on to him, like a five year old.

She buried her face in his neck. He could feel the dampness of her tears as they soaked through his shirt and onto his shoulder. He tried to put his arms round her, but she was just too large, and he couldn't get them more than half way round. It was like comforting a whale. Eventually he couldn't breathe and had to push her off him. He went into the kitchen and got hold of some paper towels. He brought them back and wiped her face and dried her eyes.

He decided to tell her everything. If anybody in the world was going to believe him, it was Persimmon. As soon as Eldridge began to tell his story she stopped crying. She stared at him with her eyes wide open, hanging on to his every word. He started with his first suspicion, and his decision to investigate the attic. He described the way in which he'd stumbled onto the tapes. When he got to the part about the funeral of Joseph and the missing tape her mouth dropped open in astonishment. When he told her about Felix creeping up behind him and standing over him with a poker in his hand, she half raised her arm as though trying to protect Eldridge.

Eldridge told her everything he knew. He laid out his every doubt and misgiving. He ended by telling her that he was sure Felix had kidnapped Darius.

Persimmon was transformed. She ceased to be a fat blubbery sponge. Now that she'd been given an explanation for what had happened, she became much calmer. She trusted Eldridge. She had no trouble believing Felix was a fake and an impostor. She'd always suspected that he was using Darius to advance his own career. But she didn't care about Felix or his motives. There was only one thing that mattered for her... Darius.

"Do you think he's alive?" She asked.

"I don't think Felix killed him up in the attic. I'd have found blood or something. Felix probably hit him over the head and bundled him out of the cottage unconscious."

"But still alive?"

"Maybe."

"Where to?"

"I don't know. I don't think Felix had any of this planned. The discovery of the tapes was probably as much of a surprise to Felix as to Darius. If Felix had known anything about them, he'd have got rid of them long before he ever gave us the cottage."

"He wasn't expecting to find Darius up in the attic?"

"The way I see it," he said, "is that Felix visited Darius yesterday afternoon on one of his regular routine visits. He wasn't thinking about the attic or the tapes or anything except Darius' state of health. Then, in casual conversation, Darius mentions about how he'd being playing around with his cassette the previous night. He may have told Felix about the pile of other tapes up there. Maybe Darius had already looked at some of them and told Felix what he'd seen, or maybe Darius hadn't looked at any of them. Whatever it was, something set alarm bells ringing in Felix's head. Felix suddenly realised there were tapes up there, and he'd have guessed what they were, and that one of them showed him murdering Joseph."

"But if Darius hadn't seen anything, why did Felix need to kidnap him?"

"Probably just bad luck. Felix decided to get hold of the tapes and smuggle them out before Darius or anyone else could take a look at them. He came back in the middle of the night, but he was too late. Darius was up there again. So Felix had to wait for Darius to finish watching his concert. But instead of going down to his room, Darius started to fiddle around with the other tapes and play some of them. Felix waited and watched. When Darius stumbled on the murder scene, Felix had to act. He was probably standing right behind Darius."

"And hit him over the head?"

"And bundled him out of the cottage taking the murder tape with him."

"Where to?"

It dawned on both of them at the same time. If Felix hadn't planned to kidnap Darius, there was only one place to take him... Felix's house in town.

They raced out the cottage. Eldridge jumped into his car and started it up. Persimmon came galloping after. She couldn't get into the passenger seat. It was a small car and her bottom spread over the gear shift making it impossible for Eldridge to drive. In the end she got out the car, slid the passenger seat forward, and put herself into the back.

Eldridge slammed his foot on the accelerator and sped out the drive heading for Cambridge. They had to get to Felix's house before Felix. There was a chance Darius was still alive. Things were happening fast, but they were happening just as fast for Felix. Maybe Felix hadn't killed Darius. Not yet. Maybe he hadn't had time to work out how to get rid of him.

Eldridge raced into the city, past the red bricked Edwardian houses in the suburbs. He ignored the speed limits, jumped the red lights. He didn't care about being followed by the police. He'd probably need them by the time they got to Felix's house.

There was nobody about. It was a Sunday morning. Most people were having a lazy breakfast at home. There was virtually no traffic. An elderly gentleman, walking his dog along a wide tree lined pavement, wagged an admonishing finger as they sped past.

Eldridge screeched to a halt in front of a small common. It was a bit like a village green. On one side was a charming crescent with a terrace of Georgian town houses. Felix's house was on the end. There was no sign of his sports car. He hadn't come and gone, there hadn't been enough time. He'd probably driven straight to the Science Park from the cottage, and was busy planning his Venice trip with Harry and Bismarck.

Eldridge parked in front of Felix's house. He jumped out and went round to the passenger door to unplug Persimmon.

They stood looking at the house. It was a two story narrow building, probably no more than four small rooms. Eldridge had no idea of its layout, Felix had never invited him inside. In the early days, when they'd been negotiating the partnership deal with Trust, Eldridge had often dropped him back home after a hard day at the office. But Felix never invited Eldridge in, not even for a drink.

The front door gave onto the pavement. Persimmon went straight up to it, and pressed the bell. There was a tiny little tinkle from the hallway and then dead silence. Persimmon waited a moment and then hammered on the knocker.

"He's not at home," Eldridge said.

"There may be a cleaner."

"It's Sunday."

"Or a lover."

Felix kept his private life top secret, but Eldridge didn't think he had a lover.

Persimmon hammered again and again on the knocker. After each go, she stopped and put her ear against the door to catch any sound coming from inside the house. She was listening for a noise, however faint, coming from Darius.

The blows from the knocker resounded round the common. They could be heard in every house along the crescent. Eldridge noticed an occasional net curtain being pulled to one side and the odd shadowy face appearing at a neighbour's window. But no one came out to ask what they were doing. The English are a reserved race, especially on a Sunday morning.

"We'd better break in," he said.

There was no way in through the front. The door was thick and unyielding. The ground floor front room was shuttered, and they needed a ladder to get to the first floor.

They went round to the side of the house. It was on the edge of a small path beside some waste land leading down to a canal. There was a tiny fan light at ground level, barely big enough for a child to get through and nothing else. Eldridge climbed the wooden fence leading to the back of the house. Persimmon watched through a crack in the woodwork.

Eldridge found himself in a small patio, with wild plants along the borders like a herb garden. It was completely secluded. The slope of the crescent meant that the back of the neighbouring houses were out of eye shot of Felix's garden.

Eldridge had hoped for a back room like at the cottage with easy to open French doors. But it wasn't anything like the cottage. At ground level there was a stout wooden door which probably gave off the kitchen. The principal back room was shuttered, just like at the front. Eldridge needed some sort of battering ram to break through.

The only way in was through the first floor bedroom window. But how to get up there? There was a small shed at the bottom of the patio. Eldridge rifled through it to see if there was anything that could serve as a ladder. It didn't have anything except for trowels and weed killers and gardening junk.

Eldridge needed Persimmon to help. He tried unbolting the fence door to let her through to the back, but it was padlocked. He climbed back over the fence and joined her the other side. The fence was only four foot something but she was just too big to climb over. He tried pushing while she pulled. He put his shoulder under her bottom and heaved. It was like a Laurel and Hardy movie. She kept slipping off his shoulder. There was so much of her he just couldn't find any point of leverage. Eventually she managed to get one foot level with the top of the fence and Eldridge gave a mighty heave. She went crashing over to the other side, bringing the fence down on top of her. Eldridge crawled over towards her. It was a shambles. They lay in each other's arms giggling like two naughty schoolchildren.

It took them a couple of minutes to regain their composure. Persimmon was half crying half laughing. The stress of knowing Darius was nearby made her almost hysterical.

Eldridge got her to her feet, and they went round to the back of the house. He found a brick in the garden shed and stuck it into his jacket pocket. Now the tables were turned and it was Persimmon's job to support him while he tried to climb up to the first floor window and smash his way in. She put herself under the first floor window near a drainpipe. She braced herself with her back against the wall of the house. She clasped her hands in front of her. He placed his foot into her cupped hands, grabbed hold of the drain pipe and hauled himself up. He could feel her arms trembling under his weight. But she was a strong girl and absolutely determined. She held firm. Fortunately it was a genuine Georgian house with low ceilings. Eldridge managed to grasp on the bedroom window sill. It relieved some of the strain off Persimmon.

But he was stuck. He just wasn't high enough to break the window and clamber inside. He needed another two feet.

It was probably the thought of Darius that gave her the strength. Suddenly Eldridge found himself rising in the air. Persimmon was raising him up like a weight lifter doing a snatch and lift. Eldridge let go of the window sill and grabbed the brick from his pocket. He smashed the window. He could feel her arms trembling. She was about to let go. He hurled himself at the gap in the window. Persimmon gave a scream of relief as he tumbled into the room.

The bedroom was empty.

Eldridge ran from room to room opening doors looking in cupboards. It was a tiny house. It took only a few seconds. Darius wasn't there.

Eldridge unbolted the kitchen door and let Persimmon in. She rushed through the house.

CHAPTER 8: LOST TO FOLLOW UP

Eldridge was in the downstairs living room, she was upstairs, when he heard her give a yell.

"Come quickly," she screamed.

Eldridge ran up the narrow stairs to the front bedroom. She had the cupboard open and was throwing out clothes.

"There's something behind," she said. "It's like a secret panel."

She was right. There was a space behind the back panel of the cupboard. It was about eighteen inches deep, just enough room to hide a body. The back panel was a concealed door. It had a tiny keyhole.

Eldridge went back to the kitchen and brought up as many knives and implements as he could find. He began hacking away at the panel.

Persimmon threw herself on to the bed and began beating at the bed clothes. She'd become desperate. She dreaded discovering what was behind the secret panel.

It was hard work. It took Eldridge an age to make a hole big enough to see through.

Then Eldridge saw him. Through the gap, he saw Darius. He was strung up like a dummy. He was dangling from a clothes peg like a piece of dead meat, his long hair cascading down his back.

Eldridge hacked away at the panel. Persimmon lay on the bed hardly breathing. She sensed what Eldridge had discovered. She didn't want to come and look. She knew without seeing.

Finally Eldridge made a hole large enough to get his hand through. He tore away at the panel. He broke and splintered the wood. He reached forward and grabbed hold of Darius. As Eldridge managed to drag him free, he heard a scream in his ear.

Eldridge stopped, he became rigid with fear. The scream terrified him. Then he realised it was him. It was Eldridge. Eldridge was screaming.

Darius had disintegrated in his hand!

****

It wasn't Darius. Eldridge had pulled out a wig. There was nothing behind the secret panel except clothes and artefacts. Eldridge thought he'd got hold of Darius' head, but it was just a long chestnut wig.

He stopped screaming. He braced himself, forcing himself to get over the shock. His hands were trembling. He fished out everything from behind the panel. It was a hidey hole stuffed full with grotesquery.

He took out a whalebone corset, and a set of handcuffs, and black silk stockings, and bondage straps, and ebony candles and women's panties. He brought out reams of latex and black leather. He'd discovered a stash of Felix's clandestine possessions, a sort of treasure chest of furtive fetish gear. It was the wig that threw him. He thought he'd grabbed hold of Darius' head, but it turned out to be just a moth eaten piece of old junk, a theatrical hair piece.

He sat on the bed with Persimmon and stared at the collection on the floor. They didn't speak, just sat and stared, horror and relief mingling in their heads.

The objects obviously belonged to Felix. They must have stumbled across Felix's pet perversion. He probably dressed himself up as a woman and had someone come round to whip him while he was bound up. Or maybe the other way round, and he whipped them. Whichever, whatever, it was pathetic.

But they weren't interested in Felix's fantasies.

Where was Darius?

****

"The Science Park," said Persimmon.

She was already running down the stairs.

She was right. If Felix hadn't brought Darius to his home, he must have taken him to the office. Eldridge cursed himself. He should have guessed it when they'd arrived at the house and seen that his car wasn't there. Felix would never have left Eldridge to look through his home if Darius had been there.

Eldridge ran after Persimmon. She'd already stuffed herself into the back seat by the time he got to the car. Eldridge was about to get into the driver's seat when he stopped and turned. He went back to the house and up to the bedroom. He grabbed hold of some of the objects from Felix's secret cache. He picked up the black silk panties with the leather zipper at the crotch, the vermilion lipstick, and the handcuffs.

"Why?" asked Persimmon, after he'd returned to the car and set off for the Science Park.

Eldridge didn't reply. He was trying to get his thoughts together, preparing for the confrontation that awaited him. He imagined the scene; Felix deep in conversation with Harry and Bismarck; Eldridge and Persimmon bursting in on them; Eldridge denouncing Felix as a murderer and kidnapper; Felix smiling sweetly; Bismarck scowling; and Harry ordering the men in white coats to cart Eldridge and Persimmon off to the funny farm.

"Why?" She asked again.

"Credibility," Eldridge replied.

CHAPTER 8: LOST TO FOLLOW UP

Felix's sex habits had nothing to do with him being a murderer, but it certainly dented his image. Right now it was his word against Eldridge. By bringing along his fetish items, Eldridge would raise enough doubts about his sanity to be taken seriously.

They entered the Science Park, and drove past the other businesses. There was hardly any one about. Eldridge drew into the car park for Therapeutic Pathogens. The first thing he noticed was that Felix's red Triumph sports car was sitting in its space marked "President", Harry's car was parked alongside in the space marked "General Manager". There were also lots of bikes about. It looked as though Harry had called a crisis meeting.

Eldridge helped Persimmon out the back seat. They walked up the ramp to the front entrance. Eldridge made straight for Felix's office. Persimmon followed. She didn't know the layout of the offices, she'd spent all her time with Darius up at the cottage.

Eldridge opened the door to Felix's office. There was no one there. He moved on to Harry's office. The door was open. Harry was sitting at his desk with about twenty of his team pushing and shoving to get into the room. Harry was sending them off on search parties to find Darius. He was giving his final orders. Eldridge waited with Persimmon outside the room until Harry had finished. He wanted him alone.

Harry ordered one group back to the cottage to search the fields and lanes. He sent another to scour all the hospitals, police cells, and hostels in the County. The last group was sent to enquire at the hundreds of bed and breakfasts scattered across the Cambridgeshire countryside.

The last group departed, and Harry was left alone with Eldridge and Persimmon. Casually Eldridge asked about Felix's whereabouts. Harry said that Felix had left the Science Park. He'd driven Bismarck back to his hotel to help him collect his bags for the trip to Venice.

Eldridge was in a hurry. But he didn't tell Harry anything about his suspicions. He didn't want hours of explanation, and he didn't want incomprehension. He wanted to get on with finding Darius as quickly as possible.

"Why don't we have a look around Therapeutic Pathogens?" Eldridge suggested.

"You think Darius might be here?", answered Harry, obviously astonished by Eldridge's suggestion.

"It's a possibility", broke in Persimmon. "Darius knows all about this set up. Maybe he got it into his head to come here and see it for himself."

"But why would he be hiding?"

"Perhaps he's fallen asleep somewhere. Or he could have got himself locked up in one of the labs or storage units and can't get out."

Harry shrugged his shoulders, puzzled by the idea, but he was prepared to give it a go. There was nothing to lose by having a quick look through the place.

They began to search the offices and the labs. Eldridge made sure Harry took them to all the cold rooms and freezer depots. He had it in mind that Felix might dump Darius in a cold storage unit until he got a chance to dispose of him. Each time Harry opened a sealed room, Persimmon gave a little gasp. It was like when Eldridge was hammering at the secret panel, she was expecting the worst at every moment.

After a while Harry began looking at them strangely. Eldridge could tell his mind was changing gear. At first he thought they were hysterical, chasing after chimera. But bit by bit he began to realise something was up. They were too expectant to be on a wild goose chase.

They'd completed the search of the animal houses and were crossing the car park on the way to the virology lab when they were approached by one of the van drivers.

"Where's my van?" the driver asked Harry.

"Felix took it," Harry answered.

It was like when he was at the movies. Eldridge's mind's eye darted from cut to cut. First a close up on Harry, then a pan across the car park, finally a zoom in on Felix's little red Triumph sports car still parked in the spot marked "President".

"You told me Felix had gone to Bismarck's hotel," Eldridge said.

"Yes," said Harry.

Eldridge's eyes were focused on Felix's little red Triumph sports car. What a fool he'd been! It had been there all the time, but he hadn't asked the obvious question.

"Why's his car still here?"

"Felix drove Bismarck off in a van," said Harry. "He said he needed something bigger to carry Bismarck's luggage."

Eldridge did a quick flash back to last night. Of course Felix hadn't driven to the cottage in his own car. He'd taken a van. He'd been expecting to cart out the videos and God knows what else from the attic. He'd taken a van in case his car was too small. That's where he'd put Darius! He'd bundled him into the back of the van. He'd left him there all night. Darius was in the back of the van right now.

"When will Felix be back?" Eldridge asked.

"He should have got back by now."

That's why Felix had come straight to the Science Park. He had to get to the van before Eldridge. He had to drive it away, before Eldridge had the chance to find Darius stuffed in the back.

Eldridge led Harry to his office. He sat him down in his easy chair and told him the whole story. Persimmon interrupted from time to time, to fill in the details. She was calm and rational. Eldridge wasn't sure if Harry believed. He didn't say a word. Eldridge could tell he was struggling to find alternative explanations for what had happened.

Eldridge took Harry through to the end; he told him how they'd broken into Felix's house and discovered the secret panel. When he got to the part about the fetish paraphernalia, he laid the objects he'd brought with him on the table. Harry didn't like to see them. He was distressed. Eldridge put them back in his pocket.

"What do we do now?" Harry asked.

"Find the van," Eldridge said.

"You think Darius is in the back of the van?"

"Yes."

Harry picked up the phone and telephoned to Bismarck's hotel.

It was a quick conversation. He spoke with the concierge. Bismarck had checked out half an hour ago.

Harry sat at his desk, stroking his chin. He was finding it more and more difficult to cope with the situation. Felix should have returned long ago.

"We have to call the police," Eldridge said.

Harry shook his head. He sat frozen at his desk. He wasn't in the business of reporting his boss to the police.

"I'll call them if you won't."

Eldridge walked over to the phone by the window. There was a red light flashing. Harry jumped up.

"Wait," Harry said. "There's a message!"

While they'd been out looking for Darius, someone had phoned in and left Harry a message.

"It may be Felix," Eldridge said.

Harry pressed the play button and sure enough the voice of Felix came out of the tape. It was a long rambling message, something about Bismarck having to meet someone on the Continent, something else about Felix needing to get to Venice in time to prepare for his talk.

The long and the short of it was that Felix had set off for Venice in the van with Bismarck as his passenger.

****

They spent the next few minutes arguing, trying to work out a plan of action. The trouble was they couldn't agree on anything.

Harry was convinced that they had got it all wrong about Felix. He conceded that some strange things had happened, but he refused to jump to conclusions. As far as he was concerned, there was no evidence linking Felix to Darius' disappearance.

"It's all guess work," he pointed out.

Also Harry didn't think there was anything odd about Felix deciding to set off for Venice. He wasn't prepared to accuse Felix of anything on the basis of what Eldridge had told him, let alone find him guilty.

"You've no proof he's done anything," Harry insisted.

Persimmon was all for calling the police and getting them to stop the van.

"We've got to find the van," she pleaded. "Darius could still be alive."

Eldridge sided with Persimmon of course, except for one thing. He felt sure the police would agree with Harry. Eldridge had no evidence. The police wouldn't buy his story. They might even try to stop Eldridge from doing anything on his own.

They were arguing backwards and forwards. For Eldridge, it was like being in a nightmare when you see yourself hurtling towards a precipice but you're paralysed and can't avoid the disaster.

Eventually it was Persimmon who broke the spell.

"Let's follow him," she said.

"Who?" Harry asked.

"Felix."

"Where to?" Eldridge asked.

"Venice."

"Who says he's going to Venice?" Eldridge said. As far as Eldridge was concerned, Felix was a liar, his message was a load of junk. He could be doing anything, going anywhere.

"He's got Dad with him", said Persimmon. "He's not going to abduct Dad as well as Darius. He's got to act normal. If he said he's taking Dad to Venice, I think that's exactly what he's doing."

Eldridge was about to snap back a reply. But he stopped as it dawned on him that Persimmon was absolutely right. Felix hadn't planned any of this. He was improvising, plotting and scheming to stay ahead of them. He was probably as panicked as Eldridge and Persimmon. It made sense for Felix to drive Bismarck down to Venice. It kept him in charge of the van, and gave him the opportunity to dump Darius en route, at a stop-over while Bismarck was out of sight. That way he'd get rid of all the evidence against him. Without the tape and without Darius, there'd be no proof of anything. He'd arrive in Venice with a clean slate.

Harry liked Persimmon's suggestion, but for different reasons. He wanted them to find the van. It would clear everything up, once and for all. If Darius was in the back of the van, so be it. But if Darius wasn't there, then Felix was innocent, just like Harry firmly believed.

"Can we catch him?" Eldridge asked.

Harry took them through to the seminar room. There was a map of Europe hanging from the wall. The route to Venice was pretty straight forward, down to the South Coast of England, across the channel, through France, and into Italy. But there were lots of options. Tunnel or ferry? Paris or Reims? Mont Blanc or Monte Carlo? More to the point, where was Felix going to stop?

Felix wouldn't drive to Venice in one hop, nor would he want to. He'd persuade Bismarck to stop at a hotel somewhere for the night. That would give him his opportunity to dump Darius. Felix would wait for Bismarck to go to bed, then he'd steal out the hotel and drive the van to some lonely spot in the countryside. He'd bury Darius in a field, then back to the hotel, a good night's sleep, breakfast with Bismarck and on to Venice, with nobody the wiser.

Persimmon saw Eldridge struggling with his thoughts.

"We have to go after them now," she said. She was thinking exactly like Eldridge. They'd already spent too much time debating. Felix had barely an hour's start, and he was driving a slow van. They could catch him, if they set off right away.

Harry marked out their best route on the map. They'd drive down to Folkestone, and take the shuttle through the channel tunnel. After that they'd take the motorway from Calais to the junction near Lille.

"You'll catch up with him long before he branches off for Paris or Reims," Harry said.

Harry promised to call Eldridge if he received any messages from Bismarck or Felix. Eldridge knew Harry would be true to his word. Harry wasn't a liar. Anyway he wanted them to find Felix. He was as keen to see Felix cleared as they were to see him caught.

Harry escorted them to the car park. He pointed out a cream coloured Ford van, sitting near one of the loading bays.

"It's identical to Felix's van," Harry said.

"Same colour?" Eldridge asked.

"Everything except the licence plate."

Harry wrote down Felix's number and gave it to Eldridge, "P 628 GMT."

Persimmon got into the back seat of Eldridge's car. Eldridge started it up and they waved Harry goodbye. He was their friend, he just hoped they were wrong.

The first stop was to collect Persimmon's passport from her room in the small hotel near the cottage. Eldridge always kept his on him. Next they drove to Stansted. It was on their way to the South Coast. It was Sunday, but the airport car hire was open and Eldridge wanted to change his car. He needed a new car, one with more power, one that would beat the van as far as speed was concerned. Also, he needed a large limousine so that Persimmon could sit up front with him without spreading out all over the gear shift. It was going to be a long journey. They might as well be comfortable.

He swapped his compact for a Mercedes. It was the same model George used to drive Bismarck. They left the airport and sped down the motorway towards the south coast ports. Eldridge switched on the radio and tuned into the local stations. After about an hour, as they were by-passing Canterbury, they picked up a station broadcasting a Darius track. Eldridge noticed the tears welling up in Persimmon's eyes, he slipped his hand across, she took hold of it, he gave her a squeeze.

As they neared the channel tunnel Eldridge spotted a van up ahead going at top speed weaving and threading its way through the slower traffic. He got a bit closer and saw it was the same make and colour as Felix's van, but it had a different registration.

"Felix could have changed the licence plates," said Persimmon.

They decided to check it out. Eldridge put his foot hard down on the accelerator and in a minute they were right up behind it. Eldridge was preparing to overtake when it veered left and took a slip road off the motorway. Eldridge followed. They drove nose to tail for about five miles down winding roads. It eventually stopped at some traffic lights in a village. Eldridge drew up alongside. He looked at the driver, an Indian, he didn't look anything like Felix.

They raced back to the motorway. Chasing after the wrong van had put them back twenty minutes. Eldridge guessed Felix was already out the other end by the time they set off on the channel tunnel shuttle.

They arrived in Calais and were waved through French customs with barely a glance at their passports. They made for the motorway. At first there were hardly any cars. It was flat dreary countryside, and they sped along the route between Calais and the junction with the A1 near Lille. Eldridge kept his eyes peeled on the road ahead. He was going fast. He half expected to see Felix's van at every bend and turn.

They were just nearing the junction for Paris when Persimmon gave a scream.

"There they are!"

She'd seen a van. It was a Ford, and it was cream coloured.

Eldridge got closer and was able to read the registration.

"P 628 GMT."

They'd found him. It was Felix's van.

They'd caught him just as he was switching to the right to join the traffic on the A1 heading for Paris.

Eldridge followed. The new motorway was jammed with traffic. Eldridge wasn't able to maintain his speed. Felix was about a hundred yards ahead. But Eldridge wasn't worried. Now he had him in his sights there was nowhere for Felix to go except straight ahead.

"We'll get him when he stops at the toll booth at the end of the motorway," Eldridge said to Persimmon.

"Can't you stop them right now?" she pleaded. She was biting her lip. The idea of waiting another hour or so before freeing Darius was too much for her to stomach.

"If I get a clear run, I'll push them off the road."

But there were too many cars and lorries. It was the main Paris-Brussels highway and they were all going at the same speed with every lane packed with traffic. There was no way of edging Felix off the road without causing a multiple pile up.

Eldridge followed the van. Twenty minutes later they passed the turn off for Peronne and the traffic suddenly eased. They were alone on the motorway, just two lorries between Eldridge and the van half a mile ahead.

Eldridge put his foot hard down on the accelerator. He hurtled along the motorway. He overtook the two lorries and was coming up fast on the van. He was just about to pull alongside when there was a blast in his ear.

It was a siren.

Two motorbike cops had crept up on him and were signalling for him to stop.

"Shit!" He banged the steering wheel in exasperation and pulled off into the service lane.

It seemed to take an age while the cops parked their bikes, removed their leather gloves, adjusted their helmets and came lumbering slowly towards them.

"Tell them what's happened," said Persimmon. "They'll understand. They'll help us."

Fat chance. It took forty minutes before they could extricate themselves. The cops were bored and cynical. Also, they didn't like a black man driving a fancy car. Eldridge had to go through the whole procedure, passport, driving license, issue of speeding fine. When the cops threatened to take Eldridge back into Peronne and keep him in custody until the fine was paid, Eldridge decided to cut his losses, pay the massive fine with a credit card, and get on with the chase.

They got back on the road to find it jammed with traffic. Also the two cops stayed right behind on their motorbikes, eager to pounce if Eldridge exceeded the 130 km/hour speed limit again. Eldridge ended up driving towards Paris at the same speed as every other vehicle on the road.

It took nearly two hours. Eldridge slipped into the queue of traffic at the toll booth, and the two traffic cops departed. There were lots of booths. Eldridge strained to see if Felix's van was anywhere to be seen. Persimmon wound down her window and paid the toll charge with her credit card. The Mercedes was a right hand drive for UK driving, and the toll machines were on the left, on her side.

Eldridge pulled into a petrol station and refuelled. He gave Harry a call.

"Where are you?" he asked.

"Just outside Paris."

"And Felix?"

"We saw him, but we got stopped by the cops before we could do anything. Now he's a good hour ahead of us, probably well past Fontainebleau."

"Will you catch him?"

"It depends on the traffic... and the French police."

"Good luck."

Eldridge skirted Paris on the périphérique and set off along the A6 in the direction of Lyons. Once he had passed Orly the traffic eased and he put his foot flat down on the accelerator. He decided to ignore being stopped by traffic cops. He had nothing to lose. He wasn't going to catch Felix any other way.

They sped past Sens and Auxerre and Avallon. The clear Spring sun illuminated the wine bearing hills of the Burgundy countryside and the vineyards of the Côte d'Or. Eldridge pointed out to Persimmon the famous names like Chambertin and Meursault and Nuits Saint Georges.

A couple of hours after leaving Paris, they approached Macon and the turn off for Geneva. Eldridge wasn't sure. Maybe Felix was still up ahead? Maybe he'd stopped for lunch with Bismarck, and was now behind them?

"Keep going," said Persimmon.

It was the toss of a coin.

Eldridge continued as fast as he could along the A40 towards the Mont Blanc tunnel and the Italian frontier.

If he hadn't been so preoccupied with looking out for the van it would have been a great drive. The motorway was spectacular. Near Nantua, it leapt out of the mountainside and was suspended high above the valley like a magic carpet before disappearing again into the mountain on the other side.

There wasn't much traffic on the road, and still no sign of Felix or his van. They approached the outskirts of Geneva. The motorway skirted the Swiss frontier, keeping just within French territory. They came to St. Julien-en-Genevois. It was the last stop before Mont Blanc. They'd arrived at the end of their journey. Had they missed Felix along the road? Had he gone another route altogether?

Eldridge pulled in at a roadside cafe. He ordered a coffee. Persimmon didn't want anything to eat. She was studying the map. Eldridge called Harry.

"Any news?" he asked.

"Not a word," Harry said.

"We're near the Italian border."

"Will you go on?"

"I don't know."

Persimmon was still busy with the map. She slid it over in Eldridge's direction.

"Are we far from Lake Annecy?" she asked.

Eldridge looked at the map.

"About thirty minutes."

Eldridge wondered what she had in mind.

"When I was a kid," she said, "my Dad used to take me and my Mom to Lake Annecy for a couple of weeks every Summer. We stayed at a village called Talloires at a neat hotel. It was very old fashioned. Dad loved it."

"You think Bismarck may have chosen the spot as a stop-over?"

"It's a possibility."

They got back in the car. Eldridge filled it up with petrol and they set off cross country. It was barely thirty miles to the town of Annecy, and then another few miles going clockwise around the lake to Talloires.

Forty minutes later they drove down the tiny road which led to the lake shore. The *Auberge du Père Bise* came into view. It was an old world type resting hole, the sort of place which would have appealed to Bismarck's taste for unostentatious luxury.

Eldridge looked at the parked cars. They were mostly expensive limousines with French or Swiss licence plates. There was no sign of Felix's van.

The hotel was on the lake shore. The water lapped up against the lawn where guests were gathering in evening dress to sit at the terrace tables and sip their champagne cocktails before dinner.

Eldridge recognised the location. He'd never actually been to Lake Annecy but he remembered it featuring in a movie by Eric Rohmer

He told Persimmon to wait in the car, and went through to the lady at the front desk.

"Have two gentlemen checked in?" he asked. "An American and an Englishman?"

"There were two English speaking gentlemen," she said, "about an hour ago. But I was full."

"Do you know their names?"

"They did not give me their names."

"What did they look like?"

"One was an elderly gentleman, the other was much younger, even younger than you."

"Do you know where they went?"

"I telephoned to Monsieur Veyrat. He runs the hotel further down along the lake. He took them."

Eldridge raced back to the car.

"What's happened?" asked Persimmon. She'd noticed Eldridge's excitement as he started up the engine.

"I think they're at the *Auberge de l'Eridan*."

Eldridge explained to Persimmon about there being no room at the *Père Bise* and that two men, fitting Bismarck's and Felix's description, had checked in instead at Marc Veyrat's hotel which was barely ten minutes away. Marc Veyrat was one of the world's great chefs, his restaurant at the *Auberge de l'Eridan* was a gastronomic shrine.

"You think it's them?"

"Could be."

Eldridge doubled back towards Annecy. He'd actually passed Veyrat's hotel on the way to Talloires, but he hadn't paid it any attention.

They arrived five minutes later. He slid down the slip road and pulled up at the side of the hotel. The car park was full of Rolls Royces and Ferraris and Lamborghinis, preposterously over priced cars owned by wealthy clients coming from Geneva to dine out at one of the great restaurants of France. Veyrat's restaurant was altogether more fashionable than the *Père Bise*, and also more glitzy. Eldridge guessed it wasn't really Bismarck's cup of tea.

Felix's van wasn't in the car park. But the space was already full. It was possible that Veyrat's staff had another spot for overflow, where they parked the less flashy cars.

Eldridge left the Mercedes with a valet and went inside.

"I am so sorry Monsieur," said the man at the front desk, "but we are now completely full."

It turned out that the two English speaking gentlemen had taken the last room.

Eldridge asked who they were.

"I cannot tell you sir, such information is confidential."

Eldridge tried to explain that they were his friends. But the man at the front desk was having none of it. He was used to having shady guests, oil sheikhs and arms dealers, and he wasn't in the habit of doling out potentially incriminating information.

"Did they come by road?" Eldridge asked.

"I cannot tell you, sir."

"Did they come in a van?"

"I really think it would be better if you ask your friends yourself."

"Let me speak with them."

He called up to the room, but there was no reply.

"They are probably changing and showering for dinner. They will be down soon. Why not wait for them in the restaurant?"

There was no point insisting. He wasn't going to tell Eldridge anything. They'd just have to wait and see.

Eldridge and Persimmon went out onto the terrace overlooking the lake. The waiter came to take their order. Eldridge chose the gastronomic menu for two. He was starving, he hadn't eaten anything all day. They were in one of the great restaurants of the world. They might as well enjoy themselves.

After a cocktail, they were taken through to the dining room and shown their table. Persimmon was too nervous to do anything except pick at her food. Each time a waiter entered the room she thought it was them. She kept turning her neck and craning and fidgeting.

The table next to them was empty. It was laid for two. They were going to be sitting right next to them. They waited for them to arrive. They knew this was their last chance. If it wasn't Felix and Bismarck, that was it. They had nowhere else to go.

"You've done the best you could," Persimmon said to Eldridge, as though reading his thoughts. She said it simply and sweetly. Eldridge was completely bowled over. She had so much to lose, and yet she wanted to reassure him in case he'd got it wrong.

Courses came and went, and still they didn't come. The food was magnificent, served in delicate offerings on enormous china plates. Each dish was flavoured with its own herb and served alongside its flower which had been picked from the Alpine slopes by Monsieur Veyrat himself earlier that day. Eldridge vowed that if they ever made it safely through this ordeal, he'd bring Persimmon back, and they'd order a meal which she could really enjoy.

Monsieur Veyrat wandered between the tables chatting to his diners. He wore a splendid Savoyard hat, but his costume was more impressive than his conversation. Eldridge got the impression that the guests were happier just eating the food and not having to listen to the theory which went with it. Eldridge told Persimmon to pretend she couldn't speak French in case they were cornered by him.

They were just being served an aniseed flavoured mille feuille of foie gras, pommes de terre sautées, and truffles, when they came into the dining room.

They were shown to the table next to them.

They sat down.

The older man turned in their direction.

"You were looking for us?" he said.

Persimmon burst into tears.

She couldn't stop herself. She just started blubbing at the table.

It wasn't Bismarck, and the younger man wasn't Felix.

They were just two Americans on a tour round Europe.

Persimmon left the table. She went to the bathroom to try and get control of herself.

The Americans looked shocked. They were a gay couple. They guessed they'd caused Persimmon some sort of distress, but they couldn't fathom what it was about or why.

Eldridge made excuses. He explained that it wasn't anything to do with them. He ended up by telling them the truth. He told them Persimmon had been expecting to see her father and a friend, and that she was upset because they weren't who she was expecting.

The American couple relaxed when they realised that Persimmon's reaction was not directed at them personally. They made small talk while Eldridge waited for Persimmon to come back. He told them that they were on their way to Venice.

"What an extraordinary coincidence," said the older man, "so are we."

He was a university teacher and the younger man was his student. The young man looked frail and fevered. Eldridge let slip that he was a doctor and the older man proceeded to tell him their life story. He insisted on telling Eldridge everything, how he'd been teaching a course on post modernism at Berkeley, how the young man had attended his course, how they'd become lovers, how the young man was already HIV positive when they met, how they'd decided, when the end was near, they'd travel to Venice. The young man wanted to die in Venice.

Eldridge sat and listened while the older man told him all about it. He felt he should have been touched by the story, but he wasn't. It was a bit too self conscious and sentimental for his taste. The idea of travelling to Venice and planning your death like the last act of an opera struck him as profoundly unmoving. Eldridge knew what had inspired them. It was Visconti. The older man saw himself as Aschenbach and the young man was Tadzio. It was pure kitsch, a bit like the decor in Monsieur Veyrat's restaurant where the marble floors clashed hideously with the rustic Alpine furnishings.

Persimmon came back from the bathroom. She tried smiling but it was all she could do to keep from bursting into tears again.

They sat staring at their mille feuille, pretending to listen to the gay couple, and watching the sun set over the lake. They didn't speak to each other. They had nothing to say.

Time was slipping away. At this moment Felix and Bismarck were sitting together just like they were. At this moment they were finishing their meal just like they were. Soon Bismarck would bid Felix goodnight. Soon Felix would take the van. Soon Darius would be gone forever.

Tears were trickling down Persimmon's cheeks.

Eldridge had failed her.

She had failed Darius.

The battle was lost.

****

Eldridge stepped out of the dining room on to the terrace to answer a call from Harry. Harry told Eldridge he'd just spoken with Bismarck.

"Is he with Felix?" Eldridge asked.

"Yes."

"Going to Venice?"

"Yes."

"They've stopped for the night?"

"Yes."

"Where are they?"

"Vonnas."

Eldridge ended the call, paid the bill and was in the Mercedes with Persimmon by his side, heading back to St. Julien two minutes later. The gay American couple were left speechless by the speed with which they said their goodbyes. Monsieur Veyrat was shocked. They'd ignored his mille feuille. He ran after trying to persuade them to have some dessert, but they were out the door before he could finish his pleading.

Eldridge explained what had happened to Persimmon as soon as they were on the road.

"Your Dad phoned Harry."

"Why?"

"Something to do with a ticket for somebody he's meeting in France."

"Where is he?"

"A hotel in Vonnas. Felix booked them a couple of rooms and they're checked in."

"Vonnas?"

"We passed right by it. It's off the A40 just a few miles outside Macon. They probably left the road just before we would have caught up with them."

"They're there now?"

"Yes."

"How long will it take us to get there?"

"An hour or so."

Persimmon was biting her lip again. They had no time to lose.

"I think it'll be OK," Eldridge said. "Your Dad's been with Felix the whole day. He even complained he was sick of the van. He told Harry he was thinking about staying in France a couple of days and letting Felix go on to Venice alone."

"What if Felix leaves right now?"

"I don't think so. Bismarck said they were getting ready to go down to dinner."

"Dad and Felix?"

"That's what he told Harry."

Persimmon continued biting her lip. She wasn't altogether reassured. Eldridge didn't blame her. He wasn't either.

Eldridge retraced the route they'd taken. They zipped cross country to St. Julien-en-Genevois. It was getting dark but he did it in fifteen minutes. They joined the motorway and he increased his speed to well over a hundred miles an hour. He kept his eyes glued for traffic cops lurking at the side of the slip roads. They sped past Nantua and roared along the motorway heading for a small turning between Bourg-en-Bresse and Macon.

It was completely dark by the time they arrived at the exit for Vonnas.

Eldridge turned left off the motorway and dropped his speed to a crawl. They were on a tiny road. There were fields to either side. Two minutes off the motorway and they were in the heart of the French countryside.

"Why Vonnas?" asked Persimmon.

"It's a bit like Veyrat's place. We're in the belly of France. This whole area is littered with great restaurants."

Eldridge had guessed the sort of place they'd stop at. It was a pity he hadn't chosen the right one straight off.

As Eldridge drove along the country road, he realised why Felix preferred Vonnas to Annecy. They were in the middle of nowhere. It wasn't a tourist route. The place was surrounded by pastures and meadows. There were any number of spots for Felix to dump Darius unobserved.

They entered the village. Vonnas was lit up with street lamps, and every house and street corner was decorated with window boxes. The whole place was overly neat and tidy, like a creation from Disneyland. The village had become a sort of appendage for one of the most famous restaurants in the world. Georges Blanc had succeeded his mother, in her day it was known as *La Mère Blanc*, now it was a place of pilgrimage for elite gastronomes.

They reached a small wooden bridge with a fairy tale river. The restaurant ran alongside. It was like a temple to food, with scores of white coated acolytes bearing burnished silver platters between kitchen and table. Most of the guests were already in the dining room. Some had finished and were walking along the wooden walk way returning to their opulent rooms overlooking the river front.

They drove past the garden at the back. There was a floodlit helicopter pad and a chugging sound. Eldridge wound down the car window and heard the noise of a helicopter coming in to land. It was probably bringing late arrivals from nearby Lyons.

Persimmon gripped his hand. She squeezed it tight.

She'd seen what Eldridge had seen.

Standing alongside the pad, illuminated by floodlight, was Bismarck.

Persimmon squeezed his hand even tighter.

Coming out the shadow was Felix.

Bismarck and Felix were standing side by side watching the helicopter land.

Eldridge drove on and rounded the corner at the front of the hotel. There was a small open square where cars were parked. The first thing he noticed was a cream coloured Ford van.

"P 628 GMT."

Persimmon read out the licence plate. She was squeezing his hand so tight it was hurting.

The car park attendant opened the barrier. Eldridge drew in to the square and parked the Mercedes next to the van.

"Get rid of him," he said to Persimmon.

She got out the car and slipped.

She gave a yelp of pain.

The car park attendant came running up. She lent on his shoulder and got him to escort her to the lobby.

Eldridge jumped out and looked round the car park. There was nobody else watching over the cars. He went up to the Ford van. He tried opening the driver's door and the passenger's door. They were locked. He went round to the back of the van. It was even more securely locked, with a sort of bolt across its two doors. He cursed himself for not grabbing a set of spare keys from Harry. He rattled the back doors. They were bolted tight. There was nothing to do except bust it open.

He went to the trunk of the Mercedes and pulled out a spanner from the tool kit. He put the spanner under the bolt at the back of the van and tried to lever it open. The bolt was a solid piece of steel and didn't budge. He got another spanner from the trunk and used it as a purchase on the first. He could hear Persimmon's voice coming from the lobby. She was kicking up an almighty fuss, making sure everyone was fully occupied worrying about her ankle.

He gave a heave and the first spanner buckled. Sweat was pouring down his face. He went back to the trunk and rifled around. He found a crowbar near the spare tyre. He took the crowbar and prised it under the bolt. He gave a grunt and pushed hard. The bolt bent slightly. He tried easing it away but it had jammed against the back doors even more tightly.

He heard Persimmon give an enormous shriek. He guessed that the car park attendant was about to leave and she'd had to distract him again.

He put the crowbar under the bolt and threw his full weight against it. Suddenly the bolt snapped and he was hurled forward on to the ground. He landed on his face and cut his forehead on the gravel of the car park.

The back of the van swung open. The bolt was the only thing keeping it closed. The doors had opened by themselves.

Eldridge got to his feet, and wiped the pebbles from the palms of his hands.

He began unloading the van. It was full of all sorts of junk, mostly projection equipment and poster displays for the Venice Conference. He took everything out piece by piece. He worked his way systematically towards the back. He was nearing the back of the van. There was virtually nothing left. There was just one large poster screen. He got hold of it.

There was a howl.

It was Persimmon. She was kicking up an ever greater rumpus in the lobby. He dragged out the poster screen. He saw him straight away. He was lying face down, covered in a sort of shroud.

Eldridge crawled into the van and turned him face up.

It was Darius.

He didn't move. He seemed dead. Eldridge got hold of him and carried him out the van in his arms. He laid him down on the gravel. He tore off the shroud. He was still in his pyjamas. Eldridge put his head to his chest. He couldn't hear anything. Eldridge's pulse was beating too fast; it was drowning out everything else.

Dead or alive?

He put his face to his mouth. He tried to feel if there was any sign of breath. He felt something blowing against his cheek. He couldn't make it out. Was it the breeze from the trees? He put his ear to his lips. It was coming from Darius. He was trying to say something. He was so weak, he just couldn't get the words out.

Eldridge told him to be calm, that he was going to take him straight to hospital, and that he'd be alright. Darius' eyes opened. He looked at Eldridge. Eldridge told him about Felix, how he'd kidnapped him, and been planning to kill him. Darius nodded his head. He understood what Eldridge was saying. He was struggling to say something in reply. Eldridge put his ear to his mouth. He was expecting to hear him whisper something like "thank you."

It was very faint, but he heard him clear as a bell.

"Asshole."

****

Eldridge wasn't sure if the comment was directed at Felix for wanting to kill him, or at Eldridge for taking so long to find him. Anyway Darius wasn't dead... Far from it.

Eldridge picked him up and laid him on the back seat of the Mercedes. He covered him with the shroud to keep him warm. As he put the shroud over him something fell out. It was the tape. Eldridge couldn't believe it. Dopey Felix had kept the tape. He'd been intending to bury Darius and the tape together. Now Eldridge had both.

Eldridge heard Persimmon coming back to the car park. She was talking to someone, probably the car park attendant. He piled the poster screens and projector equipment back inside the van. He shut the back doors and slipped what was left of the bolt into the socket to keep them closed.

Eldridge had got everything stowed safely away when Persimmon came round the corner of the barrier. She was clinging to the car park attendant, slowing him down. The back door of the Mercedes was open. Darius was lying across the seat clearly visible. She took one look and gave a scream. This time it was for real. She came hurtling towards the car like a boisterous hippo. The car park attendant was left at the barrier his mouth open in astonishment.

"He's OK," Eldridge said to her. "He's alive."

She got in the back of the car and put her arms round Darius to cuddle him.

Eldridge started the engine and drove off fast. He wanted Darius in hospital as quickly as possible. He hadn't had anything to eat or drink for more than a day. He needed urgent attention. Eldridge headed straight for Lyons. The University Hospital was as good as anywhere in the world. Persimmon was clucking and cooing over Darius all the way there. Eldridge watched her through the rear view mirror. She was almost delirious with pleasure.

They arrived at the hospital. Darius was wheeled straight to ITU. Eldridge spent a couple of hours with the doctors checking him out. He was fine. There'd been no real damage, just slight bruising where Felix had hit him over the head, but nothing serious.

Eldridge left Persimmon looking after Darius and made his way back to Vonnas. He was alone, he wanted Felix all to himself and was looking forward to it.

He drew up outside the hotel. The villagers were in bed and asleep. The car park was locked but Eldridge could see the cream coloured Ford van still standing where he'd left it.

Eldridge waited an hour. He expected Felix to come out at any moment. At about one in the morning, Eldridge became impatient. Maybe Felix was going to put it off? Maybe he'd decided to dispose of Darius tomorrow? After all he'd be on his own if Bismarck stayed behind.

Eldridge got out of the Mercedes and walked silently to the hotel. He looked through the glass doors of the lobby. There were lights on inside. A few diners were still hanging around having liqueurs and coffee at the bar.

He slipped inside. One of the guests saw him, but paid no attention. He went to the front desk. There was no one there. The barman was the only staff member on night duty. The registration book was lying on top of the desk within easy reach. Eldridge opened it and flipped through the pages. There he was, on the last page, the Honourable Felix Langsbridge, room 203.

Nobody was paying Eldridge any attention, as he left the entrance lobby and walked along the wooden platform beside the river. He could hear the sound of the waterfall in the distance. He passed rooms 180-190, and then rooms 190-200. He arrived at room 203.

There was no way in, just a solid wooden door and bell.

Eldridge continued to the end of the walkway and went round to the back of the hotel on the garden side. He counted the rooms from the end trying to work out which room was which. Room 203 was on the first floor. It had a balcony. There was a small tree near the balcony. It was simple for Eldridge to climb the tree, the branches were like steps. He eased himself off an overhanging bough on to the balcony.

He hadn't made a sound. Nobody stirred. The windows from the balcony to the room were ajar. Eldridge felt in his pocket for the handcuffs he'd taken from Felix's secret stash. It was poetic justice, he'd cuff him with his own implements. Eldridge approached the windows and pushed them apart.

He stepped into the room. He was in a lounge area. In front of him were the hallway and the front door. To his right was another door. It was closed. Eldridge went through to the hall and opened the front door. He read the number. Room 203. He'd found the right room. Eldridge closed the front door and tiptoed across the carpet to the door to the bedroom. He opened it quietly and slipped inside.

Eldridge saw Felix lying in bed asleep. He could hear him breathing. He crept up to the bed and stood over him.

Felix stirred in his sleep. Eldridge brought out the handcuffs from his pocket. Felix moved his arm from under the sheet.

Eldridge grabbed hold of it. It was soft and fleshy, like a corpse.

Eldridge locked the handcuff on his wrist.

Felix gave a high pitched scream, like a witch.

Eldridge struggled to grab hold of his other arm.

Felix thrashed about on the bed, like a demon.

Eldridge grabbed the other arm.

Felix was shrieking and squealing, like a stuck pig.

Eldridge locked the handcuff on his other wrist.

Felix thrashed around, screaming and yelling. He sounded like a girl.

Eldridge turned on the lights.

He was a girl.

He was Trudy.

Trudy was sitting up in bed, her eyes open wide in terror, her wrists handcuffed in front of her.

CHAPTER NINE

GUINEVERE

It took a couple of seconds before Trudy realised it was him. She'd thought she was being raped. Eldridge unlocked the cuffs and explained what had been happening.

After she calmed down, she gave Eldridge some explanations of her own. It turned out she was the mysterious guest Bismarck had planned to meet on the Continent. He'd flown her in to accompany him on his trip to Venice. He'd organised her flight from LA to Paris, and then Paris to Lyons. When Eldridge spotted Bismarck at the helicopter pad, he'd been waiting to greet her. She'd taken the helicopter from Lyons and was coming in to land.

So, what about Felix? Trudy explained how the hotel had been full, and because Bismarck didn't like her sleeping in the same room as him, Felix had offered his room which was adjacent to Bismarck's, and gone to stay at the hotel annexe down the road.

Eldridge went straight to the annexe. It was early morning, and by the time he got there Felix had long since disappeared. In fact he'd discovered about Darius being missing from the van while they were still at the University Hospital in Lyons, and had taken a taxi to Macon and vanished into thin air.

Eldridge came back and spent the rest of the night talking with Trudy, telling her everything that had happened. He sat on the edge of her bed.

In the morning came the explanations with Bismarck. He was furious to discover he'd been duped by Felix. He didn't care about Darius, and didn't even bother to phone the University Hospital to speak with Persimmon. Instead he went back to the States in a huff, leaving Trudy to follow on her own. He took the helicopter to Lyons and a flight to London and a connection to San Diego. He was back in La Jolla, in the security of his Green Room, with Isabel by his side, that same evening.

He left Eldridge to sort out the shambles.

First, Eldridge telephoned Harry and told him what had happened. He was surprised by Harry's reaction. He transferred his allegiance to Eldridge in one swallow. It was all or nothing with Harry. Harry had been Felix's devoted disciple for so long as Felix was worthy to receive it. But Felix had betrayed the Company. Harry was a Company man. Now Eldridge was running the Company, so Harry became Eldridge's man.

Later that day, Eldridge arranged for the video tape to be played inside the Commissariat of Police in Lyons. The police gathered round as he put the cassette into their device. The tape was one of those time lapse recordings where everything is in slow motion, where people move around in jumps and starts. The strange eerie movements only served to highlight the grotesqueness of what they were watching.

Eldridge explained to the police how the security firm had set up a monitoring device in the attic of the cottage in Cambridge. The video cameras were activated automatically and everything was stored on tape. There were some innocent pictures, like Martha baking her pies in the kitchen. There were mischievous pictures, like when Samuel tripped Izaac at the foot of the stairs. And, then there were sinister pictures, like when Felix entered Joseph's study at the bottom of the garden.

They watched as the flickering images showed Felix entering the study. The camera was lodged in the right hand corner of the ceiling. It gave a view of Joseph, with his back to the camera, sitting at his desk. He was writing. Felix came into camera face on, entering through the door opposite Joseph's desk. Joseph was wagging his finger at Felix. It looked as if he may have been laughing. Then Felix moved. The slow motion effect of the recording made it seem as if Felix had pounced from one end of the study to the other. The images followed in quick succession like a macabre slapstick comedy. Joseph with his body bent double coughing and spitting, Felix holding the handkerchief against Joseph's face, pressing it against Joseph's mouth and nose. Joseph struggling and writhing like a snake desperate to escape from Felix's grip, Joseph kicking and lashing at Felix's shin, Felix smothering Joseph with his handkerchief and frothy spittle oozing through on to his fingers, Joseph slumping to the floor, Felix holding the handkerchief over Joseph's face as he lay motionless on the floor, Felix withdrawing the handkerchief, Martha coming into the room and discovering her husband dead.

The police made several copies of the tape and put out an Interpol alert for Felix's arrest.

The next thing was to sort out what to do in Venice. The doctors in Lyons reported that Darius was recovering well. It really looked as though the cure had worked.

"You're the boss" Harry urged Eldridge on the phone. "We have our slot at the conference. Someone has to do it. Why don't you?"

There was only one thing bugging Eldridge. Where was Felix?

CHAPTER 9: GUINEVERE

****

If Eldridge went to Venice, why not Trudy? Trudy jumped at the idea. Eldridge got the impression she was a bit annoyed with Bismarck, bringing her all the way to Europe only to send her straight back home again. At any event she seemed as pleased as punch to make a detour to Venice before returning to the States. She was as excited as a little kid. She'd never been to Italy, and was thrilled about visiting Venice.

They landed at Marco Polo airport in the late afternoon. Harry was waiting for them at the exit. Harry had arrived earlier that morning to set up at the conference hall.

"There might be a problem," said Harry.

"What?" Eldridge asked.

"Felix. He's here, hiding somewhere in Venice. He phoned the Conference Centre and told them you weren't giving the talk."

Eldridge felt a sudden chill. The police forces of Europe were out searching for Felix, and yet he was still meddling in their affairs. It made Eldridge nervous. Why hadn't Felix disappeared like that other English murderer, Lord Lucan, and left them to get on with their lives? Why was he still hovering around? Obviously Felix didn't want Eldridge giving his talk. Did that mean Eldridge had become his number one target?

Eldridge told Harry he'd talk about it tomorrow. He was devoting the rest of the day to Trudy. He'd decided to give her a treat. He hired a taxi. She giggled when she realised the taxi was a launch.

As they boarded, he scrutinised the boatman. He had a vision of Felix in disguise ready to leap out at him with a carving knife like a demented Norman Bates. But the boatman turned out to be a surly old gnome who metamorphosed into a courteous sprightly gallant the moment he set eyes on Trudy. He was enchanted at the thought of helping the "signorina" on board, and he eyed her in a way which was much more blatant than back home. Eldridge stood with Trudy in the stern. The launch was in immaculate condition, all burnished wood and sparkling metal. The old man eased it out of the mooring and then... whoosh! The prow was high out of the water, with the propellers churning up a siphon behind. They roared down the water lane. Trudy was jumping up and down in glee. The wind took hold of her hair and blew it in a train behind her. It was as if she was posing for an ad in a fashion magazine, a stunning girl in a startling location.

Trudy waved as they passed the buses chugging their way slowly towards the lagoon. She got a kick out of being in her own private launch, and she loved it when she saw the passengers in the public boats waving back. Eldridge got a kick out of having her all to himself.

The launch slowed right down as they approached the main island. They made their way through the canals behind the Ospedale. Trudy was ecstatic. The sun was low in the sky, the evening had a warm springtime feel to it. The Venetian mommas were gathering in their washing from the balconies, the poppas were unloading their cargoes at the fondamenta. It was enchantment, a world apart. Trudy was pointing at everything around her like a child in Fairyland.

The taxi picked up speed and they came out of the canal into the bacino. Trudy gasped. It was extraordinary. Wham... San Giorgio Maggiore on the island in front... Santa Maria della Salute on the island to their right. The launch took a long wide sweep and the landing for the Piazza San Marco came into view. Trudy said nothing. She just stood and stared, her mouth wide open in disbelief. The sun was setting, giving a pink warm glow to the Doge's palace. It was a scene as pure and as perfect as at any time in history. They could have been two sailors from the fifteenth century.

Eldridge held her hand as they made their way down the Grand Canal. She was trembling. Eldridge squeezed her hand, and she leant over and kissed him on the cheek.

The taxi drew up at the landing stage of the Gritti Palace. Eldridge eyed everyone carefully before he disembarked. There was no one who looked like Felix. They were taken through to the reception area.

Eldridge booked a suite, a bedroom and salon. They'd be together and Trudy could still be faithful to Bismarck. The bill was on Trust. He liked the idea of Bismarck paying for them, Venice isn't cheap at the best of times, a five star palace hotel and the price goes into orbit, a suite and you head for outer space. They were escorted to their rooms, porters bowing and scraping at every corner, and bank notes scattered like confetti. But Eldridge was on edge all the way. He had a feeling that Felix was lurking behind every corner and cupboard.

She asked about Venice, how it was built, why it was important. She was avid for knowledge. He told her about Marco Polo and the trade routes to the East before the circumnavigation of the globe.

"Let's go and visit the city," he suggested.

She gave him the sweetest smile. It was fun being with her.

He took her to the Ca' Rezzonico. He wanted to show her the frescoes.

"Giandomenico..."

"Son of Giambattista."

She was laughing. She'd never heard of either an hour before and now she knew the difference between father and son. They were looking at Tiepolo's series of frescoes with Pulcinello against a background of tumblers and satyrs. She stood up against the wall, her mouth open in awe. She loved them. She had a pleasure in art which took Eldridge's breath away. He realised her quest for knowledge wasn't to store away and to impress, another two weeks and she'd be teaching him.

They moved on to the fresco of *The New World*. It was an extraordinary composition, a crowd of onlookers huddled together and staring at something. You couldn't tell what. They were painted from the back, and whatever they were looking at was hidden from view by their tightly packed bodies. It seemed an allegory for what they were going to encounter at the conference.

****

Eldridge woke early. He'd left the curtains open and the shutters pulled back. The early morning light and the chugging noise of the motoscafi entered his troubled dreams, and he was soon wide awake.

He crept down the corridor and peeked into her bedroom. She was fast asleep. The bedclothes were pushed aside and she was lying on top with just a flimsy night-dress as a covering. She was curled up on her side, her eyes were tight shut and she was sucking her thumb. Trudy reminded him of Carroll Baker, she was the very image of *Baby Doll*.

He showered and went down to have his cappuccino at the terrace restaurant overlooking the Grand Canal. The concierge was at his desk. He was a magnificent specimen, about fifty five, silver haired, courteous to the point of parody, and in a uniform that would have done justice to an Admiral of the Fleet, a bit like Janning's doorman in *The Last Laugh*. He bade Eldridge good morning.

"Did dottore have a good sleep?"

"Fine."

"And the signorina."

"Even better."

"The signorina is... how can I say..."

"... a very beautiful lady." Eldridge finished his sentence for him.

Americans get high on business deals. But, at any time, on any occasion, Italians are obsessed by only one thing, women. The concierge insisted on accompanying Eldridge to the terrace restaurant. He had more to say. It wasn't small talk, it was a necessity. He had to compliment Eldridge on the quality of his companion. There was no envy, just a need to express his appreciation. As they walked side by side, he discoursed on the merits of youth versus the maturity of age. He reflected on the fact that a woman's beauty ripens with time. He talked about Trudy like she was a vintage wine. Eldridge got the impression he thought she wasn't yet at her best. Another two years in the barrel and she'd be perfect.

Eldridge sat at a waterside table and bade him goodbye. He left regretfully. He could have gone on talking about Trudy indefinitely. The waiter brought him his coffee. There is no greater pleasure than drinking fine coffee at the water's edge of a palace hotel in Venice.

It was while he was being served his second coffee that he heard the concierge return. At first he thought he'd come back with some further reflections on Trudy. But he was fussing over someone else. Eldridge had his back to them. The concierge was busying himself at the table behind him, finding the most comfortable chair, worrying about the position of the sun, in a delirium of obsequiousness, as though he were seating royalty.

"If Lord Langsbridge will sit on this side..." said the concierge, "I am sure his Lordship will have a better view."

Eldridge felt goose pimples down his neck.

Lord Langsbridge.

Felix.

Felix was standing behind him. It was like in the attic, he had crept up behind him without Eldridge noticing. Eldridge had been too busy thinking of Trudy, he should have been looking for Felix. Now it was too late. He was standing behind Eldridge with a poker, ready to bludgeon him.

Eldridge jumped to his feet and turned. The concierge gave a gasp. He thought he was going to strike. But of course it wasn't Felix. Felix was an Honourable. "Lord" Langsbridge was his father. It was Felix's father.

Lord Langsbridge looked startled.

Eldridge made his apologies. He told him he thought he was someone else. Lord Langsbridge gave Eldridge a dismissive nod, as though he were a troublesome servant, and set about reading his paper.

Eldridge could see the resemblance. He was a tall man and he had the same lantern jaw.

Eldridge returned to his coffee. He remembered Harry telling him that Felix's dad was in Venice and was going to preside at the conference. Suddenly Eldridge realised why Felix couldn't let him give the talk. This was meant to have been Felix's big moment to impress the world. Everybody was assembling in Venice. The entire cast of characters were gathering for the dénouement. It was like the final chapter of a book. Felix was completely mad, if he couldn't give the lecture, he certainly wasn't going to let anyone else. He wasn't going to let Eldridge steal his thunder, he'd kill

Eldridge as soon as he got up to speak in his place.

Eldridge began to feel light headed. It was partly a sense of trepidation. It was also the coffee. It was so strong, it was positively intoxicating. He finished breakfast and telephoned Harry. He told him to meet him at police headquarters. It was a short walk from the Gritti but Harry was already waiting by the time he got there.

"You think Felix is going to kill you?"

"The guy's nuts. He thinks I've cheated him. He probably thinks I've masterminded everything to steal his glory from him. The moment I get up on the rostrum to deliver the talk he'll kill me."

They entered police headquarters and were escorted to an office on the first floor. The chief of police greeted them. He was a relaxed and amiable man. He didn't seem in the least put out that Eldridge wanted to review the security arrangements.

"I will order my officers to be waiting at the landing stage at San Giorgio," the chief of police reassured them. "If he comes by public or private transport he will be apprehended immediately."

"What if he lands somewhere else on the island?" Eldridge asked.

"I will have men at the doorway to the conference hall. The Cini Foundation used to be a monastery. It has only one entrance."

"What if he has a gun?" Eldridge didn't really expect Felix to fight his way in. But he didn't want to take anything for granted.

"My men are armed. I have also put some marksmen on the roof of the Foundation. They have orders to shoot if there is any sign of violence."

"How will they recognise him?"

The chief of police pulled out a photo.

"This photo is being carried by every officer in Venice."

Eldridge looked at it. There was no mistaking Felix. It also looked a bit like dad. Eldridge wondered if a dopey policeman might arrest dad by mistake. He quite liked the idea and decided not to warn the chief of police of the possibility.

Harry asked the chief of police about security before the conference began.

"I will arrange to have two men watching Dr. Kwanza at all times," he said immediately. "They will guard him from the moment he leaves this building until he has safely delivered his talk."

The chief of police was as good as his word. Two policemen followed as Eldridge walked back to the Gritti with Harry. The next step was to warn the conference secretariat about what was happening. They were based on the Lido. The concierge ordered a taxi, and the two policemen accompanied Eldridge and Harry. The launch pitched and lurched in the choppy waters. It took a good twenty minutes before they even came near the island of Santa Lazzaro with its secluded colony of

Armenian monks. Then another ten minutes making their way alongside the Lido and down the narrow waterway to the landing jetty at the Excelsior. Eldridge ducked as they came under the last low slung bridge.

The concierge had phoned ahead to have everything ready for when they arrived. The Excelsior was closed but a car was waiting at the landing with another for the two policemen. They got in and drove up the ramp and out of the grounds of the empty hotel. It was still too early in the season to welcome tourists. The whole island was like a ghost town. They drove down the main road and there wasn't a single shop open, just an occasional cafe with two or three people inside.

They arrived at a modern building. It was the conference secretariat. The Director was pacing up and down outside the building waiting for them. He was bemused by Eldridge's arrival with two policemen. He escorted them into the building. The two policemen waited outside his office while he took Eldridge and Harry inside.

Eldridge felt sorry for him. He was a light weight dermatologist from Padua with a passing interest in AIDS research who'd been landed with the job of organising the meeting. When he'd heard about Felix's work he'd agreed to let Felix give the opening Plenary Lecture. Then the day before yesterday he got a call from Harry that Felix wasn't coming and Eldridge was giving the talk instead. Then yesterday he got a call from Felix telling him that Eldridge wasn't giving the talk. He was agitated. He didn't understand what was going on. He was uneasy about the policemen outside his door. Eldridge didn't blame him. He began to put him in the picture, and told him about the warrant for Felix's arrest.

"You mean he's a murderer?" The Director couldn't believe his ears.

He pressed the intercom and shouted for his assistants. They came rushing in. The Director spoke to them rapidly in Italian. Each time he muttered *assassino assassino*, the two assistants quaked. They gathered behind the Director's desk. Eldridge got the impression they were expecting Felix to burst past the policemen and gun them down, and were getting ready to duck.

Eldridge reassured them there was no cause to be nervous.

"He's after me," he explained.

"But he called here!"

"He'll try and kill me when I get up to speak."

"You really expect him to come?"

"I'm sure of it. He's completely mad. He'll try to kill me when I give the talk, but the police will stop him before he ever gets anywhere near the conference centre. They have his photo. As soon as they see him, he'll be arrested and taken away."

"You are certain?"

Eldridge nodded his head.

But he wasn't that confident. Everything was a bit too pat. Felix wasn't going to just turn up at the conference as though nothing had happened and let the police arrest him before he could do anything to stop Eldridge. Felix might not be the world's greatest criminal master mind, but he wasn't a fool. Eldridge couldn't help feeling he was missing something.

The Director was wringing his hands in despair. The idea of an embarrassing fracas at the opening talk of the conference was distressing him. He imagined his more senior colleagues shaking their heads in reproach, and banishing him back to the skin diseases of Padua.

Eldridge bade the Director goodbye. The two policemen accompanied Eldridge and Harry to the bus stop. They took the water bus back to Venice. Eldridge left Harry at San Marco and made his way to the Gritti with the two policemen in tow.

The conference was going to open at four PM.

Eldridge was due to give Felix's talk at four thirty.

Everything would be settled by evening

****

Persimmon and Darius had checked in. Darius looked great. He'd put on another couple of pounds since he'd been in Lyons.

Trudy gave Darius a kiss. Eldridge gave Persimmon a hug.

The concierge looked on from behind his desk. He didn't say anything, he was truly lost for words. The contrast between Trudy and Persimmon was too great for comment. Trudy took them out on to the terrace and ordered tea, while Eldridge told them about Felix being in Venice.

Persimmon began biting her lip. She was worried. She thought it meant that Felix was planning something new against Darius.

"Felix isn't interested in Darius." Eldridge told her. "He doesn't matter to him any more. The police have the tape, that's all that counts."

"Why is he here?"

"He's after me...," Eldridge pointed to the two policemen at the doorway. "... He hasn't forgiven me for unmasking him, and he's enraged at the idea that I'm taking his place at the conference."

"But if he tries to kill you, he'll be arrested," said Persimmon.

"Everything's gone wrong for Felix. He'll be arrested whatever happens. His career is finished. He'll spend the rest of his days in jail or in an asylum. He's got nothing to lose in getting rid of me before he goes down."

"He could run away," said Darius. "That's what I'd do."

"He's got nowhere to go," Eldridge said. "For Felix life is over. This afternoon will be his last act as a free man."

"He must really hate you," said Persimmon. She was biting her lip. Eldridge could tell she was scared. Eldridge was scared. But there was no going back. It was time to face up to whatever the future had in store.

Eldridge was planning to take Darius and leave the girls, but Persimmon wouldn't hear of it. She wasn't letting Darius out of her sight, especially now. She was adamant. She was going to stay by his side. Eldridge knew what she was thinking. If Felix started shooting at Eldridge he might hit Darius instead.

Once Persimmon decided she was going, there was no stopping Trudy.

"I'm coming too," she said.

"No you're not," Eldridge said. "It's got nothing to do with you."

Persimmon and Darius went on board the launch, leaving them to fight it out alone.

"Yes it has," she said.

"Why?"

Eldridge was becoming impatient. The launch was bobbing up and down on the jetty. Persimmon and Darius were beckoning for him to join them.

"I love you."

Eldridge was walking towards the jetty. She was by his side. It dawned on him what she'd just said.

Eldridge stretched out his hand. She grabbed hold and stepped on to the launch. The two policemen jumped aboard and they were off to San Giorgio.

****

They arrived at the landing stage. The place was alive with journalists clambering to interview the streams of delegates disembarking from the motoscafi. Cini Foundation meetings were always prestigious events, guaranteed world wide coverage in the scientific journals.

This meeting in particular was drawing the attention of the world's press. The fact that it was an AIDS meeting made it front page news. But the rumour had been spreading for a couple of days that a big story was about to break. There was a buzz of excitement about the place.

Felix had been right about one thing. It was the perfect place to announce the cure.

The TV reporters were stopping the more eminent scientists as they crossed towards the conference hall. It was a bit like movie stars besieged on their way to the Oscars. Eldridge spotted Felix's dad being interviewed by RAI. He had his young teenage son with him. Harry had told Eldridge about Felix's dad remarrying after he separated from Felix's mom. Felix's dad put his arm round the boy's shoulder as he answered the journalist's questions. The boy basked in his father's glory. Eldridge wondered if Felix was jealous of his step brother.

Harry was waiting for Eldridge as he got off the launch.

"The official programme's still got Felix to give the lecture," he told Eldridge as they made their way towards the conference hall. "They haven't had time to change it."

"Who's going to introduce me?" Eldridge asked.

"The Director. He'll get on to the podium and make some excuse about Felix being indisposed, and then he'll ask you to come forward and take his place."

"Everything's set for my talk?"

"I've gone through the slides with the projectionist and they're fine."

They made their way from the jetty to the entrance to the Cini Foundation. The two policemen were right behind Eldridge all the way. He put his arm round Trudy's waist. He was looking everywhere for Felix. If he caught sight of him he was going to push Trudy out of harm's way.

But there was no way Felix was going to get inside, let alone do any damage. There were police everywhere. They were stopping and searching all the younger delegates. Eldridge spotted the marksmen up on the roof. They had machine guns. The chief of police had done his job.

They entered the conference hall. Eldridge and Darius were made to show their IDs. The police were stopping all the young males whether or not they looked like Felix.

They had reserved seats in the front row.

The mayor of Venice was up on the platform with the dermatologist from Padua and Felix's dad. Eldridge looked round the conference hall. It was filling up. The delegates had nearly all arrived and they were occupying the first twenty rows. The medical and scientific journalists were sitting in the back part of the hall behind the large desks that had been set up for them.

The Director introduced the mayor who made a short and spirited speech about the reputation of the Cini Foundation. He spoke about how Venice used to be a great trading centre for the exchange of goods and materials and how now, thanks to the Cini Foundation, it was a centre for the exchange of scientific information.

The mayor spoke in Italian. There were earphones at each seat offering a simultaneous translation. The official language of the meeting was English, but the local dignitaries were allowed to speak Italian.

The mayor finished and there was an appreciative round of applause. The place was full. There were even delegates standing in the aisle.

Next came Felix's dad. He strode up to the rostrum. He was president of the meeting and he gave a long opening address welcoming the delegates. He spoke just like Felix. He had the same clipped muffled speech. Trudy was on one side of Eldridge, and Persimmon on the other. They both gave a start when they heard him speak. The resemblance was uncanny.

Eldridge scanned the conference hall. He noticed Felix's step brother sitting in the front row, a couple of seats further along from them. He was a young man, no more than seventeen or eighteen. Harry had told Eldridge that Lord Langsbridge had tried to make him his heir at the expense of Felix. Lord Langsbridge nodded and smiled in the young man's direction from time to time during his address.

The delegates were all engrossed in Lord Langsbridge's peroration. Eldridge examined the faces to see if Felix was hidden amongst them. He craned his head to look at the back of the hall. The journalists were all typing away at their portables. There was nothing strange happening anywhere. Felix wasn't there.

Felix's dad finished his speech. The delegates gave him a round of thunderous applause. He stepped down from the podium and sat at an empty seat in the front row next to his son. The boy gave him a pat on the back. They were obviously proud of each other.

Eldridge noticed a striking tall girl in the doorway. He was surprised to see her standing, he wondered why no Italian had been gallant enough to offer her his seat. She was breathing strangely. It sounded as though she was having an asthma attack.

The Director stepped forward to the podium. Eldridge rose from his chair. Trudy whispered "Good luck."

There was definitely something odd about the girl in the doorway. Her face had too much makeup. She looked like a tart.

The Director mentioned Felix's name and the tall striking girl in the doorway stepped forward.

The Director stared at the girl coming towards him.

There was complete silence in the hall.

Eldridge heard her wheezing as she passed in front of him. He sat down. He had recognised the tall girl the moment she stepped forward. He recognised the vermilion lipstick, the long chestnut wig, the lantern jaw.

It was Felix.

He was in drag.

And suddenly it dawned on Eldridge. Felix wasn't going to kill him. It had nothing to do with him. Felix had come to give the talk himself.

Felix tripped on his way up the steps to the podium. He was wearing black leather boots with long stiletto heels, and one of the heels buckled on the step.

Eldridge heard someone snicker.

Felix stumbled towards the podium. He turned and faced the audience. He looked directly towards his dad sitting in the front row.

It was obvious that Felix had come to Venice because of dad.

Felix had come to impress his dad.

EPILOGUE

FULL CIRCLE

Felix mounted the podium. He turned and faced his audience. He was about to address a congregation of the greatest scientists in the world.

He stood at the lectern and looked directly at his father who was sitting in the front row. Father stared at him, anxious and bewildered. Felix gave him a reassuring smile. He'd done it all for father.

Felix began to speak. There was total silence in the conference hall.

Felix told them about his discovery.

At first there were a few stifled cries and gasps. Then, one by one, the members of the audience rose to their feet. Uproar broke out. They were giving him a standing ovation. Some were clapping, others were yelling their approval.

Felix had discovered the cure for AIDS.

Even father was standing, even father was proud of him.

Felix could hardly make himself heard above the hubbub.

It was the consummation of his life's work.

But Felix couldn't speak. Something had happened to his throat. He felt a tightening around his throat as if he'd been paralysed. The more he struggled to free the words, the more his throat tightened. He was gasping for breath. He was unable to breathe, The words wouldn't come, they were locked inside his lungs.

And the members of the audience weren't applauding, they were laughing. There were gales of laughter every time he opened his mouth and tried to speak.

The mayor was bent double, rocking backwards and forwards.

There were hoots from the delegates. The Italians were making rude gestures and the Americans were shouting obscenities.

Felix went bright red. He couldn't control his blush. It was as if his face was on fire.

He stretched out his hands towards his father in supplication.

At last father recognised him, and the expression on his face changed from astonishment to contempt. He shook his head. He was ashamed of Felix.

Felix's face reddened even further. If it had been dark it would have glowed like a furnace.

Father stared back at him in disgust.

Felix staggered. He made a desperate effort to keep upright as he stumbled towards father, but one of his heels had broken and he tripped and fell to the ground.

Father moved forward. Felix thought he might be coming to comfort him, but father turned away and spoke to the young man sitting by his side.

Father escorted his new son from the conference hall without a backward glance in Felix's direction.

It was like that time outside the church. Felix lay on the platform gasping for breath while father went off with his new family, abandoning him, leaving him to choke to death.

Felix crawled to the edge of the platform, with froth dribbling from his lips, and not a breath of air able to enter or leave his lungs.

Kwanza sat in the front row a few inches from him. He wasn't laughing. He was a black maggot. Black maggots don't laugh. Trust's whore was sitting next to the black maggot. They were slime. They deserved to be crushed underfoot.

The tension was building up inside him. He couldn't contain it. He needed release.

He closed his eyes.

The slime disappeared and Felix was enveloped in blackness.

He was safe at last.

The sound of laughter faded. Instead he could hear the wind howling. A storm had come up, and was banging the branches of the trees against the window pane, making a pattering sound like the fluttering of moths struggling to get in.

He was naked and alone, shadows dancing across his body, his skin white as alabaster, smooth as cream, the flagpole rising from the jet black fur between his legs.

He was soothed by silk stockings and lace garters.

The flagpole extended itself. It produced tiny droplets in celebration of the rubber straps and whalebone stays.

And her face was powdered and her cheeks rouged.

And her hair.

Golden chestnut hair.

Guinevere!

She couldn't breath. She was choking.

There was a pounding outside. At first the cry was "First Principles... First Principles..." then it became "Police... Doctor..."

But that was miles away in another world. What mattered was here and now.

Guinevere struggled and writhed in her chains. The flagpole reared its head, and wept in sympathy.

She was in her death agony, her fingers clawing at the floor, her face smothered beneath the cellophane mask, her body writhing and contorting in pain.

Father straddling her...

A furnace in father's loins...

Father entering her...

There was a hammering on his chest. It didn't matter. It was somewhere else.

Father penetrating her...

Bitch!

Not a breath of air... choking... gasping...

No release. This time no release. Guinevere condemned to death.

Father watching as she chokes...

Father watching as she dies...

A final hammer blow on the chest.

But too late.

Guinevere is gone.

****

Darius' mother couldn't accept that Darius had been honoured for his contribution to the cure.

"Oh now come on now, you weren't born yesterday - everyone knows an Honorary anything's just something they give you when you're not good enough to get the real thing; like with your father when they gave him that Honorary Membership to the Music League here in town which only entitled him to pay expensive dues and come and hear the bands because he wasn't good enough to actually play in them; and in your case we both know why they gave it to you; for no other reason than that you probably just drove them crazy until they just said, 'Oh, just give it to the little S.O.B. - anything to shut him up'."

And, most of all, she didn't understand what the fuss was about.

"I can't help thinking what a shame it is that they didn't come up with a cure for Cancer or something decent that normal people get..."

****

After her trip to Venice, Trudy left Bismarck for Eldridge. She enrolled in college to study Fine Arts, majoring in Renaissance painting and architecture. She graduated with flying honours, and was even invited to do a spell as visiting curator at the National Gallery in London.

At first, Eldridge couldn't make up his mind about marrying Trudy. On the plus side, he was living with the woman he loved and who loved him; on the negative, he was plagued with the image of himself as a corrupt pimp flaunting his Blonde like a diamond encrusted platinum Rolex. He might have continued in this state of indecision indefinitely if he hadn't overheard a conversation between two African diplomats. They were talking about him, one was telling the other how clever Eldridge was in not marrying Trudy, how it wouldn't do his career any good to be officially linked to an ex call girl. That settled it; the idea that he was being complimented because he'd chosen to distance himself from an inferior was hateful. He immediately bought a ring, dropped to his knees and proposed.

The real problem was where to live and what to do. Trudy had no objection to settling in Africa and supporting Eldridge in his new life as a village doctor. But Eldridge was now a celebrity and feted the world over as the doctor who'd discovered the cure for AIDS. If he went off to some outpost in Africa, he'd end up like Albert Schweitzer, a man so unctuous about his self-sacrifice that it reeked of arrogance and pride. Eventually Eldridge found a solution of sorts. Trudy became the senior partner in their life, and he followed to wherever her work as an art historian took her.

****

Bismarck basked in his glory.

At first there had been critical comment about Felix's death. Bismarck never properly understood how it happened. Kwanza said it was something to do with an acute asthmatic attack. But that didn't explain why Felix had turned up in women's wear, or indeed why he'd shown himself in public at all. The worst were the hideous rumours surrounding his death agony. Some were saying that he ejaculated at the final moment. They said he spread his legs wide open and spurted it into the air in full public gaze.

Fortunately it was just rumour, and the debacle with Felix was quickly forgotten in the general jubilation.

Darius's recovery signalled the beginning of the end. The treatment still had to go through a series of carefully controlled trials, but these were just formalities. The treatment would soon be freely available to everyone suffering from AIDS.

Bismarck's vision and determination had been vindicated.

He was feted everywhere. The President welcomed him at the White House with a special gala in his honour, and the gay community treated him as their hero. The terrible ordeal of the trial was effaced for all time.

And yet...

There was still one thing worrying Bismarck.

Kwanza summed it up on the day of the press conference, when he gave his warning, "Remember it's a cure for AIDS, but a disease for everything else."

It was all because of that cursed incident with Tiger.

He'd been tested again and again, and the results were always negative. He'd seen doctor after doctor, and they all gave him a clean bill of health. They said he'd been lucky. But Bismarck didn't believe them. After what had happened, he knew he'd been contaminated. He had to be HIV positive. No matter what the doctors said, he felt it growing inside of him.

But it was a mistake to have panicked. It seemed sensible at the time. With Darius kidnapped and the police involved, there was every chance that the lab at the Science Park would be quarantined and the HTLV viruses confiscated, possibly destroyed. But why hadn't he just stolen a vial of viruses, and kept them for a rainy day? Why had he rushed to inoculate himself with the leukemic virus?

He should have discussed it with someone.

He should have waited.

And now?

The fever was taking hold of him. Even Isabel was getting worried. Last night she'd had to change the sheets three or four times. They were drenched in sweat. On the last occasion she'd begged him to call a doctor.

You're sick", she'd said, "... You must see someone."

She was right. The night sweats were becoming intolerable, and he was beginning to lose weight.

He had leukaemia. He'd given it to himself!

And there was no cure.

Except, maybe, HIV?

Robert Silman is a doctor/scientist, for many years Senior Lecturer and Honorary Consultant at St. Bartholomew's and the Royal London School of Medicine where he authored scores of research publications in the major scientific research journals, principally on the role of the pituitary hormones ACTH and endorphin in pregnancy and parturition, and the pineal hormone melatonin in growth and puberty. Before medical school he obtained a degree in Philosophy (Licence ès Lettres) at the Sorbonne where he co-wrote a political thriller, *Assassination*, under the pen name Ben Abro, published by Jonathan Cape in the UK and William Morrow in the USA. The book gave rise to a libel action with a celebrated French politician. The book was withdrawn during court proceedings and was republished in April 2001 by the University of Nebraska Press (ISBN: 9780803259393) with an extensive historical addendum on the accompanying libel action.

Steven Froelich is an actor/playwright. His first play, *They Offered Bob and Wilma Cash*, had Sylvia Miles in the lead with Steven playing opposite as her son. His second play, *Weekend In Rio*, was work shopped at the Steppenwolf Studio in Chicago with Laurie Metcalfe in the lead followed by public performances at the Edinburgh Fringe Festival where it received two Best Actress nominations. His first true life travel journal, *Moscow to Havana* (ISBN: 9780957296602), was published in 2012.

For more information on the authors go to:
www.buggoingaround.com

Lightning Source UK Ltd.
Milton Keynes UK
UKOW05f0614221213

223452UK00002B/10/P

9 780957 296626